DESTROYER ANGEL

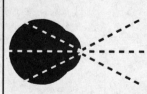

This Large Print Book carries the
Seal of Approval of N.A.V.H.

DESTROYER ANGEL

NEVADA BARR

WHEELER PUBLISHING
A part of Gale, Cengage Learning

GALE
CENGAGE Learning·

Farmington Hills, Mich • San Francisco • New York • Waterville, Maine
Meriden, Conn • Mason, Ohio • Chicago

GALE
CENGAGE Learning®

LIBRARY OF CONGRESS CATALOGING-IN-PUBLICATION DATA

Barr, Nevada.
    Destroyer angel / by Nevada Barr. — Large print edition.
        pages ; cm. — (An Anna Pigeon novel series)
    ISBN-13: 978-1-4104-6691-4 (hardcover) ISBN-10: 1-4104-6691-4 (hardcover)
    1. Pigeon, Anna (Fictitious character)—Fiction. 2. Women park rangers—Fiction. 3. Canoes and canoeing—Fiction 4. Kidnapping—Fiction. 5. Missing persons—Fiction. 6. Large type books. I. Title.
    PS3552.A73184D48 2014b
    813'.54—dc23   2014006246

Published in 2014 by arrangement with St. Martin's Press, LLC

Printed in the United States of America
1 2 3 4 5 6 7 18 17 16 15 14

For Sherry, Dianne, and Barb,
who provided me with all the ingredients
for this book, then threw in their
friendship to boot

ACKNOWLEDGMENTS

Thanks to BlueSky Designs in Minneapolis, Minnesota, for their technical expertise, Dominick for his durable sanity, Julie for her insight, Mr. Paxton for his constancy, Scot for his practical courage, and India for, year after year, quietly making me look much smarter than I actually am.

PROLOGUE

Paul Davidson was stopped on the overpass outside of Denver International Airport, amused as always by the statue of the great blue Gumby horse rearing against the white peaks of the terminal roof in the background. The peaks were meant, he assumed, to look like the Rocky Mountains. They always reminded him of a momma sow lying on her back.

His wife's plane was scheduled to leave at 11:15 A.M., nonstop to Minneapolis. This was the first vacation Anna had taken since their honeymoon. After a summer fighting wildfires, she needed a long weekend with the girls.

He'd been glad when Heath Jarrod invited her on this float trip. Some years back, Heath had saved Anna's life. Anna wasn't the sort to forget that kind of thing, and they'd become fast friends. Anna was godmother to Heath's daughter, Elizabeth, though if the church knew the kind of spiritual guidance Anna would provide, the minister might have balked.

Paul smiled. He loved his wife's irreverence. Even after three years of marriage, he never rested easy when she was away. He kept his fears to himself. A man might put Anna on a pedestal, but she would only leap down, snatch up a chain saw, and cut it up for firewood.

Three jets that might have been Anna's left in quick succession.

The great Gumby horse's eyes glowed an infernal red. Paul was glad he was an Episcopalian. A less rational belief system might have seen that as a bad omen.

"Vaya con Dios," he whispered, then got in the Nissan for the drive back to Boulder.

ONE

Hands thrust deep in the pockets of the absurd checkered hunter's coat — protective coloration in northern Minnesota — Charles stared at the campground. Gray ash, blown into ripples, exposed an old campfire ring. On the edges of the clearing the ash melded into gray hills, low and still in death. Black spikes, the last rebellion of living trees, thrust up through the misery of destruction.

Giving God the finger, Charles thought. Never a good idea. Like most Catholics, Charles prayed to Jesus and Mother Mary when he bothered to pray. Jesus was in the redemption business. Not God; God was in the smiting business.

"What're we gonna do, Dude?"

Charles slid his eyes toward the Fox River. The fire had been stopped by the water. Its final act of destruction was the campground. On the far bank, vegetation was a lush mockery; verdant greens, rich golds, and loud reds thrust out over the water like so many jeering faces.

"What're we gonna do, Dude?" repeated the goon, slouching between Charles and the river.

Known facts automatically played in Charles's mind: Sean Ferris, small-time muscle. Philadelphia, Chicago, then Detroit. Served three years for rape. Obedient, loyal. Attack dog. Ferris was old for this work, and fat. The black leather coat and pointed-toe boots stuck him in the sixties, too overdone even to pass for retro.

Charles took his cell phone from the pocket of the blanket coat and pushed the number three.

"Calling Mr. Big?" asked another of the goons Bernie had stuck him with.

James R. Spinks, forty-one years of age, out of Detroit, Michigan, connected to what passed for Mafia. Scum for hire. IQ of 84. Went by the name Jimmy. Grown men who liked to be called by little boys' names needed to be hung by their tiny dicks, Charles thought.

Bernie picked up on the second ring. The fool must be hunched over the phone, waiting for news of his cunning foray into crime.

"Campground is burned," Charles said.

"Nothing to acquire." The job was supposed to be a clean smash-and-grab. Bernie, *Mr. Big,* hadn't done his homework. The fool actually believed Charles had no idea who was the so-called brains behind this caper. Bernard Iverson, forty-six, Edmondson, Canada, marine equipment, massively over-extended, net worth five million dollars and still not worth the bullet it would take to kill him.

"One second, please," Bernie said.

Unblinking, Charles waited, listening to a clatter that suggested Bernie was using his cell phone as a hockey puck. He gritted his teeth, his jaw muscles bunched into hard knots. This was the only outward show of emotion he allowed himself. Humans were masters at reading faces. A second's hesitation, a flick of the eyes, a smile at the wrong time telegraphed weakness. Even people who didn't understand what they were see-ing retained enough feral instinct to home in on any chink in the armor. From that day forth they hammered at it until the chink became a crack and the crack a break. Once the soft flesh was exposed they went for the entrails with talons and tongues as sharp as harpies'.

The only earth the meek inherited was six feet down and capped by a stone.

A final scrimmage and Bernie was back. "There's a second campsite about four miles north on the same side of the river. It looks like it didn't burn. They probably stopped there."

Charles kept waiting. Four miles, no trail, probably: not good enough. The whole setup was Mickey Mouse. Bernie didn't know Charles, but Charles knew him. Michael had once said the so-called *Mr. Big* was nickel and dime, undermining unions, cutting corners, slighting on materials. That was why they'd bought him out. When it came to fundamental criminal activities, Charles doubted if he could steal a peek at a nudist camp. Given half a day, Charles could have come up with a better crew than Bernie's bottom-feeders.

"I'll get a bird's-eye's and call you back," Bernie said finally.

Charles punched the disconnect. Jimmy, dressed in a coat identical to the one Charles wore, but with a matching hat and earflaps, spit a stream of tobacco juice into the ash. Mostly into the ash; a drop or two of spittle remained in the Ted Kaczynski–style beard he sported.

"What's the deal?" Jimmy asked. His teeth were stained brown.

Charles looked away. "The target may be

four miles upriver. The pilot's doing a flyby. We wait here until we have a positive ID."

"Then what?" This from Reg.

Reginald Waters, African American, thirty-one, Detroit. Ex-gangbanger, low-end drug dealer, con man. Into bookies for a hundred and seventy-three grand. Last call for repayment before the bad boys came for him.

"If the target is located, we move to acquire it," Charles said without looking at Waters. Eye contact was an invitation to intimacy. Flee, fight, fornicate, or, Charles's least favorite, ask stupid questions. Open honest intercourse was not a paradigm for leadership that appealed to him.

"Even with others he works alone."

Charles's brother had said that. A photograph of Michael clicked onto the screen in Charles's mind, the black-and-white glossy taken for his senior yearbook. Next to it appeared the picture of the target lifted from the Internet.

Payback is going to be a bitch, Charles promised his little brother.

Two

One hand buried in Wily's ragged fur, Heath gazed into the fire, marveling at the concept of camping out, canoeing a river, building a fire, and eating and sleeping in the wilderness. This was a fine and wonderful thing. Boy Scouts did it, park rangers and hunters and hikers did it, photographers and dishwashers and presidents did it.

And now cripples did it, she thought. Hooray for our side.

Their camp was on a bluff above the river. Dishes and hands were washed well inland. No human effluvia would dirty the waters on Anna Pigeon's watch. Excretions were buried, the soiled toilet tissue put in ziplocked plastic bags to be packed out. This Heath was exempt from. She was testing a chamber-pot-sized camping toilet, super lightweight, watertight, and ergonomically designed to improve the aim of even the most inept user. Come morning the fire

16

would be doused and stirred. Ashes and burned stick ends would be scattered, the burn mark raked, and the area rehabbed with forest duff.

Anna had lived by the law of "take nothing but pictures, leave nothing but footprints" for so long she no longer even carried a camera; she took nothing but memories. Tonight she was storing them up on a solitary float on the Fox. Heath would have enjoyed a ride with her old friend, but Anna needed solitude. Like a dolphin in the ocean, Anna could submerge herself in the sea of humanity for long periods of time, but if she didn't surface into her private universe every so often, she would suffocate.

"You look like the Cheshire cat who ate the canary in the catbird seat," Leah said in her usual scratchy murmur. Leah always carried an internal echo, as if she were talking to herself. Too many hours alone in labs breathing toxic fumes, was Heath's guess. Leah had two doctorates, one in chemistry and one in electronic engineering. She was the research and development genius behind Hendricks & Hendricks, a high-end sports gear and clothing manufacturer based out of Boulder.

Heath met her when Leah was looking for paraplegics willing to play guinea pig to test gear she'd designed to make wilderness access easier for the disabled. This trip was a shakedown cruise for a chair, a canoe, a lifting device, and selvane, a chemical compound that was lightweight and strong, and dramatically decreased friction.

At the moment Heath was lounging in a camp chair designed for wheelchair users. Twelve and a half inches from the ground, and as stable as if nailed to the earth, it allowed Heath to move easily from chair to wheelchair and back. The arms were sturdy enough to do handstands on — Elizabeth had done several just to prove it, though, since she weighed about the same as the average golden retriever, it wasn't the best of tests.

H&H was already successful, but if selvane was all Leah hoped it would be, it would revolutionize the industry. It would revolutionize a lot of industries. God forbid the sinister uses the military would find for it.

"Lost in thought," Leah said. It was less a question, it seemed to Heath, than a statement of personal choice.

"I was contemplating your genius," Heath said truthfully.

"Oh." Evidently, people often did that, and it had ceased to be of interest. Leah

18

went back to studying the wheelchair. The wheels were larger and softer than those on street chairs, and it weighed next to nothing. Leah had designed it to be folded so it could fit easily into a canoe or strapped onto a backpack. Firelight flickering on the lenses of her glasses gave Heath the illusion of witnessing mental gears turning as Leah mulled over her design, seeking out flaws.

Elizabeth, Heath's daughter, had named her wheelchair Robo-butt. This new miracle of modern engineering was dubbed Robo-butt ATV.

Taking a drag from her cigarette, Heath watched her daughter. Heat rising from the campfire twisted the air, and she saw E as if through antique glass. The first time she'd laid eyes on this amazing creature who was to be her child had been in the woods at night. Elizabeth and two other little girls had stumbled half naked, bleeding and mute, out of the forest near where she and her aunt were camping in Rocky Mountain National Park. Heath had thought they were a bear come to dine on the helpless crippled lady. Instead, one of them became her salvation.

After the accident that broke her back, Heath had given up on herself. Along came Elizabeth, and Heath discovered she couldn't give up on herself without giving up on Elizabeth. That was unthinkable.

From a bitter drunken cripple, Heath had grown into a semicivilized paraplegic. From a scrawny frightened limpet, Elizabeth had grown into a confident beauty. Still, her eyes were the eyes of someone much older — a thousand years older. Ghosts could be seen in those depths. Shadows moved there even on cloudless days. Heath liked to think her adopted daughter was an old soul who had visited the realms of the living in many incarnations.

Before she'd asked E on this trip, they'd talked long and hard about whether a sojourn in the woods would bring back the nightmares. E was in favor of facing one's fears. Where her daughter was concerned, Heath sang the praises of running away.

"You're doing it, Heath."

Elizabeth had caught her in the act. Mothers should not be obviously smitten. E told her once in mock seriousness that it undermined discipline.

"I am not," she lied as she wiped the doting look off her face.

Elizabeth rolled her eyes.

"Doing what?" Katie asked. Leah's daughter, Katie, was thirteen. Heath had hoped they would be company for each other on

20

the trip, but Katie looked and acted far younger than her years.

"Looking all warm and runny inside," Elizabeth said. "You know, Mother Gooey?"

Katie's white-blond eyebrows, nearly invisible on her pale, heart-shaped face, drew together in confusion. When it cleared Heath saw bitterness. "Right," she said. "Maybe if I had titanium parts."

Katie stabbed a marshmallow through the heart with a twig. "These have got to be covered in germs and squirrel poop," she said with a grimace.

"Organic," Elizabeth kidded her. "Costs a fortune at Whole Foods."

"Daddy gets fits if Tanya lets me eat anything that isn't organic. 'Organic' is Latin for boring." Katie thrust the skewered marshmallow into the fire and watched keenly as it caught and burned, the skin turning black and crusted.

"Who is Tanya?" Heath asked.

"Warden," Katie said.

"Au pair," Leah said without looking at her daughter.

Katie tilted her head until her baby-fine blond hair fell forward and curtained her face. Heath suspected she was mortified. Who has a babysitter in the eighth grade? What kind of a mother mentions it in front of another girl, and a high school girl at that?

"A pair of what?" Heath asked.

Katie raised her eyes from the charred corpse of the marshmallow. Katie didn't grace Heath with even a hint of a smile. Heath had known Leah's daughter for twenty-four hours and had yet to see her smile. Katie might be accustomed to manipulating adults by withholding approval. God knew most mothers would wag themselves to death for a pat on the head from their kid.

"You shouldn't smoke," Katie said to wreak a kind of revenge. "Secondhand smoke kills people."

"It's okay. Mom doesn't exhale," Elizabeth said.

Leah said nothing. Heath had been raised by her aunt Gwen, a pediatrician. Rudeness, particularly to adults, was not tolerated. Heath had never tolerated it in Elizabeth. Leah just glanced at her daughter as if she were the ill-mannered child of a stranger.

Wily sighed in his sleep. Heath ran her fingers up his pointed coyote-style ears. Maybe Anna was right, maybe animals were better people than people. Then again, Anna didn't exactly work and play well with others. She should be roasting marshmallows and celebrating the night on the river instead of floating somewhere in her damn sacred solitude. A true friend would be drinking wine and keeping Heath from getting too involved in other people's business.

"E, would you go see if you can see Anna's canoe?" Heath asked. "Tell her we're making s'mores. That should bring her in out of the cold." Elizabeth rose with a fluid grace Heath could barely remember. Movement was language for E. Often she'd forgo use of her own legs to experiment with new ways Heath could get around. They installed monkey bars in the living room and performed monkeylike antics on them. Elizabeth was an ace with Heath's wheelchair. So as not to seem a drag, Heath learned to pop wheelies, entered races, and was rear guard for the basketball team Rolling Thunder.

The leaves, rich reds, yellows, and oranges during the day, were black with coming night. The last light of the day limned the edges with silver. Leaning back, Heath looked for the first star of evening amid sparks rising lazily into the air, then winking out like fireflies. Campfires and Wily were two of the reasons Heath preferred to camp on Forest Service rather than Park Service land. Much as she loved Anna's parks, the NPS was not dog- or fire-friendly. There were times Heath didn't want to conserve for the use of the next generation; she wanted to pretend there was enough of everything wild, that it would go on forever, and humans were too insignificant to do any real damage. Camping with a good fire and a good dog helped that illusion.

"Are these things any better roasted?" Katie asked. She was holding up one of the mushrooms Leah had picked earlier in the day. Raised north of Duluth, Minnesota, the only child of two mothers, both of whom were concerned with natural foods and sustained harvests, Leah had grown up hunting mushrooms and gathering wild rice.

Before Leah could respond, Katie had jabbed the orange fungus with a stick and poked it into the flame more as if she were torturing than cooking it.

"Don't do that," Leah said softly. Katie kept doing it. Leah looked away.

"Leave a few, at least," Heath said. Lobster mushrooms had added a nice zest to the prepared foods they'd brought.

"Never eat a mushroom I haven't okayed," Leah said. "Some are deadly."

"Oh right, like I'm going to mistake an Amanita for a lobster," Katie sneered.

"They look like deer mushrooms, not lobster," Leah said mildly.

"Do you see Anna?" Heath asked Elizabeth, a sharp silhouette on the bluff overlooking the water.

"Nope. Nada."

Feeling abandoned, Heath swallowed a slug of bourbon. It definitely tasted better from a tin cup than from a crystal glass. She wondered if that would be true inside four walls. Definitely a double-blind test in the offing when they returned to Boulder.

A crashing in the woods interrupted Heath's meditation. Katie dropped the mushroom she was burning with such determination.

"Wolf?" Elizabeth asked hopefully. "It would be so cool to see a wolf."

"More likely a bear or a moose," Heath said. "Get Wily's leash, would you, E?"

Elizabeth ducked into the tent with the enviable ease of the young and limber, scooped up the leash, then knelt, legs folding smoothly like the self-lubricating hinges on Leah's high-tech inventions, and clipped the lead to Wily's collar.

"Probably a deer," Leah said absently.

Too many years without predators had allowed the deer herds to outgrow their habitat. In winter, they starved and died of disease. Wherever humans were known to give handouts, they begged. Without food,

25

even Bambi could become aggressive. Wolves had reinhabited northern Minnesota, but not in sufficient numbers to do the thinning work.

Wily's neck hair stiffened under Heath's hand. His body went rigid. A growl, so low she more felt than heard it, began building in his chest.

"It's people," she said quietly.

THREE

All forms of sorrow and delight, All solemn Voices of the Night. The words seemed to form from the soughing of the wind in the dying leaves. The mystical ululation of a loon, a sound that seemed to Anna to linger on the water long after the bird had ceased to call, punctuated the thought.

Wadsworth? Frost?

The air was a delicate balance. The last of summer rested on the skin as the prickle of coming winter brushed the mind. Anna could taste the fertile loamy scent of leaves, fallen and readying to return to the earth, and the lingering smell of warm grass, dust, and pine. Mated with the spicy scent of campfire smoke, it triggered a longing for sometime, someplace, someone that never existed, but was nonetheless exquisite, and to be deliciously mourned.

Enjoying nostalgia, a luxury she seldom allowed herself, she lay back in the stern of the canoe as it drifted down the Fox River as light and quiet as a leaf on a pond. A new moon, a dime-sized wraith barely edged with light, was almost lost in a dense sea of glittering stars. This far north, this far from neon, fluorescent, incandescent, and halogen, this far from television screens, stars and sky appeared simultaneously close and impossibly distant. If Anna let her fingers loose from where they relaxed around the gunwales, she might fall up and forever.

There was nowhere she needed to be, no one she needed to serve. The owner of the convenience store at the put-in said the camp they'd planned on using had been burned over by a forest fire, so they stopped a few miles upstream. Anna reveled in the extra time to do absolutely nothing productive. She knew she should be missing Paul. A better husband than Paul Davidson would only serve to make a woman feel chronically inadequate.

It wasn't that she didn't enjoy his company; they'd been married several years and she was still crazy in love with the man. Catching his smile in a crowd never failed to make her heart skip a beat. The thing was, when she was alone in wild country — or as wild as country got in these United

States — Anna didn't miss anyone, not her friends, not her dog or cat, not her sister, Molly, not her husband.

Early imprinting, she supposed. In her thirties she'd been pretty well deconstructed by life. In solitude and wilderness she'd been put back together. Perhaps it wasn't so odd that she felt at home here, complete.

Paul was different. He moved through the world of people with the ease of a water snake across a calm lake. Human constellations, in the form of neighborhoods, clubs, or congregations, came to his orbit, drawn by his warmth and honor.

Anna admired it greatly but couldn't live that way every day. Now and then, she needed to breathe air that wasn't someone else's exhalation. Even this trip was somewhat overcrowded for her taste, though Leah seemed nice enough for an extremely wealthy person. Money was like sugar; too much of it sickened people.

Leah didn't talk much, which was a plus, and her voice was so soft. It had been the first to fade as Anna drifted farther and farther from camp. Heath's went next, and E's. High and sharp, Katie's was the last to be nullified by the gentle susurration of the river.

In blessed solitude and silence, Anna

drifted. Heaven. To dream of anything else was sacrilege — if one believed in sacrilege.

Gods were tricky business. Anna seldom gave them a thought, nor, if they existed, did she expect they pondered much upon her comings and goings. This amiable standoff ended when Paul retired as sheriff of Adams County and moved to Colorado, where she was a district ranger at Rocky Mountain.

Before he was a sheriff, Paul had been an Episcopal priest. He was an Episcopal priest again, working interim at St. Aidan's in Boulder. Tired of pursuing the bad guys, he said he needed to pursue the good guys for a while, for the sake of his soul. Father Davidson was not the sort to press his wife to attend church or to embrace Jesus. That would have sent Anna screaming for the hills.

Paul Davidson enjoyed the simple gift of faith.

When Anna asked him in what way and why, he said people needed to believe in something. Not necessarily the patriarchal smiting god, or the white-washed western-ized vision of the carpenter's son, not even in miracles. In the twenty-first century miracles were commonplace. People couldn't get excited over a man walking on water when they'd seen a man walking on the moon. Paul's contention was that to fend off despair and embrace life, humanity needed to move beyond miracles. They needed to believe the impossible: that there was an end to suffering, that their emptiness would be filled. That they were loved.

Since the beginning, churches had used all that was deemed holy to get their victims to collude in their own destruction. Regardless, churches were where people sought the divine. So Paul served his grand scheme of love from the altar.

Trailing her hand in water grown cold with early rains in Canada, Anna wondered idly what she served.

A low thrumming clatter of grouse wings applauded.

A sign, she thought. She smiled.

The applause continued, the sweet cacophony punctuated by the grouse clicking low in his throat. Then something alien, a wrong note in the symphony of the woods, metal swallowing metal. Anna sat up straight, suddenly alert. Nothing in nature made a sound like that.

Faintly, far away, and unmistakably, a pistol had been manually cocked, a wheel gun probably, a big one, .45 or .357. Maybe a .38. Because she was on vacation — and flying commercially — Anna hadn't brought a weapon. Heath had no interest in firearms.

Whoever it was had not come from downstream. Anna would have heard them snap-crackle-and popping through the downed leaves and twigs.

Hunters? Possible. It might be deer season. Outside of the parks, Anna was unsure of the rules and regulations. As far as she was concerned, hunting season was when rangers hunted poachers.

A chance encounter? A lone and twisted individual happening on helpless-looking women while pursuing a moose? Opportunistic cruelty of the kind portrayed in the movie *Deliverance*?

"Squeal like a pig" sliced out of Anna's memory.

Thieves? Thieves would be nice. Thieves liked to take things and slip peacefully away. Property crimes were common in parks and forests. Cars were clouted and pockets picked, but seldom this far from civilization. Hikers carried little of value, but for their gear, and gear wasn't easily converted to cash.

There was little hope for a nice honest robbery. Unfortunately other forms of low-lifes — denizens of horror films and fever dreams — often chose to be paid in the currency of screams, investing fear into the depleted accounts of their sorry, miserable, stinking lives.

Anna turned the canoe's nose upstream and began paddling hard against the current.

FOUR

In a public campground, a KOA — any place where people gathered — the approach of human footsteps would not have been frightening. Alone, in the backwoods at nightfall, there was no reason for pedestrian traffic. No good reason.

A man, dressed like a lumberjack in a red-and-black plaid coat and black jeans tucked into new boots, materialized out of the charcoal gray of evening beneath the trees. A gun that looked the size of a small cannon, the hole in the barrel as wide and deep as a well, was held close by his thigh. Admittedly, Heath's eye level was less than three feet off the ground; still, he was huge. He had to be close to six-six. Beneath the layers of flannel and wool, his body was thick. Like the blade of a shovel, his jaw was wide at the top and came to a spade point below a small mouth. Dark hair formed a widow's peak on a low, broad forehead. In some lights the face would appear ruggedly handsome. In others, dimorphic and hideous, the top half that of a he-man, the bottom that of a woman.

"Good evening," Heath said, hanging on to the vain hope these were hunters and this an unexpected social call. "What can we do for you?"

"Hendricks, Leah," the man said in a flat cool voice, his eyes flickering over Heath and dismissing her.

"I'm Leah Hendricks," Leah whispered. Her face, always pale, was gray where blood had fled the skin, and orange where the glow of the fire hit her cheekbones and the ridge of her nose. The effect was disturbing, feverish.

"Hendricks, Katie," said the man.

"What is this? Is Gerald okay?" Leah asked. Gerald was her husband.

"Hendricks, Katie," the man repeated.

"Is something the matter with Daddy?" Katie asked. "Are you a cop?"

His eyes, just holes in his face from where Heath sat, sparked as they moved in Katie's direction. "Yes," he said. "Katie Hendricks?"

"Here," Katie said and raised her hand as if she were in school.

"Aunt Gwen?" Heath asked in the barest

scrape of time, when she could believe that the police had sent forest rangers with bad news.

"This is it," the man said in a louder tone.

"About fucking time," came another male voice. Seconds later a smaller, bearded man, dressed almost identically, stepped into the ring of firelight. He carried a rifle.

"You're not the police, are you?" Heath asked. Two more men emerged from the dark fringe of trees, one with a handgun. Overkill, Heath thought and wished she hadn't. The men spread out, making four points of a box around Heath and the others.

"Are you lost?" Heath inquired politely, trying to force the situation to normalcy. "About all we can offer you is a cup of coffee."

"You and you." The tall black-haired man, the leader most likely, indicated Katie and Leah with the barrel of the pistol. Katie's eyes grew so big she looked more like a lemur than a human child. "There. Sit." He pointed at the feet of a black man who, in a black hoodie and black sweats, formed a shadow against the trees.

"Sean's got the ties, Dude," the black man said. Sean was the fourth man, the last to enter the clearing. He looked like an extra from the road show of *Grease* who hadn't aged well. He saw Heath staring at him and smiled with small, crooked, very white teeth.

Terror stampeded over Heath. It was happening, the worst-case scenario; she was crippled and helpless and monsters had come for the children and she couldn't do one damn thing to stop them. Not one goddamn thing. Visions of Elizabeth bleeding, clothing ripped, men in the midst of gang rape burned through Heath's mind too fast for the eye to see, but not for the soul to feel.

"Stay close, stay close," she whispered, reaching out to clutch Elizabeth's leg. Heath had to hold herself together. If nothing else, she could witness, she could memorize the faces. Sean, that was one name. She could listen for more so they could be tracked down. Heath's eyes tried to catch detail, find meaningful marks, but flickering light and pounding pulse and the enormity of the size of horror of the men of the guns cracked her vision into a kaleidoscope of images.

A story Anna once told flashed in her mind. A man in a bunny suit, shooting blanks from a revolver in one hand and waving a carrot in the other, charged into a Crime Scene Investigation class. He hopped around the room and out the door. When the students' eyewitness accounts were read aloud, they did not agree on whether the shooter was black or white, male or female, if it was a rabbit or a kangaroo, or how many shots were fired. The only thing on which they agreed was that the intruder had guns in both hands.

The point: Eyewitnesses were unreliable.

There would be no eyewitnesses left after these men had done whatever they'd come to do. That reality struck Heath with the force of a two-by-four across the back of the head.

"Run!" she hissed at Elizabeth and surged to her feet to put her body between the guns and her daughter's flight path. She flopped from the camp chair like a landed trout. Her mind had forgotten her legs no longer worked.

The gang leader, the tall man, straightened his arm, the pistol extending from his huge hand like a black finger pointing at Elizabeth's midsection.

"Nobody move," he said in a tone as hard as cast iron. Elizabeth, Heath, the rustle of the leaves overhead seemed to freeze. Time took a breath. The black guy froze. The bearded man with the rifle was still as stone. Everything but the fire stopped moving. A silence, closer to deafness than quiet, swallowed the camp. Heath was afraid she was going to start laughing or crying or screaming.

Over the water slow applause mocked the scene. The clapping grew louder, faster. A disapproving tongue clicking crept into the clatter.

The black man jumped. "What the fuck was that?" he demanded as the noise faded.

"Keep your pants dry, Reg," the bearded man said. "Probably just an old rat or a squirrel messing around."

"I never heard no rat sound like that," Reg said.

"It's a grouse," Elizabeth told them. "They drum this time of year."

Heath scowled at her. *Seen and not heard* echoed in her head. Invisible and gone would be better.

Reg looked at Elizabeth as if he were trying to figure out who she was calling a grouse, him or the creature that made the eerie sound.

"Finish securing the Hendrickses. Get this one, too," the leader said, his gun still aimed at Elizabeth. "Soon as it's light, we go. Reg, cover them with the Walther. Sean, secure them."

The black man, Reg, had the "Walther," a

pewter-colored handgun. It was a kind of gun that shot more than six bullets. That was the extent of Heath's expertise with firearms. Reg held it like a man who knew how to use it.

Sean pulled an unopened package of plastic cable ties from the pocket of his jacket.

Beneath Heath's hand, Wily was trembling. Or maybe she was trembling; she couldn't tell where she ended and the dog began, where reality ended and nightmare began.

Ties in hand, Sean said, "Put your pretty little wrists together so nice Uncle Sean can make sure you don't get into trouble."

Leah held out her hands, wrists together.

Wily began to bark wildly.

"Shut the dog up," the big man said to Heath. "You, with the others." He laid a heavy hand on E's shoulder. Elizabeth stumbled, then fell to her hands and knees.

Leash trailing like the tail of a comet, Wily shot from under Heath's fingers as if he'd been born in the Alaskan wilderness and just laid eyes on his first reindeer calf. Growl became roar, and his slink a lunge, as he went for the throat of the man who'd dared lay hands on a member of his pack.

Wily's heart was that of a young wolf; his

bones were those of an old dog. The man swatted him down as if he were a mosquito, then kicked him hard in the side. Wily's limp form flew through the air. With a crack of bone that snapped Heath's heart in two, he slammed into the bole of a tree.

FIVE

Wily's body slid down the trunk and pooled around the bottom as lifeless as a dropped towel.

"You miserable son of a bitch," Heath said, unable to comprehend such meaningless evil. From the corner of her eye, she saw Elizabeth rising to her feet on a tide of fury.

"Stop!" Heath cried. "No! No!"

Like an avenging angel, Elizabeth flew at the man. Pistol in hand, the man's enormous red-and-black-clad arm rose.

"Don't shoot!" Heath screamed.

He didn't shoot. He clubbed Elizabeth to the ground with the same easy violence he'd shown when dealing with Wily. The base of her skull struck the duff first, and she went as limp as the dog.

"God damn you, you son of a bitch, you goddam son of a bitch," Heath yelled. Worthless legs tangling, she scrambled to her daughter's body. Damaged nerves were sending so many mixed signals Heath couldn't feel a pulse in E's neck. She pressed her ear to Elizabeth's back. Rapid and strong, a heartbeat.

"Damn lucky for you, she's alive." Heath spit the words at the big man. A flicker of something crossed his face. Maybe amusement. Heath wanted to strike him down so badly she hissed like a snake.

"Whoa! Got us a she cat," said the bearded man.

"Hey, at least the dog shut up," said Sean. "Turn around," he ordered Katie.

"Don't you dare touch me, scumbag!" she snapped, jerking an arm the size of a toothpick from his thick-fingered hand. "My father will kill you. Do you know who my mother is?"

"I know exactly who she is, sweet cheeks. And I know just what you rich little twats are good for." He leered cartoonishly. On him it looked natural.

"Do as he says." Leah's voice was a cold thread of sound.

Katie glared at her mother, tears glittering like rubies on her cheeks. "Not so tight," she cried as the plastic was pulled taut on her wrists.

"Not so tight, Sean," the big man said.

"Dude, you can't loosen these things. I gotta cut 'em off and do new ones."

"Then cut them off," the dude said reasonably.

"Pain in the ass," Sean muttered, but he did as he was told.

Scraping, a noise, paddles on the gunwale of a canoe, grated through the panic and despair boiling inside Heath's skull.

Anna. She was returning to camp. In a minute she would beach the canoe and walk up the path to the bluff.

"You'll never get away with this," Heath yelled and flailed her arms, making as much noise as she could. "We're expected back tomorrow morning. If we don't show, the entire country will come after you, guns drawn!"

Sean stopped in the midst of cutting Katie's bonds. The thugs looked at her as if she were behaving boorishly, as if they'd never attacked and kidnapped such a disgusting barbarian.

"Crazy," Reg said, shaking his head sadly, the yellow hoodie beneath the black flashing in bright parentheses on either side of his dark face.

"Stay away from us! You hear me?" Heath shouted. "Stay the hell away!"

Six

"Stay the hell away!"

Heath.

Anna quit paddling.

Adrenaline spiked her blood and she nearly dropped the paddle into the river. Skin prickled, hairs on the back of her neck stirred, nostrils flared. As her body absorbed the level of threat, her ears felt as if they grew venous and quivering like those of a bat.

Taking a deep breath, she held it, consciously slowing her heart rate. The bluff blocked her view of everything except the glow of the fire. Shadowed red and gold leaves on the underside of the canopy shuddered in the breeze, pallid echoes of the flames beneath.

Hugging the bank, she let the canoe drift back downstream. The night had been transformed from star-filled and gentle into dark and full of menace. A man's voice.

Heath screaming obscenities. One man? More than one. Males who were announced with screams and curses tended to travel in packs, like jackals.

The canoe had drifted far enough. With a deft twist of the paddle, she nosed into the bank downstream of a tree. Roots undercut, it had fallen into the river and lay with a crown of desiccated foliage bobbing in the stream.

Anna leapt over the bow onto dry land, then pulled the canoe far enough out of the water that the tug of the current wouldn't lure it away. For insurance, she tethered it to the exposed roots. At present, the canoe was her most valuable asset. When she'd gone for a solo paddle, she hadn't planned to be out for more than an hour. Consequently, she hadn't brought anything with her, not so much as a water bottle. Her camp shoes, good moose-hide moccasins from Ely, Minnesota, were house shoes with soft leather soles. These and the clothes on her back were the sum total of her survival gear. She didn't even have her Swiss Army knife. Having lost so many to TSA, when she flew, she left it home. In lieu of major ordnance, she lifted a paddle from the canoe. A paddle was as good as a baseball bat and boasted a longer reach.

Seated on the trunk of the downed oak, she removed socks and moccasins, stuffed the socks into the shoes, tied the moccasins together by their laces, then slung them around her neck. Using the paddle as a staff, she waded back into the river.

Despite what cowboy authors had written regarding the stealth of the average American Indian, it was not possible to travel through dry leaves without making a sound. This Anna knew from experience. When she was seven and her sister, Molly, twelve, they had spent many a fall afternoon trying to perfect a method to do it. This was during what they later came to refer to as their Arapaho Autumn.

Water traverse would be quieter. The scrawny fingernail moon afforded little assistance beneath the overhanging riverbank. Like a blind woman, Anna felt her way with paddle and toes, hoping she wouldn't fall into a hole and dunk herself, or walk into an old strainer and skewer herself on a stick. Looming, unseen, the riverbank weighed on the right side of her brain. Water flowing over her knees was black as squid ink and had a viscous oily quality. Stars receded until they were mere pinpricks of ice in the sky.

Perceptions not provable in a lab informed

Anna that the pure nastiness of humanity was polluting the Fox River. Pure nasty humanity was the problem she had with Paul's God of love. Too many people were involved. Had love of one's neighbor referred only to those with fur or feathers, she might have become a believer.

Fifteen yards from the campsite, she waded out of the water. A ribbon of sand and gravel lined the riverbed. Like dry leaves, gravel was almost impossible to walk on without making a racket. Stepping with great care, she reached the rising bank where soil crumbled down from above and a short scruff of grasses grew. Grass was more forgiving of human trespass.

A man's voice rumbled downriver, chasing the crying of a woman or girl. No barking or growling. Where was Wily? As he aged, his joints had grown stiff, but his hearing was still keen.

Leaning on the paddle in the dark of the bank's shadow, Anna closed her eyes and pictured the camp. Atop the low bluff was a triangular clearing, the longest leg facing east over the river. The north, west, and southwest were thick with deciduous trees, mostly maples and oaks. The forest floor would be deep in leaves, the ferns crisp with autumn. Nearest the river, beside the cut leading to the Fox, was a large stand of white pine.

Pine needles had been one of the few success stories for the Indian scouts of the Arapaho Autumn, a success Anna had duplicated many times in the years since. Even white women could move across pine needles with a minimum of noise. Piney woods had it all over hardwood forests when it came to surveillance or surprise attack.

Since the vagaries of fire and flashlight beams would catch white flesh and red hair more surely and startlingly than the steady burn of electricity, Anna skinned out of her dark blue jacket. Underneath she wore a long-sleeved black T-shirt and a red tank top. She wriggled her arms free of the T, then pulled it up until the black cotton hid her hair and most of her face, leaving the neck hole as her window on the world. Ersatz burnoose complete, she slipped the jacket back over her tank top. There was little she could do with her hands. The Fox's was a sandy riverbed, stingy with its mud.

As camouflaged as she could manage on short notice, she silenced her thoughts, as she always did when she wished herself invisible. Tracking everything from grizzly bears to skunks, she'd become convinced animals could sense a clamorous mind.

People, not so much; still, she waited for inner quiet before walking quickly over the parched grass toward where the glow of the campfire touched the river.

Water soaked from her trouser legs and squished beneath her bare feet, seemingly as loud as whales mating or ten thousand jellyfish going under a steamroller. Five nerve-stripping yards, and she was beneath the bluff where Leah's oversized canoe, a product in testing, was beached. She nearly barked her shins on the gunwale. With only a new moon, little light came from the open sky above the Fox. Beneath the trees ruled a darkness rivaling that three miles underground in Lechuguilla Cavern.

A social trail, cut by human and animal traffic, had eroded into a miniature ravine that led from the water to the top of the bluff. On a canvas of exposed roots and rocks, firelight painted a stairway that might have been done on one of Dalí's bad days.

On hands and feet, Anna made her way up the gully far enough that her eyes were level with the top of the bank. Nose at root level, her senses were washed in the wholesome scents of soil and hay as she peered through the coarse grass covering the bluff.

Four men were visible; the nearest was a head taller than his companions. Orange and green half-dome tents, dwarfed by his height, gave the impression he stood in a magic mushroom patch. He wore the red-and-black checked wool coat favored by hunters, but the clothes fairly creaked with newness, a costume acquired for this event. Short black hair was combed back from a sharp side part. A predatory nose hunched over a luxuriant mustache that reflected the red of the flames where it curved over the corners of his mouth. In his left hand was a Colt. Anna couldn't determine the caliber but trusted it had sufficient stopping power.

Not a duck or grouse hunter's weapon.

He held the gun firmly but comfortably, as if he were shaking the hand of an old friend. The barrel was pointed at the back of Heath's head. These were not hunters of deer or elk or moose. These were men who stalked alleys, bars, and city parks.

Elizabeth was prostrate, her cheek pressed to the ground, her girlish mouth twisted into a moue. A trace of black was smeared between her nose and upper lip. In the shadows there was no way to tell if it was blood or dirt. A slight rise and fall of her chest let Anna know she was alive, either unconscious or playing possum. Heath was draped over her in a protective curve of motherhood.

Not hunters, not woodsmen: These guys wouldn't have come by river. They were motorboat types, not canoeists. A back road, maybe, an old logging or mining road. Yet they hadn't driven. As still as the night was, Anna would have heard an engine. Their clothes were speckled with leaves and twigs where they'd pushed through vegetation. They'd traveled by foot and for quite a long way.

Beyond the big man covering E and Heath with the Colt was a man no more than five foot eight and clad in a red-and-black coat identical to the big man's and augmented by a matching plaid cap with earflaps. Had it not been so creepy, this mini-me would have been comical. A dirty-brown beard hid most of his face. In his hands was an old pump-action .22, the kind of rifle any self-respecting Mississippian would call a squirrel gun. He held the .22 out from his body and too far forward, more like a divining rod than a rifle. Saturday night specials, straight razors, and pool cues were likely his weapons of choice.

The muzzle of the .22 was pointed at a place on the ground behind the tents. Leah and Katie, Anna guessed. Good news. Dead people didn't need to be held at gunpoint.

The remaining thugs had not tried to

change their spots with Eddie Bauer's best. They were dressed like miscreants snatched off any city street. One was slender, black, and around thirty. He wore blue Converse high-tops and black drawstring pants. For warmth he'd layered two hoodies, one over the other, black over yellow. Both hoods were up; his hands were stuffed into the pouch pocket on his stomach. Without daylight, Anna could tell little else about him: whether he was light- or dark-skinned, handsome or ugly, or even if he had hair. If he was armed, whatever he carried fit into the pocket of a sweatshirt.

The last of the quartet was an excessively white middle-aged man. A beer belly the size of a seven-month-old fetus pushed his jacket out. Astraddle a red-veined nose sat glasses with rectangular lenses in brown plastic frames. The temples sank into the man's flesh. The lenses were so thick his face appeared squeezed in, his eyes the size of watermelon pips. Newer, lighter, thinner lenses had been available since the eighties. The too-white guy either liked the look or hadn't bothered to update his prescription in thirty years. His jacket was black leather with zippered pockets. On his feet were half boots with elastic inserts on the side, the kind fashionable in the seventies.

He stood several feet from the bearded man with the rifle, also staring at the place where Anna assumed Leah and Katie sat. He had no gun, but an oversized hunting knife hung from his belt in a leather sheath.

Sudden and awful dread rushed into Anna. Poison, cold and acidic, burned her brain. Sweat broke out on her palms. Light-headed, she clung to a root for fear she would stumble back into the gully. Twice before had she gone sick with a fear she didn't understand. Neither time had there been any real threat in sight. The first was in Mississippi. She'd pulled over a beat-up Ford sedan for going twenty miles per hour in a fifty-mile-per-hour zone. The driver was a young female, pathologically obese, her short brown hair like a bathing cap painted on a white billiard ball. Her eyes, beady and black, were buried in folds of flesh. The passenger was as dried up as a mummy, old and wrinkled and tiny. Neither wore a seat belt. Neither said a word.

When Anna had leaned down to speak to the driver, something so evil gusted out the driver's window that she rocked back on her heels, her insides quaking. She'd given them a warning, then scuttled back to the sanctity of her patrol car, certain there were the dismembered bodies of infants in the trunk, and just as certain she wasn't going to try to find out if that was true.

The second time was at Isle Royale in Lake Superior when she was checking fishing creels. She'd boarded a fishing boat tied to the dock on one of the islands in Washington Harbor. Three men were in the boat, three creels, and a sense of something so palpably wrong, Anna leapt back on the dock without counting their catch.

This paunchy, absurdly dressed man emanated the same ordure; the stink of heroin in the veins of a child whore, slit nostrils, cats run over for fun.

As the physical terror swelled, and Anna felt she must shed her skin like a snake, E's eyes suddenly popped open the way Lucy's always did in Dracula movies. A laugh, or maybe a scream, was startled to life in Anna's throat. It took an effort of will to keep it from escaping.

Elizabeth was staring beyond the firelight where the pines crowded close on the northern side of the bluff. Anna followed her gaze. At the base of a venerable old white pine lay a shadow, gray-brown and wadded up, the way a man's coat might fall if he tossed it at a hook and missed. It was Wily. He hadn't been barking his fool head off because he was dead. There had been no reports from a gun. He must have been clubbed or kicked to death, his faithful body struck by a booted foot, or slammed into the unrelenting bark of the tree. Fury burned the overweening terror from Anna's mind. Her eyes ached with tears that turned to steam before they reached the ducts.

Two teenaged girls, a slightly mad scientist, a paraplegic, and an old dog: Anybody who would prey on such as these would stomp kittens and dry-swallow ducklings.

Elizabeth had long suffered nightmares, scars from her brush with a psychopath. Anna doubted she could survive a second brutal encounter. Katie was a poor little rich girl who had probably never faced any adversary more daunting than a recalcitrant nanny. Leah had a high-voltage brain, the kind that easily short-circuited. If anything happened to E or Wily, Heath would probably dive back into the ocean of self-pity and bourbon where Anna had first found her.

If Anna went for help, it would be thirty-six hours minimum before it arrived. Thirty-six hours would be too late.

Monsters weren't known for deferring gratification.

With luck, and the good wood of a canoe paddle, a lone gunman could be taken down by five women. There would be a cost, but it could be done. Richard Speck, the rapist and murderer of eight student nurses, had taught women a hard lesson; better one or two die in a hero's rush than all die slowly and horribly.

Four gunmen was a different story. Still Anna would stay, would watch. She would wait for an opening, a chance, then she would take it. Too many years rescuing lost hikers, mourning friends, and seeking justice for the dead had passed for her not to know she was, and always would be, her sister's keeper.

SEVEN

Heath's guts felt as if they had been dumped in a blender set on "puree." She was so scared she thought she might have wet herself. Not that she could feel it. Pissed her pants. There went her foolish pride, the petty superiority she allowed herself when contemplating those whose backs had been busted a few vertebrae higher than hers. At least I can control my bladder, she'd think. At least I don't piss myself.

Pride cometh jeering at the most inopportune moments. Still, she hoped she hadn't wet her pants, that she wasn't panicking. She'd been a climber, for Christ's sake. It was not a sport for cowards. At least not physical cowards; there had been a time she'd been afraid of life, afraid to live without two good legs, but that was years ago, before she'd fallen in love with the little girl who was to become her daughter.

Now it was E who was turning her craven.

Overcoming fear for one's self was a piece of cake compared to overcoming fear for one's child.

Pushing up on one elbow, she took most of her weight off of E's back while managing to stay between her and the gun. Not that her scrawny body would do much good. Though she'd never owned a gun, never shot one, and never wanted to, Heath had lived in Colorado all her life. She couldn't help but absorb a modicum of ambient knowledge. Fired at close range, a bullet could go through one person and kill whoever was behind. Still, as insubstantial as she was, she was better than nothing. She might get lucky and if the dude — Lord! To be shot by a man called "the dude"; she'd die of shame before she had time to bleed to death — if the dude pulled the trigger, maybe her bones, a zipper, or a button would deflect the bullet and save E.

Until Anna could rescue them.

That was the thought she wouldn't articulate to herself. That was a hell of a burden to put on one small, unarmed girlfriend. Heath couldn't help but hope: Anna was smart; she was resourceful, with a couple of miracles and a lot of luck . . . Anyway, Heath was careful not to raise her eyes to the woods, listen too intently for the soft fall of moccasins on leaves, or otherwise telegraph Anna's presence. She prayed that Leah, Elizabeth, and Katie would have the good sense to do the same.

A sensible person would have hopped in the canoe and paddled for help, but Heath knew Anna hadn't. She couldn't, no more than Heath could shut off her fear for Elizabeth. Anna was out there. As long as the four jackasses of the apocalypse didn't realize that, there was a chance.

Elizabeth wouldn't give Anna away. Heath could count on her. Trauma had not destroyed E, it had made her wiser than her years. Leah might be the smartest human being on the planet, but Heath had no idea what the scientist would do when she and her daughter were the lab rats. If Heath, who'd once made her living leading difficult climbs, had very possibly pissed herself in terror, what must an other-worldly brainiac be suffering?

Leah didn't share her inner self with the world, not even, apparently, with her sole offspring. Docile as a robot with the power switched off, she was watching the potbellied scumbag retie Katie's wrists with plastic ties. Shock, Heath told herself. Leah was wasn't used to not being in control.

After a day and a half with Katie, Heath

guessed Katie would offer Jesus Christ up to the Romans if she thought it would get her an extra hour of TV a night. Katie would give up Anna in a heartbeat if she saw any profit in it. Then again, if there was nothing to be gained, Katie might keep the secret to her grave just to spite the riffraff who dared handle her so roughly.

Putting her lips so close to E's ear she could smell the wood smoke in her hair, Heath whispered, "Elizabeth?" Beneath her cheek Elizabeth's head nodded fractionally.

"Play dead." Foolish as it might be, E flat to the ground, not moving, not looking in the direction of the men, made Heath less afraid for her. Rather like pulling the covers over your head so the monster in the closet won't eat you, she mocked herself.

"Get up," the dude said in a voice so conversational, so easy, it bored a hole in Heath's mind that sucked the sane universe through into a place where water ran uphill and the sun set in the east.

"What do you guys want?" Heath demanded. "What in the hell do you want from us? Whatever it is, take it and go." The thug, Sean, laughed an ugly grunting laugh.

The dude said nothing. He stepped closer, melding in with the dark canopy of leaves, as tall and unknowable as a giant redwood.

Nostrils flared black. Cavernous eyes were deep behind cheekbones sharp as knives. Heath was seeing not the man but the skull under the flesh. Nothing shone behind the eye sockets, nothing. Windows to the soul opening onto a room inhabited by cobwebs and cockroaches. The dude would shoot her and Elizabeth where they lay rather than repeat himself.

He nudged Elizabeth's shoulder with the toe of his boot.

Heath swatted his foot away. "Let me," she said, glad to have a reason to turn her eyes from his face as she shook E's shoulder gently. "E, wake up. Get up. Seriously rotten ice. Get up."

Rotten ice was what caused the fall that crippled Heath. "Rotten ice" was the phrase they used when something was deadly serious. Not that E wouldn't realize armed men appearing out of nowhere and killing the family dog was a serious situation; Heath said it to cancel out her previous order to play dead.

Elizabeth got to her hands and knees, then wavered to a standing position. Grace and agility gone, she moved like an old drunk. Weaving, she found her feet. Blood dripped from her nose to her upper lip. The bastard had hit her so hard it made her nose bleed.

Furious, Heath wanted to fly at the dude and rip him to pieces. She hated being confined to the earth like a worm, gazing up at nostrils and armpits; hated being unable to kick the son of a bitch in the balls. Frustration turned to tears and poured down her face.

Crying like a fucking baby, she flagellated herself as her eyes flooded, blurring the looming man-beast. "I'm not crying because I'm afraid of you!" she yelled, though that was not entirely true. "I'm crying because I can't have what I want. Your head on a spike."

Reacting to her outburst not at all, he pocketed his pistol, then closed his oversized hand around Elizabeth's upper arm, fingertips meeting on her bicep. His nails were clean and clipped. His cuticles were healthy and whole, not cracked like those of a man who worked with his hands.

"What are you doing out here?" Heath asked, trying to sound reasonable, civilized, a person other people didn't kick or kill.

"Jimmy," he said, ignoring the question as well as the questioner.

That, at least, Heath was accustomed to. People had a lot of reasons not to see a woman in a wheelchair, let alone one flopping about in the dirt. As she was trying to think of a way her invisibility might work for her, the small bearded man trotted over and pointed the rifle at her head.

Dragging Elizabeth with him, the dude moved to where Leah and Katie knelt. Reaching down with his free hand, he grabbed a handful of hair and lifted Katie effortlessly to her feet.

"Leah!" Katie cried.

"You didn't have to do that," snapped Elizabeth.

Leah scrambled up awkwardly, her hands bound.

"Leah!" Katie cried again.

"Do what they want," Leah murmured, not even trying to move closer to the child.

Katie's fine blond hair, usually tucked behind her ears, fell over her face in a veil. Without her hands she couldn't push it aside. Acutely aware of how it felt when suddenly robbed of abilities one never considered crucial until they were taken away, Heath wanted to shout at Leah to sweep the hair out of her daughter's eyes for her.

"I have money," Leah said in just over a whisper. "I can pay you if you let us alone."

The dude turned his skull back in Heath's direction, his sleek mustache moving like a drugged ferret as he said, "Now you," in the same tone a bored receptionist might say,

"Have a seat."

"Dude," said the bearded man, the one with the rifle trained on Heath. Umber specks, spit out with the word, added to a brown freckling on the front of the new coat. He jerked his chin. The beard, grizzled with gray, dark brown streaks running from the corners of his mouth, poked out of the neck of his jacket, pointing at something beyond the fire.

Robo-butt ATV, her wheelchair.

"Bitch is a crip." Jimmy sounded affronted, as if Heath had ceased using her legs for the sole purpose of making his life harder. He spit a stream of tobacco juice into the fire, where it snapped and sizzled. The last drop trickled into his beard, adding to the brown stain. "Be doin' her a favor." Sober concentration slowing his chewing, he made tiny circles in the air with the barrel of the rifle, making a game of where he would put the first bullet.

The dude's cheekbones and chin lifted, the invisible eyes shifting in their shadowy sockets. "Are you crippled?" he asked.

Please pass the salt. Did you get all your classes? How's the wife and kids? Are you crippled? I have a great big gun.

Heath shook her head, trying to rid herself of the unreality swarming around her ears

65

and eyes like a plague of gnats.

"Whose chair is it?" he asked, mistaking her intent.

"No," Heath managed. Her voice was as weak and breathy as if she'd run a mile rather than crawled two yards. The tears had been humiliating enough. She'd not yet found the courage to look and see if the crotch of her trousers was wet. Willing her voice steady in an attempt to retain some shred of dignity, she said, "The wheelchair is mine."

Her voice was firm, clear, much better. As this self-scrutiny flickered through her thoughts quick as summer lightning, she realized how desperately she wanted to be brave for E, and for Anna, who she prayed was even now pulling a miracle out of thin air to save them.

"Are you crippled?" he asked again, using the exact same modality he'd used the first time, the way a Chatty Cathy doll would say, "I love you," each time the ring in the back of its neck was pulled.

Nothing behind the eye sockets. Nothing behind the voice. No sympathy to play on. No guilt to trip. No heartstrings to pluck.

"I can't walk," Heath said, startled at what sounded like defiant pride in her voice. "I broke my back. My legs are paralyzed."

"Hey, Dude," Reg said, his voice deep and filled with life compared to the dude's.

Unexpected, close, the sound shattered Heath's brittle facade of courage like a stone shattering glass. She jerked and squawked. Elizabeth echoed her.

Ears full of the noise of her daughter's heart breaking, Leah's murmured offers, and the thoughts crackling in her head, Heath hadn't heard the black man move from the other side of the camp.

Having circumnavigated the clearing, Reg was standing staring down at the crumpled form of Wily. The pewter-colored gun — the Walther, she remembered — was held loosely in his long-fingered right hand. He tapped the barrel absentmindedly against his thigh in waltz time — *one,* two, three, *one* — the way Heath's aunt Gwen would tap her pen against her teeth when she was thinking. In her late seventies, Gwen predated computers. She'd grown up with a pen in her hand. Reg looked as if he'd grown up with a gun in his.

"Dude," Reg said again, louder this time.

"What?" The dude had lost no composure when she and Elizabeth squeaked, lost none when Reg interrupted him, but Heath thought his virtually affectless voice was flatter than before. Could a man of hollows, holes, and empty places get angry? Heath thought not. He would only become more efficient. Unlike the rattlesnake, or the hissing cat, he would give no warning beforehand.

"Dog's not dead, man," Reg said, squatting and reaching toward Wily.

Wily's growl was more beautiful than a choir of angels. Heath started to cry again. She pushed the palms of her hands hard on the ground in the hope that the bites of small stones would distract her from another embarrassing outburst.

"Wily!" Elizabeth cried.

"Don't," the dude said before she could run to the dog.

Elizabeth didn't.

Good girl, Heath thought. E had always been a quick learner.

"Maybe you just knocked it out. One back leg's kinda weird, but it's not dead. You're not dead, are ya, boy?" Reg said.

Again Wily growled. The sound was stronger this time, and it made Heath absurdly happy in an absurdly terrifying world.

"Shoot it," the dude said flatly.

"No!" Elizabeth screamed at the man with the pewter gun. In the same breath, Heath screamed, "No!" at her daughter, trying to abort any impulsive action that could get

68

her killed.

"Man, I ain't shootin' no dog," Reg said.

Reg, the black man, born with a silver gun in his mouth, the man Heath had dismissed with the half-formed tag "urban gang-banger," didn't want to kill an old dog. A rush of gratitude strong enough to be mistaken for love washed over her. Stockholm syndrome went from theoretical historical to practical possible.

So the bastard didn't jump at the chance to shoot a dog, she told herself. That was not enough on which to base a long-term relationship.

The dude grunted, but not like a pig. It was more like the sound Heath imagined when characters in Dickens's books said, "Harrumph."

A moment passed; the silence stretched thin. Heath imagined that the man called "the dude" was deliberating whether he would kill Reg for insubordination or let him live. The drama of it kept her eyes on the big man's face. In the life of everyone there could come a time when a watcher chooses whether to kill or rob or rape. If the choice is not to, one walks on never knowing that a devil had set crosshairs on one's life.

Reg didn't take his eyes off Wily, but he

must have sensed a bit of what Heath was reading into the dude's pregnant stillness. "I mean, like, you know, people might hear the gunshots and shit," Reg excused his inaction.

"It's hunting season," said the avid troll keeping a rifle bead on Heath. "Nobody'll think nothin' about guns going off."

"No shit?" Reg asked. "Bubba's going to be blasting at everything that moves?"

Reg wasn't from the urban enclaves in Minnesota, Heath guessed. More like Chicago, New Orleans, or Houston. Other than the inner-city cant, he didn't have an accent. It was possible he'd been bounced around the circuit: Los Angeles, Chicago, Jackson, New Orleans, Los Angeles as trouble and fed-up relatives moved him on. In their own way, people who had grown up on that path had voices as homogeneous as the Twin Cities' newscasters.

"Better put on something red," Jimmy said. "You're looking a lot like Bambi."

"Shut up." It was the flat voice of the dude.

Reg shut up, postadolescent attitude shut down. Jimmy didn't say another word.

"The dog," said the dude. "One of you shoot it, club it, or stomp on its head if you want to. Just kill it."

Eight

Reg, the black man with the Walther, walked away. The one they called the dude stood basilisk-like, staring at the fallen dog. His eyes shifted from Wily's body. Anna let her breath out slowly.

After her initial reconnaissance, she had gone a ways upriver, climbed the Fox's bank, then made her way back over the whispering pine needles. Behind a red pine, thick and spiky branches making a rood screen she could peek through, she spied on the camp. Wily's resurrection, and subsequent death sentence, had taken place no more than six paces from the tree she had chosen.

Wily was coming around. She watched his eyeballs moving beneath the brown fur. First one eye opened, then the other. For a short space of time, they had the fogged look of a dreamer. Nostrils quivered, scent informed, and his eyes not only cleared but fixed on her tree. His tail thumped the ground, and his ears pricked.

Wily had a lousy poker face. There was no point in moving. Anywhere she was near enough to observe, he would be able to smell her. Maybe he'd have some kind of animal instinct not to betray her presence. Then again, he was named for a trickster.

Hoping out of sight would be out of mind for her canine friend, Anna quit spying, turned her back to the tree's trunk, then sat down, careful to keep all of her parts out of view. Leaning her head back against the rough bark, she tried to formulate a plan. With the men awake and watching, there was little she could do. If three slept while one kept watch, she might be able to kill the lookout, get a firearm, then kill the rest.

"Kill" was the word she used in her mind, not stop, disable, or detain but barbaric, irreversible, unforgivable killing. Time and life were the only true riches humans had. To waste either was a crime and a sin, if sin existed.

People had died before at her hands. Once she accidentally killed a woman in a fall. Occasionally Anna still fought up from dreams, flailing in an attempt to alter her trajectory so she would land anywhere but on the woman's neck. Never had she slunk up on people as they slept and shot them through the back of the head in cold blood.

Still, she would slaughter these men if she got a chance. She would kill them all. This was not the time or place for knocking people out, tying them up, then hoping they stayed knocked out and tied up. There were too many of them, too few of her, and the stakes were too high. When it was done, she would have unclean hands. Paul would smell the blood on them. Like Lady Macbeth, she'd see the stains in her dreams.

Nightmares would be a small price to pay for Heath, E, Leah, and Katie.

And Wily. She wouldn't forget Wily.

Anna shook off the morbid thoughts. As things were there wouldn't be an opportunity to enact the imagined bloodbath. Something would come up. A better plan. Jimmy, the pint-sized spitter of tobacco juice, struck her as stupid. Mean and stupid, that was a volatile combination in a member of one's own team. In the enemy it was an advantage. Though they passed guns around like college kids passing joints, Jimmy seemed to be the main keeper of the .22. If Anna could get the rifle, many options would become available.

The dude and Reg did not seem in the least stupid. The black guy was a fish out of his own murky waters, but he was alert — maybe even hyperalert — to his surroundings. Anna doubted either of them would make an opening she might slip through to save anybody in the near future.

The belly-twisting creep, Sean, was a cipher. He might be a Rhodes Scholar or have the reasoning ability of a chimpanzee. It was hard to get a read on him when she couldn't bear to look at him. Like quicksilver in the palm of her hand, any thought regarding him beaded up and ran off of her brain.

When she'd worked in Mesa Verde, Anna had stopped at a tent because she thought she smelled dope smoke. As a rule, she didn't care what campers used for recreation as long as it left no stain on the park, but she did insist on discretion. As it happened, the woman was burning sage, smudging her tent.

A self-proclaimed witch, she told Anna that smudging, plus a spell or two, warded off psychic attacks. Believing no more in witches than in angels, Anna had forgotten about it until the incident with a toxic sedan in Mississippi. What she had felt then was identical to the experience the campground witch described as a psychic attack. It was what she felt when she first saw the potbellied Sean. Just thinking his name brought back the willies.

"I ain't carrying no cripple on my back." Jimmy said this.

Anna knew their names and voices as well as she knew her sister's or her husband's. They'd only had to speak once and the section of the cerebral cortex responsible for storing vital survival information recorded them for all time, at least all of Anna's time.

"We're not taking the cripple," the dude said. "Three adult females, two underage females. Where is the other female?"

Anna couldn't tell of whom he asked the question, but it was Heath's voice that answered. "Anna Pigeon was the fifth member of the party," she said. "She backed out at the last minute. Family problems."

Somebody snorted. Evidently even felons had family problems.

Stealthy as a shadow, but for the cracking of her knee joints, Anna rose to stand with her back to the tree. If a search was ordered, she would walk straight into the black of the forest. The muscles of her stomach clenched as she waited for the hue and cry of hunters. Wanting to see and hear, she'd come too close. Six paces. Why hadn't she just gone and sat on the dude's lap?

Jimmy sneered, "Lucky Pigeon shit," and

laughed as if his words were so witty they would eventually be attributed to Dorothy Parker.

That was it. They were moving on. The dude took Heath at her word. At least it appeared he had. He hadn't seemed the trusting type, but Anna couldn't think of any profit to be made from his pretending he believed her.

The lie had been impressively simple, and Heath had told it well. Often Anna forgot she and other women of a certain age were not seen — at least by men — as dangerous. Heath had everything going for her should she choose a life of crime and deceit: She was white, well dressed, female, middle-aged, and disabled. Few suspected this group of sinister or underhanded motives. If Anna ever decided to run contraband, all her mules would have at least three of those attributes.

"Name," the dude said.

"Elizabeth Jarrod. The *cripple* is my mother."

Anna winced. E was too smart not to know what sort of men she was dealing with. Given her history, one would have thought she would have realized that cruelty and indifference had been man's natural state since he was an oyster cracker floating in a bowl of primordial soup. Perhaps the resilience of youth had allowed a mustard seed of faith in her fellow human beings to resprout.

"Want me to kill the cripple and the kid?" This was the mellow bass of Reg, the guy who wouldn't shoot Wily. He sounded perfectly happy to shoot Heath and Elizabeth. That should scorch the earth beneath Elizabeth's mustard seed.

A man laughed, three short barks, each starting on a high note and stopping an octave lower. Anna had no idea who it was. She had not heard much in the way of laughter. The voice that followed it was that of Sean.

"You won't shoot a crippled dog, but you're okay with shooting a crippled woman. Don't they have therapists in Chicago?"

"It's different." Reg sounded defensive, almost sulky. "Dogs don't talk. Dogs don't be thinkin' of ways to get back at you. No sense killin' a dog."

"To keep it from suffering," the dude said, not as if he believed it, but as if he read it off of a strip of paper from a fortune cookie.

"Yeah, right," said Reg. "Tell that to the dog."

"I'll shoot that goddam dog." That was

Sean. "I hate dogs. Dogs get rabies and shit. Goddam fleabags. I'll cut its throat if you don't want to waste a bullet."

"Reg, dispose of Miss Jarrod and the cripple," the dude said. "Sean will dispatch the dog." He sounded like a patient kindergarten teacher dividing up chores.

Hoarfrost grew down Anna's spine. She turned and peeked through the matrix of dead pine branches and needles. Sean's hands were occupied touching Katie. No doubt he would have called it "frisking" the thirteen-year-old. A Paul Bunyan–sized hunting knife hung in a nylon sheath on his belt. Taking the place, no doubt, of a drastically foreshortened and shriveled penis. That would be the knife he planned to use to slit Wily's throat.

"I'll do the crip and the kid," Jimmy volunteered excitedly. Anna heard the metallic swallowing sound of the pump action on the .22, followed by a faint thud and Jimmy's "Shit." There had already been a live round in the chamber. He'd just ejected into the grass.

"Reg," the dude said with a faint hint of weariness in the north wind of his voice.

The next bullet would not be frittered away. Stepping back from the tree, Anna drew a deep breath. If she charged into the

78

midst of the men, she might be able to knock Jimmy down, maybe even wrest the rifle from him, but she would die.

Then Heath and Elizabeth would die.

The only hope was to distract and divide. If she could draw a couple of the thugs into the trees, get them to chase her, she might be able to split them up, let the darkness confuse them. Anna was at home in the dark. The darkness had always been her friend. Maybe an opening just big enough to let one of their lives out would present itself. Maybe a chance for Leah, Katie, or Elizabeth to run.

As she drew breath to shout, a whining cadence cut through the momentary quiet, as sour and cleansing as the juice of a lemon.

"God, you are so lame. Heath's got ten times as much money as Leah."

Katie. It was Katie Hendricks. The only child of wealthy parents, she would have known of the danger of being kidnapped from an early age. She would realize why men would take only her and her mother and "dispatch" Heath and Elizabeth.

"You're so stupid you're going to flush millions and millions of dollars down the toilet and it serves you right." Katie's spoiled-girl whine segued into spoiled-girl spite.

Anna cocked her head, inadvertently mimicking Wily's characteristic pose. She hadn't thought Katie would put herself out to save others. Maybe Katie really thought Heath was rich; maybe she wanted Heath and Elizabeth for company in her sufferings. Or maybe Anna had underestimated her.

"Is that true?" asked Jimmy, eyes wide and excited under the brim of the absurd cap.

For an interminable second no one spoke. Anna feared the dude was simply deciding whether to shoot the smart-mouthed kid along with E and Heath or make them dig their own graves first. She quit breathing.

Jimmy's nasal tones sawed away the silence. "Dude, that money would be all ours. We'd have to cut the pilot in to keep him from blabbing. That'd make it a five-way split, but millions? Nobody'd ever have to know we even had it."

"It'd make this shit worth it," Reg grumbled.

"You're being paid," the dude said.

"Paid, yeah. Money, but not, like, *real* money," Reg argued. "If she's not shittin' you about the crip having dough, that could be real money."

"Big money," added Jimmy.

Anna watched the big man. His face was as unreadable as the face of a granite cliff. There was no way to tell what he was thinking.

"The Hendricks child is lying," the dude said.

"Am not," Katie murmured, sounding so like her mother, for a second, Anna wasn't sure which one had spoken.

"Elizabeth Jarrod," the dude said. "Do you have millions?"

"No," E said.

"Are we done?" the dude asked the other thugs.

"My great-aunt Gwen has the millions," Elizabeth said.

"See, Dude, it ain't no lie! Auntie will pay up, sure as hell," Jimmy said.

The Dude slowly looked from Jimmy to Reg to Sean. Before, the air between the men had been charged with fear of the dude and fear of the wilderness. That had suddenly changed to an almost audible hiss of greed.

The minions, at least, believed Heath might be too valuable to murder.

If the dude destroyed this perceived windfall, he could risk losing hold of his merry band.

Anna dared not move. Since she didn't have a line to God, she prayed to her husband, Paul, to lean on the Almighty.

The forest hushed as if listening: no owls, no night creatures, no insects chirring or stirring. Pressing her palms and her forehead against the rough bark of the tree, inhaling the faintly sweet odor of the sap in the cracks of the rough bark, Anna waited for the gunshots. "Suit yourselves," the dude said finally.

Anna breathed.

"They are now your problem. If they delay us, they — and you — become my problem. I don't like problems. Clear?"

"Clear," said Reg with such audible relief, Anna guessed he feared the dude as much as she did.

"Clear," said Jimmy happily, not clever enough to be afraid.

"We cut it five ways," Sean said. "You two, me, the pilot, and the dude." There was a short silence during which Anna imagined Jimmy counting on his fingers.

"Five ways," Reg agreed.

"Yeah. Fair's fair." Jimmy sounded more childish than Katie.

Anna had dealt with intelligent criminals, average criminals, and criminals who bordered on idiocy. These four were a different breed. They hailed from a world of thuggery with which she had no experience, a place where men had devolved beyond bad and good into a creature so basic she would have said they were less like people than vicious animals.

Except that would have been a disservice to the animals — and, she suspected, to the dark intelligence of the dude.

NINE

Cluster fuck was the correct phrase, Charles thought. There was a reason he had sworn off working with fools and amateurs. They got people killed — the wrong people. He should have left this alone, but it had seemed a God-sent opportunity. One he'd been waiting for a long time. Even so, he should have walked away the moment they'd arrived at the burned-over camp and found the targets missing.

Greed, that's what had undone him. It's what got everyone in the end. Greed for money, life, sex, power. A suitable revenge. Not the glib and momentary bullet to the base of the skull, a feast, a harvest festival, a play with five acts. Greed had tempted him to buy Bernie's statement that the targets were only a short walk downstream, a couple of hours at most. Bernie had either been lying or obliviously optimistic. Night had nearly overtaken them in the woods.

No food, no flashlight, it could have been a miserable ten hours waiting for the sun.

Charles could only blame himself. If you knew you were taking the word of a fool as gospel, then who was the fool? Some plans were hatched, some unfurled, some led; this one would be bench-pressed, shoved up by force of will and muscle every inch of the way.

He surveyed his partners in crime: a dribbling idiot, a rapist, and an ex-gangbanger who wouldn't shoot a goddam dog. That one had taken Charles off guard. African Americans weren't supposed to like dogs. A racial memory of the baying hounds and the slave-masters chasing them through the swamps or something. Times had changed. Reg probably had a Pomeranian named Peaches waiting for him at home.

The dog didn't matter one way or another. Its leg or maybe its back was broken. Whether they killed it tonight or a wandering bobcat killed it tomorrow was of no importance. The dog had been an object lesson. A man who will kill a dog will stoop to anything. That is a man to be feared with bowel-loosening intensity. That is a man with no soul. If the dog had died when it hit the tree, Charles would have been happier. Since it didn't, when Reg refused to shoot the thing, he'd put a spotlight on himself as the weak link. Hostages were drawn to the stench of compassion like flies to horse dung. He'd seen it in the cripple's face, the dawning of hope that one of her captors was nice, a good person who liked animals and children, a person who might help a poor little crippled woman.

Charles could have shot Reg. That would have underscored the point that he was to be feared and obeyed without question, but he wasn't sure he could afford to lose him yet. The targets had to be transported to the airplane. Bernie's master plan had not been brilliant: acquire the targets, dispatch the peripheral individuals, and move the targets from camp to vehicle to airstrip via trails and logging roads. Every change in venue was a risk for one side and an opportunity for the other. Change of venue meant exposure and possibility. Bernie had factored more changes into this job than Charles would have accepted.

If he hadn't been blinded by greed.

Spilt milk, blood under the bridge, this was the hand he'd been dealt.

According to the GPS, they'd bush-whacked four miles along the river from the burned-out camp to the targets' actual location. Venues were now changed.

They could canoe back upriver. The canoe looked big, but he guessed more than four would be dangerous. That meant two men remained behind and two accompanied the targets. Charles had never been in a canoe and doubted dumb, dumber, or dumbest had either. That meant forcing the females to paddle at gunpoint. Not only was the river too public at this time of year, but Mrs. Hendricks or Miss Hendricks might think to roll or swamp the boat, and then, all bets would be off.

Hiking the targets back to the original pickup location was another option. That would mean another four miles bashing through the bushes with the targets, then three miles on foot along rough roads with the targets from the original pickup to the vehicle, and another stretch in the vehicle. A lot of exposure, many chances to be seen, to be interfered with, to be betrayed. Bernie's little gang had come close to mutiny fighting their way through the shrubbery on the walk down the river.

Sighing inwardly, Charles surveyed his temporary duty station. Because he had ordered it, the dog had to die. The cripple and the older child would be disposed of before they left this place. Bernie, God rot his soul, hadn't mentioned one of the disposables was crippled. Charles abhorred broken things, broken people. He'd had to abandon the park he'd eaten lunch in every sunny day he was in town for over ten years because someone got the bright idea of bringing retarded children to play there at noon every day. Observing the mentally retarded made him physically ill, nauseated.

People who weren't whole needed to be taken out of the equation.

This cripple, with her too-thin legs that fell to one side, with shoes on her feet as if she could walk, made his skin crawl. The legs moved jerkily of their own volition it seemed, small erratic motions like those of an insect. The wheelchair filled his nostrils with the stink of old people, sitting in their urine, drooling on their hospital gowns, hair dry as straw, eyes vacant.

Charles would choose to burn in hell rather than sit in a wheelchair. He had chosen to burn in hell. Occasionally, he still went to confession to unload a few sins, but there were things God could not forgive.

Dragging his gaze off the trappings of hospitals and nursing homes, he considered what the cripple had told him: The fifth female had opted out of the trip. One canoe, four females, four tents. There was nowhere else to be but this camp or the river. Why wasn't he surprised that Bernie hadn't known of this development either?

"Finish securing the hostages, then find something to eat," Charles told the men. Food would go a long way toward heading off any thoughts of mutiny Bernie's little side trip might have fostered. As Michael used to say, the world looked better from the bottom of a plate.

Walking to the edge of the bluff overlooking the Fox River, Charles took the cell phone from its holster on his belt beneath the heavy blanket fabric of the new coat. He punched in the speed-dial number for Bernie. Briefly he outlined the choices for moving the product. "Any ideas?" he asked when he'd finished. Bernie floundered around awhile, Charles listening to him talking to himself as he pawed through what sounded like a pile of nails.

"Okay," he said when he finally came back on. "Have you got a GPS on your phone?"

"Yes."

"I Google Mapped it. You have four miles back along the river, three to the car, then five by road to the strip and a last mile or two on foot. The road is there, but might be impassable in a car."

This was information Charles had just given to Bernie.

"Yes," Charles said again and amused himself with the thought of killing Bernie for nothing when this thing was over, a little lagniappe for putting up with such a pain in the ass.

"It's only six total if you go cross-country from where you are to the airstrip. That'd save you time. There's no huge mountains or rivers as far as I can see."

Charles considered the idea. It was shorter. The going couldn't be much rougher than it had been along the water. Six miles. Half a day. The crippled female wouldn't make it; that was a plus. The greed that had the goons believing she was of monetary value would wane quickly enough if they had to carry her on their backs. Let them choose when to dispose of her. That would leave him out of the negotiation and keep resentment from stiffening their spines.

"Have the plane there by noon." Charles punched the OFF button before he had to listen to Bernie get whatever last word he planned on getting.

He turned his attention to their primary target.

Leah Hendricks, Boulder, Colorado. BS, MS, PhD, thirty-five, five feet nine inches, one hundred eighteen pounds. Net worth unknown, estimated between three and seventeen-point-five million. Hair light brown, dyed black. Eyes gray. Skin white. *Mrs.* Hendricks. Charles had seen her picture many times. Photos didn't show how thin she was, wide-hipped but narrow.

When she turned sideways and stuck out her tongue, she'd look like a zipper. Michael's childhood joke would have made him smile had those muscles not atrophied from lack of use. For a supposed outdoorswoman, she was pale to the point of anemia, blue veins visible on her temples. He knew her dirty little secret. As dirty little secrets went, hers was fairly pathetic; still, he enjoyed knowing it. Leah Hendricks hated camping, backpacking, and all the other outdoor sports she designed for.

That she was a fraud didn't impress him one way or another. She was cattle on the hoof, money to purchase Michael's passage out of hell, a repast of dishes best served cold. The more quickly he got his goons fed and through the night, the more quickly he could get this business finished.

He pointed his pistol at Mrs. Hendricks. A little scut work would do the multimillionaire's soul good.

"You. Help Sean with the food." He had no qualms about using Sean's name. The damage was already done. The fools had been bandying names about. If Hendricks was as smart as she was supposed to be, she'd realize that was tantamount to announcing they didn't expect witnesses to survive. Victims who didn't expect to survive took more chances than those who thought good behavior would win them a gold star and a few more mundane years of their mundane lives.

If she read the unstated bad news, she didn't show it. Mutely, she nodded. Charles couldn't tell if she was scared speechless or if she wasn't the talkative type. He hoped both were true.

TEN

There would be hell to pay when the thugs discovered that not only was Heath not a multimillionaire, she still had forty-three thousand in medical debts. Given that there was already hell to pay, she was grateful for the reprieve, grateful she and her daughter weren't going to be shot down like dogs. Try as she might, she couldn't think of a way to get Wily included in the reprieve, but at least at the moment, Scan was too occupied with Katie to cut Wily's throat. She dared hope, somehow, this save would be permanent for E, that she'd live to grow up and have a whole new set of issues from this second violent trauma in her world.

Heath doubted her reprieve would keep her alive more than a day longer than her dog. She and Wily could keep each other company on the ferry ride across the River Styx. Had these men the dedication and stamina to work as hard as it would be to carry a one-hundred-fifteen-pound woman, half of her dead weight, through the wilds of northeastern Minnesota, they would have made their pile in honest jobs by now. The instant she became a burden, it would occur to one of the louts that Elizabeth would probably bring as good a price as they'd get for the both of them anyway.

From the dude's abbreviated phone conversation, it sounded as if he intended to take them cross-country for six miles. Before this trip, Heath had never been to Minnesota. She had no idea what the cross-country hiking was like. In the mountains around Boulder, Colorado, in the older pine forests, there were places where she would rate hiking off trail from doable to joyful. Here, what she'd seen as they glided past in the canoe was a different matter.

The forest was mixed evergreen and deciduous: red fir, aspen, red and white pine, white fir, maple, balsam and oak, aspen, tamarack, and alder thickets that truly earned the title "thicket." Beneath the forest's canopy bracken fern, tansy, aster, wild roses, sumac, and more grasses than an amateur naturalist could identify tangled together.

It would be difficult to navigate on foot. Impossible in a wheelchair.

Lacking wheels, Heath's most efficient mode of travel was backward, on her butt, using her arms in place of her legs. Palms to the ground, she could lift the weight of her body and move her buttocks back a few inches. Being strong and practiced, Heath's personal best was ninety feet, and that was over smooth surfaces. More than that and she began to burn out her shoulder muscles. Six miles cross-country might as well have been six thousand.

Elizabeth would exhaust herself trying to help. Worse, she would endanger herself by annoying the thugs. When the time came to shoot Heath, Elizabeth could not be trusted not to throw herself in the line of fire and take the bullet for her. Her daughter had a selfless streak that time and inexperienced mothering hadn't been able to eradicate.

The only escape Heath could envision depended on getting Elizabeth out of camp while there was still enough darkness to cloak her. Anna would find her. They would take Anna's canoe downriver and get help. On her own, Anna would never leave. With Elizabeth's well-being to consider, she'd have to.

Help had better come fast, to save even Leah and Katie. Kidnapping was often simply murder postponed.

The bearded thug staggered up from the canoe with a loaded cooler. The thugs attacked the food like ravening beasts, ripping into plastic containers of potato salad, bread, cornflakes, and milk cartons. Tops were popped off canned chili and stew. Jimmy didn't bother with a spoon, the dirt on his fingers apparently providing added zest. As they were pillaged, paper plates, plastic wrap, bottles, tins, cups, and napkins were tossed aside or into the fire.

Anna would be appalled.

The dude ate sparingly and without sitting down.

Sean dragged Katie down by his side. Kneeling, her face hidden behind the screen of blond hair, her hands tied together on her knees, she sat immobile while she was treated to a monologue about the quality of the food. Leah did not look at Sean or her daughter. Sitting, knees up under her chin, bound arms around them, she looked like a side of beef trussed for slaughter. Her face expressionless, she stared at Heath's wheelchair. Remembering Katie's crack about being loved only if she had titanium parts, Heath wondered what kind of relationship Leah had with her daughter. What inspired a thirteen-year-old girl to call her mother by her first name?

"Save the sleeping bags," the dude ordered when he'd finished. "Salvage food for tomorrow. Burn the rest."

Sean licked his fingers in a parody of seduction. When he'd done, he stood and unbuckled his belt. Nausea threatened to make Heath's supper come up as he took Katie's pale bird-boned hands in his paw and drew them toward his crotch.

"Hey!" Heath shouted. She'd not meant to, didn't want to draw attention to herself and, therefore, Elizabeth. It just happened. "What the hell do you think you're doing?"

"See-cure-itty," Sean drawled, showing teeth the size of BBs. He drew his belt between Katie's arms and rebuckled it, attaching her to his waist. "You want to get free, all you gotta do is open my pants," he said.

"As if," Katie snapped. Sean laughed. Leah did nothing.

The fabric of the first two tents went up in a colorful column of chemical flame. Poles shrank and grew distorted, like bones aging on fast-forward. Small, startling explosions rocked the air as tubes and bottles of whatever the women felt they couldn't live without exploded.

"Five sleeping bags, Dude," said Jimmy as he crawled, ferretlike, from the last tent.

The dude, standing with the pistol loose at his side, eyes raking the campground and the woods with the professional dispassion of a Secret Service bodyguard, turned his stare on Leah.

Leah said nothing. Her eyes, unfocused, remained fixed on the wheelchair. On climbs, Heath had seen that vague look in the eyes of climbers who panicked and mentally opted out of the adventure. Abdicating, it was called. When people abdicated responsibility for themselves, they became the responsibility of the rest of the party. A burden that could not be trusted.

"Five bags," the dude repeated.

"My back," Heath said. The dude didn't like looking at her; she'd figured that out. Now he stared at the point in the middle of her forehead where the third eye is rumored to reside as if weighing her veracity against some internal measure, the way the ancient Egyptians were said to have their hearts weighed against a feather when they died.

People who didn't like to look at disability wouldn't want to hear about it either. Heath didn't care what he thought about her, just so long as he stopped thinking about the number five.

Feigning enthusiasm for the subject, Heath started saying whatever came into her head. "The way my spine fractured made it so the weight that my rib cage used to support now rests on my bladder. A lot of us have catheters, up the urinary tract — or the rectum, you know, fecal matter and all that shit. Well, I guess, technically shit is fecal matter, but anyway —"

"Throw the bag on the fire," the dude said abruptly.

Heath had found, if not an Achilles' heel, at least a small breach in the stone in which the dude had encased himself. Weakness terrified him. Four men, four women, four sleeping bags. The women were destined to sleep on the cold ground. Since that was infinitely superior to having to share bag space with the bastards, Heath chose not to mind.

Reg's head popped up in the wash that accessed the river. It was dark and he was dark and his hoodie was black. When the roaring fire caught his eyes Heath felt a jab of terror as old as mankind, a horror of the monsters of the night.

"What about the canoe and all the shit they got in it?" Reg asked. "Burn that, too?"

"We'll sink it in the morning. Not near shore. Chop a hole in it and drag it out till we're sure it goes down."

Reg's orange-and-black eyes vanished.

Heath's scalp began to crawl down from where it had climbed to the top of her head.

"I need some things," Leah said softly. "To make it easier to move Heath."

Leah had not abdicated; she had been studying the chair, thinking of how it might be altered so Heath wouldn't be left behind with a bullet in her head. She'd been planning a way to take her with them. Relief flooded Heath. She had not wanted to die, not wanted to sacrifice herself for the greater good.

For what seemed a long time the dude said nothing. His face betrayed no emotion. The hand with the pistol was as relaxed as ever. His stillness did not feel like calm. It felt like the counted seconds between when lightning strikes and thunder cracks.

"Leah can do it," Katie said, still attached to the creep by cable ties. "Leah loves mechanical things. She wishes I was a robot."

"That's not true," Leah said, but she didn't take her eyes off the chair.

"Reg," the dude said.

Reg's wicked-looking eyes glowed back from the darkness below the riverbank.

"Cut Mrs. Hendricks loose," the dude said. "She needs tools so you can roll your new investment overland. See to it she gets

100

nothing else." The tip of his pistol moved an inch toward the Fox. From him it seemed like a sweeping gesture.

Like one in a dream, Leah walked around the fire to the shallow ravine leading to the water. Katie watched her mother walk out of the light. Despair made her face seem that of a spirit no longer tethered to the earth, a balloon come loose and liable to float up into the branches had she not been tied to the thug's belt.

"Katie's only a little girl," Heath said mildly. "Her hands are tied. She can't hurt anybody. Would it be okay if she sat over here by me?"

The dude rotated his eyes to settle them just above Heath's head. She made an effort to keep both fear and pleading off of her face. Sean was the sort that would feast on a victim's fear. The dude seemed beyond even that twisted recognition of their humanity.

"No," he said.

The destruction of the camp continued. Heath had hopes the invaders would build the fire so high that the Forest Service would send someone to investigate.

Minutes passed. Fire burned. Through the leaping, devouring light, Heath could see that E, hands bound like Katie's, had dropped to her knees. Her head was bent forward, in a pose unsettlingly like that assumed by a woman about to be beheaded.

Heath rubbed her face, trying to pry loose the terror. She needed to clear her mind, look for weaknesses, opportunities, think like a heroine. The effort was in vain. Fear clouded her vision. Uncertainty made every considered act a potential path to destruction.

She realized she was praying; then she realized she was praying not to God but to Anna. Horror of theistic retribution froze the unvoiced words. Sorry, God. Sorry, Anna. She sent the thoughts up into the night with the sparks from the all-devouring fire.

Leah returned, trailed by Reg carrying a red toolbox. He set it on the bank between the camp and the river. Heath knew the box. Leah always carried it. She was as faithful to the battered metal box as Heath's aunt the pediatrician was to her black leather medical bag. Like a doctor's bag, the toolbox opened in the center and folded out into two cascading trays, each with several compartments. The larger tools were in the bottom.

"Open it," the dude ordered. Reg opened the box and sorted through it.

Jimmy peeked over the black man's shoulder into the toolkit. "Dude, bitch has a saw in there!"

Reg picked it out of the box. In his hand it looked Barbie-sized. "Stay back," he said. "She's liable to give you a manicure."

Sean snickered. Jimmy sulked. The dude showed nothing. Heath wondered if his lack of affect went clear to the bone, if he was without imagination or humanity.

"I'll need two paddles from the canoe, the LED lantern, and someone to hold it," Leah murmured, her eyes on Heath's wheelchair as if nothing else mattered.

"Jimmy, get the lamp," the dude said. Jimmy sprang to the small pile of items yet to be burned, salvaged, or stowed and picked up the lantern.

"Where do you want it, Dude?" Had he been a dog with a tennis ball he couldn't have been more pleased with himself. He all but wagged his tail to be of service.

Thinking of tails, Heath dared a glance to where Wily lay. She'd been careful not to look, not to remind the thugs he existed and was still awaiting execution. Wily's head was down and he wasn't moving, but the bright brown eyes that met hers assured her he was still alive.

"Get the lamp going and set it beside Mrs.

Hendricks," the dude ordered.

The chore proved too much for Jimmy.

Leah turned the lamp on.

Leah on the bank, Heath by the fire, Katie tied to Beer Gut, Elizabeth on the other side of camp. Heath wondered if isolating them, not allowing them to comfort one another, was coincidence or a control mechanism. Her observation of the dude suggested he instinctually divided and conquered. A natural Machiavelli.

"Elizabeth, could you bring me my cigarettes?" Heath asked her daughter.

Without looking to the dude for permission, E rose gracefully despite the bound hands and the knock on the head. Circling around the fire, she surreptitiously petted Katie's hair as she passed Sean. Heath doubted that at the age of fifteen she would have had the sense to comfort another girl in shared misery.

The cigarettes were beside Heath's abandoned camp chair. Elizabeth retrieved both cigarettes and chair, then came and sat next to her mother.

The dude watched but did not stop her. The isolation had been coincidental, not inborn cunning. Heath felt better with E close, and better knowing the dude was not as all-seeing and all-knowing as his sphinxy face would lead one to believe. She moved her poor old butt up onto the kind seat cushion and smiled at her daughter.

Reg fished the Walther from his trousers. He'd stowed the gun in his waistband in order to carry the toolbox. As inner-city fashion decreed, he wore his pants low and baggy. The gun had been swallowed and come to rest in the nether regions of his drawers.

Leah sat down in the wheelchair and stared into the fire. Heath had seen her go into creative trances a couple of times before. Under the guns of evil men, it seemed unlikely, unless work was where she hid when she was frightened. That would account for Katie being given over to nannies while Leah spent her life in a lab. Working with living creatures was far more angst-ridden than working with metal and plastic.

The fire died to a stinking smoldering heap of melted nylon and blackened tin, the occasional gout of flame darting up as proof of life. Heath wondered if Anna's red metal fuel bottle, the one in which she traditionally carried a nice Cabernet, had been found and tossed on the fire. She really could have used a drink. For a moment, she fantasized about getting the men drunk, then sidling up to them in good old succubus style and slitting their throats with Sean's great big knife.

Leah continued to sit motionless in the wheelchair, the toolbox at her feet, her eyes on the dwindling fire. Heath began to lose hope that she was absorbed in the problem at hand and worry that she had gone catatonic. Either way, she envied Leah her absorption. The only respite she herself had from worrying was the endless fussy complaints of her legs. Every minute or so she had to shift her weight to keep the pressure from cutting off the blood flow in any one part of her butt more than another. Fatigue and tension were causing more spasms than usual, her feet kicking out. It was a cruelty she'd not been warned of, that legs, deaf to her commands, would, of themselves, flip about with such vigor.

Through the distortion of the heat, she could see Katie. The altruistic Sean had finally let her go. He'd even given her one of the remaining sleeping bags. She lay on her side, her hands beneath her cheek, her eyes closed. Heath hoped she slept.

"Try to get some sleep," Heath murmured to Elizabeth. "I have a feeling you'll need it."

"Why don't you lie down and let me keep watch?" E returned.

Until then, Heath hadn't realized that that was what she was doing. She was keeping the watch. She could not overhaul a wheelchair; she could not keep Sean's eyes from Katie, or the dude's fist from Elizabeth, or a bullet or knife from Wily. Witnessing was the only act she could do, so she would witness.

Sunrise was five hours away.

Heath tried to enter into Leah's world, or the world she imagined the engineer had retreated to, a place of sprockets, cogs, and fighting friction. Leah had created the wheelchair for rugged sports. The seat was a single unit, a molded cup of hard plastic that could be snapped off the lightweight titanium frame and used with other devices. The twenty-inch quick-release wheels were wider than those customarily used in civilized settings and had a deeper tread.

Clamped to the side of the chair was one of Heath's indispensible items. The manufacturer called it a Tilt 'n' Turner. Elizabeth dubbed it "Jack," as in jack-of-all-trades. It was a custom-designed mechanism that could support up to a hundred and forty pounds and could lock in any setting at any angle. Heath used it to support everything from her cell phone to a 1949 Harley engine she was rebuilding. The Harley engine transport had not been a success. Jack had not failed; the engine just weighed more than Heath and tipped over the chair.

"Two sleep, two watch. Two-and-a-half-hour shifts," the dude announced. "Sean, Reg, you're up first."

The dude and Jimmy retired to lie on two of the sleeping bags. Reg squatted near enough to Leah that he could shoot her before she could run him over. Sean paced, rifle in hand, looking out as Reg looked in.

Each time Sean passed by where Katie lay, his eyeballs stayed on her inert form a little longer, eyeing her the way a rat would eye a piece of cheese in a trap, trying to get up the courage to go for it. Heath dragged Elizabeth's bound hands onto her lap and held them tightly.

"I'll be okay, Mom," Elizabeth whispered. "I think I'm too old for him."

Heath thought she might be right. Katie was thirteen, but she looked no more than eleven. Heath told herself it wasn't bad to be happy a monster selected a child other than hers.

Sean's passes grew slower. Finally he stopped and stared hungrily down at Katie's small body. When he raised his head he caught Heath and Elizabeth watching him.

"I'm gonna kill that fuckin' dog," he said

abruptly.

He must have seen the judgment in their eyes, Heath thought. Now he would murder Wily to punish them.

Rifle tucked under his arm, he stalked around the fire, took a ball-peen hammer from Leah's tool box, and moved toward the tree where Wily had fallen.

Elizabeth closed her eyes and hid her face on Heath's shoulder the way she used to when she was a little girl. Forcing herself to keep her eyes on the thug so she might witness Wily's passing, Heath made solemn promises to kill Sean one day.

The thug stopped, stared at the ground, then into the woods, then at the ground again.

"Hey, Reg," he said. "The dog's disappeared."

Reg's features quaked slightly, as if he'd walked into a glass door. "Stuff doesn't just disappear, man. Something takes it."

"Wolves," Elizabeth said.

ELEVEN

"Wolves," E said.

Anna saw the wisp of a smile that blew across Heath's face. Safe in the black bosom of the woods, on a slight rise no more than thirty paces from the camp, she smiled unseen back at her friend as she smoothed down the fur on Wily's neck.

Dressed and hooded in dark colors, perched on a downed tree, her back against an upthrust limb, she knew herself to be as invisible as she felt. Wily, too, had all but disappeared. He was designed with protective coloration in mind, his uneven fur brown or gray or gold — the color seeming to shift subtly depending on the background.

"Wolves'd be scared of the fire," Reg said uncertainly.

"The fire's almost dead," Heath noted.

"Shut the fuck up about wolves," Reg snarled. Through a few intervening branches, Anna saw him stuff the gun into the pouch pocket of his hoodie. Hands free, he began tossing pieces of deadwood on the fire.

"Leave it," Sean said. "Dog just crawled off to die. Dogs do that."

"I wish people did," Reg said sullenly.

"Maybe it was the windigo," Heath said.

This was a story Anna had told around campfires on Isle Royale when she was a young ranger. She'd told it to Heath when she'd invited her to northern Minnesota, where the windigo lived.

"What the fuck's a windigo?" Reg asked, sneaking glances at the woods.

"It's a legend in these parts," Heath replied.

"Not to the people who've actually seen it," Elizabeth said in a low voice.

"Cut the crap," Reg said.

"The Algonquin Indians believe that if a person ever resorts to cannibalism — like the Donner Party — the demon of the windigo takes them over. Afterward they crave human flesh. They hunt the woods of these parts at night," Heath said.

"It's not a demon, Mom. That's stupid," Elizabeth said. "It's like an infection. The reason the stories happen is because the winters are so bad up here, people do eat people and get infected."

"It's just a myth," Heath said to Reg.

"There was that guy in Duluth . . . ," Elizabeth said.

"That was never proven," Heath returned.

Anna had noticed Reg was on edge the moment she laid eyes on him. The others weren't comfortable in the wilderness, but the man from the mean streets was downright scared. The grouse thrumming spooked him. Elizabeth's talk of wolves spooked him. Reg probably didn't get out of town much; the very intensity of the darkness and the depth of the night sky would spook him.

Reg struck Anna as a man who was used to being the scariest thing in the room, a king in his own country — however small that fiefdom might be. He didn't take the dude's orders with the lickspittle gratitude of the other two. A flunky for the dude, operating out of his area of expertise: He would have had to be desperate to take this job, in deep with loan sharks, drug dealers, or the local gang boss.

Whatever shark nipped at Reg's heels, it must have inspired him to snatch at the idea of Heath and Elizabeth being worth millions. Greed was like hope on steroids, ready to see the object of desire where it did not exist.

"You gonna work or what?"

Reg's demand snapped Anna out of a half-doze she'd slipped into without realizing it.

Leah didn't reply.

"She is working," Heath said.

Half an hour crept by. Anna fought to stay alert. If an opportunity presented itself to free any of the hostages, it would come while the dude was sleeping.

"What the fuck?" Reg. No one replied.

Heath slid down in her camp chair, letting her head rest against the back.

Sean, no longer pacing, stood on the bluff over the river where the entirety of the camp was under his eyes. Reg, pistol hanging like a living appendage from the end of his arm, moved to stand beside Sean.

"This is fucked, man," Reg said. "Three of us could've sacked out. Don't need two to watch this shit."

"Dude said two," Sean replied.

"Yeah. Yeah."

Another silence followed.

Reg stepped over behind the wheelchair and pressed the bore of the Walther PPK to Leah's left temple. "Fuckin' do something!"

TWELVE

Leah had never been good with people. People were predictable, but they weren't consistent. That was anxiety-making, as if gravity quit working one day in a thousand. Never knowing when that day would come, life would be one long terror of suddenly being spun off into space. Education didn't help. What was true about a person Monday might no longer be true on Thursday. Committing to a relationship was complicated when the person one committed to might be transfigured into another person.

SUBJECT TO CHANGE WITHOUT NOTICE

That should be tattooed on the foreheads of newborns.

Leah could not even vouch for the fact the language people spoke did not change from moment to moment. Many times as a child she'd ventured out onto the playground where the other children were bunched together and heard them chattering like magpies. Not metaphorically; to her they literally sounded like magpies.

Separating out one thread and following it to a sense of meaning took concentration.

She surmised the magpies had trouble understanding her as well. Murmuring had become habitual because, other than when she talked design or development, no one listened to what she had to say.

Mathematics, physics, chemistry: Numbers didn't change without warning. Didn't judge and condemn. One never had to hide from numbers. In math two plus two always equaled four. In English literature two plus two could equal two above ground, one in a tomb, and one swallowing poison. Philosophy, sociology — the studies of why people felt as they did and did as they did — were even worse.

The magpies knew why jokes were funny, why Juliet drank the poison. Not Leah. They wore bright colors and waved their hands, emotions flashed across their faces, teeth showed, cheeks puffed up, hair was tossed over shoulders. There was nothing wrong with her eyesight, but she'd worn glasses since she was eight. The clear lenses helped hold the world at a distance, imposed a kind of visual silence.

To survive, she'd learned ways of shutting

that world out.

As a child she'd lived in terror of her inadequacies coming to light until she'd found her home in the design studio. For the past years she'd practically lived at her lab, working with physical matter and intellectual challenges, working out the bugs in selvane and experimenting with its possibilities.

Leah was a genetic unknown. Her mothers moved and worked in the human race with zeal and ease. They took Leah hiking and camping and mushrooming. She'd loved them too much to tell them she didn't like the vagaries of nature, only the being away from people. They told her she was just shy, that she was more than adequate, she was loved.

Leah wasn't related to either of her mothers. As a teenager, she'd speculated that her DNA had come from another solar system. She'd taken to astronomy, looking for home. That had led to science fairs and scholarships, then to designing for the disabled.

Leah was comfortable around disabled people. She envied them the fact that their disabilities didn't excommunicate them from the human race. By studying them, helping them to regain lost abilities through science, she might discover what in her had suffered from a birth defect, gone under-nourished, or been excised as worthless by some psychic surgeon.

These creatures who had smashed the night, hacking and snapping with words and guns, had driven her back into her mind. The big man, the dude, was hauntingly familiar, though Leah was pretty sure she'd never met him, but then she seldom truly looked at people. Those cold changeless eyes she would have remembered. Maybe. Maybe he just resembled a man from TV or the movies, a B-movie actor who made a living playing mobsters and Second Thug. Leah seldom watched either. She couldn't be sure. Seeing him made her mind want to slam shut.

When the men took over the camp, every connection she'd forged with Heath and Elizabeth had been trampled asunder. Heath was a mother and Elizabeth was a daughter and they spoke as mother and daughter. Katie no longer even looked to her to be a mother. That was best. Leah could seldom think of anything to say to Katie.

In this crisis, part of her wanted to step up, be an adult, a parent, but she didn't know what to do, what was expected, how to act. There were too many unknowns. The men who'd captured them did not behave according to any rules Leah had memorized. Any action she took could worsen the situation. Even making eye contact with Katie might spark the child to do or say something wrong, or provoke the men to do or say something harmful.

Enclosed in the prison of her skull, peering out through the portholes of bone, she watched the horror unfolding around her but had no way of breaking through.

Then it became clear they would murder Heath because she could not be transported with sufficient ease.

Leah could fix that. Maybe there was nothing else she was good for, but she could make Heath a chair they could move through the woods. That had always been the way. That was why Gerald had married her, why he had wanted her child. Shutting out all else, she put her mind where it could function, where the component parts didn't change from moment to moment.

By the time the man, Reg, put the cold gun barrel to her temple, she knew what she needed to do.

Slowly, colorlessly, movement ingrained from years of wanting to go unnoticed, Leah rose from the wheelchair.

Reg and Sean reacted as if she'd exploded from a cannon. Both guns came up.

Leah waited to see if they would shoot her. Her mind could picture the strike of the firing pin, the explosion, the spin and velocity of a bullet, the sound waves coming slightly behind the slug, the lead penetrating her brow bone and spinning her brain into a froth. She should have been afraid, but death had never held any terrors for her. When the trigger was not pulled, she announced quietly, "I need six cable ties."

Reg and Sean looked at her as if she had spoken an unfamiliar language. Leah was used to this. "The plastic strips you used to bind our hands," she explained.

"The dude didn't say anything about giving you shit," Reg said. "Should we wake him up?" he asked Sean.

"No. Give her the ties. We've got a ton of them. She can't do any harm with ties. Let the dude alone."

"Right. Let sleeping dudes lie," Reg grumbled as he fetched a plastic bag full of cable ties Sean had been carrying.

Leah took the ties and knelt beside the wheelchair.

"You're welcome," Reg sneered.

Regardless of how evil the deed and how small the favor, everybody believed they deserved gratitude. Leah didn't understand this, she only knew it to be true.

"Thank you," she said. The man huffed as he took his due.

Moving efficiently, she went to work. Pressing the buttons on the hubs of the quick-release wheels, she removed them from the snap-lock brackets that attached their axles to the wheelchair's frame. The smooth click that accompanied the act satisfied her on a primal level. The Tilt 'n' Turner slid out of its brackets as easily as a sword from a sheath, and Leah felt the universe of order reasserting itself. The chair's seat was designed to be moved from venue to venue. Leah removed it, then set out her pieces on the grass as neatly as a meticulous child arranging the clothing of a paper doll. Pattern informed action. Neatness mattered in mathematics and physics. With the pieces in place, the whole was visible in her mind.

Using a wrench from the toolbox, she unbolted the axles' quick-release brackets from either side of the frame. The chair was titanium, but the tubing was hollow to keep the chair lightweight. In minutes she had the first dock removed and had started on the second. The flow of the parts, each piece coupling and uncoupling precisely as she had designed them to do, moved through her hands and mind like music through a conductor's baton.

The quick-release brackets, in their metal housings, were added to the pattern of parts.

The wheelchair's cushion, customized with variable contouring and foam layers used by NASA, was part of the equipment she was testing. Using the Tilt 'n' Turner tray as a template, she marked the seat cover with a pointed scribe. Cutting into it caused a moment's ripple in her working dance, but it had to be done if the seat was to be mounted to the tray of the T 'n' T. Using a small cordless drill, she bored holes through the six-thousand-dollar prototype seat and cushion.

The whine of the drill bit brought the dude up from his sleeping bag gun in hand with the suddenness of a ghoul disturbed from a grave. The gun was not pointed at her, so Leah didn't stop working. By the rude glare of the Coleman lantern, she saw Heath's right leg begin to spasm. Leah looked away. That was how her mind felt when she tried to be the mother Katie needed.

"It's just a drill, Dude," Sean said quickly. "One of those battery jobs."

"You said she could have the toolbox,"

Reg added. "The drill was in it when you looked." His voice was gruff.

The dude joined his cohorts watching her work. She felt them looming. With the ease of long practice, she shut them out and affixed the plastic seat to the top of the long square aluminum arm of the Tilt 'n' Turner.

THIRTEEN

The filthy beasts were caught up in Leah's project, all but Jimmy, who slept the sleep of the innocent. Heath and Elizabeth had been talking quietly. Anna hadn't caught on until she'd noticed E was taking forever to straighten and settle Heath's legs, her back, her chair, her cigarettes. They were using the close physical activity to speak unheard.

Elizabeth raised her head from her work and quickly scanned the dark curtain of trees. Anna waved. In the dark, her wave went unseen; still, E and the others knew she was out here. Heath said something. E moved to the pile of items that the thugs had saved from the conflagration. It was near the edge of the camp opposite the river. First she looked at the backs of the men watching Leah and her magic tricks. Then she studied the forest again.

From the pile, she pulled the last of the saved sleeping bags, then laid it on the ground between Katie and the woods, as close to the darkness as she could. Heath nodded. Elizabeth lay down. Heath searched the trees and nodded again.

Gently Anna lifted Wily from her lap, slid off the log, then settled him in the duff nearby. By the peculiar glow of Leah's LED lantern, Anna could see his eyes. Huge black pupils surrounded by a halo of gold, flecked with brown. Holding a finger to her lips, she made the universal sign for silence.

Wily tilted his chin up, his lids lowering slightly over his eyes. Anna was jolted with the completeness of the knowledge and connection she read there. Unsure whether she'd witnessed an arcane moment of interspecies unity or was going mad, she turned and crept toward the light of the camp.

Her moose-hide moccasins would have provided little protection over rough ground. Through the soft soles, she could feel the sharpness of sticks fallen from the pines. The mocs were, however, ideal for walking softly through the forest. One of the reasons, she supposed, various American Indian tribes had adopted them.

No one in camp was moving or speaking. The fire had settled to a murmur. With no cover noise, Anna was forced to move slowly. Since she had only a vague idea of what she might do when she got close to the people, the delay didn't concern her. Fifteen feet out, and still well screened, she stopped behind the kindly bulk of a tree trunk and watched.

Leah had used the cable ties to fasten the wheels together so they formed one wider wheel. Their short axle rods poked out several inches to either side. Now she was drilling holes in the long arm of the Tilt 'n' Turner opposite the end to which she had affixed the seat. That done, she bolted one of the quick-release docks designed for the axles to the T 'n' T bar.

Anna hated the fact that a mind such as Leah's could be shut down by the likes of Jimmy, Sean, Reg, and the fucking dude.

Suddenly she wished he had a name, wished it almost as much as she wished him dead. The need to call him something other than "the dude" was so strong it stopped her breath for a second. Names mattered. Bob, Harvey, even Jason, anything would be less frightening — and less infuriatingly banal — than "the dude."

Leah clicked the axle rod of the double wheel into the quick-release dock. Holding it up, she spun it experimentally. The unified wheels whirled around with a purring noise.

The creation resembled a unicycle, the seat on the top of the Tilt 'n' Turner directly above the wheel. The short horizontal bar that gave the Tilt 'n' Turner its L shape protruded near the middle of the wheel, providing a rest for Heath's right foot.

Leah laid the thing down again, then bolted a C-shaped metal part, previously attached to one of the wheelchair's front wheels, onto the left side's protruding axle. The unicycle now had a footrest to either side of the wheel.

"Hand me the canoe paddles," Leah said in her drifting way. Without a single gripe, Sean bent down and retrieved the paddles for her.

Anna got on her belly to reduce her silhouette, then slithered slowly closer to the edge of the camp where Elizabeth pretended to sleep. Once Anna got her in the sheltering black of the night woods, she would lead her to the river. When the Fox took her, E would be home free. Elizabeth was a good enough paddler to negotiate the flat water of the Fox. In a day and a half she'd reach a working phone. If the law of supply and demand held in this situation, the three remaining hostages would be of greater value. Maybe it would keep them alive longer.

■ ■ ■ ■

Anna reached the end of the pine-needle blanket. Seven feet of crackling, creaking, crunching autumn leaves separated her from where she could signal E. She rose to her feet. Never had she felt so tall and bright and obvious, like the Washington Monument at sunset. No one noticed. Carefully, she took the first step. Leaves and twigs went off like firecrackers on the Fourth of July. Anna froze, waiting for the camp to erupt in an uproar.

Heath began squirming around as if Elizabeth had settled her in a nest of fire ants, making scuffling noises as her feet moved in spasms, grinding her knuckles into the ground and scooching her chair forward, grunting and grumbling. Noise for Anna. Anna raced the few steps to the edge of the clearing nearest Elizabeth, then dropped to her belly behind a big old rotten tree trunk covered with lichen and fungus.

As Leah applied the drill to the blade of the first paddle, Anna found a stick and tossed it at the top of Elizabeth's head. Stick tossing from a prone position, and on the sly, was an awkward business. The third stick made contact. E lifted her bound hands to her hair and surreptitiously studied the trees at the edge of the clearing.

When they made eye contact, it startled Anna. Though it had been only a few hours since she had become the ghost in the darkness, the sense of alienation was far advanced. It occurred to her, had it not been for Paul and the National Park Service, she might have gone feral years ago.

Anna looked past E. The men were absorbed watching Leah bolting the blade of a paddle to the side of the cupped plastic seat, the long handle sticking out in front like the tongue of a wagon. This might not be the best time — the dude was awake — but Anna doubted it was going to get any better. She motioned for Elizabeth to come to her.

Elizabeth silently pulled her knees up to her chin and rolled herself onto them, positioning herself as if she prayed to Mecca. Anna was suffused with pride. Heath was the one who had saved Elizabeth in every way that mattered, but Anna had been there from the first night when she had come mostly naked and bleeding into Heath's life. Elizabeth had been young then, and afraid of everything. In a mere few years, she had transformed into this beautiful, courageous young woman.

On elbows and knees Elizabeth began a slow crawl toward Anna.

Leah attached the second of the paddle blades to the side of the seat. Finished, she stood between the long handles, raised them, and pushed forward. The conveyance rolled like a wheelbarrow. Leah turned around, pulled, and it became a one-wheeled rickshaw. Heath applauded loud and long. Elizabeth inchwormed toward the log.

Katie woke. Anna saw her head come up, the white-gold hair a halo of orange against the light of the fire. She half turned. "Shh," Anna hissed.

"Leah!" Katie called.

Every eye turned.

Expressionlessly, the dude raised his pistol, his arm ramrod straight, his hand steady.

"Run," Anna whispered.

Elizabeth scrambled to her feet and bolted into the forest, leaping over Anna like a hurdler, crashing from sight in the lightless woods. Anna hoped E wouldn't bash her brains out on a tree branch in her zeal.

The report of the Colt was followed by the lesser crack of the .22 rifle.

Jimmy woke and began yelling, "Dude! Dude! What's happening, man?"

Another round slammed into the log near Anna's face. Powder, comprised of bark, mildew, fungus, and lichen, blasted into her eyes and nose.

Blind, forcing coughs to stay in her throat, Anna crawled down the length of the log. Her eyes burned as if she'd been pepper-sprayed, hurting too badly to even consider opening them. When she banged into the upraised tangle of roots, she burrowed in. Sticks jabbed at her hands and body. Being skewered was better than being shot. She pushed herself until she could go no farther, then rolled into a ball like a frightened sow bug, hiding feet, hands, and face in her dark clothing. Until she could see, she could do no better. With luck, the chase would go in the direction Elizabeth had run, and Anna would be an unnoticed black shadow, a rock half covered by the rotting roots of the fallen tree.

With luck.

FOURTEEN

Icy fingers closed around Charles's heart and squeezed. He had let his guard down. Control had slipped away. The cripple was yelling, writhing around at his feet, banging on the arms of her chair with a wrench she'd managed to get. Jimmy was hopping up and down, brown spittle frothing at the corners of his mouth, yelling, "I think I got her, Dude. I think I killed the bitch."

"You killed a log, Jimmy," the dude said coldly. "Shut the cripple up."

Jimmy jumped to where Heath Jarrod was doing her one-woman-circus act on the ground. Reversing the rifle in his filthy hands, he clubbed her on the side of the head with the butt. "Got her!" he crowed as she slumped over, as proud as if he'd downed a battalion of marines with a dull Boy Scout knife.

Charles snatched up the lantern. "See nobody else moves." He walked into the woods where the girl had run, stopped, and listened for movement. She had gone to ground. Without light, she couldn't have gotten far.

Holding the lantern high, so he wouldn't blind himself, Charles moved into the trees. Forests bore no resemblance to parks. There were no long vistas beneath an even canopy. The pruned and ancient forests of southern France resembled cathedrals, arched ceilings reaching to heaven. Here coarse, half-dead vegetation clawed up from the earth. Wiry arms and bent fingers scratched down from above. The lantern ignited a never-ending spiderweb of twigs, needles, and branches spinning down to a floor of rubble from past lives and new bizarre lifeforms.

The girl could be lying in a hollow twenty feet from him. One man, one lantern, he would not find her. Stumbling about in the mess would make him look the fool. Control would be further eroded. Charles was accustomed to working with a higher quality of muscle, men who could be controlled with reason, logic, fear, intimidation, promises: the sticks and the carrots.

Years before, Michael had warned Charles that Bernie was the sort who left steaming piles that other people stepped in. The oafs Bernie had unearthed from beneath one of his rocks were amateurs. One never knew what an amateur would do. One never knew what an idiot would do, or a lunatic. With the three stooges, all those bases had been covered. The moment he no longer needed them he would do his good deed for the decade and add them to the list of disposables.

He turned out the eyeball-searing glare of the lamp and walked back toward the firelight of the camp. Letting the girl go was an option. He doubted she and the cripple were worth much in the way of ransom. By the time she found civilization and sent a rescue party, he and his would be long gone. The difficulty lay in the next twenty-four hours. He needed the stooges to move the product. The stooges were motivated by the belief that the cripple and the girl were of value. Herding the two of them would give the fools something to focus on besides their bellies and their peckers.

Charles didn't doubt that when the time came, Sean or Jimmy or Reg would kill the cripple for him. The decision theirs, his hands clean of their little drama. That would help foster what passed for loyalty with this sort of scum.

Stepping back into the firelight, he set the lantern down, then crossed to where the cripple sat, her head in her hands, still dazed from the impact of the rifle butt. He stood behind her low chair and steeled himself to touch her. The thought of it made his skin creep. A pool of sick formed in the bottom of his gut.

Grabbing a handful of hair, he jerked her up. The trousers looked half empty, like those of a scarecrow, as the legs followed, the heels of the shoes dragging along the ground.

Holding her by the hair, the fire blazing, he thought of the comic books he and Michael had read as kids, the natives holding up shrunken heads for the shock and titillation of eleven-year-old boys. Ah Michael, he thought, the things I do for you. I should leave you where you are. At least then we'd see each other again.

Not wanting his pistol to touch the cripple's head, he kept the barrel a few inches out and pointed it at her ear.

"I have a gun pointed at your mother's head. If you do not return to camp by the time I count to twenty, I shall kill her." He hadn't shouted; he'd used the voice he saved for when he needed to penetrate steel.

"One."

FIFTEEN

Faint whispering trickled through the trees like smoke. Anna tried to open her eyes against the pain. "E?" she whispered.

"Here."

Blinking furiously, Anna tried to follow the tiny trail of sound. In darkness and tears, she saw nothing.

"I have to go back," came the breath of an answer.

"No," Anna hissed because she dared not wail. "Come here," she begged. If she could get hold of Elizabeth, she wouldn't be going anywhere Anna didn't want her to go.

"They will kill Mom. You don't know him, the dude. He will."

The thread of sound was thicker. Elizabeth was moving back toward where Anna hid, to the camp. "Yes. Yes, he will kill your mother. He will kill her. Then he will kill you," Anna said. "They will kill you all. Stay with me and live. Heath wants you to live."

"I'm over here," Elizabeth said loudly. "I'm coming."

Anna rubbed her eyes with both fists, squeezing out water and flecks of rotted wood, desperate to clear her sight.

"No!" Heath screamed. "Don't you dare. Run, God damn you! Ru—" The voice was cut off with a thud.

Anna peeked between the roots. Through a watery veil she could see that all eyes were on Elizabeth as, straight-backed as any Englishman who ever faced a firing squad, she marched into the clearing. Through the prismatic lens of tears and rotten dust, Anna saw the dude holding Heath at arm's length by her hair, knees inches from the ground. She showed no more life than a sack of laundry. He cast her aside with an indifference that offended Anna more than the cruelty.

A prop in the theater of the absurd, Leah still stood between the pulling shafts of her creation, as unmoving as a statue, eyes blanked by reflections on the lenses of her glasses.

Slowly, with dignity, Elizabeth walked around the fire toward the bluff.

Heath pushed herself to her elbows. Her face was a mask of pain. "Damn you, Elizabeth. Damn you." The words were slurred.

Forgetting all she'd learned about effective self-locomotion, Heath hurled herself forward, an outflung hand closing around the dude's ankle.

"It was me, it was my fault," Heath said, the words coming so fast they were hard to understand. "I will do anything. Kill me. Let me lick your boots. Wash your feet. All I have, all I will ever have, I beg you . . ."

Pleas tumbled from her tongue like the toads from the mouth of the cursed fairy-tale princess. Anna understood. Pride was not worth the life of a single human being. If she could have traded hers for Elizabeth's life, she wouldn't have hesitated either.

"I'm sorry, Mom," Elizabeth said. She stopped in front of the dude.

Fear poured out of the clearing. It boiled off of Heath, pulsed from Elizabeth, and bent Katie's little rat shoulders. This blast of horror altered Anna's view of the dude. Firelight played over the planes of his face. His eyes fell away into tar pits of unfathomable depths. Flat cheeks and broad brow shifted like continental plates, as he assumed the size and indestructibility of a hellacious mountain range.

The thugs, the women, the forest, even the sky receded. The dude was all that remained.

"Kneel," the dude said in the voice of a dead god.

Elizabeth knelt.

Anna found herself praying that he would only force her to give him a blow job. A woman could survive a blow job. A woman could bite off the penis of the enforcer. There would be possibilities.

The dude's hand shot out with remarkable speed and closed around Elizabeth's throat.

The mountain that fear built began to heave, great shoulders hunching into dark hills against the underlit canopy as the dude closed the fingers of a hand as big and heavy as an anvil.

"No!" Heath screamed.

The anvil slammed into Elizabeth's chest.

It struck Anna's mind with equal force. She fell into the burst of roots.

"No!" she heard Heath scream again. She went on screaming as, with the unstoppable regularity of a pile driver, the fist pounded her daughter.

Anna counted seven blows before she heard Elizabeth fall to the ground.

SIXTEEN

Heath was no longer screaming on the outside. Inside, every nerve shrieked, an internal cacophony that scrambled thought. Her skull burned; her brain matter was made of double-edged razors. Had there been anything in her stomach, she would have vomited. Had there been anything in her bladder or bowels, she would have fouled herself. Her arms unable to hold her up, she lay across the curled form of her child weeping in dry-eyed silence.

The dude's boots appeared before her eyes. A swarm of swear words, more felt than heard, pelted her, from Reg's direction.

For the second time that night, Heath listened for her daughter's heartbeat. "Thank God," she said as she heard it, strong and regular, if too fast. "I'm squashing you," she muttered and tried to lever herself off her daughter. Her arms had as much strength as overcooked pasta noodles. Consciousness teetered on blades of agony. Terrified she would fall and suffocate Elizabeth, she croaked, "Help me! Help me, you goddam bastards."

The goddam bastards ignored her. "Please," Heath begged, not even hating herself for groveling. Hands closed coolly around her shoulders. Leah helped her roll free of Elizabeth.

"She's alive," Heath said. "Listen to her heart."

"Okay," Leah murmured. Heath couldn't bear to take her eyes off of Elizabeth. Leah retrieved the camp chair, set it beside Elizabeth's body, then helped Heath into it.

Heath could feel the thugs as thick and dangerous clouds above her, like the shadows of coming storms. Shutting them from her mind, she concentrated on Elizabeth. "Wait!" she said as Leah started to roll the girl over.

Wiping her face hard to stir up the memories, she again saw the dude's giant fist smash into Elizabeth, once in the side and again in the face. If E's spine had been damaged, it would be near the base of the skull in the first three or four vertebrae. Climb guides were well versed in the emergency treatment of back and head injuries. Heath dug for the old knowledge. "Stabilize her head," she said finally. "Ease your arms under her so her head and neck are cradled by your forearms, then drag her by the collar of her jacket."

Washing garbage.

The phrase shot into Heath's mind so jarringly she could see the words in the air between her and Leah. Stabilize the neck of a kidnap victim who would be moved or shot the following morning. If she was lucky. If not, the dude would take up where he left off.

It ain't over till it's over, came another cliché, and Heath let go of futility. The fat lady could sing and be damned, she thought. Anna was out there. As long as that was the case, only a coward or a fool would give in.

"I need a sleeping bag," Heath snapped without looking to see who heard, then waited for the expected blow.

Instead, the dude said, "Sean."

Pot-gut leading, Sean brought a sleeping bag into Heath's peripheral vision, dragging it by the tail like a great blue neon worm.

"Leah, could you lay it out beside E? I'll stabilize her neck, then we can roll her together."

"Mom?" Elizabeth was coming around.

"Don't try and sit up," Heath begged.

141

Elizabeth sat up.

"I guess you were right about the running thing," she said. "I could be halfway to somewhere by now."

"Damn straight," Heath said, but she was too delirious with joy that Elizabeth was alive to put any power behind it. "Sit still," she ordered as she ran her hands over E's body and face.

"Broken rib or two," Heath said when she'd finished. "That's my best guess. Your nose isn't broken, nor the bones around your eyes. Most of the blood is from the cut over your right eye. His ring must have gouged the skin there."

Elizabeth leaned over and threw up a thin stream of bile.

SEVENTEEN

Anna was too far away, and the light was too fickle, for her to tell if there was blood in Elizabeth's vomit. Taking comfort where she could, she rejoiced that the girl could sit up without assistance and speak in coherent sentences.

High sorrowful howling drilled through the cold night air.

"Fucking wolves!" Anna heard Reg yell. Then came the din of a gun firing wildly as he shot into the trees surrounding the camp.

Abruptly, the howling ceased.

It had been howling, not barking, yet Anna knew it was Wily. He'd reached back into his ancestry, leaned his head back, and howled with such heartbreak she wanted to howl with him.

From much farther away, howls began to haunt the night. Wild wolves answering the sorrowful call of their civilized brother. Reg's gun hand shook. He reached into the pocket of his hoodie and pulled out another magazine.

The dude stared at him. Reg didn't acknowledge the look, but he didn't begin firing into the dark again either.

Elizabeth was alive. Even had she been dead or dying, there was nothing more Anna could do. Her eyes were too full of filth even to watch and weep. Using the cries of her friends and the excited gabble of the thugs as cover noise, she crawled into the greater darkness in search of Wily.

She did not find Wily; Wily found her. He had dragged himself nearly to the camp, and his family. The thumping of his tail on pine needles announced his presence. Anna felt for him. The familiar touch of his fur, and the lack of any warm wet places on his hide, reassured her he'd not been hit by a stray bullet. Cross-legged, she gathered him onto her lap. Wily found her eyes and began licking. "Gross," she whispered, but she didn't stop him. His tongue was soft and wet and felt good cleaning what had to be a double handful of cockleburs from beneath her eyelids.

Jimmy was yelling about having shot a wolf. The wolves — the real wolves — were miles away. Much as she'd love to see a wolf, a half-blind woman and lame dog might look sort of tempting. Regardless of the logic, she wasn't afraid. Part of her believed wolves, mountain lions, bears — all the creatures of the wilds — would give her a bye. Too much Disney as a girl, she suspected, the creatures of the forest nestling in Snow White's skirts.

"You hit shit, dickwad," Sean said.

"Let's go," Anna whispered in Wily's ear. Tail feathers brushed over her forearm where it curled around his hindquarters. Eyes still stinging and tearing, Anna worked her way to her feet in stages. With no light to tell up from down, she was afraid she might fall. Enough strange noises and eventually even these thugs would get suspicious a creature other than a windigo or a wolf skulked in these woods. Once sure of her footing, she bent down and lifted up Wily. Wily wasn't a big dog; still, he weighed close to thirty-five pounds. That was the upper limit Anna allowed herself in a backpack if she was going any distance.

Clutching the compliant dog, she made her way slowly away from the river deeper into the trees. Every few steps she looked back to see if the glow of the campfire could still be seen. It was the only way she could judge whether she and Wily would be out of sight of the thugs when the sun rose.

145

When the orange glow was entirely swallowed, and Wily's weight had grown onerous, Anna stumbled into the umpteenth dead-and-down tree and declared it home for the night. Sitting on it, she swung her legs over, then slid to the ground. Wily's weight resting on her thighs, her back against the log, they shared body heat. Fatigue and shock helped Morpheus drag her fast and deep into sleep.

Approaching footsteps woke her. Gray diffuse light proclaimed coming sunrise. Their cloak of invisibility was gone for another twelve hours. A growl, more vibration than sound, came from beneath her hand. Wily neither let the growl grow, nor did he bark. Anna should have been surprised, but she wasn't. By the glare of an LED light, she had seen inside him, and he inside her. They were comrades in arms. Words no longer mattered.

The steps closed in on the log she and the dog sheltered behind. After hours immobile, on the cold ground, with thirty-five pounds of dog flesh on her legs, Anna doubted she would have a chance leaping to her feet and running. Even if the thug didn't shoot her in the back, he'd catch her almost immediately.

146

Playing bunny rabbit, she closed her eyes and hugged Wily. Bracken snapped. Asters, touched by frost, creaked as the man came closer. He wasn't hollering to his pals. He wasn't trying to move quietly. Ergo, he didn't know Anna was there, didn't know the bunny was frozen just beyond the log, its furry little brain convinced if it remained still enough the hawk would not see it.

The footsteps halted. Anna hadn't the courage to open her eyes. Whoever it was was standing right on the other side of the log. The top of her head would be visible. Red-with-gray hair, a mess from her nightly adventures — the crown of her head might pass for a spray of lichen or frost-burned weeds. Thinking weedy thoughts, she waited for the cry of denunciation that would end her freedom and Wily's life.

What came was the gentle sound of splashing, an intermittent stream of water striking an uneven surface. A thug was pissing on her tree. Explosive giggles threatened to boil up her throat, hysteria trying to burst forth. With an effort she kept breathing slowly and made not a sound. To calm herself, she imagined that the urination was intermittent because the bastard had prostate cancer. Advanced prostate cancer.

Eventually her listening was rewarded by

the zip of a zipper and the noise of footsteps retreating through the snap, crackle, and pop of the frost-rimed undergrowth. Cold as she was, much as she, too, felt the need to empty her bladder, she dared not move until there was sufficient racket from the kidnappers and the others to cover the racket of getting herself and the dog up off the ground and into the day.

Losing their trail, or keeping up with the thugs, was not a concern. Regardless of no food and a gimpy dog, the day she could not follow a pack of city boys through the woods would be the day she'd find an ice floe upon which to sit and wait for a polar bear with her name on it.

Eighteen

Katie, Elizabeth, and Leah lay on one sleeping bag, another spread over them. Jimmy was on watch. The dude had retired to the woods for his morning ablutions. Heath sat in her camp chair. She had not slept.

By the grace of God, Elizabeth was not badly injured. Her back and right thigh were bruised, and her stomach was sore to the touch. Her face was an advertisement for obedience: the right eye swollen shut, the lid shiny and veined as a peeled grape. Lips were clown-sized, the lower split and seamed with black blood.

Her teeth were all accounted for; the vision in her left eye was unimpaired, no blurriness, and she had no signs of mental confusion. She had slept without signs of nightmare.

The dude had not hit any vital organs. Not for a moment did Heath doubt he knew how to beat a person to death with his fists.

She was convinced he had pulled his punches. Not because he harbored any vestiges of goodness, but because he needed Elizabeth mobile.

The damages Heath had not yet been able to measure were those to Elizabeth's spirit, her sense of self. As a child she had had that systematically taken from her by a psychopath who'd abducted and imprisoned her and two other girls for several weeks.

With the help of an excellent therapist, and an internal strength Heath could only marvel at in a child so young, Elizabeth had not only recovered but built a new self that was strong and brave. The "brave" she had proven last night. What the dude's beating had left of the "strong" remained to be seen.

E's spirit was not the only one in imminent danger. After the aborted escape attempt, Leah would not speak a single word. Nor would she meet Heath's eyes, or anyone else's, for that matter. This went beyond her normal self-absorption. Heath wondered if she was ashamed that her wealth had attracted the thugs to the party.

As she thought of the scientist, Leah's eyes opened. From habit, Heath whispered, "Good morning."

"Why didn't you send Katie with your daughter?" Leah whispered back with a malice that took Heath off guard. "They never would have shot me."

So that was why Leah had turned to ice. Heath bit back the urge to snarl, "Without you, none of this would be happening." Instead, she said, "I couldn't reach Katie."

"Elizabeth could have woken her."

The horrible truth was, Heath had never given Katie a thought. Elizabeth had taken up all of her mental energy. "Did Katie rat E out?" she snapped before she could stop herself. "She saw what Elizabeth was doing."

Leah reached for her glasses and put them on. "She didn't see," she said flatly.

Heath was not sure of that.

"I know she didn't," Heath lied. As Benjamin Franklin had said, if they didn't hang together, they would all hang separately. "I should have tried to get them both out of camp. We have to stick together if we're going to make it."

Before Leah could take the white flag — or burn it — the dude returned to camp.

"We leave in twenty minutes," he said. "Do what you need to do."

Breakfast was whatever cold canned food had escaped the conflagration of the previous night. Sean, Reg, and Jimmy fished the food from the cans with their fingers and stuffed it into their mouths. None of the captives were offered food. There wasn't enough for eight when four of them were swine.

Elizabeth managed to snag a can of peaches. She offered it unopened to Leah. Heath was so proud of her she felt tears prickle in the corners of her eyes.

Their trek along the river the previous day hadn't taught the thugs they needed to carry water. When they thirsted, they drank from the Fox. They would have headed cross-country with nothing but hostages and what was in their bellies, had Heath not found the courage to speak up before the water bottles were destroyed along with everything else.

Personally, she would have loved to see them perish of dehydration, but the minute they got thirsty, they would suck down the water she, the girls, and Leah carried. Heath consolidated their water into two of the bottles, then gave the remaining two to the dude, who sent Jimmy and Sean to fill them. The water filter had gone into the fire.

Heath could, and did, hope the unfiltered river water would give them many nasty parasites. Sadly, there was no hope it would cause them to die miserable deaths.

Leah rescued a loaf of bread, lunch meat,

and Katie's day pack. The dude turned the pack inside out. Finding it empty, he let them use it to carry the food and water.

For the morning's ablutions, the cable ties binding the girls' hands were cut. Such was their relief, it leaked over into the realms of gratitude. This was ameliorated by the fact that the dude did not let them retire to the privacy of the woods to relieve themselves. After some negotiation, he permitted Leah to dig a shallow hole and two to stand as a human screen while another used it. During her backcountry career, Heath had lost most of her delicacy in the area of toileting. If she had to go, she would declare any small shrub as sufficient screening and do what needed to be done. What modesty had survived the outdoor life was destroyed when her back was broken and she was, for a time, dependent on others for everything.

Leah, and especially Katie and Elizabeth, were another matter. Elizabeth was at the age where she locked the bathroom door to blow-dry her hair. Katie was probably even shyer about her personal needs. To imagine the likes of Sean and Jimmy watching the girls relieving themselves made Heath's stomach tie itself in knots.

The idea of the dude watching didn't sicken her as much. The dude cared so little for so much, she doubted he noticed life around him as anything other than convenient for the dude or not convenient for the dude. Reg didn't quite exhibit that level of sociopathic behavior, but he struck Heath as a businessman. Watching girls peeing or humiliating women wasn't his business. His business was getting money.

Sean and Jimmy were avidly trying to peek around the two standing guard so that they might see the miracle of elimination. Modern-day sin-eaters who did it not to cleanse the souls of others but because they were greedy for the taste of degradation, humiliation, and fear. Like *Dracula*'s Renfield, they gobbled down innocent lives, growing fat on the leavings of those more evil than themselves.

Reg and the dude would kill. Sean and Jimmy would do much worse. On sunnier days, Heath would have said there was nothing worse. Dead was dead. Life was hope. Yet Sean and Jimmy were black holes into which hope drained away. Heath had come to grips with the level of helplessness imposed upon her by her physical disabilities. This was a new brand of helplessness, and the depth of the glimpsed abyss made her palms sweat.

Anna was out there, possibly wounded, if

any of Reg or Jimmy's wild shots found her. Wily was wounded or dead. Heath wanted to communicate with them so desperately it manifest as an aching hunger of the heart, but she didn't dare leave a note or scratch a message into the dirt. If the thugs found it, it would tip them off to the fact that there was another woman, one on the loose. Heath was even afraid to look at the woods more than absolutely necessary for fear it would give Anna away.

If Anna could follow, she would. Heath comforted herself with that thought. Once Heath had heard a man say Anna could track a duck across a pond a week after it had flown. For Anna it would be child's play to trail eight people, four of them idiots, and one in a wheeled cart.

"Show's over," Sean said with a leer as he lowered himself into Heath's camp chair. She glared at him. Puckering up, he made kissing noises. The thick distorting lenses of his glasses, complemented by the fish lips, would have been comical if he'd not been so vile.

Fear cooled to hatred and formed a cold iron-hard rod down Heath's spine as she watched the evil fish-faced thing remove its pointed-toed ankle boots and peel off its socks. Blisters the size of quarters bloomed on its heels.

Forcing a look of mild interest, Heath said, "I'm an EMT. If your buddies haven't sunk the canoe yet, there's a first-aid kit in it. I can patch up your feet." Inside her head, her voice echoed faraway and hollow. Sean lost vibrancy, as if viewed through dirty glass.

His hard round belly held like a basketball between his chest and knees as he cradled his foot, he stared at her suspiciously. "Why would you do that?" he asked.

Pushing with the heels of her hands, Heath straightened her upper body. She wasn't an EMT. Once she'd been a first responder. As a guide she'd been religious about the refresher courses. Since the accident she hadn't bothered. "Habit," she said. "Maybe hope that if I take a thorn out of your paw, you won't eat me."

Sean snorted. "What the hell," he said and rose to limp to the edge of the embankment. "Reg! Hang on a second. There a first-aid kit in that thing?"

As soon as Sean turned his back, Heath looked to Elizabeth. Moving stiffly, back and legs aching and sore from the beating, she was gathering up the toilet paper, then putting it in a plastic bag the way Anna had taught her.

"E," Heath mouthed. "Wily's briefcase." In her penchant for naming things, Elizabeth called the dog-poop bags "Wily's briefcases," because they were carried when he did his business.

Without question, and with the sureness of a person who followed bizarre orders under deadly circumstances as often as James Bond, Elizabeth dropped the bag containing the used toilet paper, then shunted it over to Heath with the side of her foot.

Though none of her DNA had been used in the project, Heath congratulated herself on having such a smart, quick child.

Someone, presumably Reg, tossed a white metal box to Sean, who fumbled but managed not to drop it. He returned to Heath's chair, shoved it with his foot until it touched her thigh, then flopped down hard in it. Opening the latches, then the lid, he removed the three-inch scissors and tucked them in his coat pocket. Thrusting the box and his feet toward Heath, he said, "Try anything hinky and I'll snap your neck like a dry stick."

Box in her lap, Heath opened the hinged lid between herself and her patient so he couldn't see her slip Wily's briefcase in with the first-aid supplies. Balancing on her bottom while working on Sean's feet was a trick rather like riding sidesaddle on a palsied horse, but she managed.

After donning latex gloves, she carefully broke open the blisters, then, taking the used toilet paper from the ziplock bag, made a show of thoroughly cleaning the open wounds. When she'd done as much damage as she dared, she bandaged his heels. She'd doctored enough feet in her time that she had the knack of bandaging blisters so the bandages would stay on for a day's rough hiking. Sean's would not. They would peel off in an hour, two at most.

During this peevish rebellion, Heath watched herself from above and to her left, an out-of-body experience. Since the accident, she occasionally abandoned her corporeal self. Smearing urine and feces in open wounds was scarcely more efficacious a revenge than spitting in the soup was for a disgruntled waiter, yet she instinctively knew that many slaves before her had done the same.

Until one could overthrow the master, one would undermine him.

NINETEEN

Leah wished she could take back her snipe about Heath not saving Katie, wished she could take back not only the words but the silence that preceded them. While Heath had connived to free her daughter from danger, Leah had dismantled and remantled a thing of metal and rubber. A grown woman playing at Transformers while the world went to hell around her.

Ostensibly she had done it to help Heath, to save her life. In reality she'd done it because she hadn't the wits to do anything important. She knew she could make a new design, craft it for the job described. Despite the sufferings of Gerald's child, the battering of Heath's, she couldn't but think that in its utility, it was beautiful.

Rick Shaw, as Elizabeth had named it, was a creation to be proud of. The frame was strong, the seat balanced close over the double wheel, the paddle handles mounted where the center of gravity would be once Heath was seated.

Heath had tried to save her child's life.

Leah had turned a thing into another thing.

The night before, until Katie had called her name and the shooting started, working with the wheelchair had made Leah happy. Standing between the handles of the machine she had built, she'd forgotten she had a daughter, forgotten she was a hostage. She was showing off her work, and she was happy. There must be holes in her soul. If her mothers had lived, perhaps they'd have found a way to knit them up.

Admiring Rick Shaw, Leah murmured, "Katie, you are going to have to help."

For a moment, Leah thought Katie would refuse. A familiar mutinous look marred her perfect face. Leah and Gerald's DNA had designed this child; she had built this human being, a creature perfect in form and function. Why couldn't she take pride in her daughter?

Katie was so like her father, blond and ethereal on the outside, grasping and manipulative on the inside. Leah had been twenty-one when she met Gerald. Just out of grad school and knowing nothing of men. Gerald had a partnership in a business in

Montreal designing and selling outdoor equipment. He believed in her, bought out his partner, and used the money to build her a lab in which to work.

Within three months of the wedding, Katie had been conceived. That was the last time she and Gerald had sex, or nearly the last. Gerald had his own life. Leah designed; he sold. That he did other things had ceased to interest her years ago.

Had Katie purposely called the attention of the thugs to Elizabeth's escape? Had Gerald done something? Had she done — or not done — something that twisted Katie's mind?

"It's not too bad," Elizabeth said to Katie. "Not heavy exactly."

Katie moved to take her place, each girl on a paddle handle like dray horses readying to pull a wagon.

"Thank you," Leah said. "You're a good girl," she added, because that was what Heath would have done.

"Just part of the machinery," Katie said in a voice like treacle.

"Ready?" Leah asked.

"Ready as I'll ever be," Heath said with a smile.

Heath believed Katie had nearly gotten Elizabeth shot, yet she smiled. Leah had never been able to tell if smiles were real, what they tried to communicate.

"Hold Rick Shaw steady," she said to the girls. She helped Heath get into the seat. Once she was settled, Leah took a roll of duct tape from her toolbox, then taped Heath to the chair at waist and chest.

For the minutes this took, Leah lost herself again in the rhythm of building, testing what she had built, seeing its use taking shape. Taping done, she put Heath's feet on the makeshift foot rails and attached them firmly.

"These are for balance," she said, retrieving two straight pieces of tubing she had salvaged from the original chair's frame. Duct tape was wound around one end of each to give Heath a better gripping surface.

Using them like ski poles, Heath balanced herself above the single wheel. "They sure as hell don't teach this in therapy," she said.

"Dude," Reg said. "Weapons."

The dude turned slowly, his eyes no more fathomable in the light of day than they had been in the dark of night. Leah couldn't even tell what color they were: the color of a stormy sky, mud, a sandstorm, the oil slick on the garage floor? Leah felt a strange kinship for this cold, colorless man. He, too, lived in a world by himself. That he chose to destruct rather than to construct didn't make them opposites.

"Balance poles," Heath said and tossed him one. She didn't throw it but tossed it with obvious gentleness. Heath was on borrowed time, living because Katie had said she was wealthy. Leah wondered if Katie had lied from kindness or habit, or if it mattered.

It wouldn't take much for the thugs to choose to divest themselves of Heath. Though given the choice between dying and bushwhacking six miles in Rick Shaw, escorted by homicidal maniacs, Leah might have chosen the dying, Heath would never choose death. Heath knew watching her murdered would permanently damage Elizabeth's psyche. Leah didn't think the same would be true of Katie.

The dude neatly caught the pole in his right hand. He was ambidextrous. A weird sense of déjà vu washed through Leah. For a moment the dude held the pole, balancing it on his palm. It weighed next to nothing. "Keep it," he said. No attempt was made to toss it so Heath might catch it. He just dropped it for them to retrieve as they wished.

Reg picked it up. "Dude, I tell you, this is a weapon."

"If she starts knuckle-dragging after you with those things, you can shoot her. How's that?" the dude said dismissively.

Leah saw the insult slap Reg's cheeks and flash in his black eyes. Reg was not good at taking insults — or orders. Evidently the dude was so used to hurling both at people he'd grown inured to their reactions.

"Stabbing," Reg said through stiff lips. He jabbed at the air with the untaped end of the bar to illustrate his meaning. Reg would know about stabbing with found weapons: pens, broken bottles, sharpened sticks.

Reg dropped the pole.

Ignoring him, the dude took his cell phone from the wallet on his belt, punched a button, and held it to his ear. The look was incongruous to the point of perceived anachronism.

Heath had banned cell phones on the trip. Heath's first excuse was that there were many places along the Fox where there was no cell reception. Her second was that the girls wouldn't be able to leave them alone. The real reason was that they offended her friend Anna.

"Yeah," the dude said into the phone. "We're headed out. Six-point-seven miles. Should be there in a few hours."

Reg was shaking his head, grumbling.

"Took us a fucking lifetime to get here, and we were following the fucking river."

Gutter language was not a part of Leah's life. Of course she had heard the word "fuck" before. She'd just never heard it used as a verb, a noun, and an adjective, often in a single sentence.

The dude didn't put his phone back in its holster but held it in front of him, watching the GPS map on the screen.

"Let's move," he said.

Stepping between the poles, Leah took over for Katie. "You push," she said to Elizabeth. Too late, she realized she had marginalized Katie, disincluded her. Had she always done that? Had Katie chosen to keep her distance? Had Gerald orchestrated their relationship? The arrangement had once seemed to suit everyone concerned.

Their little train began to crawl out of the clearing, the dude leading, Reg behind him, Leah pulling Heath, Elizabeth behind pushing. Katie was nearly treading on Elizabeth's heels, keeping as far from Sean and Jimmy as she could.

The first fifty yards, where social trails had been stomped into the soft earth by summer campers relieving themselves or searching for firewood, were comparatively easy. The chair moved smoothly on its doubled wheel, and there was space enough to each side for Heath to use her poles to maintain balance so her weight didn't shift and jerk on the pulling handles.

Then the short honeymoon ended. Underbrush, laced with a loose weave of fallen twigs and branches, made movement a muscle-wrenching struggle. Hard physical labor was another thing that was not part of Leah's life. Had the dude not been slowed up by fighting through thick vegetation, she, Heath, and Elizabeth would have been unable to keep up. Rick Shaw would have been abandoned, and Heath gotten a bullet between the eyes.

As time passed, Leah almost wished for it. In tight places the chair had to be pivoted on its wheel and pushed like a plow, Heath's back serving as the blade that cleaved scrub and low branches.

Elizabeth, and even Katie, pulled, one on each paddle handle, while Leah pushed. Then Leah pulled and Elizabeth pushed. Over the bigger logs it took all three to lift the chair. Heath worked with her poles and thanked them again and again. She told them they were the most beautiful women she had ever seen, that should she die without sin and be ushered immediately into heaven, the angels that greeted her could be but a dim reflection of their glory.

The compliments seemed to fuel Katie and Elizabeth. Leah shut them out. They were not angels, they were not beautiful. They were sweating and grunting, bruised and bleeding, wrestling with a problem that, ultimately, could never be solved. People problems never could. The thugs would kill them, sell them, or ransom them. The thugs would be caught, imprisoned, put to death, or stay free to live like kings. Life had no solutions; it was a series. Once the issues were solved, the series was over, dead.

Leading with his cell phone GPS, the dude continued in a straight line regardless of difficulty. Reg grumbled, but he was strong and young. Sean and Jimmy didn't do as well. Jimmy was short of breath. Sean, almost crippled with blisters and inappropriate shoes, minced along last, his mouth set in a hard line.

From the look on Heath's face when she caught sight of him, Leah knew she took satisfaction in the creep's suffering. Leah took satisfaction in the fact that Rick Shaw was proving up to the rigors of the terrain.

After three hours even this small pleasure was buried.

Heath asked Leah to duct-tape her hands to her makeshift ski poles because her

167

fingers no longer had the strength not to drop them. Katie quit helping and reverted to nonstop whining. The paddle handles Leah thought she'd used so cleverly came to look like the oars in a slave galley, she and Elizabeth the unfortunates condemned to pull them until they died on the benches where they were chained.

The thugs did not volunteer to help, nor did Leah or Heath ask them to. Heath, undoubtedly because to be tended to by the kidnappers was a worse fate than breaking the backs and ripping the skin of friends and family.

Leah didn't ask because she knew the answer would be no.

TWENTY

Such was her exhaustion, it took Heath a
few seconds to realize that they had stopped.
Through eyes bleary with sweat, she peered
ahead. Reg was squatting on his heels, his
chin up, watching the dude. Over his shoulder, Heath could see the dude in profile
standing in a small clearing, staring down
at his cell phone. Though his face was as
blank as ever, the muscles at the corner of
his jaw bunched as if he gritted his teeth.

"Rest," Heath said.

Leah and Elizabeth dragged Rick Shaw to
where they could set its handles on a rock,
keeping Heath on the level, then both
dropped to the ground as if shot. Heath
started peeling off the grubby duct tape that
affixed her hands to the poles. Katie came
up beside them, then sat down a little ways
away, her back to her mother, and began
picking at the blisters on her palms.

E was bleeding from a long gouge in her

shin where a footrest had torn through her pants as she wrestled Rick Shaw through a bad patch. Scratches from the low dead branches thrusting out from every pine tree like spines from a porcupine cross-hatched the unbattered half of her face, her neck, her hands. Leaves, gold and red with autumn, tangled in her hair. Sweat darkened her jacket beneath her arms and in the middle of her back. Her face was so red it frightened Heath.

Not once had she complained. It wasn't that Elizabeth was an abnormal teen. At home she could be as annoying as anyone else her age. This trauma was so reminiscent of the one that had brought them together that Heath feared it would break her. Instead, it almost seemed she had prepared for it. E had worked with a wonderful therapist Aunt Gwen recommended. Apparently Elizabeth had not only hunted down and faced her demons but had chosen how she would act should more demons come.

Wise, Heath thought. More demons always came.

"Lunch," the dude announced abruptly.

Lunch; such a civilized activity, mundane, a thing taken at a small table on the mall in Boulder, or while reading in the sun at the kitchen table. Under the circumstances, the word had little meaning for Heath.

Sean shoved past. With a grunt, he fell to his butt, leaned back against a tree, and pulled off his boots. The bandages were off. Heath would have liked to see nasty suppurating sores, but it was too soon to expect that.

Reg went to stand by the dude and stare down at a creek cutting through the woods. Maybe fifteen feet from steep bank to steep bank, not deep, but running fast.

The bunching of the dude's jaw indicated something more ominous than a river crossing. Heath watched him as Elizabeth crawled over and began ripping the duct tape from Heath's ankles. Heath started to thank her, caught a glare from Katie, and resisted the impulse.

The dude was glancing from his phone to the abbreviated horizon of half-nude tree branches. Pacing the bank of the creek, he moved his phone up and down and side to side in an unconscious parody of a devout Catholic crossing himself.

He'd lost service, Heath realized. He had no signal, no GPS. They were lost, or, if not, they soon would be. She couldn't decide if that was good or bad.

Finished with the duct tape, Elizabeth wedged her shoulder beneath Heath's left arm. "Ready?"

"As I'll ever be."

As Elizabeth helped her lower herself to the ground, Heath watched herself kick her daughter, then absorbed the sharp end of a broken branch. "Sorry," she said to Elizabeth. "I hope I didn't hurt you."

"No, but the branch will think twice before messing with you again," Elizabeth gasped.

Heath knew the branch had won. Blood was probably pooling in her sock below the puncture. Shorted circuits in the lower half of her body didn't register pain as did the upper half, but she could tell when she'd sustained an injury. The only way she could explain it to the able-bodied was that it *almost* hurt.

"Damn it," Heath said. Her heels were drumming against the ground.

"Possessed by an Irish clog dancer," Elizabeth said. "Call the exorcist."

Heath laughed. It felt both marvelous and inappropriate.

"Gimme your bag."

Jimmy shattered the moment of transient pleasure. Before Leah could take the pack off, the bearded troll grabbed it and yanked roughly backward.

"Hey!" Heath yelled before she could stop

herself. She'd learned any wrath she brought down upon her own head would likely also be visited upon that of Elizabeth.

"Shut up," Jimmy said and proceeded with ripping the pack from Leah's shoulders. When he'd finally freed it, Leah was sprawled in the dirt. Her face, always pale, was so colorless, it looked more like bone than flesh. Katie was whimpering, the small awful sound baby animals make when frightened.

"Katie," Heath said. "Your mom is okay." Katie flung herself onto Heath's lap, knocking the air out of her lungs. She was long-legged and coltish, no longer lap-sized. Heath stroked her hair, looking over the top of her head at Elizabeth. E shrugged. Katie was an enigmatic pain in the ass, the shrug said.

Reaching out, Elizabeth gave Heath's shoulder a reassuring squeeze. Heath wished it were Elizabeth on her lap, wished she were still young enough to think her mother was safe as houses. E began pulling off her boots and socks the way she always did on hiking stops. Anna had convinced her that feet needed to breathe. Leah was watching Heath comfort her daughter. An emotion more like confusion than jealousy shadowed her eyes. She made no move to come collect her weeping offspring, just watched with what appeared to be befuddled interest.

Jimmy had taken the day pack to the edge of the sunken stream. Inside were three-quarters of a loaf of white bread, a package of sliced bologna, and a package of individually wrapped Kraft American cheese slices. For reasons known only to genius engineers, this was the lunch Leah took to work every day. When Katie saw it in the cooler, she said, "Well, at least Leah won't starve." This childhood food relic, sneered at by foodies from L.A. to New York, was currently being fought over as might be fine caviar in a discount fish market.

Reg had one shoulder strap, Jimmy the other, and they were worrying it between them like two dogs with a bone. Jimmy's rifle, slung across his back by a strap, was flopping about with such vehemence Heath dared hope it would go off and blow their brains out.

The skirmish distracted Katie from her tears. Wiping her eyes with the back of her arm, she pulled out of Heath's embrace. Curling her legs under her, she leaned back against a tree and pretended to close her eyes. Heath could see small shining crescents where she peeked from beneath her lashes.

Elizabeth stood and, in bare feet, walked toward the skirmish.

"E," Heath called desperately. "Never mind. We aren't hungry."

Elizabeth pretended not to hear. Stopping close to the grapplers, she waited. The peculiar nature of her nearness and silence brought the tug-of-war to a halt, though neither Reg nor Jimmy relinquished the strap he'd captured.

"What do you want?" Reg asked.

"I'll make the sandwiches for you."

"Right," Reg said, "and spit in them." Heath was startled to hear her thoughts on the petty vengeance of slaves come from the mouth of a man whose great-great-something was probably among that number.

"I won't," Elizabeth said. "You can watch. You're smashing the bread, and nobody will have anything." Her voice was calm, a little obsequious and shaky. Fear or exhaustion, or both. For once Heath was unable to read her daughter's emotions.

"You want a sandwich, I suppose?" Reg asked.

"That would be nice," Elizabeth said meekly.

"Fuck off," Reg said to Jimmy, as he put the heel of his hand against Jimmy's sternum and casually pushed the smaller man down. "Make 'em," Reg said, putting the pack in Elizabeth's arms. "I'll say who gets what."

He almost shot a glance toward the dude but stopped himself. Heath noted only a slight jerk of the head.

"We'll say who gets what," he corrected himself.

With no mustard, no mayonnaise, and no plates, the making of sandwiches was akin to dealing cards. Jimmy and Reg watched unblinkingly as Elizabeth dealt out bread, then bologna, then cheese until she had six sandwiches assembled. Heath noted approvingly how careful she was not to do anything sudden or fishy, to keep her hands in sight so the men watching wouldn't suspect her of anything. She also noted, and without approval, that Elizabeth was sucking up to them. Perhaps there was no harm in that, and maybe some good — even if it was only a sandwich to eat. Still, she didn't like it.

Reg took a sandwich for himself, then carried another to the dude, who continued to pace by the creek. Heath wondered if any of the others had yet reached the conclusion she had, that they had lost their electronic guide.

Jimmy jammed his sandwich into his mouth where he stood. Elizabeth brought two sandwiches to Heath to be shared among the four of them, then carried the last to where Sean sat morosely gazing at his torn feet.

"Eat fast," Heath whispered as she handed one of the sandwiches to Leah. Heath was riding, she reasoned, she didn't need food. She shoved the sandwich into her coat pocket for Elizabeth. The pocket was not a particularly sanitary place for food storage, but Heath had no doubt, once the men finished their sandwiches, they would grab anything not yet eaten. She was determined to keep Elizabeth's few bites safe.

E delivered Sean's lunch. She didn't just hand it to him, she folded down cross-legged on his right side. Her bare toes were close enough to his thigh that, if she flexed them, she would touch him. "I brought you a sandwich," she said.

Or somebody said. The voice was E's from five years past, the E who had been a scared little girl, innocence lost, and nearly her mind with it. This Elizabeth was tiny, smaller than Katie, and no more than nine years old. A pit yawned inside Heath. Dizziness threatened to topple her into it. Elizabeth had seemed so strong, so able. Had Heath been fooling herself, projecting what she wished to see? Had she blinded herself to the fact that her daughter was regressing in the face of this second brutal attack?

The thug took the sandwich with a grunt.

Just as if he had said "thank you," Elizabeth said, "You're welcome," in the old small voice. He ignored her. She stayed where she was. After a moment she said, "Your poor feet. They must hurt awfully."

The abyss that had manifest did not vanish from Heath's mind. It merely changed shape. E hadn't regressed, not unless she had regressed all the way to Jane Austen's day. Elizabeth would never say, "They must hurt awfully."

Relief that her daughter's mind was sound momentarily canceled out the fear of what she was up to. Sean had shown a nasty appreciation of the slight, small, girlish Katie. Heath couldn't forget the way he'd pressed his belly and, if it could be reached, she presumed his cock, against the child's back as Leah was being bound, how he all but drooled on her sleeping body. Elizabeth had seen it, too. With the prevalence of information, even girls younger than E knew what a man like Sean's preferences were.

"Life's a bitch," Sean said.

"And then you die." Those words, in the scared-child voice, gave Heath the creeps. She could feel them like insect feet creeping down her spine and over her scalp. Her left leg shot out, the toe of her boot banging into a stone.

Sean shuddered as well. Before Heath could consider that he might actually possess a soul, she saw what had caused his reaction. It wasn't the little lost child act. It was Elizabeth's toes. She was wiggling them the way a nervous little girl might, and they were tickling Sean's thigh. Sean was liking it very much. E was pretending not to notice.

Heath was trying not to have a heart attack.

When she realized just what it was that Elizabeth was up to, she did have a heart attack. Or felt like she did, given the sudden painful crushing sensation in her chest. The girl's quick eyes had noticed something Heath's had missed. As Sean threw his sorry ass down, the great long pig-sticker he wore on his belt had been forced partway out of its sheath. The holding snap popped open, and two inches of blade extruded from the leather. While distracting Sean with sexually deviant fantasies, Elizabeth's bare toes were working the knife from its sheath.

There could be no happy ending to this. If E managed to get hold of the knife, she wouldn't — or couldn't — drive it into a man's heart. Even if she pulled off that gruesome and magnificent stunt, she would be shot by one of the others.

"Elizabeth!" Heath tried to call. What came out of her mouth was a papery whisper. Her daughter ignored her. "Elizabeth!" This time she found voice. "Come here. I need you."

"Leave her alone," Sean growled. He grabbed E by the shoulders and pulled her across his chest. It was the opening E needed and Heath dreaded. Elizabeth pulled the knife free.

"Break it up." The dead and deadly voice of the dude put a stop to everything. Even time, or so it seemed. Sean let loose of Elizabeth. Elizabeth, in her scramble away from the thug, managed to push the knife behind the tree on which he leaned, half burying it in the duff.

Heath could have cried with relief. Elizabeth wasn't arming herself, she was arming Anna.

Elizabeth crawled back to Heath, and Heath hugged her hard. Into her ear she whispered furiously, "Stupid, stupid risk. A lot of bullets were fired. Anna might not be coming."

"She's coming," E whispered so fiercely Heath felt the heat on her eardrum. "Nothing stops Anna."

TWENTY-ONE

Wily in her arms, Anna glided to the edge of the clearing. Stopping, she searched the area. A mess. Nothing remained: no tents, no camp chair or wheelchair, no porta-potty, sleeping bags, or clothes. The fire pit was smoldering with items never meant to be destroyed by burning. Leah's state-of-the-art canoe was gone. In an hour or two, when the smoke cleared, river traffic floating by wouldn't know that just above their heads four lives had been violently uprooted.

Come evening, if canoeists chose to camp here, there would be evidence of an upheaval, illegal dumping or burning, but not enough to send them back on the river at night to report it.

The scorched white metal of the first-aid kit lay at the edge the fire. It had been kicked into the burn area but hadn't caught. Anna set Wily carefully on the ground, then fished the box out with a stick and left it to cool. The bones of Heath's camp chair were charred, but possibly usable. A metal World War II army canteen, the green canvas burned away, the aluminum charred, was settled bent and soft-looking in the coals. That, too, she fished out with her stick. A can of Dennison's chili had exploded, spewing beans on the ground. The can was cool to the touch. Anna scraped out the last half inch of beans and licked them off her fingers. Nothing else appeared salvageable.

She moved Wily to where he could reach the beans in the grass, then began walking around the fire in circles of ever-increasing diameter, letting her feet, as well as her eyes, search. Near the edge of the clearing, nearly hidden under an aster still flaunting a few blue flowers, she found a headlamp and band. One of the women — or girls — had thought to toss it into the bushes for her to find.

Anna retrieved it with silent thanks. Nights in the woods were not the half-dusk of nights in towns, fields, or deserts. Unless the moon was full, nights in the woods were blackout, bat-blind dark. The moon was new. Come sundown, Anna would be glad of the headlamp.

A few feet farther out she came across a

piece of nylon fabric from a lime green sleeping bag — Katie's, she thought — the edges melted, the shape irregular and about two feet by four in size. This she picked up to add to her trove.

Salvage left under Wily's protection, Anna cleaned what was left of the chili can in the river, drank, refilled it, then took it to Wily. She sat down beside him and, gathering the beans he couldn't reach, said, "This is it, old buddy. A scorched first-aid kit is our greatest treasure. Drink up." She held the can of water to his snout, and he lapped greedily.

"The doctor is in."

Wily was a trooper. Anna palpated his right hind leg. The fine grating sound of crepitation, the noise broken bone ends made when they rubbed together, made her teeth itch. He whimpered the least of whimpers. "Sorry, guy," she said. "It's broken. I was hoping for a sprain. Lots of dogs I know do just fine on three legs with a sprain. A break hurts too much. Shock would kill you — or me."

Opening the first-aid kit took a while. Heat had deformed the metal, and the latches didn't want to release. A fist-sized rock, firmly applied, finally sprang them. The lid was eight inches by nine. She bent it back and forth, forcing the hinges, until it broke free. A canister the size of her thumb rolled out. Aspirin. She unscrewed the cap, shook two into the palm of her hand, then swallowed them with the last of Wily's water.

It wasn't her habit to drink out of toilet bowls or doggie dishes, but things had changed. The night before, Wily would have been killed by the thugs, had she not stolen him away. Had he not slept curled on her lap and chest all night, she might have suffered hypothermia. They were family now. Besides, given the situation, she didn't think the worst threat to life and limb was going to turn out to be dog spit.

She shook out a third aspirin and held it out to Wily. He took it neatly and made a great show of swallowing. The second she turned her head, he spit it out. "Saw that," she said. She plucked the pill out of the dirt, dusted it off, then put it back into the tube.

The box held rolls of cloth tape, gauze, bandages, a small bottle of peroxide, a two-ounce bottle of hand sanitizer, half a dozen alcohol wipes, and a rubber bulb syringe for the ear. Nearly every one of the many first-aid kits she'd used over the years had a bright blue ear syringe bulb. Never once had she used it. "Today's the day," she told Wily.

Back at the river, Anna filled the syringe and squeezed water into both gritty eyes until all the brown and black shrapnel the bullet had blasted from the log was washed away.

Wily was next. She talked him through it the way she had talked a hundred park visitors through her medical machinations in the backcountry. Wily listened better than most and, she was willing to bet, understood more.

"Your femur is broken, if dogs have femurs. The big bone just below the hip." Gently, she folded his leg, then laid the smooth metal box lid over it. "I'm going to tie it with the gauze, Wily, stabilize the leg so it won't move. It will hurt a lot less that way, I promise. Since we are not exactly on our way to the vet, I'm going to tape it as well. So when we get out of this, and your fur is being pulled out by the roots by some sausage-fingered vet tech, remember I did this for your own good."

Wily yawned. She was boring him.

When she'd finished and helped him to stand on all fours, she said, "Give it a shot." Wily walked several feet on three legs. "What a sport," Anna commended him. "We'll save the walking for when it counts." The terrain would be too rough to traverse for an old dog with a broken bone, but she didn't tell Wily that. He had his dignity.

Using a hot metal rod, once a tent pole, Anna melted slits in both ends of the elongated piece of nylon she had found. She settled Wily in the center of the fabric, sat down with her back to him, then pulled a hole over each arm, drawing it up until he was strapped to her back papoose-style. Wily laid his chin on her shoulder. A warm canine sigh woofed into her ear.

"De nada," she said.

She filled the charred canteen with river water and dropped it and the half chili tin over her shoulder into Wily's sack. The first-aid items she stored in various pockets. Then they walked into the autumn woods.

Anna didn't so much track the kidnappers as follow the highway they had bulldozed. Despite the fact that eight bodies had broken trail, snapping off twigs and trampling shrubs, the going was hard, yet in a couple of hours she was close enough to the kidnapping party that she could hear them — and they could hear her.

From that point on, she and Wily dared move only when the kidnappers moved. Stopped, Anna realized she was hungry and thirsty. Having removed Wily from his sack, she shared a cup of river water with him.

For the hunger there was nothing to be done. Since it wouldn't prove fatal for a month or more, she banished it to the back of her mind.

Thirty minutes later, she heard the noise of the kidnappers and her friends on the move. "Time to go," she whispered to Wily. Misunderstanding her, intentionally or not, he resignedly got to his three feet and hobbled a few feet away to pee on a tuft of grass.

"Good idea," Anna commended him and followed suit.

The noise of the kidnappers continued but grew louder. They were moving, but evidently not in a linear direction. Leaving the track they'd trampled into the duff, she climbed a gentle slope that ended in a bluff where the land dropped away precipitously, the soft sandy banks undercut by a small swift river thirty feet below.

Leaving Wily resting on the nylon cloth, she crawled to the edge of the bluff. The dude was downstream on the far side of the small river. Leah was duct-taping Heath into the rickshaw.

They should move Heath and the chair separately.

The current was too swift.

There was too much torque.

Anna quashed the urge to rush down and help, or stand up and shout instructions.

Twenty-Two

The dude was on the opposite bank. From chest to boots he was soaking wet. The water had to be close to three feet deep in the middle of the channel. Strainers made from dead limbs and other detritus attested to the fact the river was at or near flood stage from rains farther north. Whether the dude finally got a signal or just decided to follow his nose, he had ordered them to cross the fierce little river.

Taped into the chair, unable to move anything but her arms, Heath fought down her fear as Leah and Elizabeth began lowering her down the embankment, one on each of the paddle handles. Clawing at the crumbling bank, Heath supported as much of her own weight as she could. Dirt clods rained down on her face as she grabbed at anything that looked like it might hold. Her knees and feet loosed small avalanches of soil into the water below.

Heath felt the wheel hit bottom, a stability of sorts. She watched the water rise over her trapped feet and her legs, brown foam creaming her knees, but felt neither the wet nor the cold.

Elizabeth and Leah were kneeling on the bank, their arms stretched full length, the paddle ends in their fists. The wheel of the rickshaw was in the water. No longer able to reach the bank to help them, Heath looked up. The paddle handle was slipping from Leah's sweating hands.

"Katie!" she yelled. "Help your mom!" Katie, face a mask of distaste, skinny arms crossed over her chest, didn't move.

"Mom!" Elizabeth cried as the current twisted Rick Shaw, ripping the other handle from her hands. The paddle handles shot skyward. Heath and the chair plunged backward. Tea-colored water swirled over Heath's shoulders. This she could feel.

The cold shocked her, driving the breath from her lungs. The Fox River had been just as cold, but in the sun, in a fabulous canoe, with friends and family, Heath hadn't noticed. Now the sun sulked behind sullen-looking clouds, a cold disk of white on a gray sky. Friends and family were dead or in danger, and the water was just damn cold.

Up on the bank, Jimmy and Sean laughed

uproariously. Heath hadn't heard such roaring belly laughs since Aunt Gwen had taken her to the road show of *Spamalot* in Denver.

"Mom!" Elizabeth was sliding. She stumbled into the water, throwing her body across the paddle handles, fighting the current with her weight to keep the chair level and upright. Leah jumped down after her.

With one on each handle, the chair came level, the wheel on the bottom.

"That was exciting," Heath said.

"Katie, we need you," Elizabeth called.

"If I get wet, I'll be cold," Katie called back.

"If you don't help, wet isn't all you'll get," Elizabeth snapped.

"You have to cross anyway, Katie," Heath called before either could utter words that couldn't be unsaid. "You'll be safer if you cross with us." Katie was so small, the current would snatch her away if she tried it on her own.

Mincingly, and with many squeals, Katie entered the stream and hesitantly took a paddle handle. Leah moved behind Heath and grabbed the double wheel.

"On three, lift the handles. I'll lift the wheel," Leah murmured. Heath could barely hear her.

Katie repeated her mother's words as if

she had to translate them from a language the others weren't familiar with.

"You're going to tip backward, Heath," Leah said. "Girls, be sure you keep her chin above the water. Okay? Then you walk backward. Slowly. One, two, three."

Though forewarned, Heath yelped with vertigo as the chair tilted backward and the cold water rushed over her chest and throat.

"Easy, baby steps," Leah murmured.

Heath began to move backward, the water slopping over her shoulders. "Whoa," she gasped as the stream sent icy fingers over her breasts and down her pants.

"Are you okay?" Elizabeth asked.

"You mean other than being disabled, dunked, and abducted?" Heath asked.

"Yes. Other than that."

Elizabeth was so tired Heath could feel the trembling of her muscles through the paddle handles and the plastic of the seat, yet she found the strength to pretend her mother was amusing. What a girl.

They'd made it to midstream when the left side of the chair, the upstream handle that E was holding, dipped precipitously. Heath felt her weight slew to that side and the chair lurch. The wheel between Leah's hands began to turn from the vertical. They were losing it. The current was spinning the rickshaw, trying to flip it over.

"Pull up! Pull up!" Heath yelled at Elizabeth.

"I'm trying. Dammit!"

Katie's paddle handle lifted out of the water, her hands like small white starfish, glued to the shaft. Water foamed over Heath's upstream shoulder. She had to twist her neck to keep her face above water.

"Don't let go, Katie!" Elizabeth cried.

"Push down, Katie, get the paddle down!" Heath said. Water poured into her mouth, and her words were lost in a fit of coughing.

"She's drowning!" Katie screamed.

Leaning as far upstream as she could with her body taped to the back of the seat, Heath reached over and grabbed at the bottom of the chair, bowing her back in an effort to use her weight to right the rickshaw.

"Up, up," Leah was shouting. The upstream side of the chair bucked up and down as E worked to raise the paddle handle and bring the apparatus to level.

Though the shout had been meant for Elizabeth, Katie responded. She lifted instead of holding her handle down. The center of gravity shifted, the double wheel caught the water like a tiller, and the chair spun.

"I can't hold her!" was the last thing

194

Heath heard before she went under.

She'd gotten a breath and closed her mouth. Her eyes were open. Nothing but brown showed. With fingers that felt as responsive as if they were made of clay, she scratched at the tape across her chest.

Remembering her horror at being taped into the wheeled death trap, futile fury lent her an erg of power. She had said nothing. Leah and Elizabeth — even Katie in her way — worked so hard for her, she couldn't bear to criticize or make special requests. Because Aunt Gwen had drummed good manners into her, she was going to die a horrible gurgling death.

The lower part of the chair struck a submerged rock. Heath began cartwheeling downstream. Hands, scrabbling pitifully at the wet tape, forgot their business and tried swimming. Her head was snapped back by the spin. Her mind flashed on the county fair, back when it was small potatoes, a showcase for the local cake bakers and curtain makers, 4H calves and sheep, boys and girls sleeping in the stall with a loved prize animal, vying for a blue ribbon, then slaughter. Tilt-a-Whirl. That was the ride. Heath had chipped her front tooth on the safety bar before barfing cotton candy all over the wide-wale corduroy trousers of the boy of her dreams.

Light slashed her eyes as the chair rolled her faceup. The colors of autumn smeared in with the gray of the sky and the tears of the river. She'd just had time to suck in another lungful of air before she was under again.

Abruptly, the spinning stopped. Heath was saved. Then she wasn't. The bottom of the river was in front of her face. Craning her neck as far as it would go, she could see the lighter shade of the surface. Not helping hands but the handles of the chair had arrested her tumble downriver. One or both had jammed in the soft mud of the bottom and the side bank. She was caught in a strainer designed by a genius engineer, and would drown as neatly as a rat in a rain barrel.

Pressure built in her lungs until they felt full to bursting, not empty. Soon she would no longer be able to hold it in. She would gasp it out. Silty water would rush in and fill her lungs.

A sharp bony finger raked across her cheek, tearing into her ear and tangling in her hair; a branch, maybe attached to an anchor — a tree or a larger branch. In the way of drowning men grasping at straws, Heath grabbed it with both hands and pulled. Not far above was light. She willed her face toward it, strained with arms and shoulders worn to threads by the morning's trek.

The river dragged at her legs. The current toyed with the paddle handles, digging them deeper, then lifting them up. Where her body began to sense pain, low on her spine, seared above the numb, but not forgotten, sensations of the dead weight below. It would be worth breaking herself in two if she could get her nose above the surface for even an instant, a breath.

With the last of her strength, Heath jerked her chin toward the light and managed a sip of air, enough to prolong this hell for half a minute more. Her fingers opened without her permission. The branch, no bigger around than her thumb, scraped through, cutting her palms. The knowledge that Elizabeth would take her death hard spurred Heath to one more desperate snatch at the branch. Her fingers closed again around the black tendril, but she hadn't the strength to hoist her shoulders up the three inches it would take to get her lips to the surface. She watched her hands opening as if they belonged to someone else, watched them float out from her body on arms that could not move without the aid of the current.

The force in her lungs, the desperate hunger for air, couldn't be denied any longer.

Through the murky waters a pale ghost drew near, a star shape, as amorphous as a jellyfish. The flashing of her life before her eyes had been a disappointment. If this was the light one was supposed to go toward, death was going to be a drag, she thought as she blacked out.

TWENTY-THREE

Hallelujah, Charles thought as the cripple went under. Maybe his luck was changing. Michael, if you have any leverage with your landlord, get him to drown her. One less malformed abortion taking up space that could be utilized by whole men. Though Charles had to admit this cripple was a fighter. She'd fought longer and harder and with less complaint than any man he'd worked with. If she'd been whole, she would have been a force to be contended with. If she'd been whole, he would have had to shoot her the minute he'd walked into camp.

Half running, half swimming, the cripple's daughter was forging after the rolling machine that held her mother. Not a second's hesitation, the dude noticed. The apple showed nearly as much courage as the tree.

Across the water, atop the steep bank, the idiot Jimmy raised his toy rifle to his shoulder. A squirrel rifle. Jimmy boy had probably kept food on the table with his peashooter until he infected his whole damn family with mad squirrel's disease. Shooting the daughter while the cripple drowned would have been a neat solution to a number of Charles's problems, but Leah Hendricks was between Jimmy and the daughter, and Jimmy was a lousy shot.

Anger always simmered in the caldron of Charles's chest. Negative emotions — pity, sadness, guilt, lust, envy — were instantly transmuted into anger. Anger was stimulation and fuel. Showing anger was weakness. This ill-begotten, ill-fated circus of the damned he found himself ringleading had spawned a surplus of anger, fuel for weeks to come.

Drawing a sip of the heady brew, he raised the Colt and fired off four shots in quick succession. Explosions of dirt blossomed in a line four inches below Jimmy's boots. The bank crumbled, the .22 fired. Arms pinwheeling, rifle flung aside, the bearded man tumbled into the stream.

Charles allowed himself a small interior smile.

The cripple's daughter had reached the inverted chair. Plunging her arms under the water, she shouted, "Help me! I've got her."

The Hendricks woman, who, like the

riffraff on the other bank, had been gaping at the spectacle, hesitated, then started toward the daughter. Charles considered stopping her with a well-placed warning shot, but he'd become interested in seeing how the drama unfolded.

Together, Hendricks and the daughter got hold of the chair and lifted until the cripple's head was above the surface of the river. Lifeless as old seaweed, the cripple hung from the duct tape. Drowned.

"Hold fast, Leah," the daughter shouted, then let go of the chair. Grabbing her mother's face, a hand on either side of her head, she bent and clamped her lips over those of the cripple.

A healthy body putting lips to a broken piece of meat turned Charles's stomach.

The girl's head snapped back. She spit, then a clearly audible "Eeeww" came up stream on the slight breeze.

Charles felt his gorge rise. The cripple, back among the living, had vomited in the daughter's mouth.

"Reg, Jimmy, get that contraption up here," he yelled. Enough time had been lost. "Sean, get the Hendricks girl across."

Holding his ridiculous boots in one hand and Katie Hendricks's arm in the other, Sean gingerly tiptoed across. Several times it looked as if the current would do with his belly what it had done with the wheel on the cripple's chair, but he made it without a dunking.

Charles's luck had run dry.

Wet clothing, no food — when darkness came they would all be in a sorry state unless he could get them to their destination. GPS systems didn't work off cell towers. They triangulated off satellites. The make of phone he carried required the transmission of a cell tower in order to keep streaming. A civilized nation shouldn't have any dead zones. Bernie was just the fool to find one.

With no GPS, he reasoned he'd have to keep going north by northwest, the direction they'd been headed when the cell phone went dead. It couldn't be far. A few miles at most.

The Hendricks woman and the cripple's daughter scrambled up the bank. Gasping, they fell to the grass. Reg and Jimmy wrestled the chair with the cripple in it up the incline. All three were coated with thick terra-cotta-colored mud. Along with its burden, they dumped the contraption on its side, then sat down, breathing hard.

The cripple had spilled half out of the seat, supporting her torso with one shaking arm. Water streamed from her hair and snot from her nose. Charles stepped over to her.

"Why don't you die?" he asked with genuine curiosity.

The cripple stared up at him with sharp hazel eyes.

"You first," she said.

TWENTY-FOUR

Carrying Wily in her arms like a baby, Anna walked the short distance from the bluff to where the others had crossed the river. A bread bag, squares of paper from presliced cheese, and a plastic envelope that had once held "heart healthy bologna" were scattered around. An insane need to pick up the litter consumed her.

Priorities, she told herself. She was following kidnappers, carrying a dog, intent on rescuing friends from psychopaths. Time was of the essence.

The compulsion was too great. Having put Wily down on a nice pad of pine needles, she picked the trash up and shoved it into her pockets.

Guessing where ground zero of the lunch had occurred, she again walked her concentric circles. This time she found nothing. Hopping along, grunting through the pain movement caused his broken bone, Wily followed the scent of Heath, E, or a bologna sandwich to a large stone beside a red pine. He whined.

"What's the matter, guy?" she asked. He looked as sheepish as a dog can look. "Embarrassed because you can't lift your leg? Got to squat like a bitch? I've got no sympathy. This is an equal opportunity forest."

Wily squatted to pee.

It was then Anna saw it. In the duff behind the rock, mostly covered by needles, was an enormous blade, the cutting edge nine inches long and an inch and a half wide at the hilt. Another gift from her girlfriends. A thousand Christmases could come and go before Anna would receive anything that brought her so much joy.

"We are officially armed, Wily," she exulted. "No more tooth-and-claw business for us. We've moved into the Iron Age. Modern warfare at its most personal."

Wily thumped his tail and nosed her pocket where the plastic from the bologna packet had been stowed.

Farther downstream Anna found a place where the little river widened and grew shallower. Having stripped off clothes, socks, and shoes, she bundled them, along with Wily, in the jury-rigged carry sack. The water came only to her waist. The fording was accomplished with creatures and paraphernalia dry.

Dressed again, Wily on her back, she followed the stream upriver to where the thugs' trail led away from the water. Over the next few hours her greatest difficulty proved to be not stepping on the heels of Sean, the trailing thug. Periodically she got close enough she could hear the rumble of dissatisfied men. Then she and Wily would have to sit and wait fifteen or twenty minutes before they dared progress.

Anna estimated the dude and his bunch had traveled three miles north-by-northwest during the first half of the day. Without a GPS, and the sun sequestered behind a white sky, they spent the afternoon doing what lost people do. They walked in a circle. It wasn't a myth that people lost in the woods walked in circles. Why this was so, Anna didn't know. Perhaps one leg was a millimeter longer than the other, or right-handed people favored that direction. Most dead hikers were found within half a mile, if not less, from the place they first got lost.

By the time the fading glow of the sun silvered a horizon scraped clean by naked branches, the kidnappers had completed their circuit. They were a couple of hundred yards from the river that had nearly killed Heath, and less than a quarter of a mile downstream.

Anna knew this because, despite Wily's weight, the slowness of their progress had made her impatient. Like a mountain lion keeping track of prey, she ranged to each side and ahead of them.

Unlike the mountain lion, she didn't consider eating them. Hunger had passed. In its place was an almost pleasant burn, as if she ran on high-octane fuel. Without the distraction of people, chatter, food, or other trappings of civilization, her senses became attuned to the north woods. The ground was not stony like that of the Rockies. Though shod only in moose leather, her feet were not sore. Anxiety, like hunger pangs, had become a normal sensation, one she did not have to rate as good or bad. Just as she didn't rate the warmth or weight of the dog slung on her back as good or bad. Future and past slipped away. What remained was the narrow focus required to wait, like a cat outside a mouse hole, for days if need be. Waiting for the kill.

"You don't know where in the fuck you are!" filtered through the trees. Reg.

A soft reply. The dude.

"It's getting dark, and there's wolves and

shit, and I got no more interest in following you through the bushes!" Reg's voice had gone up several octaves since the incident at the river. His nerves were shot.

Anna bet the dude hadn't a clue that they had looped back around to where they had started. The light was going fast. Whether the dude liked it or not, they would have to stay where they were until morning.

Kneeling behind a fallen log, she wriggled out of the papoose bag. Her black T-shirt had been shed in the heat of the day and used to better secure Wily to her back. She unwrapped the dog from his green nylon and black cotton sacking. "If you've got to go, now's the time," she whispered.

While he hobbled over to a place of privacy so she wouldn't see him squatting like a girl, Anna removed the chili tin, the battered canteen, the headlamp, and the knife from the ersatz pack.

As she had the previous night, she arranged the black shirt around her head, the neck hole open for her face. The strap for the headlamp went over the makeshift burnoose. She flipped the lens to her forehead so its reflective surface wouldn't catch the light. The chili tin she filled with water for Wily, then drank deeply of what remained in the canteen. Anything that could clank or constrain her movements she would leave behind.

"That includes you," she told Wily as he returned from his place of concealment. He lay down, put his chin on his paws, and puffed out a sigh. He hadn't complained all day. His old bones had to be aching from being trussed up like a package for so long. "Feels good to be free, doesn't it?" Anna asked and stroked his head.

Beneath the leaden sky, shadows began to coalesce in the hollows and thickets. Silently Anna rose to her feet. The knife was in her hand. Walking as softly as any creature on paws, she crept toward where the kidnappers and their victims milled and stomped and cursed. Rising as silently, Wily followed on three legs, his grizzled muzzle close to the ground as he read the news of his people. Anna did not stop him. He had as much right as she to hunt these woods.

The two of them settled in a swale twenty feet from the clearing where the party had stopped. The swale was shallow and wide. Old beetle-killed pines had fallen haphazardly over it. Undergrowth tangled along its lip. Lying belly-down to the slight rise, Anna raised her head over the edge of the depression enough to be able to see the thugs and her friends. Wily curled beside her, his chin on the back of her knees; in the failing light he trusted more to his nose than his eyes.

Heath, lying on her side, was still tied in the chair. Tanned even in winter from snowmobiling, her skin had faded to the color of an old chamois cloth, hard used and much laundered, a dirty tan that pinched to white around her nostrils. Her legs, tied to the footrests with sorry-looking remnants of tape, shivered as if they pulsed with electricity. In the cold colorless light, blood showed black on her palms and forearms. Balance poles either lost or abandoned, so that she'd been using her bare hands.

Elizabeth squatted nearby, elbows on knees, head hanging, face hidden behind a greasy curtain of hair. One of her shirtsleeves was shredded as if she'd been in a fight with a puma. Leah sat with legs folded and hands on her knees like the pale ghost of a yogi. Her head was up and her eyes open, but she did not appear to be looking at anything. Katie stood behind her, hands limp at her sides, face blank.

The four of them were drenched. River water had dried, but sweat had replaced it. Sean and Jimmy weren't in much better shape than the captives. As the sun went down, so did the temperature, from a high of around seventy to closer to fifty. Forty before morning. Maybe freezing. They were all at risk of severe — even fatal — hypothermia.

Sean slumped to the ground. Groaning, he removed his shoes. Jimmy unslung the rifle from his back and flopped down. The dude stood still as a rock, studying the trees around him as they faded to gray in the evening light. Reg paced.

"What the fuck do we do now?" he growled.

The dude took his cell phone from the leather holster on his belt and stared at the face of it. Reg sprang toward him and snatched it from his hand. "Fucking Motorola," he shouted and threw the phone into the woods.

Shoot him, Anna prayed. For an instant it looked as if she would get her wish. The dude turned his cod-eyed stare on Reg. To her disappointment he decided to let him live a while longer.

"We wait," the dude said flatly. "We can't be more than a mile or so from the airstrip. When we don't show up, the pilot will come looking for us. The plane will lead us to where we need to be."

"It's going to be dark soon," Jimmy said. "He ain't gonna find us in the dark, Dude."

"We wait until morning."

Elizabeth had freed Heath from the rickshaw and helped her to sit up, a tree supporting her back. From the pocket of her coat, Heath took out a pack of cigarettes; she shook one out and put it between her lips. The mangled cigarette beckoned to her nose like a skeletal finger. Her hands trembled so badly, the lighter fell to her lap.

"We need a fire," Elizabeth said. Then, louder, "We need a fire."

"No shit, Sherlock," Reg said. "Fucking wolves."

"No matches," the dude said.

"Lighter," Elizabeth replied. The girl was too tired to keep the scorn from her voice, and Anna was afraid for her. The dude either didn't notice or chose not to show it.

"Reg, Jimmy, Sean. Get wood. We'll build a fire. That'll keep us until the plane comes."

"Any food left?" Jimmy asked plaintively. The dude picked up the day pack, turned it upside down, and shook it.

"Not a chance," he said. "Missing a meal won't kill you. Cold will. Get the wood."

"I can't walk, Dude," Sean whined.

"You know what happens to horses that can't walk?" the dude asked.

Muttering something about animals and PETA, assholes and feet, Sean began pulling on his socks.

Reg walked purposefully away from the others, snapping off dry twigs and snatching up pieces of downed wood as he went. Sean limped around poking dispiritedly into the brush. The dude remained where he was, his eyes on the captives, not as if he expected them to try to escape, but as if they were specimens of an animal whose continued existence he had not yet decided was worth his further effort.

Jimmy left his rifle where he'd dumped it and wandered off into the trees between Anna and the river.

"Hunting season has officially opened," she whispered to the dog. Wily thumped his tail against the ground.

Clutching the knife hilt, she rose to her feet. Matching her steps to those of Jimmy — who made more noise than a herd of stampeding elk — she followed. Shadows had gone. Trees and bushes showed black in a colorless world barely illuminated by cold gray sky. Anna angled away from the camp on a trajectory that would intersect Jimmy's racket. Within minutes she saw him.

Bent over a fallen log, he was trying to tug off a rotting limb. His back was to her as he worked it back and forth. Knife in hand, she stepped from behind the screen of trees she'd kept between them and

213

walked quickly toward where he huffed and struggled.

"Damn," he gasped and plunked his butt down on the log, wiping his forehead on the sleeve of his coat.

Cloaked only by dusk, Anna was directly in his line of sight. The breath in her throat stopped. Her heart thudded. The rush of her breathing roared like a chain saw in her ears. A childish desire to close her eyes, and thus render herself more invisible, was strong. The need to keep watching was stronger.

Jimmy sighed, turning his head to the left and right, his beard wagging over his chest. He was not expecting a human shape; his mind was on consumable fuels, and he was tired. Dark clothing and the black hood sufficed. His eyes passed over the shadow Anna had become and lit on a tangle of downed dry pine branches several yards farther into the woods.

Motionless, she waited as he gathered sticks and twigs. When his arms were nearly full she began a slow creep toward him, timing her movements to his tugs and yanks. Her breath sighed out. Thought ceased. Movement became as fluid and natural as that of a snake through familiar grasses. Her heart resumed a steady beat. Her ears stopped roaring. Nothing but the ribs in his back over his heart and the stalking existed. The knife was not in her hand but of her hand.

When she was scarcely more than a yard away, Jimmy's pile of sticks began to slide. Trying to save his harvest, he spun to the left. Before he could face her, Anna sprang, the knife held over her head in the pose Anthony Perkins made famous in *Psycho*. Putting what strength she had behind it, she brought it down on the right side of Jimmy's back, hoping to plunge through to his heart.

The knife was big, but it wasn't sharp. The weapon was cheap, probably worn more for effect than use. The blade cut through the heavy blanketing of the coat and sliced into the thug's skinny back. Already slightly bent over, Jimmy toppled forward, dragging the knife with him. The hilt twisted in Anna's hand as the blade scraped along his scapula, then jammed in a rib. As he fell, Jimmy turned to see his attacker. The hilt was wrenched from Anna's fingers as he fell onto his back.

Flinging her body on top of his, she drove him into the ground. He was squirming like a snake under a boot. "Die, goddammit," Anna whispered.

He opened his mouth to shout. Anna drove her elbow between his jaws and jammed down hard. Fists pounded at her face; fingers clawed at her hands. Beneath her, his body bucked like that of a man in the throes of passion. She rode him and cursed him in a steady whisper, and the knife worked its way farther into his body.

His teeth ground ineffectually at the sleeve of her jacket. She rammed her elbow deeper until she heard him choking. The thrashing became more feeble. Finally it stilled. Anna lay atop him, a demon lover. She was gasping for breath. Sweat dripped from her face into the dead man's beard.

Until the last of the light had drained from the day, and she could no longer see the outline of his face, she did not move. When she finally rose from her kill, his teeth ripped the elbow of her jacket as pulled it free of his mouth. The fabric was wet with spittle and redolent of tobacco juice.

She could not see the body. She couldn't even see her own feet. She looked in the direction of the group. A fire blazed. Sean was shouting Jimmy's name. Idly she wondered how long that had been going on. Time had folded in on itself and gone as black as the night.

Then her head was back, mouth open.

Howling poured from her throat as primeval as that of the first wolf. A second howl joined hers, Wily. Then, from a distance, the answering howls of a pack.

When she'd done, her face was wet. Whether it was from sweat or tears, she didn't know.

In this strange, new, ancient, familiar world there seemed to be no difference between the two.

TWENTY-FIVE

Heath's insides felt fragile, as endangered as a china teacup in an avalanche. There was no part of her that didn't hurt, but for her legs, and they complained with quivers, kicks, and that unsettling feeling that was almost pain. Rick Shaw, prison, tormenter, and, very nearly, executioner, was lying on its side like a child's hastily discarded bicycle. Hours had passed since her near-drowning, yet Heath felt the pull of the cold river on her mind, a siren song urging her to give up, accept the inevitability that these men were going to take her life.

There was a restful seduction in the idea of letting go, sliding into dark waters. Without Elizabeth, she might have given in. A child kept a woman anchored to life. A mother might not go down fighting for herself, but for her child . . .

The fire helped Heath pretend she was whole and brave and good. Light in the darkness, the theme for so many books and songs, was a potent healer of damaged souls. Heath drew the heat in through her pores. Metaphorically, she dragged herself upright, shoulders squared, rifle at ready, eyes clear, nose to the grindstone, ear to the ground, and all the other nonsense people used to buoy themselves up.

"Think of somebody worse off than you." She heard her aunt's voice in her mind. "Then help them. It always works for me."

Worse off than an aching, starving, thirsty para lost in the wilderness with four of the creepiest individuals ever to crawl out from under a rock?

Heath's eyes sought Leah where she and Katie sat cross-legged close to the fire. They neither touched nor talked. Katie had her thumb in her mouth. Heath hoped she was gnawing on it rather than sucking it, reverting to infantilism.

Leah was worse off than she; Heath had the joy of Elizabeth.

Elizabeth, hands held out to the fire, knelt between the Hendrickses. Exhaustion had quenched the rebel flame in her eyes. The lure of victimhood was working its wiles on the others as it was on Heath.

"Up," she commanded to the girls and Leah. "Up and to work. It's going to be colder than a well digger's hind pockets tonight. We need a bed of boughs between our butts and the freezing ground, and a back to catch the heat. Can we borrow your knife?" she asked Sean.

Sean was propped against the trunk of an aspen. Denuded of leaves, in the firelight, the branches reached for the sky like skeletal arms. Sean had not moved since he'd lit the fire with Heath's lighter. Freed from his shoes, his mangled feet poked toward the flames.

"Shut the fuck up," he said without opening his eyes. Heath winked at E and was rewarded with a slight dimpling, the precursor to a smile.

Sean believed he'd lost his knife crossing the river.

"Right," Heath said, pushing her luck to stimulate herself and her friends. "Never mind. We'll make do." Quickly, before Sean could decide to get to his sore feet and come kill her, Heath addressed the women. "Just get what you can."

"One of you steps out of the light, one of you is shot," the dude said.

"Buddy system," Elizabeth said, some of the punkiness back. "A new twist."

The dude didn't respond.

Leah and Elizabeth gleaned enough pine

branches to pile up a hint of shelter at their backs, and enough leaves to make a soft bed. Without a word, Katie took the snuggest place in the middle. Leah slumped on the far edge, watching her daughter from the corners of her eyes. A good sign, Heath thought. At least there was acknowledgment of existence.

Building their nest had not lifted the film of despair from any faces.

"Hot drinks," Heath said. "The wilderness panacea." The others looked at her as if she'd gone mad. "Rocks, get me rocks small enough to put through the mouth of a water bottle." Under the eyes of the gunmen and the urgings of Heath, Leah and E shook off their lethargy and rose to do her bidding.

"Katie?"

Katie glanced up, still chewing on her thumb, and looked at her mother through the hair fallen around her face. "Come help me find small stones?" Leah's tone was new to Heath. It was no longer quite so vague and dreamy. There was a note of pleading in it.

Katie shook her head and returned her attention to her autocannibalism.

Putting rocks in the fire, fishing them out, cleaning them as best they could, and dropping them into the bottle finally allowed them the illusion of control. Looking far more alive than they had, they curled up together in their relatively soft, warm nest and passed marginally hot water from one to the other.

When the last of the warm water was gone, Katie and Elizabeth curled up between Leah and Heath. Elizabeth pillowed her head in Heath's lap. Extra weight and lack of movement were going to wreak havoc on the flesh of Heath's backside, but she didn't care. Tonight she couldn't drum up a lot of sympathy for a part of her anatomy that had gone AWOL. It wasn't often a mother got to cradle her teenaged child.

"Where's Jimmy?" the dude asked suddenly. Though Jimmy had gone at dusk, and it was now full dark, he was just now realizing the little man was missing. So was Heath. Even Sean and Reg seemed not to have noticed that he'd never returned from gathering firewood.

"Taking a piss," Sean said indifferently.

"Long piss," the dude said.

Reg flashed a look of alarm as he rose to his feet, the Walther coming out of his pouch like a faithful joey.

"Jimmy!" Sean shouted half heartedly.

"Hey! Jimmy boy!"

Into the listening silence came the howling of a wolf. The sound knifed into the camp cold as an arctic wind. Heath saw the men freeze as it touched them. Another howl followed. Heath knew that howl, or thought she did. Wily. The forest stopped breathing. Then, from far away, came an eerie answering wail that built from a single voice to a chorus.

Heath yearned to howl with them: Anna and Wily and real wolves. Given twenty-four hours with the dude and his gang, even the real wolves seemed like guardian angels. Neither Katie nor Elizabeth woke.

"Wolves. Jesus fuck," Reg said. Holding his pistol in both hands, arms locked at the elbows, he turned a slow circle, trying to see into the darkness beyond the fire. "Jimmy ain't comin' back." He shoved the barrel of the pistol into his waistband and began snatching down dead branches and throwing them on the fire.

"Find him," the dude said. Sean started putting on his shoes with a slowness that would have done a recalcitrant four-year-old proud.

"Find him your own self," Reg retorted. "I'm not leavin' the fire for that little freak. It's dark, Dude, in case you haven't noticed.

Even if he wasn't dog meat, we'd never find him."

The dude took a burning brand from the fire and walked several steps into the dark beneath the surrounding trees.

"Ain't like them torches in Hollywood movies, is it?" Reg sneered, as the branch flamed out, embers dropping to the ground.

"Reg's right," Sean said tentatively. "We aren't going to find Jimmy. If he isn't dead, he'll come back. If he is dead . . ."

The dude threw the smoldering wood back onto the fire. Tilting his head back, he stared skyward as if already awaiting the plane.

"Hey, Jimmy!" Sean shouted again.

"Shut the fuck up," Reg snapped and sat down with his back to the fire, the Walther on his knee.

The shouting awakened Katie and Elizabeth.

"It's okay," Heath said. "Nothing bad has happened. At least not to us."

"It's okay," Leah echoed, her comment aimed between her daughter and Heath's.

Katie blinked with confusion, then lay down again.

Jimmy did not return.

"I'll take first watch," the dude said after a while. Sean laid down next to the fire, tucked his hands between his thighs, and slept. Reg did not.

Through the distortion of the heat, Heath watched his head repeatedly droop as he nodded off, then jerk upright, the gun bobbing to attention and making a short arc covering the darkness. Every few minutes he threw more wood onto the fire.

Heath enjoyed the heat, ignored her hunger, and willed her worthless legs not to hop about like demented frogs and disturb Elizabeth. For once, they did as she begged and were still. It took an even greater act of will to keep herself from stroking E's hair, or otherwise pestering her. The love of a child turned out to be a much fiercer thing than Heath had expected when she'd adopted the girl. She would have felt guilty about not loving Wily as much, except, she suspected, Wily felt much the same as she did about Elizabeth.

Leah, her black-framed glasses halfway down her nose, gazed at the fire with unfocused eyes. The flames lent color to her cheeks. Whether it was real or a trick of the light, Heath was relieved. Leah's paleness worried her at the best of times. This last twenty-four hours she'd looked like a ghost.

"Tired?" Heath asked, too worn out herself to care that the question was idiotic.

"Not bad" was the surprising reply. "There's two of us and only one of you," she reminded Heath. "Three, if you count Katie."

"I count Katie," Heath said, in case the child was only feigning sleep.

"Things have been . . . So much has . . . I should have done more," Leah said, sounding lost and angry.

"More than just save my life a few times a day?" Heath asked.

"How did the chair work from the inside?" Leah asked, showing her first true animation of the evening. Heath would have thought that would be the last question on her mind after fighting with the contraption all day.

For a while they talked design and function. The normalcy was a balm. Leah's murmuring voice was soothing. Heath felt herself relaxing to an extent. Just as she was thinking how nice it would be if only had something to eat, Leah whispered, "I picked some mushrooms."

Reaching into the pocket screened by her daughter's sleeping form, Leah drew out three delicious-looking lobster mushrooms and several deer mushrooms. "I've been keeping an eye out." The lenses of her glasses flashed as she shot a surreptitious look toward Sean, who was nearest, then the dude, who, back to the fire, continued to search the scrap of sky tangled in the tree branches. The man had an uncanny ability to make Heath feel he was watching even when his back was turned.

Leah pinched a small white mushroom from the pocket of her shirt and set it on the ground near the other mushrooms but not touching any of them. "Amanita," she whispered and looked meaningfully at the men. "Destroyer Angel."

For a moment, Heath's fatigued brain couldn't make sense of the word. Then she remembered the previous night, a million years ago, Leah lecturing on which mushrooms were food and which were poison. The Destroyer Angel was exceedingly deadly. A smile plucked up the corners of Heath's lips, and was answered by a grim smile from Leah. Getting the mushroom from Leah's pocket into a thug's gullet would probably prove impossible. For this minute, though, it was enough to know they had a lethal weapon. The mushroom was like a lottery ticket. Odds were a billion to one a person would win, but it bought a day's worth of dreams.

The wind changed direction. Smoke blew into Heath's eyes. When it cleared, she saw

Sean was awake and staring at them. One toe stuck out of his worn socks like a great white grub. His leather jacket was unzipped. His belly pushed toward the flames, straining the fabric around his shirt buttons. In the apertures between the edges of the fabric, white flesh and dark stiff hairs showed. Letting her gaze pass over the place where he was, Heath tried to make it seem she had not met his eyes.

Sean, like the boogeyman, or certain insane people, might become more dangerous if one made eye contact.

She'd not been quick enough. Whatever the mental switch direct eye contact flipped, flipped in Sean's brain. Laboriously, he rose to his stocking feet, then hobbled gingerly until he was between them and the fire, blocking light and heat metaphorically and literally. Grunting, he lowered himself to the ground. He arranged his feet by picking up his legs and moving them, much in the same way Heath did. She hoped infection had set in and the pain was unbearable.

A halo of orange fire surrounded his head, throwing his face into shadow. On his cheeks, wider than the back of his skull, gray bristles of a two-day-old beard shone like tiny satanic candles.

"You ladies look all comfy-like," he said.

Heath had no idea what to say to that. Did he want to chat with his victims? Was he bored? Lonely? Did he think they would care? Or was his plan to evict them from the warmth of the nest they'd made and take it for his loathsome self?

"All curled up like a bunch of puppies, nice and warm," he said and grinned. His teeth should have been crooked and stained with brown, like the bad guys' in cowboy movies. Instead, they were white and straight. If they hadn't been so tiny, it would have been a Pepsodent smile. Heath imagined how it would look after being smashed in with a steel-toed boot.

"What do you want?" she asked. She'd wanted to sound cold and imperious, the way Anna did when she suspected park visitors of killing her rattlesnakes or annoying her coyotes. What came out was the barest frightened whisper.

By the greater exposure of the undersized Hollywood molars, she guessed Sean liked it very much. Had her throat not been so dry, she might have spit in his face. What could he do to her? Kidnap her? Cripple her? Send her to bed without supper?

Elizabeth was what he could do to her.

Heath's throat grew even dryer. No longer sure she could manage even a whisper, she forced herself to hold his gaze. He didn't like that. Smile shrank, eyes slitted.

"How about I snuggle right in there between those two little bitches and get me warmed up? Puppies — bitches, get it? I'll be the big dog." He laughed.

Heath did not. She was not averse to his snuggling in, if all he intended was to sleep, because it was a sleep from which he would never wake. The moment he'd said it, the lovely image of her two hands pulling a bootlace tightly around his neck and holding it until he was dead shined like a magic lantern on the walls of her mind.

"Me and her and little blondie would just lie happy as spoons in a drawer," he said.

Heath could not tell if he was taunting her and Leah or coaxing them. Undoubtedly the former. Sean didn't seem the type who'd waste any time convincing a woman to give him what he wanted when he could take it by force. Whichever it was, his words were exciting him. Back in the day — when she'd had sex now and then — Heath had noted the twitching that penises often displayed before they committed to a full erection. The front of the thug's trousers appeared to have a small nervous animal within shyly testing the walls of its prison.

"Let me take a look at your feet," Heath

said in hope of distracting him. Her mouth was so dry she'd half expected a puff of dust to come out.

"They're bad," Sean complained and obediently pulled off his socks. The stirring of foot and fabric released the vile odor of stinking feet. Even when she'd used them daily, and without mercy, Heath's feet never stank. Elizabeth's gym shoes didn't smell. Two days in the woods weren't sufficient for this reek, not even given she'd doctored them with feces.

He thrust them toward her. Her legs jumped like those of a gigged frog. Her knee banged Elizabeth's head. The girl came awake with a startled scream.

In the mind of Sean, this was another extremely humorous event. His guffaws woke Katie. The girls would have woken soon anyway, if only from the excruciatingly creepy vibes the man gave off. His evil was such it would penetrate the unconscious mind.

Leaning forward as best she could, Heath studied his feet with pretended concern.

"They hurt like sonsabitches," Sean said plaintively. Heath hazarded a glance at his face. The thug, the kidnapper, expected them — or at least her — to pity him, to feel bad that his feet were raw and torn.

Expected it. She could tell. His face was as readable as that of a kindergartner showing Mom a skinned knee.

"I bet they do," she managed.

He waited.

Heath had no idea what for.

"Can you bandage 'em up again or something?" he asked, irritation replacing childishness.

"No bandages. Nobody brought the first-aid kit." It surprised Heath to have to say it. Could they be so unfortunate as to have been taken by insane kidnappers? Or was that redundant?

"Somebody sure as hell should've," Sean snarled, turning suddenly hostile. He threw back his head, the firelight catching the backs of his ears and turning them red. "Jimmeeeeeee!" he screamed so loudly the four of them flinched. When his head rocked back on his neck, eyes in their direction, Heath could tell game time was over.

He pointed a finger at Katie's drawn white face. "You!" he said. Before he could order Katie to do whatever he intended, Leah opened her fist and took a bite out of a lobster mushroom the size of half a sandwich.

Sean's appetite changed gears. "You've got food," he whispered accusingly. His eyes

232

flicked from side to side as he took in the whereabouts of his compatriots. Sharing was clearly not one of Sean's talents. "Give it to me."

Still chewing, Leah held it out, the crisp white semicircle of the bite she'd taken clear and cartoonlike against the rusty red of the mushroom. Sean grabbed it off her palm and, lowering it to where it was less likely to attract the attention of Reg or the dude, examined it, turning it over in his dirty hands. "What is it?"

"It's a lobster mushroom," Leah murmured softly. "I found several edible varieties of mushrooms today." Reaching behind Katie, Leah scooped the mushrooms up, then held them out toward Sean. "The white ones are deer mushrooms. The red-colored are lobster."

Of the little white ones only two were deer mushrooms; the other was the Amanita. He's a pig, Heath thought. He'll eat them all. She reached out, plucked up a deer mushroom, popped it into her mouth, then began to chew. Her mouth was so dry she couldn't tell if the mushroom really tasted like moldy cardboard or if it was only her. Uncooked mushrooms made one a little queasy, but Heath was already way beyond a little queasy.

"Hey!" Sean snapped, grabbing for the remaining mushrooms. Hope slowed time. Heath watched his blunt fingers swim through the firelight toward the Amanita. There was time to notice the broken nails, the black wiry hair on the backs of his fingers, the dirt in the creases of his knuckles, time to see Sean eat the Amanita, sicken, and die.

"Were you born stupid?" the dude asked Sean. "Or do you have to work at it?"

Startled by his sudden appearance, Sean yelped.

Reg was on his feet yelling, "What the fuck? What's happening?"

"Never eat a mushroom that doesn't come in a can," the dude said evenly.

Reg saw the mushrooms. "Were you gonna eat that wild shit, man? Even a fucking retard knows not to eat shit you find on the ground."

The dude, the very image of a god of destruction, stared down at the three of them. Then only at Leah. His fist shot into the midst of them, fast as a boxer's left jab. It emerged with a handful of Katie's hair, and Katie with it, shocked into the limpness of a rag doll.

"Don't play games with me, Mrs. Hendricks," the dude said. "Sean," he called without looking away from Leah. "Something to keep the chill off." He held the child out with the ease of one man handing a used coat to another.

TWENTY-SIX

Anna stood in the impossible night of the forest, her eyes fixed on the one spark of light, the campfire. One way or another, the body of the man at her feet had to be gotten rid of. If the kidnappers saw that their pal had been knifed, they would know they were not alone. Once they were on guard, she wouldn't be able to get near them.

Too close to the camp to risk using her headlamp, she knelt and felt for the dead man. Her hand landed on his face. His nose was warm against her palm. There was a time she would have snatched her hand back. That time was eons past. Following the lines of his body, she ran her hands down neck, shoulders, and arms. When she'd located both his hands, she drew his arms up and together.

Working blind, she tugged, trying to drag the corpse to the river the thugs had returned to in their witless perambulation.

Dragging dead weight in soft duff was harder than she would have thought. Jimmy might have been dropped in hardening concrete for all the effect she was having.

Squatting on her heels, she stared at the distant flicker of light. Dragging was a bad idea anyway. There'd be sign. Maybe the thugs would think the trail was left by the wolves carrying off their kill, but she couldn't count on it. There was no way of knowing how thoroughly they'd search. They didn't seem to give a damn one way or another, and might not bother. Again, she couldn't count on it.

She'd have to carry him. He couldn't weigh more than one-forty. Using the fireman's carry, she'd hauled bigger men when she had to. Fireman's carry, sometimes called dead man's carry; truth in advertising this night.

Anna worked herself around until she was squatting between his arms, facing the top of his head. Having gathered her legs beneath her, she lifted his torso to hers and held him in a lover's hug. His beard tickled down the collar of her coat like a nest of spiders, and she shuddered. Of all the gods' creatures, the one she was never able to come to love was the spider.

Pushing slowly, she rose to a standing

position, drawing him up with her until they stood breast to breast, knee to knee, cheek to cheek.

Her nose wrinkled at the smell of his tobacco-spittle-doused beard. Breath rasped in her throat. Inhaling slow and deep through her nostrils, she stilled it. Free of distraction, she heard breathing, quick and steady and close by. For a cold moment she was afraid she'd not killed the little man thoroughly enough, and she hadn't the strength to murder him again.

No, not murder.

This was war.

"Wily?" she whispered.

A whuffing snort came from the dark on her left. He hadn't abandoned her. Taking strength from the presence of the pack, Anna turned in the dead man's limp embrace, bent over at the waist, and let his torso drop over her hip bones. Had he been a small woman or a child, she would have pulled his inert form over her shoulders. A one-hundred-forty-plus load needed to be supported by the bones of her pelvic girdle, the center of gravity directly above her hips and thighs.

Having steadied the corpse, she turned her rear end to the light from the camp. Hoping none of the thugs were watching her particular patch of woods, she flipped her headlamp right side out, then clicked it on. After near-total darkness its brilliance shocked her. Laserlike, the beam sliced through clotted night, snatching trees out of winter sleep, firing lichen into color.

A riot of noise erupted from the camp. This was the time.

She took a step forward, then another, then another. To her ears, her passage resonated like a parade of bulldozers, but by the time the camp quieted down, she was too far away to worry. Even if they did hear the crackle of leaves, or her labored panting, they wouldn't have light to investigate.

At last the beam fractured on fast water, foam sudden and sinister in the lightless flood. Anna was soaked with sweat, her clothes sticking to her skin. If she didn't do something soon she would get chilled — too cold for even the dedicated warmth of the family dog to save her.

"Better than a lion skin," she whispered to Wily as she peeled the dead man's coat from his back. The blood was still wet. It didn't bother her.

In one pocket she found a box of .22 longs. If she could get her hands on the squirrel gun she'd be golden. The old pump-action Winchester was one of the most accurate weapons she'd ever had the pleasure of firing. In the other pocket she found the cap with earflaps. Having removed her headlamp, she put the hat on, then tied the flaps underneath her chin.

"I'm a lumberjack and I'm okay," she whispered to the dog. Apparently Wily had never seen much Monty Python. He didn't even crack a smile.

She laid the lamp in the grass so it pointed toward the body. "Turn it off if anyone comes," she said, only half in jest. Wily sat awkwardly, whined, then fell over on his side, watching her as she went through the dead man's trouser pockets. She found a ChapStick, which she fell on greedily, smearing her chapped lips without a thought to the surface the wax had last touched. The used handkerchief she left alone. In his right hip pocket was a wallet. According to the driver's license, the dead man was one James R. Spinks, late of Detroit, Michigan. The wallet also contained twenty-three dollars in cash and a wad of receipts.

"Look at these," she said, fanning the scraps of paper out under Wily's nose. "Maybe James R. thought he could write off his expenses. 'Murder weapon, three dollars and seventy-two cents.' Kidding," she told the dog as she pocketed the wallet.

Police loved receipts. They drew a neat map of where a person went, when he went there, and what he bought.

Anna took James R.'s boots off and tossed them in the river. The socks she kept, pulling them on like mittens over her hands. Her nose had become doglike. Scent registered more acutely than the day before. Judgment was suspended. There were no bad smells or good smells, just useful smells.

Having sat down next to Wily, she braced her feet against James R.'s shoulder and thigh, then shoved with her legs, rolling the body over the bank and into the water.

"Damn," she whispered after a minute. "Sorry, Wily." She should have cut off a slab of meat for the dog's supper. "Next time." A hazy memory of a former self, no more than a wraith drifting behind her left shoulder, remembered a time this would have been an alarming thought, or something not thought of at all. Anna ignored it.

A woman's scream brought both Anna and Wily to their feet. Snatching up the lamp, she started to whisper, "Stay," to the dog, then thought better of it. In their tiny pack there was no alpha. She and Wily were equals.

Half shading the lamp, she began to run in the direction of the camp. Sufficient noise from the others covered her progress. By all the laws of physics, she should have stumbled and fallen repeatedly, but she could not put a foot wrong. Campfire light appeared through the trees. She clicked off her lamp and kept running. Within minutes she had gained the periphery of the clearing and was down on her belly behind a mare's nest of fallen branches.

A devilish play was being enacted center stage, backlit by the orange fire. The dude held Katie by her hair. This was the third time Anna had witnessed the dude lifting a woman by the hair. Was he loath to touch them? Had he discovered that this mode of elevation inspired the most helpless terror?

Katie was on her feet, her little hands clutching his fist to alleviate the pull on the roots of her hair. Heath was cursing, her arms whipping around her, as she tried to get to the girl. Leah's long-fingered pale hands were clamped say-no-evil-style over her mouth. Shocked into inactivity, Elizabeth's lips formed the O of a fish gasping for breath. In her battered face, it was neither cute nor funny.

Sean was hunched over, staring at the dangling Katie like a dog salivating over a pork chop.

His great pig-sticker of a knife found its

way into Anna's hand, urging her to rush in and bury it between the dude's shoulders.

Then she would be shot.

Katie would be given to Sean.

Wily would die alone.

Retreating several yards into the dark of the woods, Anna sucked in a lungful of air, then screamed, low and terrible, the guttural shriek tearing at her throat. She screamed the way she thought the late, unlamented Jimmy would have, had she given him the chance.

The actors in the firelight froze in a tableau. Retreating a few more yards on silent moccasined feet, Anna cried out again, higher this time, ending in a wail.

"Jimmy!" Sean yelled. "Jimmy boy!"

Moving as quickly as she dared, Anna circled the camp. Her first cries had been from the east, the side where the river ran. When she was approximately north by northeast, and a good thirty yards from the fire, she began to cry like a lost child, then stopped suddenly, as if cut off by a blow.

Covered by shouting and racket from the kidnappers, she ran until she was due west of the fire. There she produced a wail that trailed off; the windigo carrying the screaming Jimmy into the frozen north to devour at leisure.

"Jimmy! Stop fucking around! Get your ass back in camp," Reg shouted.

"God damn you, Jimmy!" Sean cried.

Anna slipped back near the camp, then climbed into a white pine with the boughs thick enough to hide her should anyone look up. Katie was in a pile at the dude's feet. Leah was yelling, not a scream or a cry, simply a sustained line of sound that went on and on in a hollow aaaaaaaahhhhh.

Heath was crying the loudest. Perhaps in joy that Anna lived to be a thing that went shriek in the night, perhaps hoping the cries were from Jimmy as his nasty self was dragged away by evil spirits or strong-jawed predators.

Reg was spinning like a top, four-letter words flying from his mouth like bullets from a machine gun. His face, framed by the black and yellow of the double layer of hooded sweatshirts, was more gray than walnut. His lips, thin and bloodless, stretched back over his teeth. The Walther was held in both hands.

He began firing wildly into the dark. Sean threw himself flat on the ground and covered his head with his arms, as if meat and bone could stop a round from the Walther.

Jimmy's Winchester was propped against a tree where he'd left it. Anna had over a hundred .22 rounds in her pocket. Hopes were dashed. The dude picked up the rifle and, swinging it like a club, struck Reg across the shoulders.

Reg fell forward, stiff as a length of timber, the Walther clutched so hard in his fist he didn't let go even as he struck the ground.

Reaching out from the cushion of leaves where the women had gathered, Leah grabbed Katie's arm and pulled her back into the fold. Awkwardly, as if she'd never learned how to do it properly, she patted the girl's hands, trying to comfort her.

TWENTY-SEVEN

Sheer exhaustion had knocked out everyone but Reg. Jimmy vanishing, and the weird noises coming out of the night, had cured Sean of his appetites for both mushrooms and underaged girls. The quiet was a blessing to Charles. If he'd had to listen to Sean screwing the Hendricks girl half the night, he would have gone mad. The cretin lay passed out on his side, jacket zipped, feet nearly in the embers, hands pinched between his knees. Charles would give the child to Sean, not because Sean deserved it but because Hendricks did.

Reg was haggard, but his fire was burning nicely. He'd been feeding it most of the night to keep the wolves from eating him. That would be a sight worth seeing, Charles thought. Very Roman Coliseum, one hale and hearty urban criminal against a pack of wolves.

The first hint of dawn had alerted Charles

as to which way was east. Watching the light drizzle in, shadowless beneath an overcast sky, he thought about the eerie cries that had come out of the woods. Wolves, of course. Anyone with half an ear to the news knew wolves had returned to northern Minnesota. Loons, maybe. Mating or dying or being eaten by coyotes. Until the first night of this debacle, Charles had heard loon calls only on movie soundtracks. Cougars could sound like a woman screaming. That bit of information had been gleaned thirty years before at one zoo or another. Moose and elk bugled; PBS taught him that.

Never before had he heard any of these sounds in situ, as it were. Coming face-to-face with the denizens of this brand of wilderness was out of his range of experience. It didn't scare him. Wild animals were not fond of the companionship of humans. Should one break that rule, anything short of a grizzly bear could be taken down with a .357. Demons, demonic possession, put the fear of God into him, as Michael liked to say. The monks at the monastery where he and his brother had been dumped were modern Catholics and tended to roll their eyes at talk of exorcisms, but Charles had seen people possessed by demons. There were times in his life he believed he might have been possessed himself.

People who held up the Bible and proclaimed their belief in God, then denied Lucifer and his demons, were cherry picking. God didn't work like that. Charles had always known he couldn't take only the good parts of anything. Without darkness, light was meaningless. Without Satan, God was nothing but a schizophrenic with a cruel streak. Fools asked why God let bad things happen to good people. That was a slap in the face of God. God didn't let bad things happen; the devil made them happen. The only other choice was that God was a monster. Anyone who believed that might as well stick his head in the oven and turn on the gas.

There were angels, and there were monsters. Since Michael died, Charles had known he was fated to be one of the latter. Monsters were depicted as loving evil, craving it. It wasn't true. Insane men — or lowlifes like Sean — loved and craved evil. For those fated to it, evil was just the job they got when the time came for them to work for a living. For those who were good at their work, life could be pleasant, joyful even. This was important to realize, because the next part was true as well. Those like him would burn in hell. That was the deal.

That was what they signed on for, whether they admitted it or not.

Charles was at peace with that. He was not at peace with the idea of demons loose in the woods.

"Dude, we gotta look for Jimmy." Sean was awake.

Speaking of demons, Charles thought as he turned to look at him. Sean was an ugly man. Ugly in face, in body, and in mind. Myopic, overweight, shorter than average: He'd been born either to serve Satan as a half-assed monster, or the Lord as a court jester. "So look for Jimmy," Charles said. "As soon as the plane shows us the way, we go, with or without you."

Sean didn't leap up to search. Reg didn't move at all. Sean put on his pointy-toed boots, then stepped a foot or two from where he'd spent the night to pee against a tree.

"Ain't no plane comin'," Reg said darkly.

The plane was coming; Charles had no doubt about that. Bernie would hire the entire Canadian air force if he had to. Bernie needed not only what was in Mrs. Hendricks's wallet but what was in her brain.

The cripple was shaking her daughter. When she didn't wake up, the cripple began to panic, shaking her harder. Judging by the girl's face, she'd been beaten within an inch of her life. Charles was good at that. If he'd wanted her dead or badly injured, he wouldn't have used his fists. Even pulling his punches, and striking where there was lots of flesh to bruise and swell, his knuckles were sore. Females were more terrified by the appearance of a thing than the thing itself. It would be interesting to see if, without a mirror around to let the girl know how bad she looked, she would react differently.

"Sorry," the cripple said after she'd frightened the girl out of a sound sleep. "The airplane will be coming. We have to be ready to move." Too bad about the legs, Charles thought; there was nothing wrong with her mind. She harbored no illusions about what would happen if she lagged behind.

Charles scrutinized the sky as the hostages executed the screen-and-pee dance, relieving themselves. Sean wasn't evincing his earlier avidity, but he wasn't looking away either. The cripple, Charles noticed, didn't join the festivities. After yesterday, she might not have the strength for the process. Maybe she'd get lucky and they'd cross another small river. This time she could urinate before she drowned.

The faint buzzing of a small-engine aircraft caught his ear. Minutes later the plane flew over, low and slow, the nose wheel barely clearing the treetops. It was a single engine, a Cessna 182, high-winged, white, with a red stripe down the fuselage. Its wheels were shielded by sleek metal covers that came to a point in the back as if blown by the wind. The number painted on its side was Z552IF. The pilot wagged the wings. The nose was pointed at a right angle from the brightness that was the rising sun in the east. Charles's back was to the sun; the pilot was leading them north.

Reg and Sean were leaping, waving their arms, and shouting like maniacs.

The cripple's daughter fetched the one-wheeled contraption from where it had fallen the night before. As she bent, she winced. Charles had cracked her right third and fourth ribs.

With Hendricks helping, they began loading the cripple. They were moving more slowly than on the first morning. Charles would have to drive them harder. He had no interest in another night playing Boy Scout leader with this bunch.

The Hendricks child rose from where she'd been sitting, arms around her shins, face hidden on her knees. She walked between the rifle and Elizabeth. Stopping at her mother's side, she asked, "What can I do to help?"

That was a new slant. Charles had assumed this one had been born for the dark side. He'd give her to Sean tonight, he decided. No sense in letting her grow a spine — or a conscience — on his watch.

Again the plane flew over, pointing its nose in the same direction.

"We move," Charles said and walked into the trees, listening to the scratching and cursing as Sean and Reg hurried the hostages to catch up.

TWENTY-EIGHT

Insulated by Jimmy's coat and hat, Anna and Wily slept comparatively well. The coat was roomy enough that Anna could button it around Wily's bony shanks as he lay on her chest, his head on her shoulder, his broken leg supported by her arm. They woke before dawn, refilled their water bottle at the little river, then, muscles warmed by movement, headed toward the camp, where they could watch the others. Wily had grown accustomed to the splint and navigating on three legs. He was walking fairly well but tired easily.

Anna didn't. She should have, she realized as she scooped him up and tucked him under her arm. He struggled briefly to prove he was as strong as ever and didn't need to be carried like a puppy. It was all for show. Anna knew he was glad of the lift.

Ten yards from the fire, Anna found a hollow where she and Wily could lie unseen.

By raising her head and moving a low fir bough, she could keep an eye on the kidnappers. A camp of Neanderthals must have looked much like that of the thugs. Neanderthals probably did a better job of it, though, with mastodon steak for breakfast and a hide or two to keep the cold off.

The long-awaited plane flew over, filling the clearing with noise and metal, then vanishing, the roar of the engine drifting behind it.

Zulu five five two Ivan Frank: Anna committed the plane's number to memory. The number on an airplane was more telling even than the license plate number on an automobile, and less easily changed or disguised.

"We move," the dude said and pointed in the direction the plane had disappeared.

North by northwest, as near as Anna could tell.

Reg mouthed off.

"Stay or go," the dude said.

From where Anna lay in hiding, the dude's irises looked like steel ball bearings.

Reg chose to go.

Sean limped a few yards into the woods and shouted, "Jimmy! Jimmy boy!" Evidently that was all his conscience required, as he limped back without any serious attempt to find his comrade. Anna's efforts to hide the body had been wasted. Even bordering on the feral state herself, it hadn't occurred to her that not even a rudimentary search would be attempted.

Heath was in the rickshaw. The plastic of the seat was scratched all to hell, the canoe paddles looked like they'd been used as sharpening posts by lion cubs, and the spokes of the wheels were prickly with sticks and grass, but it was still in operating condition. Anna was impressed by its durability.

Sean shoved the barrel of Jimmy's rifle between Heath's shoulder blades for no other reason than congenital cussedness. Elizabeth and Leah began pulling the rig. Trees swallowed hostages and thugs alike; their din faded. The distant song of the rushing rivulet insinuated itself through the still branches.

Giving them time to get well ahead, Anna lay on her back beside Wily and studied the tree canopy. Less than thirty-six hours ago, she had been on a pastoral junket with friends, floating on the Fox River, stargazing. The sky had been clear, the autumn colors rich and ripe. There was food to be eaten, wine to be drunk, and three idyllic days of peace and camaraderie to look forward to.

Staring into dull pewter, scraped by winter-black aspen branches, it was hard to get her mind around time and space. In the cold light, fragments of leaf color on the maples were faded and sad-looking, spruce boughs more black than green. In the faces of battered and desperately fragile hostages, who existed at the whim and pleasure of a psychopath and his acolytes, Anna could scarcely recognize the merry canoeists she held in memory.

For thirty years Americans had been waist-deep in fictional psychopaths, bizarrely creative serial killers with motives as labyrinthine as any Greek minotaur could wish. The dude appeared devoid of creativity. The dude was as direct as a rabid skunk, single minded and single purposed, interested only in that which concerned him directly. From the outside, he seemed no more malicious than a hammerhead shark. A primeval life-form, designed to feed, a form that would die if it stopped moving forward.

The dude was taking Leah and the others to a place where they would be met by a plane. The thugs were only the hired help. Who planned the kidnapping, and intended to reap the greater benefits? Leah was so very filthily rich, money alone could be motive. Still, from among many exceedingly wealthy individuals, she had been targeted.

Kidnapping for ransom was not an American pastime. It was rare enough that the kidnapping of the Lindbergh baby was still spoken of. Of all crimes, kidnapping was one of the most abhorrent to Americans. Kidnapping a rich, white, respected, female engineer would bring the law howling down on the perpetrators. Therefore the payoff had to be very tempting indeed.

Perhaps a payoff greater than money?

Lying in the fragrant damp of Minnesota's woods, dressed in a coat stiffened with the blood of a dead man, Anna found money an alien concept. In the real world a hot bath, an apple, a cup of tea: Those things were real. Money was as meaningless as hula hoops and nose rings. Few lived in a real world anymore. They'd made a new world where symbols were more valuable than the things they stood for.

The airplane buzzed over again, lining up with the dude and the hostages to keep pointing the way. Anna lay perfectly still. Red-and-black squares weren't protective coloration anywhere outside a checkers tournament. If the pilot saw her, he might assume she was just a thug who liked alone time for meditation and spiritual rejuvenation. Since there was no phone or radio contact between air and ground, it would be a while before he could give her away.

Wily plopped his head on her shoulder and whuffed a great sigh into her ear. They lay in comfortable companionship until the third passage of the plane.

"Ready?" Anna asked. Wily sat up, his hindquarters moving stiffly. Anna followed suit. Without waiting for him to ask, she lifted him out of the hollow so he wouldn't have to fight his way up the dirt hill with only one operative hind leg. They worked their way toward the camp, each seeking information in his or her own way.

Dog nose paid off before human eye.

Anna went to where he sniffed with such interest. Half buried in the needles and leaves was the cell phone. "Good boy," Anna said automatically. She'd forgotten the black kidnapper had snatched and thrown the dude's cell phone. She slipped it into her pocket with the .22 rounds. Farther along, higher up, in a different place, there might well be a signal. 911. Lovely numbers, Anna thought.

The thugs hadn't bothered to put out the fire. Squatting near it to enjoy the heat, she scanned the area. Wily leaned against a tree. The posture was dictated by his desire to take strain off his broken leg. That didn't change the fact that he looked like a canine version of Frank Sinatra at his insouciant Rat Pack best.

"What a fine party it's been," Anna said.

Wily thought his own thoughts.

Grass was trampled in a short straight line where the dude had paced. The earth had been torn up by Reg's forages for burnable fuel. Nothing had been left behind. No gifts from the girls. The thugs hadn't had anything with them but guns. How much ammunition, Anna wondered? Reg had gone through at least a clip.

Turning before the fire like a roasting pig, she considered making it bigger. It was too damp, she decided. The cloud cover too low for the smoke to be visible. Even if she managed to get a good show of smoke, with recent rains the fire wouldn't spread. The U.S. Forest Service would let it burn itself out.

"Nothing for it but to follow the scent, good little doggies," Anna said to Wily. He cocked an ear and eased away from the tree.

TWENTY-NINE

The plane flew over seven more times. On the final two passes, they didn't see it, only heard it above the thickening clouds. The terrain they traversed was no different than it had been the previous day. Heath worried about Elizabeth. The pain in her ribs was evident. Bruising and a split lip made internal damage seem too possible. Leah, and occasionally Katie, tried to take up the slack, but Katie was not strong and was unused to work. Leah was worn nearly transparent. Half blind with fatigue, Heath bulled through, running on the bare bones of willpower.

The only thing she was thankful for was Sean. Sean and his rotten feet slowed the party more than Rick Shaw.

Reaching the dude's destination was bound to be bad. If evil persons wanted to move the victims from point A to point B, it was because point B was better for them and worse for the victims. Villains seldom transported their prey to more public spaces with better lighting.

Still, old habits died hard. Heath was pleased that she was no longer the one holding up progress, the weakest link. Her days of being the leader in physical trials had not ended when she'd abruptly hit the ground. In rehab she competed with other people, competed with herself, competed for fun and respect. Things that had been important when she was fully able were important now. All that changed was the arena.

Losing use of her legs, though a major alteration in her life, strangely enough wasn't as big a change — or as daunting a challenge — as having a child. Losing a child was unthinkable. Heath had tried groveling to no avail. Next time — should there be a next time — what? There was no trying the dude's patience; he had none. No appealing to his better nature or humanity. Those did not exist either.

The only appeal he'd responded to was when Jimmy, believing they were redeemable for cash, begged him to take Heath and E. Heath suspected it was nothing as normal as greed that drove him. More likely he needed to keep his fellow felons cohesive and submissive. Heath doubted they'd survive another hour once they outlived their usefulness.

Thirty more minutes passed. An eternity of striving.

The plane did not return.

The forest around them ended. Ahead lay a black-and-gray mausoleum of what had once been an ecosystem. Inches of gray ash covered the ground. Tree trunks were black and scored like coal. Quiescent, and sinister as alligators, logs lay beneath a sea of ash. Teeth of stone, black with soot, poked from gray gums of hills.

As the seven of them traversed this T. S. Eliot world, their feet churned up eddies of featherlike ash that coated the inside of the nose and clung on the back of the throat.

Twenty more minutes slogged past without the airplane returning to show them the way. The dude's pace slowed to a crawl. Sean, lamed by blisters, swore and groaned at every step. E was white-faced except where the dude's fist had left its mark. Her right eye was black, the lashes glued together with dried seepage. The angry red-purple faded as it flowed down her cheek in a rash of blood-clot freckles. Her split lip had opened. Blood made a single cinematic trail down her chin.

The left side of E's face was relatively whole, but made horrific by the cut on her forehead. Blood had streamed over brow and cheek nearly to her throat. Long since dried and crusted, flakes had fallen away until the stain took on the appearance of an old rotting abrasion. Ashes clung in tatters to hair, skin, and clothes.

They all looked like zombies in a post-apocalyptic horror movie.

Thin drizzle began leaking from the sullen sky. Wet, burned lichen peeled from boulders in a parody of skin peeling from a body. Drizzle turned to rain. Great oily drops fell, thick and slow as treacle, leaving scabrous-looking spots on charred wood and scarred stone.

Heath realized they must be trekking through part of the burn that had ruined the campground they'd planned on using. They were somewhere in the thousands of acres of burned area that ended at the Fox River.

The moon, the mall, Disney World: Where they were was irrelevant as long as they were under the control of the dude.

He stopped. They stopped. All listened for the plane. Sean took the opportunity to sit, dropping to the ground with all the grace of a puppet whose strings have been cut. Leah and Elizabeth stood in what would have been the traces had they been mules.

Heath reached out to tug herself another half a foot forward with the aid of a burned black claw of a limb. Realizing she did it because she was afraid if she stopped she could never get going again, she forced herself to drop her arm.

"We wait here," the dude said.

"This is fucking nowhere, man," Reg growled. "It's got nothin'. No water, nothin'. We got nothin' to make a fire with. It's all burned. I say we keep going."

"The plane isn't coming back today," the dude said. "The clouds are too low. The pilot can't see to fly. It'll lift tomorrow, and we'll go on."

"We got a couple hours' light. Let's go on now," Reg insisted.

Heath hoped the dude would punch him a few times as he had Elizabeth. He didn't.

"Mom, want out of that thing?" Elizabeth asked.

"God, yes," Heath said. The exhaustion she had been holding at bay flooded her words. E's face screwed up the way it had when she was a little thing and trying not to cry. "I mean, why thank you, E. I confess I am growing weary of sitting in Mr. Shaw's lap." She made her voice light and mocking.

The effort was akin to lifting a compact car.

To a certain extent the act was a success. Elizabeth's face unscrewed. Heath could tell it was taking her daughter as much will-power not to cry as it was Heath not to sound like she was about to pass out. At present, reality was a bitch. They were pretending to be stronger and braver than they were.

Maybe that was all courage was, pretending not to be afraid, and taking the next necessary step.

"Shitaroonie," Sean whined as he delicately eased his foot out of his shoe. "I'm all tore up. I don't know how much longer I can keep doing this, Dude. My feet are all tore up to hell." Sean wasn't into pretending to be a better man. He looked and sounded like a vicious, beastly little boy, the sort that strangles the neighbor's cat, then screams bloody murder because it scratched him in the process.

Leah, weariness paring her low voice to a whisper, said, "Rest, Katie." Katie looked around vacantly, either trying to see who cared about•her enough to suggest rest or trying to find a place that looked alluring. Leah untied Heath's ankles from the foot-rests. Heath's legs immediately kicked out.

"Kids at recess," Heath said. During the

first few years, the spasms had embarrassed her. As if they were rude, in the same category as belches and farts. When her legs "acted up," as she called it, she would apologize. E was the one who made her stop.

"It would be like me saying 'sorry' every time I blink or breathe," she'd snapped one evening as Heath was apologizing during a movie Elizabeth had been wanting to see. "It's silly. You twitch. Like anybody is going to die because you twitched at them? Twitches don't even stink or make noise."

After that Heath had ceased apologizing, because it annoyed her daughter. Over time her motive changed. She didn't apologize because E was right. Eyes blinked. Hair blew in the wind. Legs twitched.

"I can do it," she said as E started to help Leah lower her to the ground. "Your ribs must be killing you."

"They're waiting in line," Elizabeth said with a grim look at the dude.

Heath made herself laugh.

At Elizabeth's suggestion, Leah helped her upend Rick Shaw. The paddle handles were shoved into the ashen earth, the wheel braced against a burned tree trunk. Upside down, the seat formed a tiny place of shelter from the rain. Heath insisted Katie and

266

Leah use it. E disapproved, but Katie was quick enough to scuttle under. For Heath it was a small victory. This time it was she who had given comfort. It was better to give than receive, if for no other reason than that having something to give was a facet of power.

Heath found a rock and scooted back until it supported her upper body. Elizabeth sat next to her and leaned her head against her shoulder. Leah joined Katie beneath the pretense of shelter. Their shoulders touched. Heath realized that this was only the second time she'd seen them so close to one another. Both their heads drooped on their necks. Hair once black and hair once blond were now the same ashen hue. For the first time they looked like mother and daughter.

Heath dug in the pocket of her jacket to get a cigarette. The pack of Camels was mashed and slightly damp where sweat had soaked through the jacket. Smoking in the burn felt redundant, but, without food, she hoped the nicotine would soothe her nerves and give her energy a boost. Anyway, it was something to do.

As she patted pockets in search of her lighter, she remembered Sean had taken it the night before. It was a cheap hot pink Bic, and it never failed. Since knowing Heath, Anna had taken to carrying a lighter in the backcountry. Cigarette lighters weren't nearly as fashionable as small, watertight tins of ten sulfur matches, but Anna wasn't as interested in fashion as she was in function. As every smoker knew, a Bic could go through the washer and dryer and still light.

"Could I have my lighter?" Heath asked.

Sean looked up from his study in personal podiatry. "What for?"

Heath held up the cigarettes.

"Give her the lighter," the dude said.

Sean threw it. It landed near Leah's thigh. She retrieved it and tossed it gently into Heath's lap.

"Thanks," Heath said.

"Watch out for Smokey Bear," Elizabeth said wryly. "Only you can prevent forest fires."

Heath lit her cigarette. The first drag was heaven.

"Bad example, you smokin' in front of the fuckin' kid," Reg said.

"Yeah," Heath agreed. "Where do you take your kid on father-daughter day? Joliet?"

Reg was nearly as fidgety as her lower limbs. His head snapped up at every thump of a branch falling from a tree or caw of a crow. She was too tired to care if her remark pushed him over the edge. For nearly two days, she had been ringed round with precipices. There came a time when even fear got tired.

He looked away. He'd lost interest in her. She didn't scare him. The woods did, despite the fact that they were reduced to the leavings of an inferno.

"I'm telling you, dude, we gotta keep going. We'll fucking freeze to death, if the wolves don't get us," he insisted.

"So go," the dude said and began walking back in the direction from which they had come.

"What the hell?" Sean cried. He tried to shove the foot he was crooning over back into the boot with such haste he must have peeled off a layer of flesh. Squeaking like a stepped-on rat, he dropped the shoe.

"Where are you going?" Reg's hand was in the pouch of his hoodie, where he kept the Walther.

"To get firewood so the wolves won't eat you."

"Hey, wait up." Reg trotted after him.

Heath, Elizabeth, Leah, and Katie were left alone with Sean. Raindrops plopped toadlike onto the ash. Heath pulled E closer to keep her warm. Leah's eyes narrowed behind the lenses of her glasses. Her hand slipped into the pocket of her coat as if she might find a gun she had forgotten about.

Sean stopped fiddling with his feet. He watched until the dude and Reg had gone from sight.

"You girls like games?" he asked and smiled.

THIRTY

Greens and browns gave way to sodden gray and black. At the edge of the living forest, Anna and Wily stopped. There was little to tell between the wet ash and the darkling storm clouds.

"Damn," Anna muttered. "Must have been a hell of a fire. No cover left for such as we." For a moment she stood, Wily at her side, staring through gray rain at the gray landscape. "We could circumnavigate the black and intercept the others on the far side," she suggested.

Wily said nothing.

"You're right," she decided after a minute. "Chances of finding them again are slim to none."

Wily made a sound between a yawn and a cough. Anna suspected he was laughing at her. "I can't sniff people out as well as you can," she said defensively. "We wait till dark, you think?"

Wily rolled his eyes.

If the dude kept going, the hostages could arrive at the airstrip in a matter of hours.

Then what? Killing Jimmy had been a stroke of luck. All day Anna had waited, but neither Reg nor Sean so much as fell behind to take a leak.

Sean's feet were being flayed alive by his boots. If he'd straggle behind, she might be able to pick him off. Doing it in the light of day would be harder than taking out Jimmy had been, and killing Jimmy was more difficult than Anna had thought it would be. He was small, not terribly bright, she had a knife, his back was turned, she had the element of surprise. If she'd been writing a plan it might have read: (1) sneak up; (2) plunge knife into back; (3) never, ever tell Paul.

Like the king in chess, the human heart was well guarded, and, too, the little bastard had not wanted to die. Taking lives wasn't as easy as it looked in the movies.

Sean was bigger and smarter by a few IQ points. Evil hung around him like a cloud of gnats. Evil things were harder to dispatch than stupid things. Slitting his throat was an option. No coat or bones to get in the way. Sean's cheap knife should have enough of an edge for that if she sawed a little. She'd have to be directly behind him.

"Wily, would you act as bait and lure Sean over with the old injured puppy routine so I can cut his throat?"

Wily licked her fingertips. He'd do it in a heartbeat.

"Maybe we'll get lucky again," Anna said.

When she thought about it, it was surprising how many successful murders there were in the United States. Murder was a lot of work. Guns helped. Guns with gigantic ammo clips helped a lot. It also helped if the shooter thought of himself not as human but as a weapon of mass destruction, dealing death anonymously.

"We haven't heard the plane in a while," she said. "It can't fly in this stuff. I doubt the dude knows he led everybody in a circle yesterday, but he has to know he was lost. I figure him for the kind with too powerful a survival instinct to make the same mistake twice. If he has the sense of a potato bug, he'll find shelter, build a fire, and stop for the day. Get out of the rain.

"Wily, between us, do we have sense enough to come in out of the rain?" Anna asked.

Wily whined.

They backtracked to where two boulders, exhausted by geological time, leaned on one another. Soil had collected in the basin where they came together, and a maple tree had taken root. Beneath this wilderness triptych was a sheltered space about eight feet long, six wide, and four high. Plenty big enough for her and Wily.

"The lighting sucks, but so far the roof hasn't started leaking," Anna said, unloading their treasures from Wily's papoose sack.

"We don't have anything resembling a towel," she apologized as she redistributed the goods into various pockets in Jimmy's coat. "The underside of my sleeve will have to suffice. Can't have you smelling like a wet dog." While she rubbed his head, Wily stretched and groaned. "I suppose it's the pot calling the kettle odiferous," she admitted. "In this rig I probably smell like a wet sheep or a wet creep."

Discussing the merits of various odors with a moderately interested dog, she began folding the nylon she'd rescued from the shell of the sleeping bag. When she'd achieved a rough trapezoid, she used the knife to cut a slit along each of the narrower ends.

"Hold still," she said. Obediently Wily sat on her lap, his good foot on the ground, his rump supported by her thigh. She slipped his head through one slit, wrapped the cloth over his back, then slipped the other slit over his head. Carefully freeing his ears, she said, "It's called a cape. The nylon isn't waterproof, but it's water repellent. It should keep the worst of it off your fur. At least until the nylon coating gets soaked through."

Wily's tail thumped against the side of her coat as he gave her a wry grin.

"Let me see how it fits." Anna gently nudged him off her thigh. He hopped a few paces, then turned to look back at her. Before she recalled that there might be more ears around than was strictly safe, she laughed. The bright green fabric covered Wily's back and part of his tail. Over his chest it parted in a neat V that accented his ruff. With the ragged ears of a dog who'd done his share of fighting as a pup, the effect was wonderful. "Green Lantern," she said. "Who does that make me?"

Not knowing whether she was star or sidekick, and not caring, Anna rested, Wily beside her, gazing out at the destruction of what had once been a tract of forest.

This burn was probably the same that had been stopped by the Fox River. Anna vaguely remembered hearing about it. "Nearly twelve thousand acres," she said as the number rose in her mind. "Other than toward the Fox, I haven't a clue in which direction those acres are spread. Any thoughts?"

If Wily had them, he kept them to himself. He flopped down on his side with a groan and closed his eyes.

Anna gazed at the view until mist clouded her mind. Hypnotized by the soft patter of rain, her vision blurred, and for a while she was flying over the burned land. A cold front was boiling in from the north, clearing the rain before it. The winds carried her up. Spiraling over the blackened earth, she saw specks of humanity on the ash, and the golden brown of living forest around the perimeter. Somewhere a large cat was purring.

"Goddammit, hold up! I'm with you. Wood, fire, heat. I get it. Wait up!"

The baritone bellow snapped Anna back into the hollow beneath the boulders. The purr was Wily's subvocal growling.

Less than ten yards from their shelter, Reg was trotting by.

The rain had stopped. Without its blur and distraction, Anna felt exposed, the dead Jimmy's red checks blinking HERE SHE IS.

She had to be more careful, stay alert, stay in her body. Because she had chosen to ignore hunger and fatigue did not mean they had chosen to ignore her. With cold temperatures added to the mixture, confusion awaited behind every drifting curtain of the mind. This was the time climbers fell, hikers lost their way, and campers cut their fingers off with the kindling hatchet.

"Hold up," Reg yelled.

Obviously Sean or the dude had already passed by, and neither Anna nor Wily had noticed. They could have been shot like sitting ducks, fishes in a barrel.

Reg tromped into the woods out of sight. He and whoever he followed were backtracking. Anna doubted she would have missed it if the hostages had been herded by, and knew Wily wouldn't have. Leah, Katie, Heath, and Elizabeth were still out on the burn, one thug with them as guard.

Wood. Fire. Heat. Those were Reg's words.

The dude or Sean, followed by Reg, had come back into the forest to gather wood. So near the burn, small flash fires and inroads of flame had thinned the underbrush. They'd have a bit of a walk before they found anything resembling fuel.

Anna pressed her lips to Wily's ear and whispered, "Did you notice any decent shelter back a ways?" A sense of the ridiculous echoed in the back of her mind. Then she caught Wily's steady gaze. "Me neither. These rocks are it. Heath and E, they have to shelter here, or they could die. A cold front is blowing in, driving the rain southeast." Saying the words startled her. Only in her flying dream had she seen the cold front.

Absorbing an eerie shiver, she rose to her feet. Not the fluid motion of her youth, or even the willpowered muscle of recent years. She had to use the rock walls to get from a crouch to her feet. Wily wavered to a standing position beside her. Neither made a mad dash to do anything constructive. "Reg and whoever have to come back this way," she whispered. "If we point this out, think they'll have sense enough to use it?"

Wily cocked his head and looked up at her. He doubted it.

"We can't give ourselves away. No dropped dog collars or arrows made of sticks. It has to seem like their idea."

For her own amusement, Anna occasionally practiced hiding in plain sight. Placing herself in clear view, but in such a way that the hiker's eye would naturally be drawn away from her. Most people walked by without ever noticing her. Never had she practiced calling attention to herself — or an item — without using signals or signposts clearly human in origin.

While she pondered, Wily hobbled over where Reg had walked past. Sniffing, he circled. When his nose found the appropriate place, he urinated, scratched a few times with one front paw, then limped back to Anna.

"Smart guy," she said.

THIRTY-ONE

"Do you girls like to play games?"

Leah would have rolled her eyes if they hadn't been frozen in place by sheer terror. The man was a bad joke. If he hadn't become a thug, he'd have found a place as a petty bureaucrat, enjoying the power to thwart, delay, and lose paperwork. A gun and a lack of parental supervision allowed Sean's juvenile despotism to flourish to a point he could torment those he hated — everyone, Leah expected — a little bit more than he hated himself.

War let the Seans of the world step from behind their desks and counters, out of their kiosks, and into a place beyond their darkest dreams, where victims were abundant and consequences did not exist. In Hitler's Germany, Sean would have been a low-ranking Nazi; at Abu Ghraib, a sneering guard; at Guantánamo, an avid torturer.

Along her left arm and thigh, Leah could

feel the unfamiliar warmth of Katie's body. The human being, the child this creature would defile. Her child. Leah seldom thought of her that way. Usually, if she thought of Katie at all, it was as Gerald's child. Gerald's genes were clearly stamped in her coloring and features, but that wasn't why. Gerald wanted her. He had made sure Leah got pregnant right away after they married. Once he had the child, he quit work and became a stay-at-home dad.

To say Leah knew little about men would be an understatement. Raised by two mothers, whose circle of friends was largely comprised of lesbians, Leah had not known many men. Her mothers didn't dislike men, there were simply not that many around. Growing up, Leah had been wrapped in love and support the way fine china is wrapped in bubble wrap for shipping, told she was pretty and smart and strong and good.

Genetics would tell. Leah's birth mother must have been a mess. Leah believed none of what her mothers told her, except that she was smart, and then only in academia. When her mothers died in a small commuter jet crash, their community of friends closed around Leah in a protective wall. Money was raised and she was sent to Bryn Mawr. Leah was sixteen. At twenty-two she was heralded as the wunderkind of chemistry and engineering.

Then Gerald and Katie. In a fit of cosmic irony, Gerald turned out to be gay. The one man in the world who would marry her for her mind, because he knew how to spin her thoughts into pure gold. Katie was his insurance policy: community property and child custody. The only thing Leah hated Gerald for was believing he needed that.

"You're not a pawn, Katie," she whispered. "I won't let you be used in his games."

"Speak up, God damn it!" Sean said. "You talk, I wanna hear what's said. You got that?"

"I won't let you use my daughter in your games," Leah said. Her voice was so loud it startled her.

THIRTY-TWO

Finished, Anna studied it sourly. It looked like a ranger had scratched a bunch of lines in the dirt with a stick. She hoped the dude's city senses would not pick up on country deceits. Why would he? The belief that Anna and Wily didn't exist was their greatest — only — advantage. Most people didn't bother to protect themselves against that which did not exist.

As an added incentive, she dropped the stick so it fell pointing toward the rocks. Wily sniffed it. "Does it look like a big fat arrow on a yellow sign?"

Since Wily didn't piss on it, Anna decided it would pass.

"I'm following them," Anna whispered. She pointed toward the boulders. Behind them several trees, not dead yet but with roots exposed, had blown in a heap and lay piled like pick-up-sticks in the child's game. "You should be able to find a dry spot. You can stay here and rest if you need to."

Wily shot her a dirty look.

"Sorry," she said. Anna put a span of trees between herself and the trajectory Reg had been on. Running as quietly as a rabbit across the rain-damp duff, she kept on a parallel course. It was an hour or two until dark. The light was diffuse and low with tails of fog clinging to the ground as the air cooled more quickly than the earth. The forest had become a place of mists and pools without light. Unformed shadows painted trees; damp and lichen drew faces on the stones. From the dying leaves, raindrops fell in slow motion, hitting the soggy forest floor with the splat of baby frogs hitting pond water.

Anna's effortless run was short-lived. The trees grew more thickly. Her breath shortened. Beneath the coat she began to sweat. Reg hadn't much of a lead, and he was hunting and gathering. Knowing she was close, she slipped into stalking mode. Wily caught up with her just as she heard the crack of breaking branches and men's voices. Reg and the dude; they were together.

Anna didn't try to get close enough to see them. Too much light remained in the sky, and, fierce as they were, she and Wily couldn't take down two armed men.

Jimmy's coat protecting Anna's rump from the wet ground, her lap protecting Wily, they made themselves comfortable in a stand of oaks ringed with wild-rose bushes and bracken. Hunkered down to prey, the two waited with the patience of wild animals. Putting her hands under the nylon rain cape she'd made Wily, she let his fur warm her fingers. Head back against the bole of the tree, she listened to the progress of the men gathering firewood. Ears and nose being of superior quality, Wily closed his eyes and rested his chin on Anna's forearm.

Reg was performing a remarkable feat; he was whining in a baritone, and with bravado. The timbre put Anna in mind of a tractor engine with a loose fan belt.

"I don't know why we gotta wait for the fuckin' plane. We gotta be practically on top of the landing strip. I mean it's like a big old camp or shit, right? We could've got there by just keeping on."

Wily cocked an eyebrow at Anna. She mouthed, "Right."

The dude said nothing.

"Are we supposed to build a fire out there in the ashes and shit? The pilot could see it, right? If he can see it, he can land, right? If it's cloudy we could hear him, we could follow the fuckin' sound, for Christ's sake. When's the asshole coming back?"

"When he comes," the dude answered. Irritation was loud and clear in his tone. Reg kept on. Scared, Anna guessed, angry, resentful: one of those emotions that make people chatter. Scared, she bet, mostly scared, of the dude and the alien environment.

"There's like buildings at the landing place, isn't there?" Reg asked. "Some kind of lumberyard or something? I hope they got food stashed there. I'd eat anything about now, shit on a shingle, that's what my dad called it in the army. Beef on toast. How long you think it'll take us, when the pilot does his thing?"

"As long as it takes," the dude said.

Anna shuddered with cold to amuse Wily. The dude's voice could chill beer on a hot afternoon. Reg was quiet for about thirty seconds. Like grazing cattle, the men were moving erratically, but surely, past where Anna and Wily lay hidden.

"Hey, Dude," Reg said when he couldn't stand the pastoral tranquility any longer. "That's a small fuckin' plane. I never been up in a little plane like that. Shit, it looks like a toy some glue-sniffing kid built in the basement. There's no way it carries six. No way, man. I mean, he's gotta take the cripple and the kid, too, now, right? He's gotta take them. No way we can be driving around with a cripple and a kid in the car. You were like flying out, so, what? He going to take four women and you?"

"It depends," the dude answered.

Anna promised Santa she would never again ask for anything for Christmas if only the dude would snap and put a bullet in Reg's brain.

"Shit, man," Reg said, and Anna crossed her fingers. "How much of this shit do we need? You think we got enough firewood?"

"For now," the dude said in a metallic monotone, not unlike the sound the slide on a semiauto made.

One set of boot-falls crackled back in the direction of the burn.

Anna eased Wily off her lap. She stood, shifting her weight back and forth to get the blood circulating in her legs.

"Dude," Reg called. He was staying where he was, and Anna wondered why. The last thing Reg wanted — and the first thing she wanted — was for him to be left alone in the big bad woods.

"What?" The dude was farther away than

before, and still walking.

Anna began methodically clenching and unclenching her fists to loosen up her hands.

"I gotta take a dump," Reg hollered miserably.

"Yeah?" The dude didn't stop.

There was a long time with no words. Footsteps receded. Small forest sounds dripped in: water falling from branches, squirrels or small birds scratching in the leaves, the music of a trickling stream.

Through it, faint and cold, the dude's voice came, needling. "You want me to watch?"

"You're a sick bastard," Reg shouted.

The dude's humorless excuse for laughter percolated through the trees. Then even the sound of his feet on the forest floor was gone. Anna's heart rate climbed until cold stiff muscles grew pliant and ready.

Catching one of the thugs, not only alone but with his pants down, would be the most wonderful of things. She'd skin her kill. His coat would make a dog bed for Wily. His Walther PPK could make her dreams come true.

Then she and Heath and Elizabeth and Leah and Katie and Wily would go home.

Thinking of the coat and gun made Anna's mouth water. The concept of home was too insubstantial to have much allure.

Rocking forward onto her toes, she sniffed the air the way Wily was doing. Nothing but rain-damp earth registered. A part of her had expected her nose to have evolved to a higher degree of efficiency. Time and time-lessness had merged. She'd been in the forest for millennia. Her claws should have grown sharper, her pelt thicker.

Placing her feet one in front of the other to minimize the impact of each step, she slipped deftly from the copse. Wily, encumbered by his makeshift splint, fell behind. In moments, shielded by the twin trunks of two aspens that had grown together, Anna could see the thug. Reg's back was to her. Between them was a ravine, no more than six feet across and half that deep. In the bottom ran a narrow, shallow stream; the music she'd heard earlier. On the far side of the stream was a stand of firs, their lowest branches sweeping the ground.

Alone, in the woods, with wolves and night coming on, Reg had to be scared half out of his wits. Twice he started to follow the dude. Twice his bowels called him back. Under certain circumstances, men of all ages exhibit the same symptoms. Having to take a dump is one of them. Anna was willing to bet Reg's lower cheeks were pinched as tightly as his face, as fear and need warred within him. He opened his mouth to cry out again for the dude, but something stopped him. Manly pride, no doubt.

Pride cometh before the fall, Anna thought as she slid down the soft bank. She didn't bother to avoid the water. Her moccasins were already soaked. Two steps brought her to the other side. Dropping to her stomach, she raised her eyes above the rim of the miniature ravine.

Reg muttered his word of choice for all occasions, "Fuck!" He dropped the collection of twigs and bark he'd gathered. Throwing his arms up he shouted, "God damn it!"

The dude didn't reappear. Reg lowered his arms and looked around as if he might find one place better than another for the business he had in mind.

Anna watched, nerves singing like high-tension wires.

Wily slid into the ditch. Anna gave him a hand up. Belly down on the bank, ears flattened, he took his place at her shoulder.

Reg's arms hung at his sides, swaying lifelessly as he turned around several times. The hoods of his double-layered sweatshirts were down, the yellow of the undershirt bright in the dreary close of afternoon. He must have pushed them off when the work of finding wood warmed him. Now he pulled them up, both together, making himself black as a ninja, and putting two tough layers of fabric between his neck and the dull knife Anna held.

Given his terror of wolves and loons and things that go bump in the wilds, Anna doubted he would have ventured two feet from the group without the Walther PPK. In the failing light, and the black of his sweatshirt, she couldn't see whether he carried it in the pouch pocket on his stomach or shoved into the waistband of his pants.

In over forty years of movie viewing Anna had seen hundreds, if not thousands, of pistols shoved into the back of a corresponding number of pants. In the spirit of scientific inquiry, she had tried it. Her SIG SAUER 9 mm was more comfortable than her old Colt wheel gun; still, it either gouged into her back, fell out, or slid down her butt. She suspected the carry had been invented by actors. Reg didn't hold his weapon as if he'd learned to use firearms at the movies. He held it as if he used it as a tool in his day-to-day work. The gun would be in his pouch.

Not finding any place more conducive to elimination than another, Reg stopped turning. Furtively, he glanced around. Anna didn't flinch. His gaze traveled only at eye level. Threats from up in the trees or down on the ground were safe from detection. Assured he was unobserved, he half squatted, fumbling at the front of his trousers. The Walther tumbled from his pouch and struck the ground with a solid thud. Anna could almost feel the weight of it in her hand. It took concentration to force her eyes away from the gun, and to the man she had to go through to get it.

"Fuck," Reg whispered. He stood again, undid his pants, pulled them down around his knees, then squatted. Using his left hand for balance, he leaned forward in much the same position as a linebacker waiting to charge.

The time would never be better. Anna rose from the ditch like a mist. Wily was a shadow at her heels. Together, they drifted past the boughs of the fir that had hidden them. The bittersweet smell of Christmas was in Anna's nose. The knife was in her hand.

Reg was too big, too strong to rush. He had to be disabled before he knew the fight was on. Nothing fancy, a knife in his back, deep enough she could keep his hand away from the Walther until he bled to death, or she got hold of it and shot him. Four yards, then three. Eyes on the ground, he was grunting with the strain of relieving himself when he was cold and dehydrated and frightened.

Six more feet.

An indefinable ghost breathed into the clearing. Neither seen nor heard nor smelled: felt on the skin like cobwebs, a faint electricity in the mind. Anna had sensed it before. It was the unvoiced whisper that tells the stag to look up as the hunter centers him in his sight, that hushes the entire flock when the hawk flies over. Reg felt it: a brush across the nape of his neck, a bell in the back of his brain. He wrenched his head around so far it looked like demon possession. He saw Anna and Wily, screamed, and fell sideways, his legs bound by his trousers.

The gun was in his hand and he was firing before he truly hit the ground.

Anna dropped like a stone, rolled, and didn't stop until she was beneath the kindly veil of fir boughs. Wily stood his ground, growling. Reg kept firing. The sharp shriek of bullets ricocheted off stone, the reports cracking the air. Not on the firing range, no ear protection, the noise stunned Anna.

"Wily," she hissed or screamed. The dog

scrambled under the bough. A chunk of mud the size of a man's fist exploded near him. More shots and branches breaking. Half deaf, she wrapped her fist around the dog's mouth to stop him from growling. It didn't. It wasn't Wily. It was her; teeth bared, she was snarling. Unable to remember how to stop, she released Wily and put a hand over her mouth.

It didn't matter. They might as well howl. Several yards of unprotected space lay between them and the ravine. The stand of firs was an island of cover in an otherwise exposed area. Knife clutched in her fist, she crawled rapidly around the fir, slipped out from beneath, and, keeping it between her and the gunman, listened.

The knife fell from her fingers. Wily whined. Blood covered Anna's hand. Fascinated, she stared at the red, so like that of the checks on the coat, as it spread down her fingers and dripped onto the duff in bright splashes of color. Like maple leaves in autumn, she thought. Dizziness spun the world into a kaleidoscope of trees and dogs. Her knees gave way and she went down like the devout before the altar.

She'd been shot.

That doesn't mean I'm dying, she told

herself. "Shh," she shushed Wily, though he wasn't making a sound. Together, they listened.

Silence. Reg was waiting, toying with them. Anna tried to get to her feet and failed. She reached for the knife and fell on her face.

THIRTY-THREE

"Hey, blondie, ever played hide the salami?" Sean grinned. The night before, the dude had all but handed Katie over to this wretch. Had they reached the airstrip, Katie might have been saved. Another night in the woods: Heath had no reason to think the dude would keep Sean off of her.

"You've got to be kidding," she said wearily, pretending that it couldn't happen, that the idea was absurd, in the vain hope pretending would make it so.

Sean's grin hardened around the edges. "I'll let you know when I'm kidding," he snapped. "Come over here, kid."

Leah's arm went around her daughter's shoulders. Awkwardly, she dragged Katie's slight form into her lap. The look of shock on Katie's face saddened Heath and, perversely, made her want to laugh. "Leave her alone," Leah said. No murmur this time. Leah was loud and clear.

The rifle was lying on the ground next to the thug. He sat hunched over his belly, legs thrust out, the pointy-toed boots at cock-eyed angles like jackass ears. Raindrops plopped on the leather of his jacket, beaded, and rolled. He picked up the rifle and held it across his knees, the barrel pointed at Leah and Katie.

"Oil slick." Heath said the first thing that came into her mind to distract him before his affront could turn to rage. "You remind me of an oil slick. Shallow and dirty."

"That so?" Sean sneered. He moved the rifle so the bore pointed at her, a black, all-seeing eye that never blinked. "How about I shoot you? When you're dead, you won't be reminded of anything about anybody, now will you?"

Heath wasn't sure what he meant, but she was convinced he meant it.

"The dude won't be happy if you kill one of his cash cows," she said. She was seated on her tailbone, her back against the burned tree. The muscles of her lower back trembled so violently she had to put her arms to her sides for support. They were so shaky she feared her elbows would give way and she would fall onto Elizabeth.

Flipping the rifle as deftly as a professional baton twirler, Sean brought the butt down on E's foot. Both Heath and her daughter screamed. "Shut up!" he bellowed.

Heath and Elizabeth stopped screaming. Her sneakered foot in both hands, Elizabeth glared, fierce and furious, at the thug, her bruises making the scowl gargoyle-like. That level of courage was beyond Heath. Her own face, should she be able to see it, would undoubtedly be a mask of abject terror. Worse, a thousand times worse, Heath prayed Katie would do as Sean said, or Leah would order her daughter to go to him, anything to keep him from hurting Elizabeth again.

"Now, blondie, you come over to old Uncle Sean. *Now!*"

"No!" It was Heath who spoke. Command was in her voice. Strong and cold, it slapped into Sean's face, and for a heartbeat he looked stunned. Before he could recover — before she could sink back into craven selfishness — Heath forged on. "You can hammer my child into the ground with that goddamned rifle and it will not make us one iota more compliant." Scared speechless by her own outburst, Heath concentrated on keeping her shaking arms from collapsing and ruining her imitation of valor. Beside her, she could hear E breathing through her teeth, a hiss, like air leaking from a tire. She dared not look at her. Should she see betrayal in those beautiful brown eyes, she would fold, throw Leah, Katie — a whole busload of toddlers if she had them — to the devil.

"We do not negotiate with terrorists," Leah said firmly.

This new Leah startled Heath to silence. Until today, she realized, she'd not heard the woman's voice, only a feeble echo of it from the recesses of her intellect.

"Jesus," Sean said. Clutching the rifle, he jammed the butt into the ash and levered himself onto his torn feet, then limped over to where Heath sat. The rifle arced through the air. The barrel struck her on the side of the face.

"What're you? The fuckin' United Nations?" He was snarling at Leah. He hadn't dare hit her.

Still, Heath thought, he'd hit her, not Elizabeth.

We won, she exulted.

That was the last coherent thought she was to have for a couple of minutes. Pain and shock shut her down.

True unconsciousness didn't come for her — in her cowardice, she might have welcomed that. Not a blackout, but a sinking brownout, where she could not participate in the world of the living, nor could she sleep in the world of the dead. Cheek on the ground, ashes blinded her right eye. Rain fell on the upturned side of her face, unsalty tears. Gray faded in and out of her vision. Thoughts simmered in the recesses of her cranium, none rising close enough to centers of logic to string together.

When focus returned, the rain had stopped and the dude was back. Sean was still talking.

"— getting squirrelly, Dude. Wouldn't do as I said."

"We don't need another cripple on our hands. Don't bash in the feet."

"He was going to molest Katie," Leah said, her voice not as firm as it had been before. Heath understood. The dude was a black hole into which good intentions, honor, and hope vanished without a trace.

Pawing feebly at the earth, Heath managed to get herself into a half-sitting position. Elizabeth grabbed her arm and helped her until she could rest her spine against the tree.

"You know I ain't one to complain." Sean was speaking. "But what with there just being us three and them being all the trouble they are, I wanted me a little compensation was all. They'll pay for blondie if she's alive, and I don't like 'em dead." He began to laugh at this witticism. When the dude did not join him, he stopped uncertainly.

"I'm just saying, Dude. A little something on account."

"We'll see," the dude said.

Leah or Katie whimpered.

"We'll see" to the likes of Sean was a green light. Heath had known a Sean or two in her life. Deep down, they secretly believed all men were as perverted as they, that other men just didn't have the guts to act on their feelings. Anything short of a two-by-four to the head, or the federal penitentiary, was tacit permission, a just-between-us-boys wink.

"I found a dry spot," the dude said. "Get up and move if you want a fire and a place out of the rain tonight."

"How far?" Heath dared ask. If it was less than a quarter mile, she was damned if she was going to be tied back in the chair while strength remained in her hands to cling to the armrests.

"Ten minutes," the dude said. He turned and walked away, again leaving them in the care of Sean. "Not the feet," he called back over his shoulder.

Leah and Elizabeth got Rick Shaw righted. The two of them settled Heath into the seat.

Without being asked, Katie helped by standing between the paddle handles holding the chair steady.

Being a burden was heavier on Heath's heart than any of the physical hardships she was enduring. That her daughter, Leah, and Katie, exhausted, injured, hungry, and cold, had to tend to her before they could tend to themselves made her want to tear big hunks of flesh out of her own arms with her teeth. That they did tend to her made her love for them almost too great to contain. It threatened to turn into tears or acid humor, either of which would be demoralizing.

The only payment for being the cross they bore was, of course, the scarcest commodity; she could only pay her way by being cheerful, optimistic, funny when she could manage it, and only pretending to drink when the water was passed around.

With each turn of the double wheel, agony ripped the side of her face where the rifle barrel had hit. By chance, her jaw had not been broken. A couple of teeth were cracked. Cold pierced the enamel when she breathed through her mouth, and blood stained her saliva. Of these things, she said nothing. Elizabeth did not complain about the black and swollen eye or the ribs that must have hurt with each breath, or the new injury to her foot. Leah did not complain of fatigue or fear.

It wasn't entirely stoicism. Maybe it wasn't strength in any form, Heath thought as they rolled back toward the living wood. They were like the trees falling in the forest. If there was no one to hear, there was little point in making noise.

From a distance, what sounded like gunshots, too fast and too many to count, pierced the thick air.

"What the . . . ," Sean muttered, then, "Move, move!" and a cry from Elizabeth. Sean had shoved the end of the rifle in her ribs. Heath didn't look at him, not wanting to further enrage him by movement or eye contact. Leah and E pulled harder. Jolting over uneven ground, it was all Heath could do to stay in the chair.

The dude was at the edge of the living forest, his back to them, facing the direction where the shots had originated.

"Move!" Sean yelled behind Heath.

Beyond the dude, out of the trees, where the light had given itself over to fog and coming night, something was bellowing, roaring like a lion with a thorn in every paw.

Leah dropped her paddle handle. The chair fell to the left. Heath was poured out onto the ground. Elizabeth was yelling,

"Don't drop Mom!" but Mom was already in a heap, torso over the downed paddle handle, legs twisted against the double wheel.

Sean stayed behind the women, the rifle lifted to his shoulder. The dude stood his ground, not even drawing the pistol from his belt.

The roar grew louder. A creature, black as a ninja, but big, and moving fast, burst from the trees.

THIRTY-FOUR

Charles got to his feet. Brushing the leaves off his shirt, he glared at Sean. The fool nearly shot him in the back with Jimmy's peashooter. Dirt had spurted up less than a yard from his foot as the bullet plowed into the ground.

"God damn, Dude, that was close. Jimmy's sights gotta be screwed. I'd've never! God damn," the idiot babbled while Charles decided whether to kill him now or later. Later, he decided. He doubted Reg would rape the Hendricks girl. Charles certainly had no taste for that sort of thing.

"You were going to fuckin' shoot me!" Reg screamed. "I come out of the woods, and you are fuckin' shooting at me."

Charles wasn't a finicky man when it came to language. In his line of work, slaughtering the king's English was de rigueur, but after a few days with Reg, he was coming to hate the word "fuck."

Reg's face was shiny with sweat. His eyes were too wide, the white of the sclera showing around the black irises. Charles breathed in slowly through his nose to quench a sigh. Reg was scared again, wolves or pixies or windigos, or maybe, like Charles, he believed demons roamed the earth and did not yet realize he was one of them.

"Quiet," Charles said. The silence was not instantaneous. Control was definitely eroding. Not his fault. Amateurs and fools were beyond the control of sensible men. They needed to be manipulated with great care, and even then their response to anything outside their limited view of the world could render them unpredictable.

Rather than repeat himself and let this weakness show, Charles waited until they stopped gibbering.

"Reg?" he said as calmly as an executive VP at the Monday morning meeting.

"Shit, man, it was Jimmy. Coming for me. He had a knife. A big fuckin' knife, and like this weird look in his eyes. I swear to God." Words tumbled out.

"Jimmy," Charles said, wondering what the point of this exercise in imagination was leading to. Reg was not lying; at least Charles didn't think he was. His fear was sincere. Charles could smell it. The reek of fear was familiar to Charles. As was the reek of excrement. The Jimmy story could be an excuse for cowardice, or some phobia Reg didn't want to admit to. Coprophobia, fear of excrement. Now that would make for an interesting story; a man so terrified by his own feces he hallucinated dead people.

"No shit, it was Jimmy!" Reg shouted. "Wolves or whatever didn't get him, or if they got him, he ain't dead. I tell you it was like Jimmy and not Jimmy. And that knife! Jesus, that fucker was a yard long."

"Jimmy and not Jimmy," Charles said, pretending to consider the ramifications. "Like a ghost."

"Yeah, like a ghost, man," Reg said. "But a ghost with a big fuckin' knife, and its eyes were weird, man, weird."

"Jimmy boy's not dead?" Sean was asking Charles, not Reg, asking for permission to believe his erstwhile "friend" was not worm food.

"He's dead," Charles said. Experience told him the Jimmys of the world didn't have the intelligence or creativity to pull off extravagant pranks. Jimmys were cogs; they didn't run without the machinery of the gang around them. If Jimmy had been able to crawl, he would have crawled back to camp.

"No, man, I seen him. And that dog. He had the dog you busted up against the tree with him. It was like a wolf, man. All growling and showing its fangs and it had on, like, this green cape, like Superdog, you know . . ." Reg's words trailed off.

"A dead dog in a superhero's cape," said Charles without inflection. The cretin had scared himself in the haunted forest. It annoyed Charles that Reg didn't have enough respect for his intelligence to make up a decent story. "Did you get the firewood?" he asked mildly, as he let his eyes coast over the hostages.

The cripple was down, her daughter beside her. The Hendricks woman and her child stood behind them. A family of four posing for a classic portrait. They were in shock, injured, and confused. Charles had seen to that.

Something was off in their reactions to Reg's tale.

It was that they were not reacting to Reg's tale. It had all the ingredients of a good story: ghosts and animals, superhero capes and knives, and they were showing no facial expression whatever, not even the younger females.

It wasn't just PTSD from his machinations. They were hiding something, Charles knew it as surely as he knew it didn't matter what it was. Tomorrow he'd be shed of the lot of them, one way or another. His revenge to be savored, and his money invested in Michael's future.

THIRTY-FIVE

A nurse was wiping Anna's hand with a warm wet cloth, careful to clean between each two fingers. At least this was what her mind told her as it drifted back from the realms of the unconscious. Or perhaps the subconscious. Lying on her side, she had a nice view of the hand being cleaned. On the forest floor half a foot from the tip of her nose, it lay on its knuckles, the fingers half closed. Wily, his chin on his paws, was meticulously lapping the blood from it. He'd gotten all but a few patches between her fingers, and the stuff beneath her nails. Anna didn't mind Wily licking her hand. The feel was comforting, and he might get a little protein from the exercise.

"Missed some," she whispered and spread her fingers. Pain shot down from her shoulder to meet the tiny tensing of muscles. "God damn," Anna said. "The bastard shot me, didn't he?"

Wily went on with his cleansing.

"I don't believe it. The bastard shot me." Wily raised one eyebrow and studied her with his golden brown eyes.

The bastard might still be nearby.

Anna stopped talking and listened until she felt as if her ears were waving over her head on long stalks. No sound of a man creeping or charging through the shrubbery, no taunts, nothing.

Finished with her hand, Wily flopped onto his side and began washing his butt.

"He's gone, isn't he? He can't have known he shot me. If he did, he would have come and finished me off," Anna whispered. "Went to get backup? The dude and whatsis-name? That would be stupid. For all he knows, we could be a mile away in any direction before they got back."

Wily went on with his toilette.

"We scared him off?"

Wily paused to meet her eyes.

"You're making that up. You and me? No kidding? I guess we're scarier than I thought." She was quiet for a while, watching Wily continuing his ablutions. "You know what, Wily? I'm scared to try to sit up, scared to look at where the bullet hit. I'm scared I'm going to die."

Whuff, came the canine reply.

"You're right," Anna said. "We're all going to die." While Wily watched with a concerned eye, Anna sat up. "So far, so good. Help me off with the coat?" Wily chose not to, and as it turned out, Anna didn't need assistance. The coat was so roomy it slid off her shoulders easily. Fabric driven into her upper arm by the force of the bullet was plucked from the wound. Screaming without opening her mouth, Anna sounded like a suffering puppy more than anything human. Blinking back tears, she waited until the pain subsided from hurricane to tropical storm force.

There was nothing much to see. Blood soaked the black knit of her long-sleeved T-shirt. Poking around with her finger, she found the hole in the shirt and a corresponding hole beneath, which she did not probe. Dragging the shirt off over her head was beyond her courage. Using the hunting knife, she cut away from the tear in the shirt, then ripped the sleeve off.

There was no blood on the back of the sleeve. No exit wound. Her mind was clearing. She'd been six feet from the bore of a Walther: The bullet should have torn her arm off. Hunks of shattered bone should be jutting out of a mass of mangled bleeding flesh. Reg's bullet hadn't even made it through the meat of her bicep. Either she'd been hit by a piece of lead ricocheting off a rock, or shrapnel had been driven into her arm, a splinter of wood, a shard of stone.

Having removed the cap with her teeth, Anna upended the canteen and poured the last of the water over the wound. Wily kindly assisted with the final mop-up. A ricocheted bullet; the hole was as neat and round as if it had been made by a drill, which, in a sense, it had. Blood was flowing steadily, but not spurting. Experimentally, Anna bent the wounded arm at the elbow. Her internal screaming was so loud she was deaf with it. Taking a deep breath, she tried it again. No crepitus. The bone didn't seem to be broken.

"Good news, Wily, today is not a good day to die." Wily didn't so much as smile. Evidently, he had never seen *Little Big Man* either. "You've got to get out more," she said seriously.

Further examination was pointless. Discovering that it was not broken had been pointless and painful. She'd only done it to reassure Wily.

Carrying Sean's coat and her wounded arm, she led the way back to the creek they'd forded on their way to kill Reg. For the second time in two days, she used the rubber syringe, filling it with creek water and squirting it into the hole. The pain was such that, had she not been sitting down, she would have fallen. Since she wasn't going to get it anywhere near sterile with creek water, she saved herself the agony of a second baptism. Instead, she poured the contents of the little peroxide bottle into the hole, and bit back a cry as it burned down to the bone. Peroxide wasn't a particularly good antiseptic, but it was all she had. Maybe the frothing would bring out more of whatever pulverized crud had traveled in on the bullet.

She put a couple of sterile pads over the wound, then bandaged it tightly with gauze. The chunk of lead was in the back of her bicep. The lump was palpable beneath the skin. Because it was alien, part of her wanted to slash the flesh with the thug's knife and force it out of her body. The saner part of her knew the risk of infection was greater than the damage caused by leaving the slug where it was. If they survived, a nice, antiseptic doctor with a clean scalpel could do it for her. If not, what did it matter?

The canteen refilled, she washed down four of the aspirins, put Jimmy's coat back on, and put her hand in the pocket in lieu of a sling. "That does, it buddy," she said to Wily. "That's my whole repertoire. We may as well get back to work."

Wily sighed as he got up on three legs, his lime green cape still in place, and led the way back around the stand of firs. They peeked out to where Reg had been relieving himself. The space was devoid of life, the trees silent sentinels, the fog encasing everything in shrouds of gray. Sticks and twigs lay where the thug had dropped them.

"Holy smoke," Anna breathed. "We did; we scared him off. What a weenie! He had a gun. You think he shot up all his bullets?" In the center of the clearing where Reg had squatted was a smeared pile of excrement. Bowels tended to let go in extreme fear situations, readying the body for fight or flight.

Wily sniffed the dung.

"Anything I should know?" Anna asked.

There wasn't.

"This" — Anna indicated the pile with the tip of her moccasin — "indicates serious terror. Not that you and I aren't scary as hell — for a small middle-aged woman and an old house dog. Sorry, a spade is a spade, as they say.

"I do have this big damn knife. Still . . ." Anna's voice trailed off. "Something sure as hell scared him off." Twisting around, she looked at the deepening gloom in the woods behind them, half expecting to see a ring of wolves. Not so much as a squirrel flipped its tail.

"Were there wolves?" she asked Wily. He didn't seem to think so. Though they were his brothers, they would kill and eat him if they got a chance. Had there been wolves, Wily would smell them; his hackles would be raised.

"No wolves, then. What do you say we move on?" Anna asked. "Hey, we've got them on the run."

Wily had stood his ground growling as bullets fell around him like hail. He deserved a ride from the woman who'd dived under the nearest tree. It hurt Anna that she couldn't lift him and carry him in her arms. Not that he'd ever say anything. Still, it hurt nearly as much as the bullet in her arm did. She wasn't to suffer that guilt long. All of her attention was required to remain upright and moving forward. Shock; she knew the symptoms. One was that it was hard to think clearly. She couldn't remember the others, and she couldn't tell if night was falling or if she was going blind. For a time, she simply plodded after the irregular patter of Wily's paws.

When he stopped, she stopped. When he

didn't start again, she sat down. She drank some water. She put her head between her knees. Wily sat beside her in silent sympathy. At length, her mind settled, her blood pressure rose, and she could tell nighttime from blindness.

Wily had brought her back to a place near the leaning stones. They were thirty or forty yards to one side. Tangled roots of trees, killed by fire and downed by wind, screened them.

In a miracle worth investigation by the Vatican, the dude had picked up on Anna and Wily's hints. He had brought his hostages to the sheltering boulders. Leah, Heath, and the girls huddled together inside where it was dry. Reg, stiff as a Buckingham Palace guard, stood nearby, the pistol in his hand, eyes raking from left to right with the regularity of windshield wipers. Sean, limping ostentatiously, was laying a fire at the mouth of the shelter. The dude had belatedly noticed the scrim of deadfall nearby. He was dragging branches to where Sean worked.

Not one single person spoke.

"It's going to freeze tonight," Anna whispered. She'd seen ice in the cold front she'd dreamed. She would not share that with Wily. She was in no mood to be made fun of. "We could burrow under leaves, but then we couldn't keep watch." Not to mention they were an arm and a leg shy of full burrowing potential. Should they fall asleep without a fire, or some kind of external heat source, Anna suspected one of them at least would wake up dead.

"I'm good to go," she said. Wily licked the side of her face.

Making a circle behind the deadfall, they approached the boulders from the side of the burn. The northernmost boulder was by far the larger of the two, or had been. Repeated rains and freezes had worked on its veins. Pieces of stone, from as small as a toaster to the size of a Volkswagen Beetle, had been pried loose. Fallen, they lay around the boulder's base like the skirts of a curtsying maiden.

From this vantage point, Anna could see neither hostages nor thugs. After some minutes the unmistakable scent of wood smoke tickled through the maze of rock to where she and Wily waited back in the trees.

A word had yet to be spoken.

These thugs were not a quiet bunch. Sean was a regular chatterbox. This lack of thuggy banter made her nervous. It suggested something of import had occurred. Reg must have reported the existence of a woman and a dog. That could be their death knell. Wisdom forbade her to spy on them until full dark, so she listened until her ears rang.

When the fire was burning well enough that the crack and spark of combustion filled the empty silence, her aural vigil was rewarded. A voice, cricketlike in its tiny singsong, said, "Superdog." This was followed by a low wheezing chuckle.

Then came an eruption, so sudden and loud Anna jerked like a landed fish. Wily let out a voiceless "Woof!"

"I'll break your fuckin' neck," Reg boomed. "It was him! God damn it! Forget the dog and the cape and shit. I didn't see any fucking dog, okay? But it was fucking Jimmy! Jimmy. I shit you not. Jimmy dead as roadkill. Bang and he disappears. Like that. Gone."

"Faster than a speeding bullet," Sean said.

"It's not funny, you asshole. I should blow your fuckin' brains all over these fuckin' goddam trees."

Mysteries unraveled.

Reg thought she was Jimmy. Reg had seen her through a fog, both real and that made by his terror of the woods. She'd been wearing Jimmy's coat and cap, the earflaps down. Reg panicked and squeezed off half a dozen shots while falling on his naked rump, and possibly in his own excrement. When his eyes cleared Anna had "disappeared" beneath the boughs of the fir.

No wonder he'd run. Anna scratched Wily's back through the green nylon. Superdog. Green Lantern. Both of them smiled. The last wistful hint of gray was slipping away. The thugs were noisy and occupied with their fire. Anna could hear the soft murmur of the women's voices. A breeze, with teeth of northern ice, had sprung up ahead of the cold front she'd dreamed — or sensed. If she and Wily were to survive, they, too, would need a fire tonight.

Leaning down, she whispered in Wily's ear, "Time." Moving with the careful grace of a slow loris, she walked to the base of the scatter of small boulders. For the able, they formed a giant's crooked staircase to the top of the leaning stones. To a one-armed woman and a three-legged dog, they would be a challenge. A warm tongue touched her fingers.

Wily was up for it.

She squatted to gather Wily up in her good arm. "This isn't going to be pretty," she murmured. Her arm under his belly, his front and hind quarters dangling, she stood.

Despite the fact she'd not lifted it, the gunshot arm flooded her with toxic pain. For a moment, she leaned on a rock and breathed. Eventually, with no medical care, no food, no proper sleep, and other slings and arrows, she wouldn't be able to pick him up, wouldn't be able to carry him on her back. Then what? Leave him? Cut him loose? Memory flashed on a hiker who had cut off his trapped arm to save his life.

That was an arm.

This was a comrade.

Totally different things.

A day, she told herself. Two at the most. "We can last that long," she breathed. Could Wily see in the dark like a cat? Best not to ask. He was old. Old dogs, like old people, often lost vision.

"Blind leading the blind," she whispered as she awkwardly dumped him on top of the rock she was leaning against. Hitching and swallowing groans and cries, they bumped and scrambled their way to the top of the stairs.

Fifteen feet above ground level, where the rocks came together in a natural depression, a tiny island of soil had collected. The maple tree that had taken root there was taller than Anna and a little bigger around than her thumb.

In the shallow bowl in the juncture of the boulders, they curled together around the slender sapling. Worn down by hunger, blood loss, and fear, warmed by the dog and the heat, Anna slept.

THIRTY-SIX

The dude and Sean believed Reg spooked himself and ran, then made up the story about Jimmy's ghost to cover his cowardice. The part about the specter of a dead dog in a superhero's cape didn't help his case.

Heath didn't know what to think. Thinking made her head hurt even worse than the slow screaming of the nerves on her cheek and along her temple.

Her head drooped. The muscles of her upper body ached. Cold seeped from the stone, trickled down her bones, and pooled in the pit of her stomach. Lightning shot along her jaw where Sean's blow had burst the skin. Fortunately, the .22 was a small rifle, light. E's foot had sustained no lasting trauma, and Heath's jaw was unbroken.

Elizabeth was next to her, their shoulders touching. Leah and Katie sat opposite, their backs against the other boulder, their feet and legs making a cat's cradle with E's and her own. Everyone but Heath had their hands bound in front of them with the plastic ties. Elizabeth was asleep, a blessing Heath could not emulate. Her body had sustained too much trauma. Recognized pain throbbed through her upper body, while phantom pain wreaked havoc in her lower limbs. They quivered and jumped as they fought their demons. If she survived this abduction there would be medical consequences.

Leah's head was resting against the boulder, her eyes closed. Heath hoped she slept. The fire was coming along nicely; they would not freeze tonight. Heath was grateful for that. Katie was not sleeping. She was pretending to. Sean was on watch. His eyes were not on the darkness, where the deadly shade of Jimmy and the wolves lurked, but on Katie. Whenever she peeked at him from beneath her lashes, he would stick out his tongue and wag it, or pucker up his lips in a parody of a kiss. Katie didn't want to see it, but, like a mongoose near a cobra, she couldn't resist. Each time he caught her, she would screw her eyes tight shut and pretend again.

Heath looked to the dude and Reg. They were arced like parentheses, one on either side of the fire. The dude slept. Reg was too nervous. He kept popping his head up every few minutes to look for ghosts or canine caped crusaders.

Heath had finally dropped into a nightmare-infested doze when Sean's watch was up.

"Reg. Your go. Got to watch out for ghosts and shit."

She opened her eyes in time to see Sean kick the bottom of Reg's sneaker. The blow hurt Sean's blistered foot; Heath enjoyed the wince that contracted his mouth.

"Fuck you," Reg said predictably. He got up. Patting his midsection with both hands, he reassured himself the Walther was in place.

"Take this," Sean said and handed him the rifle. "I got me things to do."

"Like what?" Reg asked as he took the gun.

"Payment on account. The dude said long as I don't wreck the merchandise, it'd be okay. The way I see it, what I'm gonna do only improves the value."

"Bullshit," Reg said.

"Want sloppy seconds?" Sean offered.

"Jesus, you're a sick fuck," Reg said disgustedly.

Heath's stomach clenched. Bile rose in her throat. There was nothing in her stomach; otherwise she would have lost it. Reaching down, she found Leah's foot and shook it gently.

Sean was skirting the fire, his eyes as hot as the coals.

"Leah, wake up," Heath whispered.

Leah opened her eyes in time to see Sean, stooped, stepping into the space between the protective boulders. The man wasn't big, not more than five foot seven. Just enough to block all the light in the universe.

"Get out," Heath ordered.

Ignoring her, Sean kicked his way through their legs and grabbed Katie by her bound wrists.

"No!" Leah screamed. In the confined space, she couldn't get to her feet. She pounded at him with her fists. Screaming as well, Heath grabbed at his legs and tried to bring him down. If they could get him down, maybe . . .

With surprising strength, the troll-like Sean yanked Katie upright. Her head struck where the rock slanted inward. Sean dragged her out into the light of the fire. Heath felt a fingernail bend and snap below the quick as he shook loose from her clutching hands. Elizabeth hadn't had time to do anything but awaken and cry out.

"What's going on?"

Heath never thought she'd be glad to hear the dude's flat voice, but she was.

"He's taking Katie!" Leah screamed, as Heath yelled, "Stop him, God damn it!" Katie, scared past utterance, her pale face painted orange in the light of the fire, looked waxen, lifeless.

"You said —" Sean began.

"Shut up," the dude snapped.

Everyone obeyed but Leah. "Please, you can't do this. You bastard. You bastards! If he touches her, I will kill you."

The dude, who Heath had come to believe was more machine than man, showed a flash of humanity, an ugly one. The hard planes of his cheeks tightened. His cod's eyes lost their last shred of light.

"Fuck the lot of them, if you want, just keep it quiet. You wake me again and I'll throw you into the fire."

"Please, please," Leah begged. "I'm sorry. I'll pay. I'll pay anything you ask, please. Katie's a child, an innocent."

"Tell that to Gerald," the dude snapped. "Shut her up," he ordered Reg, then rolled over, putting his back to the fire. "If she doesn't shut up, Sean can kill the kid when he's done."

THIRTY-SEVEN

A war broke out below. The thud of blows, women's screams, and men's shouts woke Anna and Wily.

Wily started to rise, the hackles on his neck stiffening. Anna put her arm over him and whispered, "Stay." As long as they did not show themselves and made no noise, night, smoke, and elevation rendered them invisible. The fracas fifteen feet below was as clear and offensive as if the thugs stood next to them.

Katie cried out for her mother. Leah shouted for Katie to run. It didn't take a social scientist or a criminologist to figure out what was happening. Many societies continued to view women as things, objects, items to be bought, sold, used, discarded. That was proven by the prevalence of rape throughout most cultures, including that of the American military.

The objectification of slaves was old when

the she-wolf was suckling Remus and Romulus. Weaker or conquered peoples were inferior, ergo not human, but chattel to be used.

In enlightened countries, the landscape had changed, and continued to, yet rivers of misogyny flowed beneath the surface.

Anna had known it, met it, fought with it, put aside bitterness, and moved on. What differed this night was not the ancient hatred of men for women, it was Anna. As she embraced the ways of Wily and the woods, humanness slipped away. Concepts such as contempt, guilt, and sadism became alien.

An action was necessary for survival of the pack or it was not. Cruelty was not.

Sean's brutal intentions smashed through this thin veneer of naturalism and struck Anna with the same power as it had when she was fourteen and realized her father's warning was valid. Boys — most boys — were after only one thing, a thing, not a person. Girls were not welcome in their clubs, sports, or activities as equal participants, but only as the bearers of that coveted thing, the keepers of the cookie jar.

Anna had greater compassion for the stones upon which she and Wily lay than these men had for a golden-haired girl child.

As they had at fourteen, waves of confusion and hurt washed through Anna, the force wrenching loose the last tethers that tied her to her former life. What remained was the connections with the dog, the forest, and their pack huddled below.

Leaving Wily beneath the tree, Anna suited her movements to those of Sean as he dragged his victim from the firelight, and around the side of the boulder away from the cries of the women being beaten into submission by Reg and the dude. At the edge of the boulder, where darkness was infused with the faintest of orange from the flames, she saw Sean and Katie.

Katie did not struggle, scream, or weep as she was thrown to the ground facefirst. She didn't even try to break her fall with her bound wrists.

"Throw fire at me and I'll burn you where you sit," came the dude's voice. Then the light brightened and faded. "More courage than brains." The dude again, and a woman screaming in pain.

From Leah or Heath came a wordless keen that filled the crevices in the stone on which Anna stood.

"Fight, Katie, fight him," Elizabeth was screaming. "Bite —" A dull thunk silenced her.

Emboldened by the words, Katie got to her knees. Sean kicked her between the shoulder blades. She went down again, but this time she rolled and made it to her feet.

"I get it," Sean said. "You want it the hard way."

As if there were an easy way to be raped.

Panther-footed, Anna slipped along the edge of the boulder to where the drop was less shear.

Sean grabbed Katie's wrists as he had before. Anna saw the yellow of her hair shift. Sean howled. Katie had sunk her teeth into his hand.

Good girl.

Biting earned the good girl a vicious blow to the jaw. Katie fell limp and voiceless as a rag doll.

Muttering, Sean went through what had to be the litany he used to get it up when opportunity provided a victim. "You're gonna like this, you little bitch, never had it so good, that's right, old uncle Sean . . ." As he verbally flogged himself into an erection, he pulled Katie's trousers from her unresisting body. Not bothering with her underpants, he turned his attention to his own trousers, fumbling with belt and zipper.

Lust and panic wafted up to Anna's nose, a smell like musk and bleach. She sat on the edge of the sloping stone. A hitch of her buttocks and she was sliding fast over the rough rock face, the oversized coat rucking up around her waist. She sensed her wound was sending out waves of agony. They were masked by pure adrenaline. A small thunk heralded something hitting the earth. An instant later Anna's moose-hide moccasins landed as lightly and quietly as an autumn leaf.

Mumbling prayers and incantations to the god Priapus, Sean was too absorbed to notice the scraping of her descent. Anna slid her hand into her pocket for the knife. Poetic justice, that Sean should be slain by his own phallic symbol. The knife was gone, dislodged from the pocket when the coat had crumpled up. The knife was the small thunk she'd heard. She dared not spend the time it would take to find it or use the head-lamp.

"No. Please," Katie begged.

"You goddamned pigs! Don't let him. Fight, Katie!" Screams and cries and curses from Reg pounded the air.

Dropping to her knees, Anna ran her hand over the ground. The side of it banged against a rock. It was sharp-edged, a piece the size of an *Oxford English Dictionary*, broken from the boulders by repeated frosts.

Anna pried it loose, grabbed it in both hands, then raised it over her head as if it weighed no more than a cat.

She stepped around the bulge in the rock. The bullet in her arm sent a wave of fire through her shoulder; her left arm weakened. The rock began to tilt.

Sean had his trousers undone and his cock in his hand. "Holy shit!" he said.

Before her arm could give out, Anna and the rock hurtled forward. Bones crunched and breath gusted from him as the rock smashed in his face. He fell backward. Anna, carried by the momentum of the rock, fell with him, on him. She rolled to one side, came to her knees, and grabbed for the rock covering his face with her good arm to again smash it down on his skull. The left arm wasn't responding. The right hadn't the strength to lift it.

Shaking, she rose to her feet. Blood dripped from her fingertips. The bandage over the bullet wound had come off. She gathered her balance, then stomped on the rock covering the thug's face as hard as she could. Another crunch and the sound of something wet squashing.

Probably overkill, she thought. Then, prudently, stomped on it again for good measure.

Katie stirred. Anna whirled, throwing herself down on the child before she could move or scream.

Above them, as if the moon itself cried, Wily began to howl like a wolf. Anna fought down the need to join him. Hand clamped tightly over Katie's mouth, body pressed on the terrified trembling form, Anna dredged her brain trying to find the language she had once shared with her fellow humans.

THIRTY-EIGHT

Eyes closed, brows together, lips drawn back, Leah keened without uttering a sound. The side of her face raged red with swelling flesh. Heath could see muscles and tendons working in her throat as she swallowed fury and helplessness. Elizabeth, bleeding from her lip and the mouse beneath her eye, sat slightly apart from Heath and Leah, scared she would be next, Heath guessed, and not knowing what to do when grown-ups cried. Heath saw this through a haze of pain. The burst flesh on her cheek had lost in competition with the blistered flesh on the back of her arm where the dude had laid a burning brand.

From around the side of the boulders came grunts and thumps that conjured up images that set hatred frothing red in Heath's eyes. Those same images would be in Leah's mind — but they would be of her daughter. Heath would not have been surprised if Leah wept tears of blood.

The dude, whom Heath hated more than the other thugs — even the rapist whose porcine comments they were being forced to listen to — could have stopped it. The dude's crime was the greater evil. Mr. White, Heath's sixth-grade teacher, once told the class that hatred wasn't the worst emotion; the worst emotion was indifference. She'd not understood what Mr. White meant until this night.

A loud final-sounding "Ooomph!" puffed from the darkness beyond the stone.

The dude lay by the fire, his back to the boulders. If he was awake, he ignored the noise. Reg, standing ramrod stiff, back to the fire, winced. His shoulders relaxed. Heath wondered if he, too, thought it might be over, and was glad of it. Reg, who would have killed her as casually as he would swat a fly, who refused to kill an injured dog, was terrified of wolves and disgusted by the rape of a child. Vile as he was, he was human. Somewhere, somehow, someday, there could be redemption for Reg.

Not so the dude.

After the orgasmic "Oomph" came the single howl of a wolf. It seemed to descend from the skies. The windigo, the cannibalistic spirit of the north woods that flew on the storm, was loose this night. At that moment, Heath's faith in misery and death made the demon as real as those who guarded what was coming to feel like her tomb.

The howl passed overhead and died away. The woods went silent, but for the crackling of the fire. Sean did not reappear.

"It's over," Heath breathed in Leah's ear. Leah did not cease her voiceless screaming. Like Heath, she probably thought Katie was dead.

Seconds crawled by. Heath's head, already pounding, felt ready to fly apart with the intensity of her listening.

Reg paced from one side of the fire to the other. His eyes were wide and scared. The wolf — or wolves, or windigo — was near. Yet he never looked in the direction Sean had taken Katie.

Despite the great big gun, Reg was a coward, afraid of unseen predators. Heath despised him. He hadn't the courage of the two girls he let his buddies savage.

Just when she thought she would shriek like a banshee from sheer nerves, and Leah's heart would explode through her rib cage, Katie's screaming cut into the tight-stretched stillness.

"Get off me! Momma! Get off me!" and

then hysterical wordless wailing.

"Katie!" Leah cried out. Scrambling, her feet striking Heath's already damaged legs, Leah reached the mouth of their cramped cavern only to be kicked back inside by Reg.

The dude rose from his place by the fire, fluid and deadly.

Airy, scratchy, a sound nearly identical to the scuff of leaves, yet with the rhythmic beat of iron wheels on railroad tracks, sang through night branches. Katie? Singing to herself? Sean doing something unimaginable? Heath couldn't even be sure the sound was human. Ancient horrors rose in her throat and made the skin on her scalp shrink.

Katie half stumbled, half fell into the light, whispering to herself, each step awkward. Her trousers were pulled up but unzipped and sagging.

Wordlessly, Leah held out her arms. Wrists tied together, she resembled a beggar asking for alms. Staggering frighteningly close to the fire, Katie tottered, then fell into her mother's lap. "Itwasjimmyitwasjimmyitwasjimmy."

That was what the child was chanting. If blood could, in fact, run cold, Heath's did. Ice pervaded the part of her that was sensate, and a memory of winter took the bones of her legs.

Reg stepped into the entrance to the shelter. Leah dragged Katie with her as she retreated to the farthest limit of the crack, again smashing Heath's legs in the process. No matter, Heath thought. A small price to pay. Elizabeth moved so she was between the Hendrickses, and the thug in the doorway. Heath grabbed her arm, trying to force her back. Better Reg take Katie again, better anything than he take Elizabeth.

"Take me," Heath croaked from a dry throat. "I'm still . . . whole."

Reg shoved his face inside their space. In the shadows, his black skin was the same as the black of the narrowing stone chimney above: noseless, eyeless, faceless, the lightless vacuum that artists used to depict the visage of the grim reaper.

"What's that kid sayin'?" he hissed.

Leah looped her arms over Katie's head and forced her daughter's face against her chest in a bear hug.

"Nothing," Heath said.

Reg pulled the silvery gun from his pouch. In his large black hand it appeared to float in midair, catching reflections of firelight from the rock. Like magic the muzzle moved itself to Elizabeth's temple.

"What's the kid saying?" Reg asked again.

"It was Jimmy," Heath answered so quickly it humiliated her. There was no reason he shouldn't know what Katie said, but in an insane universe one couldn't tell a hand grenade from a lime.

Reg bolted upright, struck his head against the rocks, swore, then backed out of the crack. Circling the fire, his back to the flames, he scanned the woods through the gun's sight. When he reached the side of the boulders where Sean had vanished with Katie, he stopped.

"Sean, what the fuck? Sean, man, get your ass out here."

There was no response. Reg peered into the dark beside the boulders but didn't step away from the comfort of the fire. Instead, he set his back against the rock and froze, holding the gun across his chest the way police on television do when waiting for a perp to pop out of a doorway.

The dude surveyed the camp area, took in the space between the boulders, the fire, Reg standing guard.

"Sean didn't come back," Reg said.

"Maybe he's sleeping it off."

"The kid said it was Jimmy." Reg's voice was calm and neutral. Trying to keep the dude from going after him again for seeing ghosts, Heath guessed.

"The kid said Jimmy raped her?" The dude laughed. "Maybe we'll have a virgin birth in nine months. A ghost did it. Haven't heard that one in a while."

"She keeps saying 'Jimmy did it' over and over, and Sean ain't back. It's too cold for him to be sleeping it off out there," Reg insisted.

"Sean!" the dude shouted.

No answer.

"Go get him," the dude ordered.

"No. I ain't going to," Reg said. The gun on his chest jumped an inch or two. Heath hoped there'd be a shoot-out. The dude stared him down.

"Jesus Christ," the dude said, as he walked to where Reg stood frozen to the rock. "Sean!"

He grabbed a branch from the small pile of remaining firewood and thrust one end into the fire. "The middle of nowhere is too damn dark. Can't see two feet. You'd think somebody'd put up streetlights." When the torch caught, he eased it from the coals. Walking carefully, lest it blow out, he went to the edge of the light. Then Heath couldn't see him anymore, only Reg in his statue-of-a-gunman pose.

In less than a minute, the dude stalked back into the firelight. The burning brand was gone. Brushing by Reg, he knelt in the mouth of the women's shelter. "Give me the child." He held out his hand. Leah hugged Katie more tightly.

Leaning her upper body between E and the dude, Heath planted her knuckles on the ground so she wouldn't fold up like a cheap jackknife. The dude slapped her back against the rock so hard she lost sense of what was happening. Before she could recover her wits, he'd filled his hand with the front of her coat, she was out of the shelter, facedown, her right shoe smoking and stinking of burned rubber where it rested on hot coals. Elizabeth was close behind her, moving of her own volition. She snatched Heath's foot from the fire, then crouched beside her. Heath wanted to push herself up but hadn't the strength. "Run," she whispered to her daughter.

Elizabeth helped Heath roll onto her back, then worked her leg under her mother's head as a pillow. Heath reached up to put a hand to either side of her daughter's face, the burn on the back of her arm glistening wetly in the light. "Run into the dark," she whispered desperately. "They are going to kill me anyway. Please. I have to know you're safe."

Elizabeth shook her head.

Heath could feel tears dripping from the corners of her eyes and running over her temples into her hair. "You'll find a way out. As soon as we don't show up where we were expected day after tomorrow, they'll start searching. Go now! Run. It's too dark for them to follow."

Mulishly, Elizabeth shook her head. "You'd be bored without me," she said.

With that, the moment was gone. The dude backed out of the space between the boulders, dragging Katie by one arm. Leah wasn't screaming or fighting. That meant she was probably dead or unconscious.

"What do you mean 'Jimmy did it'?" the dude yelled. This was the first time he'd raised his voice. Heath had thought him incapable of losing control. Now she hoped that was true.

Katie didn't answer directly. She'd gone rag doll and hung limply from his hand mumbling, "Itwasjimmyitwasjimmyit-wasjimmy," like an idiot. The dude shook her the way a ratter will shake a rat to snap its back.

The little body was jumping, the head flopping on the slender neck. "Stop it!" Heath cried. "Stop it! You're killing her, you dumb shit." The dude dropped Katie to the ground. Regaining her skeletal structure, she re-formed into a whole child, then skittered back between the stones.

"Sean's over there with his head bashed in," the dude said, his eyes boring into Heath.

"Sean is dead?" Heath asked. This was too good to be true. "You aren't kidding? Trying to cheer me up?"

"Sean's face was smashed to jelly by a rock," the dude said. A glint of something, perhaps gallows humor, livened his matte eyes for so brief a second, Heath might have imagined it.

"Wow." Heath shook her head. "Katie couldn't have done it. How could she? Her hands are tied. She can't weigh eighty pounds. We were all here. All she'll say is 'It was Jimmy,' so I'm guessing Jimmy did it. Don't kill her. Please."

It was a bitch having to beg from a supine position. Heath's aching neck refused to hold her head up, and she found herself staring at the sky. A star stared back. "Look," she said. "It's clear. The plane will come back. One more day, and we'll be money. One more day. Please." She ran out of breath and out of words.

The dude got to his feet, spit into the fire, then went back to the far side and lay down.

Refusing Elizabeth's help, Heath made it

to the mouth of the stones and braced her back against one side. She was furious at her daughter for not running into the woods when she'd been told to. Heath was her mother. If she wanted to sacrifice her life for her child, no little teenaged twit should be allowed to challenge that.

Elizabeth went into the crevice. She settled with her back to the opening, and to her mother. Heath closed herself inside her mind and fumed until anger changed particle by particle into pride. Elizabeth was amazing. Heath prodded her gently. "Let me in."

Obligingly, Elizabeth turned. "Are you okay, Mom?"

"Never better," Heath said. "Is Katie okay?" Heath hated the feeble words, hated that Katie would never be okay again, or not the same okay as she was before Sean had hurt her.

"She is," Leah murmured. "Her panties aren't even torn. She says Jimmy killed Sean, then fell on her, and tried to make her go into the woods with him. When she began screaming, he got off of her, and she ran.

"She said Jimmy whispered in her ear," Leah said.

"What did he whisper?" Heath asked.

" 'It's me, don't be afraid,' " Leah said.

"Anna," Heath said.

"Anna." Elizabeth said it and smiled.

THIRTY-NINE

Katie had run from her. Anna had been powerless to stop her. The flow of energy that had lifted her from her and Wily's nest, and propelled her down the side of the rocks, was gone as well.

Moving more like an earthworm than a vertebrate, Anna inched up the broken stone steps to the top of the boulders. Wily lay curled, nose to tail, around the sapling. His eyes were alert. When he saw Anna, his tail whisked quietly over the stone a time or two in welcome.

The dude's shouting at Katie rose with the smoke. Anna and Wily listened to the awful ripping scream as he tore her from her mother.

"Jimmydidit."

Katie's voice was distorted and broken. The dude was shaking her.

"I tried, Wily. I'm so sorry," she whispered. "I tried to tell her it was me, to not be afraid, not to cry out, to come with me. She was so scared."

Wily licked at the fingers recoated with blood. Old and helpless and frightened, Anna stared into the night unsure what she was. Cold and damp had weaseled into her bones, rusting the joints. Tears threatened. She wanted to die with her friends in the warmth of their company and the fire.

"My arm gave out," she told the dog. "Opened up again. I was lying on Katie like a rapist, like Sean, and she couldn't hear me. I'd forgotten I had on Jimmy's hat and coat. Like Reg, that's all she saw. He's going to kill them, Wily, all of them."

Wily stopped lapping and looked up at her with an ancient liquid gaze.

"Right," Anna said. "We'll think about it tomorrow, at Tara. I can stand it then. After all . . . Never seen *Gone With the Wind*? I don't believe that." Too tired to do else, she curled down around Wily, folding him inside the coat next to her, her hands warmed by his fur.

Paul spooned her that same way. Never had anything made her feel so safe and valued as snuggling into the embrace of Paul Davidson. The thought of her husband broke a dam in her brain. All that was loving and desirable about the human race rushed through the breach.

Without warning, the flow changed. She heard Jimmy's breath hard in her ear as she rammed the knife home again and again, felt his warm blood soaking through her shirt at the small of her back as she carried him to the river. Specks of Sean's teeth or brain matter were cold where they'd splattered on her cheeks. Bodily fluids not her own rendered her hands sticky. Wily's fur clung to her palms. Her body began shaking from within. Fingers shook. Moccasined toes dug at the thin layer of soil.

Torrents of weakness drowned her. With them came a thousand thousand gossamer threads connecting her to that which was not animal but apart, the thing called humanity: Christmas carols, kisses, high school rings, private jokes, good food, laughter, bad puns, guitar riffs, clean sheets, Paul's smile, s'mores, holding hands with her sister, winks across the room, mowing grass, feeding her dog Taco, taking out the trash, rereading *Desert Solitaire,* buying red silk underwear, being disappointed and amazed, lonely and in love.

Bright paper packages.

Whiskers on kittens.

It was not God who created Man, but Mankind that held itself together when God would drag it piecemeal back into the natural world of tides, seasons, and dancing to the movement of glaciers and the shifting of continental plates.

Declaring one's humanity complicated life, made transactions more difficult. Cats ate small helpless tweety birds, and cats were okay with that. Coyotes slaughtered adorable lambkins. Deer razed old men's tomato gardens to the ground. There was no remorse; they did not second-guess themselves, or waste time parsing motives. A bear did not wonder if she was a good bear or a bad bear, if she was fair or just or kind. A bear ate, slept, mated, defended her young, lived and died without self-recrimination. Only people did that. The past was never over; the present was lost in planning for a future that promised nothing but proof of mortality.

The disturbance from below dwindled. The dude had given up trying to shake information out of Katie.

Anna's disintegration into humanity continued. This was a bad time for it. There were things that needed to be done, people who needed to be killed.

Breathing deeply through shudders, she let herself drain into Wily, felt the bridge from dog to wolf, breathed in the scent of

350

the damp earth and the smoke of the fire. The ache in her wounded arm let go of anger at the bullet, fear of infection, and became merely an ache. The hunger in her belly ceased to resent the men who'd burned its food, lost the specter of starvation, and settled again into simple hunger.

Wily was warm and the fire was warm and Anna was as the fire and the dog and the boulder, cured of the burden of what the poets and the preachers called soul.

Denned beneath the stripling maple, she and the dog again slept.

FORTY

"A fuckin' wolf and wearing a cape like some fuckin' superhero."

Remembering the words, Heath smiled. She should have known. Wily was one of a kind. No one could make up a dog like Wily, especially not wearing a glowing green cape. Knowing Wily and Anna were alive and with them helped her retain a semblance of courage and optimism. It was the least she owed Leah and the girls, and, often, the most she had to offer.

Paranoid of wolf attack, Reg had the turned the fire into an inferno. Their shelter was warm enough that Heath shed her jacket and enjoyed the luxury of wadding it up for a pillow. Leah, Katie's head on her shoulder, slept sitting up. Elizabeth lay with her feet on Heath's thighs.

They were a sorry lot, the four of them. Aunt Gwen would have said they looked like something the cat dragged in. More precisely, they looked like something the cat played with for a day or so, then dragged in. Nothing disabling, Heath reassured herself. Nothing that wouldn't heal. Her face would scar, but Elizabeth's wouldn't. That was all that mattered. Heath was not interested in men who sought external perfection.

While the others slept, she watched the wild antics of the firelight on the leaning sides of the boulders and reveled in being warm and, for the moment, safe enough. For a change, she wasn't even thirsty. They had been able to fill their water bottles at a shallow creek they'd crossed before the weather stopped them for the night. Pain from the burn on her arm was unceasing, but there wasn't a thing Heath could do about it, so she refused to admit it was there.

Reg threw a log as big around as his thigh onto the fire. Sparks exploded into stars on the stone above her. Heath didn't look out. She did not want to make eye contact with the monsters who lurked beyond the portals of this chamber. Especially Reg. Reg was frightened. Frightened men were dangerous.

That it wasn't a ghost that had terrified Reg, that it was Anna, affected Heath in a way she had not expected.

Anna was wearing Jimmy's coat and hat;

therefore Anna had killed Jimmy.

She didn't just make him vanish into thin air. She killed him. In the dark, alone, Anna had killed a man. Once he was dead, she had taken his clothes.

Of course Heath knew thugs didn't quietly go away because they were told to. They had to be convinced; had to be killed. Jimmy leaving camp alive and in good health, no corpse, no blood, coupled with the curdling screams receding into the distance, had allowed her to put the incident into the part of her mind where zombies, dragons, and ogres lived.

Knowing Anna had taken the man's life laid such a weight of sadness on Heath's chest she found it difficult to breathe. Her sorrow wasn't wasted on Jimmy. The world was a better place without Jimmy. The demise of the bearded thug made the sea of society one drop cleaner than it had been while he lived. Heath's burden was for Anna. Killing a man, his blood literally on one's hands, had to have an effect on the killer. Lady Macbeth, "The Tell-Tale Heart," post-traumatic stress disorder: people agreed, at least on the surface, that there was a terrible, psychic, soul-wrenching penalty to be paid when one took the life of another.

Would it change her to kill the dude or Reg? Two days ago she would have said absolutely it would. Now she didn't think so, not for the worse, anyway. Accidentally killing a friend or a child, that would be crazy-making. Killing these vermin might be in the same vein as poisoning cockroaches. It was a smelly business, and not without risk, but once it was done, there was only relief and satisfaction. No one lit candles for the skittery little buggers, or piled minuscule teddy bears at the scene of the carnage. They weren't given another thought until it came time to kill them all over again.

Killing Sean and the dude and Reg would be like that, Heath decided. Murder was idiosyncratic, each killing generating a unique affect, like one's first few love affairs.

The weight of sorrow lifted. Though scratched and dented as they all were, Anna would still be Anna when this debacle was over. Heath prayed the rest of them would be around to welcome her back into the civilized world. Such as it was.

She closed her eyes. One hand rested gently around Elizabeth's ankle. She slept deep and hard. There were no dreams.

■ ■ ■ ■

Sunrise was only a suggestion far to the east when the dude woke them by banging on the boulder with a chunk of blackened wood.

"Up. We're moving."

Long hours of immobility had stiffened overworked, sore muscles. Stirring elicited groans even from Katie, who was the youngest, and usually as agile as a gymnast. This morning she was a gymnast with a chipped front tooth and a bottom lip as swollen and purple as a ripe plum. Elizabeth's face had reached what Heath hoped was maximum nastiness. She was glad her daughter couldn't see it. The eye was monstrous, purple-and-black, fat with blood. Her fine cheekbone was hidden under a blob of swollen flesh in varying hues from puce to celadon. Heath doubted her own face was any more appealing, though, as far as she could tell, her skin was more broken than bruised. The burn on her arm was hideous, four inches across, with the nylon of her jacket seared into the flesh. What was happening below her belt she didn't want to think about. Pain that was not pain, but almost pain, ghosted along the old nerve pathways hinting at dire blockages, leaks, and ruptures.

No one spoke of Sean or checked his corpse — or whatever remained of it. The dude acted as if the man had never existed. Reg pointedly avoided the side of the boulders where he lay. Katie and Leah had no desire ever to see Sean again, and Heath forbade Elizabeth to look. "Face smashed in" had been a sufficiently evocative description. She wanted no visuals in Elizabeth's mind to augment the audio.

Heath wanted to see Sean's body, not for any ghoulish reason, she assured herself. Just to be absolutely sure he was absolutely dead. Her formative years had been during the post-*Jaws* era when no monster stayed dead until it had been dispatched at least twice. The thought of Sean, a mangled mess of smashed bone and skin fragments where a face should have been, leaping out at her before the credits rolled engendered within her a superstitious tremor.

Since there was no good way she could get to the corpse without involving Leah or one of the girls, she decided to take it on faith that Katie and the dude were not mistaken, and Sean was irrevocably dead.

A night's rest, and the knowledge they weren't alone, had revived them. Once they extricated themselves from between the kindly boulders and got the blood circulating, there was almost an air of giddiness. This lightening of mood was not missed by the dude. His face was tight with suspicion. As they relieved themselves, he did not turn his back or look away as he had before.

Ghosts who bashed out the brains of rapists wouldn't be a satisfactory explanation for Sean's demise for such as the dude. He seemed a practical man. Heath studied him, seeking a clue to his mental processes. Chthonic, Heath had learned that word in high school English. Until now, she'd never had cause to use it. Of the underworld, without humanity, hard, harsh: chthonic, the dude. A sidewalk was more expressive. On a good day, one might be able to carve one's initials in his visage with a sharp stick. At present, even that niggardly sign of life was gone.

She and Elizabeth would have to be very careful today. Belligerence or delay would not be tolerated. With Sean no longer around to slow the pace, Heath was the weakest link. She daren't falter. The dude would put a bullet through her brain without a second thought.

For a while it looked as if he were going to leave the girls and Leah in wrist bindings, rendering it virtually impossible for them to pull the chair. Heath was readying her mind to die with dignity when, with a shrug that could have meant anything, he cut the plastic. Raw welts oozed blood where the ties had bitten deep. Heath had to look away lest she cry.

Fog shrouded the forest. The sun rising over the treetops was a glowing dime-sized silver disk when the dude called a stop. They were deep into the burned area, the landscape cremated and scattered by the wind. Bare-toothed rocks and black amputated limbs attested to the fact there was no peace in death. E and Leah put Rick Shaw's paddle handles on a waist-high rock so Heath could sit upright. She leaned her shoulder against a foreshortened tree trunk.

The perch was gratingly uncomfortable, but Heath was afraid if she unpacked herself, when the plane flew over the dude would shoot her rather than wait until she was remounted. Should they get home one day, she would greet Robo-butt — as E dubbed her wheelchair — as an old friend rather than an odious necessity.

Leah and the girls sat in the grit of old ashes. Reg and the dude paced. Around them was nothing but the grim residue of fire: blackened tree trunks, arms burned to stumps, pointing accusingly at the dull gray sky.

"Katie," Leah whispered, "does the dude look familiar at all to you?"

Katie stared hard at the man for a minute or more. "Maybe," she said. "I don't think so. I don't know."

"Why?" Heath asked. "Does he look familiar to you?" If Leah knew him, surely she would have mentioned it by now.

"I thought he did at first," Leah said. "Then I thought not. Who could forget those eyes?"

"Carp eyes," Elizabeth said.

"Shark eyes," Katie said.

"Then last night he said something odd."

Heath had known Leah long enough to realize that, without help, she wouldn't go on. Often she didn't finish sentences. Evidently finishing them in her head was sufficient communication. "What did he say?" Heath prompted.

"I told him Katie was a child, an innocent. He said, 'Tell that to Gerald.' "

"Your husband?" Heath asked.

"I guess so. He sounded like he knew Gerald."

"Maybe a business contact?" Heath asked.

"Why would daddy know a douche bag like him?" Katie asked.

"Katie," Leah remonstrated.

"Douche bag," Elizabeth confirmed.

"You're outvoted, Leah," Heath said.

"What business? Gerald has . . . issues, but violence isn't one of them," Leah said.

"Shut up," Reg snapped at them. Then, as if it had been too long since he'd said it, "Fuck. Plane can't find us in this shit, Dude."

"Ground fog," the dude said. "It'll burn off."

The sun climbed; the fog thinned, then was gone. Sunlight warmed Heath's cheeks and hands.

No silver plane burred into the blue sky.

Reg stopped pacing. He sat with his feet planted wide apart, throwing a jackknife into the dirt and scowling. The dude removed his red-and-black checked hunter's coat and spread it on the ground, colorful side up, to make a bigger signal for the plane. He kept looking from the coat to his wristwatch to the sky.

Another hour passed. No airplane.

Heath was out of the chair, her spine braced against the stump. She still believed the dude would shoot her should she cause delay, but the pain of holding herself upright and balanced made the bullet seem the lesser evil.

By the time the sun was halfway up the sky, and clouds were beginning to show ominously in the northeast, the dude was including Heath in his geometry of vision: coat, wristwatch, sky, Heath. The pattern reminded her of a cocaine addict she roomed with briefly in college. When the stuff was available, Sarah would obsess on something else, her hair, the mirror, her makeup. Eventually, and inevitably, the coke would be factored into the pattern. That's when Heath knew Sarah had lost the battle; she would use.

Heath tried to ignore the lightning strikes of the dude's eyes. She had the eerie feeling that his drug was death itself. His emotions would crescendo, hit a set point, and he would blow her to kingdom come just to take the edge off.

Reg stripped to the yellow hoodie, identical to the black one that customarily covered it. The dude nodded approval at the bright color. From then on, Reg was configured into the pattern. Five points: sky, watch, coat, Heath, Reg; an infernal pentagram drawn in the air. Tension quivered so palpably Heath expected it to become visible, to shiver and shimmer like July heat off the Smoke Creek Desert.

Reg ceased his constant grumbling. Bereft

of the word "fuck" he did not speak. Periodically, he shot the dude hostile glances, but never when the dude was looking at him. Having nothing better to do, he glared at the women, daring them to speak.

Heath was scared to scratch, yawn, stretch, or breathe too deeply. Who knew what might bring disaster down upon their heads? This was a hideous game, and only the dude knew the rules. Breaking one carried a penalty of death or beating.

Though the plane meant nothing good for the captives, Heath found herself praying to hear the angry buzzing of the engine, anything to interrupt the high-pitched psychic whine running along the wires of her mind. Nitroglycerin ran through the dude's veins. Living each minute knowing he might explode and destroy Elizabeth or Katie or Leah was so excruciating Heath was tempted to bring his wrath upon herself simply to end it.

Unfortunately, it was Katie who set him off.

"Leah — Momma — I think I know where I saw him!" she exclaimed suddenly. "The dude. Daddy has a picture of him."

Slowly, a crocodile emerging from cold river mud, Reg raised his head. His eyes returned from whatever inner vista they'd been watching to rest on Katie.

"Dude," he said in a low voice. The pewter-colored pistol lay atop the black hoodie he'd dropped on the ground. He picked it up as he rose to his feet.

The dude squinted over his shoulder. "What?" he demanded, then rotated his body until it aligned beneath his face. Head and body seemed to move independently of each other. Heath's crawling sense that he was not human flared. Had her legs been functional, she might have run away, abandoning her child and risking a bullet in the back.

"Kid's seen a picture of you," Reg said.

The dude walked slowly toward them, a power contained, wild horses being held in check. When he reached them, he bent over to close his fist in the front of Katie's shirt. Without apparent effort, he lifted her until he was looking up into her face. "Your father has my photograph?"

"Put her down," Leah begged, scrambling to her feet. Elizabeth was rising as well. Heath couldn't reach her to drag her back down.

"We were talking about a TV star who looked like you is all," Katie squeaked. "He, he —"

"He was on *The Young and the Restless*,"

Heath said. Given all the hours she'd spent in a hospital bed she knew the classic soaps.

Never taking his eyes off Katie's face, he quietly asked, "Is that right?"

"Yes," Katie gasped. His free arm shot out like a piston, his fist punching Leah in the stomach. Her slender body folded over, then crumpled to the ground

"Are you sure?" the dude asked in the same even tone.

An eager tension plucked at the corners of his eyes like a smile so long unused it had atrophied.

"The plane! The plane!" Reg was shouting and pointing.

Heath was of the generation that could not hear those words without picturing Hervé Villechaize on the beach of *Fantasy Island.* Hysterical laughter clawed its way up her throat. Putting both hands around her neck, she squeezed to keep her esophagus from bursting. Katie was going to die, and the plane was coming to lead them into perdition, and it took every ounce of strength she had to keep from laughing until her rib cage cracked.

Instantly indifferent to Katie, the dude dropped her. Unhurt, she got to her feet and ran to where Leah was uncurling from the gut punch. Reg tore off his yellow hoodie. Waving it frantically, he shouted, "Down here! Here! Down here!" The dude stood with his hands on his hips, staring at the oncoming aircraft as if waiting to be strafed.

The metal of the plane flashed, the wings rocked; it descended until Heath thought the wheels would touch the tops of the trees. In a roar and a storm of disturbed ashes it flew over. Heath could count the rivets on its undercarriage. Two white objects, each the size of a fat bed pillow, emerged from the plane's left-side door to plummet to earth.

FORTY-ONE

Anna and Wily lay low until the thugs and hostages were gone from the sheltering stones. After helping Wily to descend, Anna found the knife. When she dropped it into the coat pocket, it clanked. The cell phone; she'd forgotten she had it. Two bars of power showed. There was still no signal.

Wily limping at her side, she trailed the thugs across the burn. Had Reg's familiar "Fuck!" not alerted her, she would have shown herself. Just over a low rise, jagged with the charred remains of trees, the dude had stopped to await the plane.

Within earshot but out of sight, Anna skinned out of Jimmy's coat. Spread like a blanket, checkered side down, it kept her and Wily off of the cold ground. She didn't bother to wrap her black T-shirt around her hair and face. Ash from the burn, coupled with soot from the thugs' fire, grimed her until she was probably much the same color as the remains of the forest.

Sharing tepid water and filtered sunshine, she and Wily listened and waited. The sun climbed, warming the air. Wily slept. Anna dozed and nodded until screams snapped her out of a fantasy of corn chowder with fresh buttered bread.

A gunshot arm made belly-crawling an exercise in self torture. On three legs, like Wily, Anna crabbed uphill until she could see over the berm of earth they were hiding behind.

The dude held Katie up high in one hand. Leah was on the ground in the fetal position. Wily smelled a stink inside the dude that made his nose wrinkle. A whine burned in his throat. Anna believed she could smell it, too, a mix of burning electrical wires and acetone.

Before Anna could piece together what was happening, an angry buzzing of enraged hornets shook the sky. A shadow struck like a fist across her eyes. Wily barked unheard as the airplane flew over low and slow. Two parcels tumbled out the pilot's-side door.

Reg ran after them. Grabbing one up, he tore it wide open.

"Food, man. Food!" he shouted with the innocent delight of a child.

In pure agony, Anna and Wily watched as

Reg and the dude devoured deli sandwiches and guzzled from little boxes with straws. There would be food left over. The pilot had brought enough for four men. Only two still lived.

Anna winked at Wily.

Heath and the others got what was meant for Sean and Jimmy. Anna and the dog watched them eat, delighting as their friends grew in strength bite by bite. Wily was sniffing: meats, cheeses, breads, and the smells of his people filling with food and hope.

"Look," Anna whispered, pointing at Heath nudging a paper-covered parcel behind the tree stump she'd been homesteading. "Lunch."

Still chewing, the dude fished a piece of yellow lined paper from one of the sacks, letting the plastic bag fall to the ground. Anna counted the separate pieces of litter the dickheads had strewn about the landscape. Wrappings, bags, napkins, juice boxes, straws, plastic utensils, packages of salt and mustard and mayonnaise.

Litterbugs.

Anna was glad she'd killed two of them.

"What's the penalty for littering, Ranger Pigeon?"

"Death, you slovenly pig."

"What is it you got?" Reg asked as he

loped over to the dude to read over his shoulder.

"Note from the pilot," the dude said.

The thugs pored over the paper for what seemed an awfully long time. "Reading probably isn't one of their job skills," Anna whispered. Wily gave her a shushing look.

Leah and Elizabeth were quickly helping Heath back into her chair. Katie was holding the handles steady.

"Clever girls," Anna murmured to Wily.

The plane flew over again. This time the group followed in the direction indicated, the dude leading, Leah and E pulling the chair, Katie pushing, and Reg bringing up the rear. Beyond a jagged black crest of a hill, they disappeared from sight. The hellborn stench dissipated.

Anna and Wily waited another five minutes to make sure nobody came back to see if they'd turned the iron off and locked the back door, then came out of hiding and trotted to the white paper sack Heath had squirreled away.

Partially squashed from the unusual nature of its delivery was a ham-and-cheese sandwich on a kaiser roll. The ants had gotten to it. Anna brushed off the ones that weren't mired in the mayonnaise, tore the sandwich in two pieces, and gave one to

Wily. Both wolfed the food down without bothering to sit.

Also in the bag, and no worse from its fall from the heavens, was a box of apple juice. Using Sean's knife, Anna cut the top off, drank her half, then set the box down and held it steady while Wily drank his share. Wordlessly they agreed it was one of the finest meals they had ever had.

"Pick up the litter?" Anna asked.

Wily kept his eyes in the direction his people had gone.

"Right," Anna said. "Priorities."

For an hour they followed the deep tracks of the group wending its way across the burn. Without the protection of trees and underbrush, rain had carved deep gullies in the soil and the wind had filled them with debris.

The end of the devastated area appeared like a benediction. Anna and Wily breathed deeply, cleaning their noses of ash with scents of moss, pine, and downed leaves.

This initial elation lasted until the underbrush closed in, forming nearly impenetrable thickets. Half-naked tree branches spiderwebbed the sky. The dry pink sandy soil of the Fox River basin was replaced with deep loam, spongy underfoot. Damp chilled the air. Moss grew on all compass points of the trees. Lichen poked antlered heads out of moist bark.

Traces of Heath's, Leah's and the girls' suffering were everywhere: scraps of torn clothing on briars, moss scraped away when Heath's chair struck a tree, heel gouges where the chair was lifted over downed vegetation. The forest was biting pieces of the captives off, tearing at them with sharp branches, coiling around their ankles and tripping them. Heath had excellent upper-body strength and an innate determination to overcome obstacles. Leah seemed fit enough. The girls were girls; though in decent physical condition, they were not athletes. Their muscles and bones were gentled with fading childhood and oncoming fertility. Soon one or two or all of them would lose their battle with the North Woods. Their strength would give out.

In the end the dude and Reg, like slave drivers of old, would herd only those fit to walk to market.

The sun had started down the back side of the day, and the air was growing cooler, when the trail Anna and Wily followed petered out at the edge of a swamp. Beaver, Anna guessed, and old. There was no telling how wide it was, or how deep the water and mud. Drowned trees, roots long rotted away, fell over the bog, trunks and branches intertwined. Isle Royale, where Anna worked early in her career, had a number of bogs such as this. They were fine places to trap a foot or break a leg.

At the edge of standing water, Anna refilled the canteen. Mosquito larvae would add protein, she told herself. That done, she backtracked a dozen paces and saw where the group had made a right turn, heading northeast along the edge of the wetlands. The note the dude and Reg had been studying must have told them to turn right when they hit marshy ground.

Given an abundance of moisture, undergrowth grew thicker and harder to penetrate. Anna hadn't gone half a mile before she saw Heath's rickshaw abandoned beside a tangle of thimbleberry bushes. That there'd been no gunshot meant nothing. The dude could dispatch Heath easily — and probably with a degree of satisfaction — using his bare hands.

Anna needed to search for Heath; her friend might not yet be dead. The dude might not have finished the job. Anna had to find the corpse and sprinkle a handful of dust on it to free Heath's soul. Anna didn't move. She didn't want to see Heath's body. Without Heath, all she had done, and all she had left to do, was drained of reality. Mouth slightly ajar, she closed her eyes and sniffed small sips of air into her nostrils.

"I don't smell anything dead, do you, Wily?"

Wily was leaning against her leg for support, his tongue lolling nearly to his knees. "You'd tell me if you smelled something, wouldn't you?" Anna asked.

Of course he would. Wily would smell Heath's death. He'd tell Anna. Instead, he tottered forward, taking the lead. That was good enough for Anna; she followed.

The terrain made it obvious why the rickshaw had been abandoned. Thickets were so dense Leah's ingenious design would be useless. Every few feet the handles would catch and hold. The double wheel would jam between the jaws of fallen trees and branches.

Carrying Heath on their backs, Leah and Elizabeth wouldn't get far. Anna thanked nature and the universe that the sun was near setting, the short day coming to a close. Without light, the dude would have to stop.

The airstrip couldn't be much farther. Back at the Fox, the dude said six-point-seven miles. By Anna's estimation they had traveled close to twelve, and five or six of those were in the right direction. Skirting the swamp had added to the original GPS reading. By how much, she had no way of knowing, but the pilot wouldn't have led them on unless he thought they would make their destination.

Could a plane take off in the dark, on a rough field or an old logging road? Anna didn't know. The clouds that had been moving in from the north obscured half the sky, bringing darkness that much closer. Maybe, while she had been dawdling, sniffing the sweet decay of the woods and trying not to catch up with the thugs by accident, they had reached the airstrip. They could be loading into the plane to be whisked away where no one could find them. Canada was only a small hop to the north. Once there, a small plane with four small women could be hidden anyplace in the vast reaches of the country.

Anna lifted Wily, holding him around the middle. His injured leg under pressure, he whined. Anna joined him as her gunshot complained for general reasons. "Sorry," she said. "We're in a hurry. I know it can't be comfortable, but you know my left arm is shot to hell. I'll carry you as long both of us can stand it."

Desperation overtook stealth. She bulldozed through the thickets. Twigs raked blood from her cheeks and clawed the remaining sleeve of her T-shirt to shreds. Sweat poured between her breasts and grew chill on her back with the going of the day. Her arm looped around Wily's rib cage made it hard for him to breathe. He was too polite to say anything, but Anna could hear him laboring. "Not much longer," she promised. "My good arm is about to give out."

Night did not so much fall as thicken imperceptibly around the trees and bushes. When Anna could no longer see to place her feet, she stopped. She had to kneel to put Wily down. There wasn't enough strength remaining in her arm to lower him gently from a standing position. Without movement, the night chilled her. She took Jimmy's coat from where she'd tied it around her waist and put it on. Together in the dark, she and Wily listened. For a while Anna could hear nothing but her heart pounding in her ears and her breath brushing against the sides of her throat.

Wily's coyotelike ears caught the sound before hers did. Tramping feet in the darkness. Tuning her ears to the noise, Anna rose and began inching toward it, feeling her way with outstretched arms and the toes of her moccasins. Vague gray light filtered through the canopy, barely sufficient to keep her from walking into trees or tall bushes.

"We're not fucking stopping!" Reg. Closer than she'd thought. Much closer than she'd thought. "I heard something. Something coming after us."

"A deer." Elizabeth said, panting. "Lots of deer up here."

"Shut up," said Reg.

Anna could see Reg's outline. For an instant she was in full view. If the thugs had stopped a moment sooner, they would have heard her charging through the brush like a moose in rut. Fortune decreed no one was looking at her particular patch of night. She faded back a few feet, putting a tree between herself and them.

"We should make a fire."

That was Heath. She and the others were a black huddled mass on the far side of the clearing. The far side was scarcely six feet from the near side. This was not a forest of meadows and grassy swards. Trees fought for space. Land and light were not wasted.

"Shut up," the dude said.

"We got to be close," Reg said. "Shit, man, we gotta be close. We can't fucking stop."

"Which direction would you suggest we go?" the dude asked.

"The way we been goin', man."

"And which way is that?"

Confusion carried on the silence that reached Anna's ears.

"That way," Reg finally said sullenly.

"Right. Why don't you go 'that way' and let us know if you find anything."

No crunching of a man trying to navigate the night woods followed.

They would go no farther. Relief swept through Anna, blowing away the last of the adrenaline rush that had gotten her to the hostages. Suddenly she was so tired she felt like throwing herself down on the ground and crying.

Dismissing fatigue as a luxury, she turned her back on her night-stranded fellows, took the headlamp from a coat pocket, and put it around her brow. Feeling her way, she counted off fifteen steps, then clicked it on. Wily didn't follow. This close to Heath and Elizabeth, his nose was too full of the scent of his family to leave. Anna felt both alone and free.

Moving more quickly without her beloved burden, she made a wide circle around the thugs and headed left of the North Star.

In less than three minutes she reached the edge of the trees. Night had halted the thugs laughably close to their destination. Ahead was a clearing as wide, and half again as long, as a football field. At the far end, a hundred and fifty or so yards from where she stood, a fingernail moon and a scatter of stars picked out the shape of a two-story building, roof gone, walls slowly rotting back into the earth. Next to it was a shed in the same condition. Alongside the shed were shadows of what was probably old logging or mining equipment. Logging, she guessed. Not a mill, maybe a camp with barracks and a cookhouse.

The North Woods of Minnesota retained the ghosts of many old ventures. At one time or another much of the state's forests had been clear-cut. Timber and iron ore were still taken, though in smaller quantities than in the glory days. Canoeing in the boundary waters, Anna had come across short railroad spurs in seemingly remote wilderness areas where nineteenth- and twentieth-century entrepreneurs had laid line to lumber camps or mines. When business went bust, rails were abandoned to be reclaimed by the land.

At the near end of this camp, no more than ten yards from the tip of her nose, was an airplane, the small high-wing. Beneath the wing was the pilot. Or so Anna assumed. All she could see was the glowing end of a cigarette.

Tobacco smoke spiced the air, the scent so familiar and mundane it snatched Anna out of the woods and plunked her down firmly in humankind. Two days of drifting through shadows with Wily had taken her into the world of spore, scent, and survival. Returning so abruptly to the reality where politicians made fools of themselves with hookers, lights turned from green to red, and the omnipresent, omnipotent, omniscient Internet had taken the place of the gods confused her. Part of her never again wanted to run in the human race.

Human ills hit her with the imaginative power of mind. The bullet wound, an injury her animal self accepted as a part of life, burned and ached, demanding hospitals and sterile dressings. The belly that had been grateful for the ham-and-cheese sandwich cried out for more. Glad Wily wasn't present to see her devolution into a human, she breathed softly and deeply until the spasms of need passed.

In the far buildings there might be something of use. A weapon. Slipping back into the trees, she skirted man and plane and began making her way toward the far end of the clearing. Before she was three-quarters of the way there she was stopped by a shout.

"Hey!"

Anna dropped to the ground. This sudden descent without regard to her injured arm undid her. Seconds passed as pain receded and clarity of vision returned. She was breathing too fast and too shallowly. Audibly, she was breathing audibly. Pressing nose and mouth into the crook of her elbow, she let Jimmy's coat stifle her noise.

"Hey!" The call came again. Anna blinked away the tears from the onslaught of nerve damage.

The cigarette man.

Clutching her wounded arm across her chest, Anna walked on her knees until she had a clear view of the black shadow that was the airplane. A flashlight beam slashed across the grass of the field, not toward her, in the direction from which she'd come. The pilot must have heard the dude or Reg yelling.

"Keep talking," she heard him shout; then the flashlight beam bounced toward the line of trees where the hostages and the dude had been stopped by nightfall. The pilot would lead the others out of the forest. The dude and, especially, Reg would want to sleep in the comfort of four walls, regardless of how dilapidated and mice-infested those walls might be. Walls high enough to keep out the wolves, if not the ghost of Jimmy.

More determined than ever to reach the buildings, Anna rose and kept walking.

FORTY-TWO

For the last eternity Heath had ridden on the backs of her daughter and her friend, her arms wrapped around their necks, her knees clutched under their arms. Her nose had been filled with the scent of their sweat and the fading perfume of shampoo. Their breath mingled with hers; their hair blew in her eyes. Their hearts beat beneath her breastbone. Heath was the largest of them, yet the smallest, Katie, wanted to take a turn at carrying. Katie was too little, so at first Leah and E rotated the duty in fifteen-minute increments, then ten, then five.

"Slow down and she dies," the dude told Reg. "Dump the cripple or keep up the pace. Your choice." Furious, Reg dropped behind and drove them like mules, whipping Heath's back and the others' legs indiscriminately.

A peculiar change came over Heath as she was piggybacked through the trees, life and mobility dependent on the love of her daughter and Leah. One hundred twenty pounds of her crushed down on their very bones. Her hands could feel the pull of their muscles as they strained to keep up the pace, to lift their feet one more time. Yet she had stopped feeling that she was a terrible burden, their cross to bear. Hour after backbreaking hour her daughter and Leah expressed their love for her. They would not leave her behind. The marines could take lessons from these women.

Heath no longer wanted to tear herself to pieces out of guilt. What she felt was awe and honor.

What she prayed for was sundown. Soon even their staunch wills would be overcome by physical exhaustion. When they fell, and she fell with them, the dude would kill her and, probably, E. With them dead, Leah and Katie would have no reason not to keep moving.

In the dimming light Heath could see Katie swaying with the effort of keeping herself upright. Leah had stopped helping Heath when it became clear Katie could not continue without her arm to support her. Finally, Elizabeth staggered and fell to her knees, her body shaking with sobs.

Heath let go of her neck and let her weight

slide to the ground. Her eyes were closed, the effort of seeing too onerous. Gravity had beaten them, beaten down their stalwart hearts.

"Don't bother to shoot me," she mumbled. "I'll die of exhaustion in a minute or two. Get up, Elizabeth. Please do as I ask. I love you. Get up. Go."

E remained on her knees. Heath didn't know if she refused to rise or was unable to.

Wearily, Heath looked up at the dude from whence her death would come. She could barely see him. He was a mere silhouette against a dour sky.

The sun was gone. As Elizabeth had fallen, so had the night.

God is good, Heath thought. Then, considering their situation, amended it to: God is not as rotten as he could have been.

"We have to stop," Heath said. "It's too dark to see, or will be in a few minutes. You have to stop."

Leah and Katie took this as permission to collapse beside Heath and Elizabeth. Reg began cursing. Reg was afraid of the dark. He had driven them hard and cruelly, but he couldn't stop night from coming, and in the end he was stranded in the wolf- and ghost-infested dark. He used the word "fuck" so many times, interjecting it even into the middle of words, that it ceased to have meaning and fell on Heath's ear like a verbal tic: um, er, you know, like, fuck. Maybe because she was glad the thug was as scared and tired as she, it struck her funny.

Because God was not as rotten as he could have been, she was too tired to laugh.

"Hey!" came faintly through the darkling wall of trees.

"Over here!" Reg shouted. "We're over here!"

Heath heard the whack of knuckles on flesh, and Reg's grunt. "We don't know who the hell is yelling," said the dude.

"Who the fuck cares?" Reg snarled. "Over here. God damn! Come get us."

"Keep talking." The voice filtered in, a little stronger. "How were the sandwiches?"

"The pilot," the dude said.

"Who the fuck did you think it would be in fucking middle of fucking nowhere? Over here!" Reg shouted at the top of his lungs.

"Get up," the dude ordered the women. Heath could dimly see the shapes of Katie and Leah drift up from the ground, as incorporeal as swamp gas.

"I can't," E murmured so softly Heath, who was sitting nearly on top of her, could barely hear.

386

"Move your ass," Reg snarled.

E stayed still and silent.

"Go ahead, sweetheart. I'll catch up later," Heath said.

The dude snorted his version of a laugh. "Yeah, you do that." His dark self swarmed over the kneeling girl and she was dragged her to her feet.

"No!" E screamed. "I'll carry her! I can carry her!"

"Dead weight," the dude said.

Heath saw a blinding flash of fire as a clap of man-made thunder knocked her backward.

Then nothing.

FORTY-THREE

A gunshot stopped Anna in her tracks. Turning, she looked back down a hundred yards or so of not quite black night. The shot had come from near where Heath and the others were.

A single gunshot.

This close to success, the dude wouldn't shoot Leah or Katie, his primary objectives. Elizabeth was still moving on her own and, as far as Anna knew, was still believed to be the child of a very wealthy family. That left Heath or Wily. Anna was glad it wasn't given to her to choose which was to die. In the real world, where gunmen stalked college campuses and wars were fought over whose god was god, where human life was deemed of great value and destroyed with industrial efficiency, she would be expected to choose Heath.

In the forest, she would choose Wily.

More shouting; then a blade of light from

the pilot's flashlight stabbed into the clearing, raked the silver underside of the airplane wing, then steadied, pointing down the field in the direction of the derelict buildings. Anna could barely make out the forms behind the bright battery-driven star. The dude, Reg, and the pilot — she knew them by their voices — walked toward where she lay. In their midst, surrounded like cattle on a drive, were the women and girls. Or woman and girls.

When they drew level with Anna's hiding place, she could see that no one was carrying anyone. Heath, then, not Wily, had been shot. Relief and sorrow canceled each other out. Only emptiness remained. Silently, she rose. Not bothering to keep to the trees for cover, she walked swiftly back toward where the women had been when she'd left them.

The thugs made enough noise to drown out her soft footfalls, she told herself. The pilot's flashlight had rendered them night-blind, she told herself. She insisted on these things because the fact that she didn't much care whether she was shot in the back or not was craven. To make Paul suffer her loss, to die when she could still be of use, was the coward's way out.

Wily would be with Heath. Anna let that comfort float foremost in her mind. No one should die without the company of a familiar.

When she'd emerged from the woods, she was on the northeastern-most side of the clearing where it narrowed. Viewed from the opposite direction, nothing looked the same. The forest was a blank wall only slightly less solid than the earth. Without Wily's nose, the odds of finding Heath were slim. Her headlamp would help, but its thin blade of light would be like a needle searching through the haystack for a fellow needle.

The men had reached the buildings. Their voices carried in the unsullied air, but she was too far to make out individual words. Three thugs, two pistols, and one rifle; that she knew. The pilot might also be armed. Cops and criminals liked their weapons.

On the black of the ruined barracks, to the sound track of their voices, a movie played in Anna's mind: Katie held by the front of her shirt. Elizabeth beaten bloody. Wily slammed into a tree. Katie's trousers ripped down to her ankles. Heath shot.

The pilot.

Reg.

The dude.

First, Anna decided, she would find Heath's body. Then she would find Wily.

Together they would go back and kill them all.

Entering the woods where she guessed she might have first come into the clearing, Anna clicked on her headlamp. "Wily! Heath!" she whispered, calling in hisses and poking into thickets with her lance of light. A logging road cut through the forest, old, partly overgrown, but navigable. This must have been what the thugs had intended to use to transport their victims from the original abduction site. For a moment, she was tempted to walk down it, not because she wished to leave her friends behind, but because she had been fighting cross-country for so long, to walk without obstacles was alluring.

She crossed and entered again into the midnight of trees.

Accustomed as she was to working in the wilderness — or as much wilderness as could be preserved when hikers, campers, firefighters, rangers, rescuers, EMTs, botanists, zoologists, and Girl Scouts used it — the forest at night disoriented her. Trees appeared in strips as her light struck them, then vanished as it moved on. The horned moon could not be seen, nor could the North Star.

Grief and fury kept her moving, whispering Wily's and Heath's names, pushing her body through the bony fingers of dead branches and the tangled stems of dying asters. Nowhere did she see a trace of her friend or the dog.

Was she intentionally blinding herself because she didn't want to find Heath's dead body?

That thought stopped her frenzied searching. Standing perfectly still, she breathed, forcing her mind to cease its stinging refrain of "Wily, Heath, Wily."

It was then that she realized she was lost. On some arrogant level, she hadn't believed that was possible, just as on some Disney level, she didn't believe wild animals would devour her, not her, not Ranger Pigeon. Never would she be the focus of a band of gleeful heroes in green and gray descending with rescue stretchers or Bauman bags. Slowly she turned in a circle, her headlamp picking out three hundred sixty degrees of nothing but trees.

North, east, west, and south were the same to her. Heath was dead or dying; tomorrow the plane would fly out with Leah, Katie, and E. Wily would die of starvation or be killed by wolves. All because Anna didn't know where in the hell she was.

Sitting down on a lichen-covered stone,

she turned out her headlamp. Lost and tired, she was hungry; her arm was killing her. Thugs were killing her friends. She would have lain down where she was and, as the childhood taunt went, eat some worms, but she had appointments.

The pilot.

Reg.

The dude.

FORTY-FOUR

Heath's first coherent thought was absurd: Night falls quickly in the tropics. Her head felt odd; she couldn't see. Not too far away Elizabeth was screaming, "I can carry her. Please."

The dude's "Shut up" was clear and close.

There was a muzzle flash and an explosion of noise, then she had . . . passed out? Fainted from terror? Someone slammed her against a tree? That had to be it. "Hello?" she said feebly.

Her only answer was the racket of many feet tromping through undergrowth. They had taken Elizabeth and gone. Left her for dead. Left in the dark. Was that a movie title? No, that was *Wait Until Dark*. She didn't have to wait. Absolute dark pressed in from every side. Dizziness, without visual spinning or distortion, gave her the sensation she was falling. Grabbing two fistfuls of duff, she held on until she could make herself believe the earth was solid and, once again, she rested atop it. For several seconds she was back beneath the water of the rushing stream, unable to draw breath, not knowing up from down.

Her fingers found a tree trunk she could not see. Hands on rough bark, she dragged herself into a sitting position. That was better; being upright was better. Gravity pulled down. Trees grew up. She was in place in the real world.

Reaching for invisible legs to pull them straight, her hand touched a warm wet patch on her trousers. She'd pissed herself. Who wouldn't? she thought, without rancor. Piss covered her fingers. Piss?

A flash of light and the deafening report of a gun.

The dude shot her.

She didn't feel anything but then, she wouldn't, would she? She had no intention of tasting the stuff. Holding her fingers to her nose, she sniffed. It smelled like metal. When she rubbed her fingers together it became sticky as it dried. Not urine. Blood. She felt around until she found a knee. The wet place was on the outside of her thigh, not the inside.

Tuning in to it, she could sense her lower body telegraphing its eerie version of "May day, may day." There was no pain, no physical sensation that the able-bodied would recognize, but a wave of wrongness so toxic it made the bile rise in her throat that swept through her in a poisonous fog. Maybe she closed her eyes. Who would know. Pressing her palm on the wound, she felt the blood warm and thick.

To bleed to death in the blind dark without feeling a thing; that was pitiful. How would she know when it happened, when she stepped through the veil?

A low airy grunt penetrated her absorption. Something warm and slimy slid along her cheek: monsters, Sean, Jimmy, crawling oozing zombies come to eat her brains. Before she could scream, a cold nose followed the wet tongue.

"Wily," she breathed. Her hands found his head and she wrapped her arms around him, burying her face in his fur. "You came back for me." Holding on to her dog made everything instantly better. Dark was still stygian. Blood still oozed, dripped, or spurted. Elizabeth was still in the hands of vicious men, but with a dog, there was love. With love there was hope. Hope was strength.

"It's not far," she told Wily. Her hand slipped down his back to strike a hard flat object. "What . . ." Wily stood patiently, licking what parts of her his tongue happened on, while she traced the outline. Sensitive as they were, fingers were not eyes. She could not figure out what had been done to Wily. Since whatever it was, Anna must have done it, she left it alone.

Male laughter rippled faintly through the brush.

"We have to go, Wily," Heath whispered. "Without their voices to home in on, I haven't a snowball's chance in hell of heading in the right direction." Her hand struck a water bottle near her thigh. She stuffed it into the front of her jacket.

Sans sight, sensation, and supplies, Heath didn't bother to try to stem the flow of blood. Either she would bleed out or she wouldn't. Ears tuned to the notes of the human voice, she began traveling backward, an inch at a time, palms of her hands on the ground, arms doing the heavy lifting.

Wily was at her feet, at her shoulder, ranging ahead, whining softly in her ears, licking her cheek when she had to stop. Even with his constant encouragement, Heath despaired, but she didn't stop. Not quite as glamorous as dying in the saddle, but she would at least die trying, and with her boots on.

Determination was wavering when she saw the light, literally. A spark of orange no bigger than a firefly flickered when she looked over her shoulder. Lest the disappointment be too great, she told herself it was a hallucination. Several more hard-won feet told her it wasn't. She'd made it to a clearing. A hundred yards or more away, at the opposite end of the field, a fire had been lit.

Heath had no plan. She'd chosen not to die in the dark because of the vague notion that she might somehow be of help to her daughter, even if that help consisted only of letting Elizabeth know that she hadn't died because Elizabeth could no longer carry her. If nothing else, she thought she could lift that burden from E's shoulders.

E was over a hundred yards away.

Glaring at the mocking glow of the campfire, Heath toppled over on her side and lay in the grass. Walking on water was a piece of cake. Inching backward more than a hundred yards would require an actual honest-to-God miracle. Rested, on her best day, in her living room, on the level, clean hardwood, her personal best was ninety-seven feet, two and a half times down the length of the room and back. In a kind world, floored in smooth hardwood, she would still only be able to make it halfway to her daughter.

Sighing noisily, Wily flopped down beside her. She rolled her eyes in his direction. Without the shroud of foliage, she could see him, or the shadow of him, and the glint of his eyes. "Good boy," she whispered automatically. Beyond Wily, hinting at the possibility of a sun in some far distant universe, the thinnest, most niggardly of moons rimed the aluminum of the leading edge of an airplane wing,

Twenty feet? Twenty-five?

By her own math, she should have at least eighty feet left in her repertoire. Heath struggled again to a sitting position, turned her back to the plane, and forced herself an inch closer to it. Twigs and grass collected under her heels as they dragged. Every foot or two, she rested, gathered the sticks and weeds, and stuffed them down the front of her jacket. Every time she stopped, she craned her neck to see over her shoulder. The airplane never seemed to grow closer.

Wily ran reconnaissance toward the plane. He trotted halfway back to the trees to act as rear guard. When she stopped to cry, he mopped her face with his tongue like a boxing manager toweling a fighter's face between rounds.

Her eyes grew accustomed to the meager light. The hard object on his thigh was a splint made from the lid of the first-aid box. Wily must have broken his leg when the dude hurled him against the tree. Anna had rescued him before Sean could finish the job.

Wily seemed scarcely to notice he had only three good legs. Being in open space instead of an endless wrangle of trees and bushes affected both of them positively. Heath breathed more easily. Oxygen, unfiltered through last summer's leaves, gave her new strength. Wily didn't quite disport himself like a puppy, but his gait was less faltering.

Inches became half inches, then quarter inches. Grass and sticks grew into a great belly under her jacket, poking out the neck until she resembled a poorly constructed scarecrow.

Night misted her eyes. A shadow within shades of black. Again she stopped, again looked over her shoulder. The plane was there. Right there. She was beneath the wing.

To prove she'd not slipped the surly bonds of earth and was only imagining the airplane, Heath reached out to touch the wheel cover. Cool smooth aluminum soothed her torn fingers. Sliding her hand beneath the metal, she touched the rubber of the small wheel. As she'd expected, the rubber was hard, unyielding. A hatchet might cut through it, but there was not going to be any poking holes in it with sticks.

During the endless trip across three yards of grass and weeds, Heath had formed a plan. It was simplicity itself. Reaching beneath the aluminum wheel cover, she felt for the air stem. She would uncap it, push the little button, and let the air out. Unless the pilot carried an air pump, two flattened tires would effectively abort takeoff. At least she thought it would.

The inner rim of the tire was smooth. The pilot had fancy Alaskan bushwhacking, tundra rolling, solid rubber things.

"It doesn't matter," she told Wily when he returned, panting, from a foray. "I'm sure the bastard carries an air pump anyway. Plan B." Plan B was neither simple nor foolproof. Don Quixote would have embraced Plan B.

Near the wheel, centered under the pilot's-side door, away from the thugs and their campfire, Heath removed all the sticks and grass she had collected on her journey. Directly above her, housed in the wing, was one of the plane's two gasoline tanks. If she could get a fire high enough, hot enough, it would explode.

Maybe it would explode.

Working mostly by feel, she laid her fire; the driest, finest grasses first, crushed and wadded, then the smaller sticks, then the larger fuel — if twigs one or two feet long and as big around as her thumb could be called such. The pile, which had seemed so enormous when packed in her coat, was pitiful when laid out on the ground. Reaching as far around as she could, she gathered a few more handfuls. Wily lay down nearby. In the wing's shadow, he was invisible, but the sound of his breathing made her feel less alone.

Her socks went on the pyre next. She set her jacket aside, then removed her shirt. With teeth and nails she managed to rip it into several pieces. The pieces went on the pile. In bra and panties, praying to Jesus and Pele, Heath took the lighter from the pocket of her jacket. Two cigarettes remained in the crumpled pack. The pack went on the fire, one cigarette behind her ear, one between her lips. Shifting her thumb on the rough wheel, she struck a light. Before putting it to the cigarette end, she admired it for a second. Light in the darkness, heat, fire was the first magic the gods had shared. According to Anna, gods had long since been banished into myth by churches. According to Paul, that didn't alter the fact that their gift still worked.

Heath sucked in a lungful of smoke, then held the Bic to the pile of grass and sticks. Tiny flames ran out to the ends of the blades of grass and died. Heath twisted the smallest piece of her shirt and lit it. One hundred percent cotton. It burned just fine. Before she'd broken her back, Heath wore synthetic fabrics. During the first year after she lost the use of her legs, she developed a paranoid fear of fire.

On a visit, Anna happened to mention that wildland firefighters wore cotton underpants because natural fibers wouldn't melt into the skin if one were caught in a burn-over. Since that day Heath had become a purist. Paranoia passed, but her panties and bras were still cotton.

Fire devoured the fine fuels with ravening tongues. Heath put her jacket on the blaze, then her pants, then her boots, then her bra. Flames reached no higher than a standing man's waist, and she was down to her skivvies.

The fire died down as quickly as it had flared up. Not once had it climbed anywhere near the wing of the plane where the gas tank was housed. Its puny heat didn't even discolor the aluminum. The gas probably hadn't even gotten warm.

Plan B had failed.

Heath had failed.

Falling flat on her back, she stared at the underside of the wing. She felt like an egg with the meat blown out; the only thing remaining was a thin, fragile shell of skin. Inside her was hollow. Too worn down to feel sorry for herself, she turned her head and, cheek on the grass, stared at the fire she had given her all to build. Knee-high, no bigger around than a basketball, it had begun chewing methodically on her coat and boots.

Heath waited for it to die, and tried to summon up the energy not to die with it. Tilting at windmills. She'd known that from the beginning. Too bad foreknowledge didn't dull the sting of failure.

Flames mesmerized her. Light spiked like the depiction of the star of Bethlehem. She blinked the illusion away. The fire seemed closer. The fire was closer. Flames were spreading. Not in a fierce wave that would destroy the airplane, in a creeping wall of fire scarcely two inches high. An able person would step over it. A clothed person would smother it with a coat. A rested paraplegic would scoot away. The best Heath would manage was swatting at it with bare hands. She wasn't even sure she could sit up again without help.

In the faint and lurid light, she saw Wily rise to his three paws. He lowered his head and growled as if he would attack the flames. As the hungry little grass fire burned toward her, Heath tried to force herself upright. Her arms were made of water. They ignored her brain signals with the numb sullenness of her legs. Muscles would not bunch. Fingers would not bend and claw.

The line of fire was only a couple of feet wide. Behind it was nothing but thin blackened grass, laid flat like the hairs on a balding man's pate. In horrid fascination, Heath watched it creep closer to her side, gnawing its thin blue and orange line. Would her skin catch and char? She didn't think so. A line of blisters, maybe, until the fire reached her underpants. They would catch. Maybe she'd only burn to her bikini line. In desperation she rolled over and tried to wriggle sluglike away from the flames, the rough weedy ground scratching at breasts and belly. Not an inch. Her very bones had gone soft.

Faintly Heath heard — or thought she heard — footsteps. Without further warning, a blinding light slashed across her eyes.

One of the thugs had seen the fire, had come, was here. Fear gave her one last ounce of strength. She used it to snatch up handfuls of dirt. Flinging them at Wily, she cried, "Run, God damn you! Run!"

Like everything else she'd tried to accomplish, she failed at getting rid of the dog, too.

FORTY-FIVE

Buoyed up by the prospect of committing mayhem, Anna strong-armed her tired mind out of its cozy self-pity. In her frantic need to find Heath and Wily, she had ignored the rules of tracking, but she couldn't be very lost. The men, the plane, Heath, open space, had to be within fifteen to thirty yards from where she sat on the rock. Opening ears and nose to the night, she waited for information. A breeze, a mere breath down in the trees, touched her forehead and cheeks. The weather had been blowing in from the northwest. She'd left the old logging camp on the northeast side. Therefore the clearing was on her left.

Heath and the others had been at the northernmost end of the open area. That meant Heath had to be ahead of her and slightly to the left. Rising, Anna turned on her headlamp and waited another minute. Very faintly, to her left and behind, she could hear a sound that was not of the wind or the trees or the night creatures: the uneven yaps of human laughter.

Breathing deeply and evenly, she unearthed patience and concentration. Breeze on her forehead, man-sound behind and to the left, headlamp trained on the forest floor, eyes alert for the smallest of sign, she moved slowly forward.

The spoor that marked the place where the thugs had stopped was not subtle. Suddenly the beam of her light ignited. Red, bright and gorgeous and loud, blood shouted up from the brown of the duff, gleamed in a great glorious ruby pool. Freshly spilled blood, still humming with color and life, was beautiful. Few appreciated it. When not sealed tightly in living containers, blood was jarring. Splashed across leaves and rocks it was obscene, graffiti profaning sacred ground.

Following smears of red, Anna quickly rewon the edge of the logging camp. While still in the trees, she turned off her headlamp, then flipped the lens so it rested on her forehead. Cloaked in darkness, she stepped from cover.

She had fully expected to see Heath in the dimly lighted expanse, but there was no woman, no dog. At the far end of the old camp, the thugs' fire burned cheerily. Several yards away from where she stood, the plane squatted, sinister with the promise of abduction. Cigarette smoke trickled through the breeze to Anna's nose. Mixed with it was the unmistakable odor of burning vegetation. Under the near wing of the small plane, screened from the thugs by the wheels, a blue snake of creeping flame curled out of the darkness, a tendril alive and seeking. Thrashing between the small horns of the fiery reconnaissance line was a dark form.

Anna ran lightly over the ground to duck under the shadow of the wing. The firelight showed her Heath, naked except for a pair of white panties with bits of grass stuck to them, floundering feebly, like a fish too long out of water. From hip to ankle, her left leg was drenched in blood. As ineffectual as a newborn baby, she was trying to drag herself from the reaching flames.

Wily, a growl rumbling in his shaggy chest, was lunging awkwardly, staggering and snapping at the line of fire. He made a strangled sound, then a stumbling rush at Anna. His teeth bit down on her ankle.

"It's me, doggone it!" Anna hissed. "Let go. Goddammit, it's me!" She turned on her light. It hit Heath, and she let out a mousy squeak, then began to keen. Wily bit down harder.

"Stop it," Anna snapped at the dog. She pulled the light out on its elastic band and aimed it down onto her face. "It's me." The keening didn't cease.

Anna removed Jimmy's hat.

"Thank God," Heath breathed, and her face hit the grass as she passed out or dropped dead.

Wily unlocked his jaws.

"About time," Anna muttered. Again she turned off the headlamp. The aluminum skin of the plane responded to the halogen light with silver lightning bolts. Somebody was bound to notice.

"And you damn well owe me one," she added as Wily's chagrined muzzle winked into shadow. Half hangdog, half cocky, he hobbled over and sat next to Heath. Hoping the moose hide was still intact on her moccasins, Anna began stomping out the flickering orange and blue line. From his mistress's side Wily watched closely until the last of the enemy had been crushed into the soil.

The main part of the fire had shrunk to the size of a softball; still, it was too big and too hot for Anna to trust her moccasins to it. First things first, she told herself.

"Move over," she ordered the dog as she knelt next to Heath. Being as gentle as she could with only one functional arm, Anna rolled Heath onto her back. Her skin was cool to the touch, eyes half closed, mouth slack. Her hands fluttered as if she were trying to help.

Anna bent down and put her lips against Heath's ear. "Can you hear me?"

"It's me, doggone it." Heath's words were so slurred as to be almost unintelligible.

Anna laughed quietly. Heath didn't respond. Heath hadn't been trying to lighten the mood; she just echoed Anna's words. Even if she didn't bleed to death from the bullet the dude or Reg put in her leg, Heath was not out of danger. Hypothermia, trauma, hunger, thirst, exhaustion: The thugs had created the perfect recipe for shock. Anna had treated dozens of cases, but few had had all the deadly ingredients.

Mouth still next to Heath's ear, Anna murmured, "We can't stay here. I have to have light." With that announcement of misery to come, she tried to manhandle Heath into the fireman's carry she'd used on Jimmy. Though Heath was twenty pounds lighter than the bearded thug, using only one arm Anna couldn't lift her the eighteen inches needed to pull her into place.

Heath moaned.

Wily whimpered grievously.

"You didn't whimper when I got shot," Anna whispered acerbically. Wily said nothing.

Working quickly, Anna shoved Sean's knife through her belt, then let the purloined coat slide off her shoulders. The fabric adhered to the blood on her upper arm. Gritting her teeth so hard she heard her jaw crack, she tugged the left sleeve down. The coat fell to the ground, exposing an arm black with dried blood. With no pocket except that in her trousers, Anna tucked the hand at the end of her injured arm in the waistband of her pants. It wasn't as good a sling as the sleeve and pocket had proven, but it would reduce movement and pain.

Working awkwardly, she spread the coat on the ground. "Sorry, soon over, here we go," she muttered as she rolled Heath onto the coat and arranged her in a fetal position. "Hug your knees. Hang on," she told Heath and, clutching the cuffs of both sleeves in her right fist, inch by inch, began dragging the coat with its burden toward the tree line.

"No," Heath gasped. "Feed the fire . . .

reach the gas tank."

Fuel to build up the fire was too far away, too hard to find in the dark.

"Never mind," Anna said. "After we get you situated, I'll get in the cockpit and start slashing wires. I'm bound to bust some-thing."

Every time the coat jerked over a rough spot, Anna worried Heath would cry out. When she didn't, Anna worried she'd killed her.

"Am I hurting you?" she asked.

"I don't feel . . . right," Heath managed.

Anna doubted any of them, including the thugs, was feeling right.

Inch by inch.

Finally, they reached the safety of the trees. Letting go of the sleeves, Anna fell back on her butt. Jarred into grievance, the bullet wound sent waves of nausea to her stomach. Wily nosed his head under her good arm. "Don't worry, buddy. I'm not quitting on Heath. Slave driver," she added, turning on her headlamp to assess Heath's injuries.

"Shot in the thigh," Anna began her cataloguing. Using half of her water and the cuff of Jimmy's coat, she sponged away the blood. "Neat entry. Didn't hit the femoral artery."

Heath made a whuffing sound uncannily like Wily's laugh.

"Right," Anna said. "You'd be dead. I don't think the bullet broke any bones. I don't know how shock works when you can't feel pain, but a broken femur registers in all other systems. Let's roll you onto your side.

"Exit wound is a nasty bugger — that's medical jargon. I don't expect you to understand it," Anna said and was rewarded by another whuff. "You lost a chunk of meat about the size of a baby's fist. Still bleeding, but not gushing." There was no point in listing the minor damages. Knowing how scraped, punctured, and bruised her legs and feet were would only serve to increase anxiety and worsen shock.

Using Jimmy's knife, Anna hacked and tore the lining out of the coat and fashioned a pressure bandage around Heath's thigh. One-armed, she piled up duff and leaves to make a soft bed, raised and warmer than bare ground, then wrapped Heath in the coat. Jimmy's coat only covered her halfway down to her knees. Her poor pale legs cold and bare, she resembled a red-and-black all-day sucker on a white stick.

"Lie down next to her," Anna told Wily. "Share your heat."

Wily shot her an aggrieved look that suggested he was going to do that anyway, then lay down alongside his mistress.

Anna was building up more leaves to elevate and protect Heath's legs when eerie high-pitched notes tickled through the trees, seeking out her ears and their whereabouts.

"Whistling," Anna realized. Her father whistled like that when he was deep in thought, building houses in his mind or laying fence line. "Whistling through his teeth," she said. She laid the headlamp near Heath.

"Wait here," she whispered to Wily, then silently slipped out of the trees. Despite having the cold tuneless whistle to guide her, it took a moment to locate the source. It manifest as the burning end of a cigarette floating through the air fifty feet or so from the airplane.

"Anything?" came a yell, weak with distance, but clear in the crisp air of the autumn night.

"Must have left a butt unstomped," was the shouted response.

The thugs had finally spotted the tiny fire behind the plane's wheels. Fortunately, the pilot attributed it to not putting out his cigarette properly.

The circle of orange vanished. He'd

turned his back.

"When I holler, you hold the flashlight for me," he shouted. "I'm going to taxi her up near the fire. She's getting lonesome out here." The burning cigarette end re-appeared, followed by the crunching shuf-fling of a man walking without sufficient light.

Behind the red ember, Anna was begin-ning to make out the shape of the smoker. He was less than twenty feet from the plane. Once the machine was parked near the thugs' camp, there would be no jimmying open of doors and cutting wires. Come daylight, the plane would lift off with Eliza-beth, Leah, and Katie.

Anna slipped Sean's overgrown knife from the belt of her trousers. Clutching it in her fist, she sprinted toward the oncoming figure. Running on pure instinct and adrenaline, no thoughts sullied her mind or slowed her reflexes.

She was on him before he realized she existed. Knife tucked firmly against her side beneath her arm, blade pointed behind her, she curled up like a sow bug and rolled into the man's legs. Hard boot leather ripped into her ear. Her injured shoulder shrieked through her bones that she was going to die. Eyesight dimmed.

With a startled "Huh?" the pilot flew ass over teakettle. The thud when he hit the ground was loud enough to be encouraging. Back on her feet, Anna staggered for the airplane, her balance out of whack, her vision doubled. The edge of the wing and the pointed tip of one wheel cover were limned in silver, rendered visible by light ten million years old. It occurred to her she probably should have killed the pilot, but in her condition it wouldn't have been a sure thing.

"Hey! Hey, goddammit! Get me some help down here. You! Get away from that! Touch her and I swear to Christ I'll cut your balls off and feed them to the pigs."

Anna was so close she could have reached out and touched the propeller when he caught her. A huge hand closed on her upper arm. Ruined flesh crushed the bullet into her ulna. Agony drove her to her knees. She willed nerveless fingers not to drop the knife. A boot slammed into her ribs, knocking her to her side. Using the force of the kick and the fall, she rolled beneath the airplane's engine, into the triangle between the nose and side wheels. Disoriented, she tried to crawl from under the plane, sticking her head out at the precise place where the pilot was standing.

A boot ricocheted off her temple. Swinging her head the way a bull does when deciding whom to gore first, she fixed on the barely flickering light from Heath's fire — no bigger than a baseball, and the flames so few she could count them — and wormed toward it.

The flames were less than a foot from her nose when she squirmed from beneath the plane. Using the wheel and the side of the fuselage, she clawed her way to her feet. The knife was still held tightly in her hand. Bracing her right forearm against the pilot's window, she stepped up the fourteen inches to the top of the aluminum wheel cover. In order to retain her balance, she reached for the strut with her left hand.

The arm was finished. It moved only a few inches. Her fingers would not flex. Had she been able to reach the strut, she couldn't grip it. She needed two good hands, one to anchor herself and one to wield the knife.

"Come out of there," the pilot shouted. "I'm going to break you in so many pieces you'll have to be vacuumed up. Help! Get me some help down here!"

Boot leather thudded on aluminum as the pilot kicked and poked under the nose of the plane, trying to locate the intruder.

"What you got?" Reg.

"Get me some light," the pilot yelled. "Bring the flashlight, God damn it!"

"Keep your fuckin' pants on, man." Reg's voice was closer. He was coming to see what the fracas was about; Reg with a Walther PPK.

Once light hit her, a bullet would hit her, or a man would hit her. Anyway she looked at it, she had about three seconds to live.

Anna put the blade of the knife between her teeth. Leaning against the cabin for support, she grabbed her wounded arm with her good hand and lifted the miserable screaming thing upward until her wrist reached the V between the top of the strut and the wing. With a scream, she jammed her wrist until the bones were wedged tight between the metal of the strut and the underside of the wing.

The arm stabilized her.

Pain had gone beyond pain into a blanketing wave, the precursor of unconsciousness. Before she could succumb, she clutched the hilt of the knife in her right hand, then stabbed upward with every ounce of strength she could muster.

The plane's aluminum skin was thin. Dull as it was, Sean's knife pierced it.

"Thankyoubabyjesus," Anna murmured.

Liquid trickled down her arm. The dangerous, sweet smell of gas burned in her nose. The drip was slow; by the time the fumes reached the fire and ignited, she would have pried her wrist from its trap and be halfway back to the woods.

A flashlight beam cut a slash of silver from the trailing edge of the wing, then a dusty swath across her belly.

"He's after the goddam airplane!" the pilot shouted.

Screaming down the pain like a wounded panther, Anna wrenched the handle of the knife, twisting the blade. Gasoline gushed out, pouring down her arm and shoulders.

Roaring wordlessly, the pilot slammed into her. Her wrist tore free from the strut. Her feet were knocked from their perch. Airborne, her body flew a dozen feet before it smashed to the ground.

A whoosh of air and blinding light illuminated the underside of the wing and the fuselage. Waving his arms and shrieking the way Anna had seen a hundred stuntmen do in a hundred movies, the pilot emerged from the glare, a man of fire, hands, head, arms made of flames.

A column of fire sprouted from beneath the burning man's feet and rose to envelop the wing. The gas tank exploded; shrapnel comprised of seared flesh, fire, and aluminum washed over Anna on a tidal wave of superheated air.

FORTY-SIX

They were encamped in what Leah believed was an old equipment shed. Three and a half walls were still standing. The corners were piled with rubble that undoubtedly housed all manner of vermin. A fire blazed where a fourth wall had faced out on the long clearing. Compared with their previous bivouacs, it was warm, almost cozy.

Expecting, perhaps, to have to spend a day or two weathered in at the camp with what he believed was four thugs and four hostages, the pilot had stocked the larder well. For two thugs and three hostages, even after the men had had their fill, there was an absolute cornucopia. Leah thought she was too tired to eat, that she didn't have the energy to lift food to her mouth, let alone chew it. The smell of cold pork and beans changed her mind.

Lunch's sandwiches, the only food they'd had in thirty-six hours, should have gone into shrunken stomachs and kept them full all day. Instead, it reminded their stomachs how wonderful food was. Leah's had started screaming for more within the hour.

Because Heath would have done it, Leah was careful to see that the girls got fed before she ate anything. It wasn't that she was a bad person, she knew that. Well, perhaps she was a bad person. No one knew what her progenitors' genetics had been. Clearly, since they'd abandoned her the day she was born, they didn't have strong parenting instincts. Leah was not accustomed to having the responsibility for feeding others. She was barely accustomed to feeding herself. Food was something a lab tech sometimes left on the workbench, and if she remembered, sometimes she ate it.

With Heath dead none of them believed they should be so callous as to be hungry. Especially Elizabeth, Leah could tell. Young, resilient, she couldn't help herself and so she ate, but shame kept her eyes downcast.

Since the dude had shot her mother, Elizabeth had either cried silently or, judging by the expressions that rotated across her face, blamed herself for being unable to carry Heath any farther, or plotted revenge on the dude.

Or so Leah surmised. Reading other

people's emotions was another chore she was not accustomed to performing for herself. Not a chore, she corrected herself, an art form. Like drafting. Except not at all like drafting.

After she'd rested she'd be better able to think.

Katie plowed into the food with the pragmatism of her father. Gerald did have emotions. He loved his daughter. Leah thought he liked her well enough. Courting Leah, he'd said he loved her. Leah believed it then. He'd never crushed her heart, never announced he no longer loved her, never had loved her. The truth came slowly, delivered in endless thoughtful kindnesses. Acts of service that masqueraded as love. Not until Leah had seen the genuine adoration in his eyes when Katie was born had she known that what he gave her was an imitation of love.

There had been sadness. Then there was work. Gerald took care of Katie. If he saw her now, hands bound with plastic ties, pouring canned peaches into her mouth between bites of a cinnamon roll — the individually wrapped kind they sell at the cash register in convenience stores — he would be running for wild-caught blueberries to counteract the toxins.

Picking out a round of sliced wiener with filthy fingers and stuffing it into her mouth, Leah realized she and the girls were in a kind of feeding frenzy. Not only were their bodies in need of fuel, there was always the fear the food would be snatched away.

"Hey! Hey, goddammit!" the pilot shouted over the distance between the camp and the plane. "Get me some help down here. You! Get away from that! Touch her and I swear to Christ I'll cut your balls off and feed them to the pigs."

Leah and the girls stopped midswallow. As one, they stood, trying for a better view. The far end of the field was shrouded in darkness, the voice of the pilot small with distance, but shriller, more alarmed than before.

"See what he wants," the dude said to Reg. Reg was leaning against one wall of the ruin, using his jackknife to scrape the last smear of deviled ham from a small tin. Having already consumed enough to send a teenaged boy into shock, Leah assumed it was more for amusement than sustenance.

"It's too fuckin' dark, man." The nonchalance was strained. He didn't raise his eyes from his ham project, didn't want the dude to see he was scared to go.

The dude picked up the flashlight and

tossed it to him. Reg glanced up in time to catch it before it banged into his head.

For several seconds the two men stared at one another. The dude's carp eyes won. Reg clicked the light on. Black clothes were sucked into black night and he vanished quickly as he walked out of the camp toward the plane. What remained was swathes of unexpected green scythed from the ground by the flashlight.

"Bring the flashlight, God damn it!" The pilot was screaming, high-pitched and angry.

"Keep your fuckin' pants on, man," Reg said.

"He's after the goddam airplane!" the pilot shouted furiously.

With herd instinct, Leah and the girls closed ranks and stood shoulder to shoulder watching the blank screen of darkness. "Anna trying to disable the plane," Leah whispered almost inaudibly. Elizabeth nodded. Her eyes welled with tears. Anna had not saved her mother. That had to be hard. Elizabeth talked about Anna as if she were Superwoman, then Anna had let Heath die. What good was the death of thugs or the salvage of Katie's innocence if she could do nothing to keep Heath alive?

The black box theater blew into shocking

life. Darkness shattered into the shape of a man on fire, a creature of fire, crying high and wild and waving its arms. A human torch staggering like a mummy, reaching for an end to pain or a victim for it. Leah placed a hand on either side of Katie's face. She tried to turn her head so she wouldn't see. Katie shook free. Leah didn't try again. She could not tear her eyes away either.

"Holy Mary Mother of God," breathed the dude. Jimmy's rifle in one hand, the Colt in the other, he walked to the edge of the firelight.

Shots rang out. The pilot hadn't had a gun, not one Leah could see. Reg was firing at someone or something. Anna. He had to be shooting at Anna. He was bellowing as he pulled the trigger.

Leah could see nothing but the burning thing. Once human, eaten by fire, it staggered several steps, then turned, the fiery face seeming to look straight into the camp. Behind it fire shot up from the ground, forming a column underneath the airplane wing. Then the plane exploded, a star-blast of fire. The creature was blown to its knees. There were no more cries. In absolute silence, it toppled over. The flames were smothered, but for an eerie blue running across the downed form, painting the shape

427

of a man. Behind him the plane had gone almost dark. The explosion stealing air from the flame.

"Momma," Katie said. Her eyes were beseeching. Leah had no idea what to say or do. She looked around for Elizabeth.

Elizabeth was not there. She had used the moment of the dude's distraction to get to the end of the truncated wall. On silent feet, she was slipping around the end to where she could escape into the night, then into the forest.

Leah should have thought of this. She should have thought to send Katie. For half a breath, she hated Elizabeth for not taking Katie with her. It was an ignoble hate. There'd not been time. There wasn't time now.

A flicker of shadow gone wrong caught in the corner of the dude's eye. Quick as a cobra strike, his head snapped around. "Stop!" he yelled. The pistol came up, straight and level and aimed at Elizabeth's retreating back.

Leah hurled the half-eaten can of beans she still held in her hands.

The beans struck him in the chest, splattering under his chin and down the front of his coat. Sending out a shower of wood chips, his bullet smacked into a rotten board where Elizabeth had been standing a second before. Elizabeth was gone, hidden by the darkness. They could hear the sound of her footsteps as she ran into the safety of the woods.

Face dead with rage, the dude turned the gun on Leah.

Utter stillness descended. With it, unexpectedly, clarity. Total clarity of mind: Leah had not known her mind was fogged, but it had been for years and years. Intricate puzzles, schematics, and plans had filled it like cobwebs filling an abandoned house. Ideas and numbers ran along the strands of the web. She shepherded them, pruned them, deleted them, perfected them. Never was her mind still.

Life had gone on largely unnoticed outside of the laboratory in her skull. Equations hooded her eyes; their mathematical music stuffed her ears. On this trip, in spite of the monsters stalking her and Katie and Heath, Leah had clogged her mind with remaking the wheelchair, with clever mechanical scenarios. When those had been ground into dust, she lapsed into a mental silence, a dead spider on a dead web full of dead flies.

At this moment, with this gun pointed at her and Katie, her child, her daughter, Leah could see and hear and think with stunning lucidity. She felt as if she'd awakened from a long, complicated dream.

"Sit down, Katie," Leah told her daughter calmly. "Finish your dinner." Stunned into instant obedience, Katie sat and, though she didn't eat, picked up the sliced peaches and held the can between her hands.

"There's no point now," Leah said to the dude. "Without the plane you can't transport us. You'll be caught. Killing us would serve no purpose."

"There's a purpose," he stated flatly.

Before Leah could ask what, or the dude could shoot her, Reg came hurtling into the firelight, gasping and gesturing wildly with his silvery pistol. "Man, Dude, this shit isn't right. There is some kind of bad goin' on, like sewer-stink bad. Fuckin' Jimmy and the fuckin' dog and Sean and shit. This is bad, Dude. We gotta get the fuck out of here."

Foam, lit by the flames, showed in orange specks at the corners of his mouth. His hands flopped as if strings attached to them were being plucked by a tone-deaf harpist.

"Who did you shoot?" the dude asked.

"What the fuck? You listening to me? We got no plane, Dude. We got no fuckin' plane! We got to get out of here. Do the hostages, and get the fuck out."

"There'll be a plane," the dude said. "Who

did you shoot?"

Reg's face blanked with confusion. "What the fuck you talkin' about, man? I ain't shot shit. This is like insane, Dude."

"Did someone else fire those four shots?" This time there was concern in the dude's tone.

"Nobody shot shit, Dude, I'm telling you."

"You mean you didn't hit anything?" the dude asked.

"Like I said, man, I didn't hit shit. That was crazy stuff. This thing all fire like in the comics."

"So you shot at the thing of fire?" the dude asked.

"Shit, yes! What a fucking nightmare." Walther in hand, Reg threw himself to the ground beside the boxes of provisions the pilot had brought. He pulled out a bottle of Jim Beam and unscrewed the cap. "Fuck you," he said to the dude and took a long pull.

"That 'thing of fire' was our pilot," the dude said.

"Yeah? Well, fuck him. I did him a fucking favor." Reg drank again. Leah waited for the dude to shoot him. The dude always disappointed.

"The cripple's child is out there," the dude said. "Got away during the festivities.

You see her, shoot her. Either one of these two moves, shoot them. You got that, Reg?"

"I got it," Reg said. He took another long drink.

"Cap it," the dude said softly.

Reg screwed the cap back on the bottle and set it carefully in the cardboard box as if afraid it would tip over and spill its precious contents.

"Where is the flashlight?" the dude asked.

"How the fuck should I know?" Reg mumbled.

He must have dropped it when he'd fired at the burning man, then run like a deer back toward the fire. At least Leah hoped it was a man, hoped the burning figure was not Anna. Surely, if the pilot wasn't dead, he would have called out. Of course, Anna could have killed the pilot somehow, then accidentally lit herself on fire trying to sabotage the airplane.

"Right," the dude said. "How the fuck would you know anything?"

Tucking the .22 Winchester under his arm, the dude stepped toward Reg. Reg flinched like a dog expecting a slap. Reaching past him, the dude lifted up the pilot's jacket. It was vintage World War II, horsehide, with cracked and fading patches. To wear a jacket like that in a tiny airplane put

Leah in mind of a lab tech she'd worked with who wore full motorcycle leathers when he rode his 49 cc scooter to work.

From one of the inside pockets, the dude fished out an iPhone. Having pushed a number of digits with his thumb, he waited a few seconds, then said, "Send another plane, *Mr. Big.* Later. Just do it, Bernie." He pushed the disconnect, slid the phone into the pocket of his coat, then retrieved the rifle from under his arm. The Colt had never left his right hand.

Again with rifle in one hand and pistol in the other, like a figure on a poster from an old cowboy movie, the dude turned his back on the lot of them and faced into the night.

Leah had lost the appetite she'd thought so insatiable a few minutes before. Katie had as well. "Reg, can we move back and lean against that wall?" Leah asked, indicating the wall Elizabeth had slipped around the end of.

"I don't give a shit. You get up on your hind legs, though, and I blow you away," Reg snapped.

"Thank you," Leah said. That she was genuinely grateful annoyed her, but she was. "Come on, Katie-did." It was the pet name she'd called her daughter when she was only one or two years old. She hadn't thought of it in a long time. Katie remembered; her face lit up. Through the dirt and misery, she smiled as sweetly as she had when she was little.

Careful to crawl and stay low, Leah and Katie moved the few feet to the wall. Leah leaned back and stretched her legs. To her surprise, Katie backed up to her. Tentatively, Leah slipped her bound wrists over her child's head, let her arms drop around the narrow shoulders, and hugged Katie to her chest.

Katie snuggled in. Leah was in awe of how much comfort her daughter was to her.

FORTY-SEVEN

The neighbor's dog was barking. Anna found it amazing that dogs never got hoarse. They could bark for hours, days on end, and never wear down their vocal cords. This dog had been barking forever. Not a vicious come-near-and-I'll-bite bark, this was a welcome-home-I'm-so-happy-I-could-die bark. Anna could not remember a time when this dog had not been barking.

Giving in to the inevitable, she opened her eyes. She had no idea where she was. Whether her dog Taco was barking, or where her bedroom window was. Frightened, she tried to picture her house. Various permutations of park housing, much of it similar, stirred together in her mind without jelling.

She'd dreamed her husband was dead.

Zach was dead. It wasn't a dream.

A whiff of something acrid startled her nose. Smelling salts?

Zach had died over twenty years before.

Paul Davidson, she was married to Paul Davidson. *Paul was not dead.*

Intense relief flooded her mind. She was lying on the ground somewhere in Minnesota, staring at a distant spark of light, a campfire, and Paul was not dead. The near distance quivered and shuddered as if there were a rift in the time-space continuum. Whatever that was.

Then it clicked into place. The fight, the burning man, the explosion. The pilot had knocked her clear of the Cessna before the fire reached the gas tank. That she still lived attested to the fact that there couldn't have been much gasoline left in the rubber bladder in the wing. The shudder of air was heat rising from the wreckage.

Other than alive, she didn't know how she fared. Without moving, she started to take inventory, then gave it up. There was no part of her body that did not hurt. Starting slowly, with her fingers, she attempted movement. Her left arm was uppermost. Moving those fingers caused her bicep to remind her, before she'd been blown up, she'd been shot. Her right arm was underneath her. Feet worked. Knees bent. Hip joints rotated. Head moved up and down and side to side.

Gathering her shredded courage, Anna managed a sitting position. Her face hurt. Burned, she guessed, but not badly. Her eyelashes were singed. The stench of burning hair — smelling salts — had helped bring her around. Her feet were bare. She'd been knocked out of her moccasins. Where her socks had gone was a mystery.

The dog quit barking.

Wily quit barking. Of course it was Wily. Anna had left him with Heath minutes ago. Hours ago. She hadn't the slightest idea how long she had been out. There was no sign of dawn. The sliver of a moon was still about where it had been when she'd come to disable the plane. Maybe half an hour, forty-five minutes.

Why hadn't the thugs found her? Reg was afraid of the dark, but he had a flashlight. The dude didn't act like he was afraid of anything. The sight of the burning man might have changed that.

Burned alive.

Anna felt acid rise from her stomach. Leaning to the side, she vomited it out. Had the man not slammed into her, she would have been the thing of fire. I didn't kill him, she told herself. Jimmy, Sean — I killed them. I did not burn the pilot to death. I never lit a human being on fire.

In truth, she hadn't. Truth didn't matter in the long run. The burning pilot was seared on her soul. She wanted to pour this out to Paul, wanted to see the endless kindness in his hazel eyes, the redemption in his smile. She wanted him so badly she hurt inside as much as she did outside, her lungs and heart swollen and aching.

She was rocking.

That was a bad sign. Rocking back and forth. Like a depressed person. Like a very depressed person. A seriously mentally ill individual. She stopped herself immediately.

"Anna." Her name was breathed on a cold wind from the north. A windigo was whispering, calling her to dinner. "Anna." It was walking up behind her on its burned stumps of feet. Heath couldn't walk. "Anna."

Scissoring her legs and pushing with her good arm, Anna fought to rise. Hands closed on her upper arms, crushing the bullet under the flesh.

Anna fainted.

When she came to, a face without a body floated over her, glowing almost blue. In an instant, it vanished.

"I'msorryMomtoldmeyouwereshotIforgot." Anna heard that. Her mind took it in, poked it a few times. "I'm sorry. Mom told me you were shot. I forgot." Mom. Forgot Anna

438

had been shot in the arm. Anna had left her headlamp with Heath. The face was E's. Must be she was still dreaming. Heath could not have rescued Elizabeth. Heath could barely hold her head up. Yet Elizabeth had the headlamp.

"Elizabeth?"

"I got away."

The pride in the girl's voice went a long way toward making Anna glad she'd regained consciousness. Elizabeth had escaped the thugs; she'd found her mother. "Good girl," Anna said. "Very good girl."

Elizabeth took hold of Anna's uninjured arm and helped her to her feet. "Are you okay?" the girl asked, keeping her voice a bare whisper.

"I assume you mean relatively speaking," Anna replied. "Your hands are still tied together."

"This plastic is made of kryptonite or something. I hope you have the knife," Elizabeth said.

Anna swayed, and E held her steady. Seeing would have helped. She could have kept herself parallel with the trees and perpendicular to the ground. In total darkness, her inner ears out of whack from the blast, she was having trouble keeping her balance. "I did have the knife," she said when the invisible world quit spinning. "Maybe I still do. Look around, but watch the light. I don't think your mom and I have much running left in us tonight."

Elizabeth turned the light on, carefully shading it with her cupped hands, and, on her knees, followed the tiny spotlight she aimed. Light helped. Anna felt better seeing E's face in the reflected glow, the warm red of her fingers, the shadow of the bones beneath the flesh. Life.

The light illuminated a moccasin. A few feet away, Elizabeth located its mate. Anna slipped them on. A deadly Indian from the Arapaho Autumn; if clothes made the man, shoes made the woman.

The knife did not reveal itself. Anna sent E to see if there were any desirable sharp or pointed pieces of wreckage they might fashion into a weapon. Ideally, Anna would have gone with her, but since the act of remaining upright was taxing her abilities, she felt E would be better off alone.

Elizabeth returned with a couple of promising-looking shards of metal. Anna accepted the offer of her arm and leaned on her as she led the way back to where Wily and Heath were hidden in the trees.

"Thank God," Heath said when they returned. "The sky went nuclear, then shots, then nothing. I thought you were dead. I thought we were all dead."

"Almost," Anna said as she slumped to the ground at Heath's feet. She took them onto her lap to warm them. Even though Heath couldn't feel it, there could be no harm in warming the blood headed back up to her friend's heart.

"Elizabeth got away," Heath said. The pride in her voice cheered Anna somewhat.

"So I noticed."

"She just slithered out when the plane exploded," Heath said.

"Smart," Anna managed. Concentrating on what Heath said was hard. Speaking in whispers was hard. Being cold in the dark was hard. "It's a hard life," Anna said.

"First thing she did was come looking for me," Heath said.

Anna wished somebody who didn't want to kill her would come looking for her.

"Wily found me," Elizabeth said fondly.

Elizabeth had set the headlamp on the ground. Between her feet, she held a strip of torn aluminum. From the shape of it, Anna guessed it was once part of a strut. Wily lay beside E, his chin on her thigh, watching her saw at the plastic.

"Good old Wily," Anna said. At the sound of his name the dog raised his eyes. Anna

441

looked into them. The darks were darker and the amber more golden in the lamp's light. "Hey," she said.

The dog gazed at her. He seemed to scarcely notice her.

"Wily?" Anna felt panic swell in her chest.

The dog turned his eyes to the face of his mistress as she sawed at her bonds.

The Wily of the woods, Anna's comrade in arms, was gone. This was just a dog. A good dog, but just a dog. Anna almost howled with loneliness. Had she been crazy for a while? If she had, she liked the part of crazy with Wily. Crazy. Killing men and running with wolves.

More battles had to be fought. No time to mourn fallen comrades. Whether or not they really existed.

Prying her eyes from the dog's devotion to his young mistress, she asked, "How are you doing with the ties?"

"Slow," Elizabeth said, "but coming."

"What do we do now?" Heath asked, a thread of sound from the murky shadows.

"Kill the dude and Reg," Anna said wearily.

"That's cold," Heath said.

"Yes."

"I'm okay with it," Elizabeth said.

"Without the plane, my guess is the dude

will try to take Katie and Leah out the logging road to wherever they left their vehicle,
then make a run for it. That or murder
them, bury the bodies, and write off the
ransom," Anna said.

"The pilot had a satellite phone," Elizabeth said. "The dude called somebody
named Mr. Big." She snorted her derision.

"Damn," Anna said. "If he has a phone,
he can get another plane. Soon as it's light,
the guy could land."

"We are so screwed," said Heath.

"Not yet," Anna said. She said it for Elizabeth. Personally, she thought Heath was
right. "Anybody have water?"

"I do. The dude left it next to my body,"
Heath said.

"What a sweetheart." Anna accepted the
bottle and drank. Life-giving, that was the
right description for water. Life poured
down her ashy throat and she was renewed.
Still damaged and miserable, but capable of
believing they had a chance. Where there
was life, there was a chance. "Anybody have
any idea how long until dawn?" she asked.

"It has to be soon," Elizabeth said. "I
don't think nights are this long in Anchor-
age in January. Got it!" She held her freed
hands up in the faint glow to show them
off, then turned out the headlamp, plung-

ing them into the total lightlessness of a cave at midnight.

"You have the strength of ten men," Anna said.

"I ate," Elizabeth admitted with audible embarrassment.

"Good," Anna said. "Times like these, eat when you can and rest when you can. Like we used to say fighting fire: If you can stand, you can sit. If you can sit, you can lie down. If you can lie down, lie down in the shade."

A small gray-blue square appeared bobbing like swamp gas over Heath's chest. Anna watched it wondering if it was a harbinger of further madness.

"It's five fifteen," Heath said. "Sun should be up in less than two hours."

Heath had found the cell phone in the pocket of Jimmy's coat. Before Anna could ask, she said, "One bar, no coverage. Clock works, though."

The dude had a satellite phone. For all they knew he could have called in the marines. Hordes of barbarians could be skulking up the logging road with Uzis and flamethrowers.

Between them, Anna, Elizabeth, Heath, and Wily had five good arms, seven good legs, one set of pointy teeth, a sharp-edged chunk of twisted aluminum, and a clock.

444

"We're all set," Anna said and closed her eyes.

FORTY-EIGHT

Charles poured two fingers of Jim Beam into one of the little waxed paper cups from the box. Lifting it slightly, he toasted the pilot.

Toasted the pilot.

The grim humor would have pleased him, had he been in a mood to be pleased. Charles had worked jobs before where the best-laid schemes gang agley, as Brother Sebastian used to say. If one stayed long in this business, it was inevitable, but he'd never worked a job as screwy as this one.

Jimmy missing, Sean killed, the pilot in flames, howling of wolves and seeing of ghosts: This was one for the record books. Charles had no doubt that demons were real. Jesus Christ himself saw and dealt with demons. The Bible was unequivocal on the demon issue. Demons did exist, did possess people and, on occasion, animals. Even if the Bible hadn't gone into such detail regarding demons, Charles knew from experience that that much was true. He also knew it was rare in the modern world. Not because demons had gone the way of the dodo and the passenger pigeon. Demons walked the streets and rode the subways in greater numbers than at any time in previous history.

Thy name is legion, Charles thought and sipped his whiskey.

Possession was rare in modern times because demons had no need to possess a resisting soul anymore. Millions of souls were awaiting with arms outstretched to welcome demons in. Why go mano a mano with Max von Sydow when boys with automatic weapons are just begging for a chance to slaughter little children by the score?

Jimmy, James R. Spinks, forty-one years of age, out of Detroit, Michigan, IQ of 84, walks out of camp, never walks back in. Charles assumed he'd gotten lost in the dark. The eerie noises could have been anything. Loons, coons, hyenas, whatever passed for wildlife in these woods. Tonight there'd been a dog barking, or a coyote, a fox, a wolf. Charles didn't know if wolves and coyotes barked like dogs or only howled. The noises could have been Jimmy in a panic. Who cared. No Jimmy was a blessing. The wolves were welcome to his stinking carcass.

Reginald Waters, ex-gangbanger, low-end drug dealer, con man, into bookies for a hundred and seventy-three grand, says he has seen Jimmy's ghost as well as the dog, whose bones had snapped audibly when Charles smashed him into the tree, and seen him wearing a Superman cape, no less. Unlike Jimmy, Reg wasn't borderline retarded, but he'd found something that scared him more than the collectors his bookie was going to send after him if he didn't come up with the cash. Reg had reached that level of terror where men gibbered. Charles had been the instrument of that kind of terror often enough to recognize it. Under the influence of all-consuming fear, nothing a man — or woman — said could be trusted.

Sean Ferris, small-time muscle. Philadelphia, Chicago, then Detroit. Rapist. The Hendricks child said Jimmy smashed in Sean's head with a stone, then tried to lure her into the big bad woods at night.

That was three; three times Jimmy had appeared.

Three might matter. Christ rose in three days, appeared to the apostles three times.

One possibility was that it was Jimmy. Not the oaf who couldn't remember which was his drink cup and which was his spit cup, but a demon-possessed Jimmy who could appear and disappear at will.

Demons.

The pilot, on fire, burning man, arms out like the holy cross; that was sufficiently demonic to set a nun's rosary to quivering.

However, what self-respecting demon would possess Jimmy Spinks's sorry self? And to what end? Demons weren't in the business of saving the virginity of female children, or offing one of their fellows. Sean was a child molester, a rapist, a demon's dream come true. Wasting Sean was wasting a good resource.

If the individual making Charles's life such a trial wasn't Jimmy, possessed or un-possessed, that left the fifth woman. Charles had not thought of the fifth woman since the cripple had told him she'd missed the canoe trip due to family issues. He'd taken that statement at face value. More fool he. The sin of pride, one of his favorites. A cripple would not dare lie to him. A cripple wouldn't lie at all. A cripple might grovel or beg, but never show the presence of mind or the cunning to lie.

Charles stared through the rich brown liquid into the bottom of the Dixie cup. Surrounded by the likes of Sean and Jimmy, guns and knives, that broken piece of human flotsam refused to quit, or even to shut up. She reminded him of something. Arnold Schwarzenegger, that was it, at the end of *Terminator* when all that was left of him was a torso and a couple of arms, and he was clawing his way along the road after the hero. That would have been Heath, clawing her way after him, if he hadn't killed her.

Respect, that's why he'd shot her in the thigh instead of messing up her face. No pain in crippled legs, and bleeding to death was a peaceful exit. Blood under the bridge, he thought. Eyes scanning the clearing, then the top of the walls, he took another sip of whiskey.

The fifth woman.

He was having trouble getting his mind around the concept — the reality — of a fifth woman. The fifth woman killed Jimmy? The fifth woman took the dog? The fifth woman dressed in Jimmy's clothes and scared the shit out of Reg? Unseen, unheard, unnoticed, this fifth woman smashed Sean's head in?

If Sean was killed by this invisible woman, why didn't the Hendricks child go away with her? Why did she insist it was Jimmy? Confusion? Was she told to lie? Could the child have the presence of mind to lie to him, say it was Jimmy, and go on lying to him?

Charles shook his head. Demonic possession made more sense.

Ceasing his constant scanning of the perimeter, he fixed his eyes on Katie Hendricks. Pale, sylphlike, a pupa of the venomous butterfly she was apt to grow into. Female children weren't his bailiwick. No females were allowed in the monastery when he and Michael were growing up. They had attended all-boys Catholic schools. Entry into the world of women hadn't come until Charles was nearly twenty-two. Adult females held no mystery for him. Female children held no interest.

Watching Katie Hendricks sleep in the circle of her mother's arms, he thought how like Gerald she looked. On the heels of the thought came a memory. Reg: *Hey, dude, she's seen a picture of you.*

The plane, the food, the trudge had knocked that from Charles's mind.

He did not allow pictures of himself to be taken. Once, that had been easy; see a camera, break it. In the age of cell phone cameras, one never knew. Possibly he was in the background of a photo some nincompoop had put on Facebook, or walking past during a video that went viral.

If the child had seen him in an anonymous context it wouldn't matter — for several days she'd seen his living face. She could describe him to her heart's content and it wouldn't matter. Bernie, even the FBI, if Bernie screwed up and got caught, couldn't do much with that, not after he'd had a shave and a haircut.

Context, connections, that's where things got dicey. Putting his face and a person, place, or thing together would eventually lead to a name. Charles was not off the grid; he had merely built himself a life in the interstices.

He tossed the cup and the last few swallows of whiskey into the fire. Walking softly, he crossed to the Hendrickses. Both were deeply asleep, exhausted. He, too, would be exhausted if he allowed himself.

He knelt beside them. Tickling Katie lightly on the back of the hand, he waited for her to wake. Eyelids fluttered, then opened. In the low light, they were the dark blue of irises in early spring. "Hi, Katie," he said in what he hoped was a kindly confidential whisper. "You saw a picture of me."

Warily, she nodded. Yes indeed, this one could lie.

"Where did you see it?" Charles could see this child, this infant, considering what would be the right answer. Fortunately for her, she decided on the truth.

"Daddy had it," she admitted.

Leah's eyes opened.

Daddy had it. Gerald Hendricks had it; not anonymous, disastrous.

"What are you talking about?" Leah Hendricks insisted. Since he'd taken her, Ms. Hendricks had grown a spine and a voice. Too bad she'd never get to exercise either.

"Your daughter says her daddy has a picture of me," Charles said in the same kindly manner. Leah Hendricks had not grown a new face. Hers was more open than her daughter's. She was startled by the question; she didn't know about the picture either. "Where did you see it, Katie?" Charles asked.

Katie glanced up at her mother. Leah had no guidance to give her.

"In a box in Daddy's closet," the child answered. "It wasn't exactly you, but like you. You were younger and with longer hair. You were smiling." This last sounded like an accusation.

"Anything else in Daddy's box?"

Katie shook her head, her blond hair, clumped with ash and sweat, writhing Medusa-like on her mother's chest. "Just the picture and a bunch of mushy e-mails from Momma that he'd printed out."

"They weren't from me," Leah said. Her face clouded. She wanted her words back.

"Why did you think the e-mails were from your momma?" Charles asked.

"They were signed 'your loving partner.' "

"Bernard?" Leah's eyes went suddenly wide with knowing. "Michael!" she said. "Michael Bagnold." Narrowing her surprised gaze, she looked hard at Charles. "Michael is your brother, isn't he?"

"Was," Charles said.

Leah Hendricks had put it together. Connections would be made, contacts, monks he kept in touch with, the church he and Michael had attended, the chapel fund in Michael's name.

Rising, he took the satellite phone from his coat pocket and crossed to the far side of the shed.

FORTY-NINE

"Momma?" Katie said, sounding confused.

"Never mind, Katie-did." Leah kissed the top of her daughter's head. Katie fell back to sleep. Not so Leah. Michael Bagnold had been one of her husband's business partners when she and Gerald met. She had met the third man only once. Barnyard, Michael had called him because he left shit that his partners were always inadvertently stepping in. Bernard Iverson, Barnyard, had only ten percent of the operation before they squeezed him out.

Michael was a twin, she remembered, an identical twin. Michael was a handsome, winsome man.

Hard to believe the dude — she couldn't bring the twin brother's name to mind — was any relation at all, Leah thought as she studied him covertly. Like Michael, the dude was tall, with a broad chest, wide of shoulder and narrow of waist. They shared the same dark hair and olive complexion. The same cheekbones. The dude's nose had been broken, probably more than once, and not healed straight. Of course, he was fourteen years older than Michael had been when Leah knew him.

Michael. The dude. It was as if she were being shown before-and-after pictures. Michael as a lovely young man, then Michael after a holocaust or some other prolonged, painful, embittering experience.

The young Michael's eyes were dove-colored and clear as glass. The corners had tiny lines from laughter. He quoted Shakespeare, told jokes, read Greek and Latin. He had a miniature wire-haired terrier named Cleo. Cleo accompanied him everywhere, her collar a string of pearls. Michael had been kind to Leah; he made her feel normal instead of like an Einstein Monster.

The dude was a cold, dead-eyed man. Age, hairstyle, the mustache, broken nose, and a hairline scar through his left eyebrow changed his countenance to a degree, but even without the disguises, Leah would never have recognized him. The difference between the brothers was as marked as the difference between a stained-glass window flooded with sunlight and that same window at midnight.

Leaning her head back, watching him through lowered lashes, Leah tried to remember everything she could about when she'd met Gerald and Michael. Gerald was thirty-two, ten years older than Leah. Michael was close to that. Michael would have been — the dude was — in his forties now. Gerald and Michael owned a sporting goods store in Montreal that specialized in camping and backpacking equipment. They were partners.

"My God," Leah whispered. The dude flashed her a glance. She closed her eyes and her mouth. Gerald had not "turned out to be gay," as she'd always believed. Five years into a lucrative marriage, with a child, he hadn't suddenly realized his sexual orientation and come out of the closet. Gerald had known he was gay when they met. Michael had loved him, Michael, the loving partner, in his business and his bed.

Details of the past were hazy. She'd been so young and so unaccustomed to dealing with anything outside academia. Gerald hung on her every word, seemed fascinated with her plans and designs and ideas. His attention swept her off her feet.

Gerald was not pushy about sex; he didn't grab or grope or implore. It had made her feel safe, made her feel as if he loved her,

457

cherished her innocence, wanted it to be "right" for her. The truth was Gerald was gay. He didn't want her, he wanted the beautiful, charming Michael. Another woman might have noticed. Not Leah, the princess recently released from the ivory tower.

In a whirlwind that left her gasping, Gerald asked her to marry him, and they eloped to Niagara Falls. The next morning Gerald had returned shaking and pale from a walk. He said he was scared she wouldn't like her wedding gift. Gerald's wedding gift was that he'd bought Michael out of the partnership and sold the store. Most of the money would go into a lab for her. The rest would go to online marketing. Their honeymoon week was spent moving to Boulder, Colorado, and finding an apartment. Leah had never seen Michael again.

The dude said he was dead.

The dude hated Gerald. When she'd begged him to save Katie because she was an innocent, he'd said, "Tell that to Gerald."

Michael had been an innocent. When in earnest, he swore by the Virgin Mary. Every Sunday he went to mass. Gerald teased him that he had to chew the host or he wouldn't have a sin to confess the next week.

Michael was her husband's lover. He was dead, an innocent, and, in his brother's mind, at least, it was Gerald's fault. Gerald had dumped Michael and run off with the golden goose to live the heterosexual life. Had Gerald cheated Michael out of his share of the business and, now that Michael was dead, the dude wanted revenge? After fourteen years it would be a very cold dish.

The dude was punching numbers into the cell phone. Mr. Big, Leah guessed. The mastermind, the person who would get the lion's share of the ransom money. The person who had looked for rich ladies who were foolish enough to wander around without protection.

"Bring my cut," the dude snapped into the phone. "I'm not going north with you." He punched the disconnect before whoever it was could reply, then turned the phone off. This was not open to negotiation; he didn't want to be called back.

Charlie, his name was Charlie. Leah remembered Michael opening half of his sentences with "My brother, Charlie." Leah knew who he was. Katie knew enough to set hounds on his trail. The dude was Charlie Bagnold of Montreal, Canada. He wanted the cash up front, and he wasn't going north with Mr. Big.

Charlie Bagnold didn't intend to leave either her or her daughter alive.

FIFTY

Anna woke only when the first light of the sun struck the field, an hour or more after dawn. On her right side, to keep her injured arm elevated, she lay beside Heath. Elizabeth snuggled up to her mother on the other side. Not to be left out, Wily curled around their two heads like a mangy brown fur hood. One of his paws was on E's shoulder. The girl's hand rested atop it. Momentarily, Anna felt abandoned. Wily had been . . .

Magic, delusion, projection: Anna's sister was a psychiatrist; she'd ask Molly when she got the chance.

Her intention was to rise quietly, stealthily, so the others could continue sleeping while she went on reconnaissance. Weakness turned those intentions into paving stones on the road to hell. During the night her arm had swollen alarmingly. The flesh was tight against the sleeve of her shirt. As she rolled from her side onto her back, the

461

arm fell off her rib cage like a sausage rolling off a chopping block, and hit the ground with much the same sound. Unable to stop herself, she cried out as her body seized with an agony she had not known the nerves were capable of.

Elizabeth was awake instantly and, nearly as instantly, on her feet. To be fifteen and whole, Anna thought. It must be like being a god. Before Elizabeth could utter the inevitable and unanswerable "Are you okay?" Anna said, "I am jim-dandy. Never better. If you have a bit of rope or a gun, please put me out of my misery."

"I was dreaming this was all a dream," Heath said. "I was so relieved, I cried."

"Good morning," Anna said. Pushing down on Elizabeth's shoulder with her good hand, she managed to rise to her knees. "Wait until you try to get up. That's when crying might genuinely become a factor." Sweat beaded on her forehead, though the morning was cold. Her breath came in shallow gasps that puffed in the air like smoke signals.

Anna pulled one knee up, rested a few seconds, then tried to rise to her feet. "Damn it!" she said, muttering, "Elizabeth, give me a hand, will you?"

E reached out to help, but her mother

stopped her.

"Wait, Elizabeth, I didn't quite hear what Anna said," Heath said sweetly.

"Mom," Elizabeth chided.

Heath laughed and, annoyed as she was, hearing it gave Anna strength. "Give me a hand up, will you, E?" she said clearly. "I need all the help I can get."

Quiet chuckling followed her as Elizabeth helped her to her feet. "Very funny. Don't even look at me, Wily. One of you is bad enough. Coffee," she said and sniffed the air. "They have coffee. Another reason to kill them."

"Even if they did, you couldn't smell it over a hundred yards away," Heath said.

"Wily taught me to find my wolf nose," Anna said, then smiled so Elizabeth and Heath wouldn't think she was crazy. "E, come with me." Looking pointedly at Heath, she added, "In case I fall down and break a hip."

"Where are we going?" E asked as they walked the few yards toward the clearing and the burned hulk of the airplane.

"Just walking, seeing if there's anything we need to see," Anna said. "Mostly I need to move, get my blood flowing. So does Heath. When we get back, make her do whatever she does. The leg is a mess, but she's got to get warm somehow."

At the edge of the trees, still in the shadows, they stopped. The field was empty. At the far end smoke curled up into a pellucid blue sky, perfect flying weather. Reg stood by the fire. The dude, Leah, and Katie were not visible. "Probably still sleeping," Anna said.

"Are we going to stay hidden until everyone is gone?" Elizabeth asked.

"That's the only logical way to go," Anna said.

"They'll take Leah and Katie?" Elizabeth asked.

"The Hendrickses have plenty of money," Anna said. "Leah's husband will buy them back."

Elizabeth's full lips thinned, and she wouldn't look at Anna. "I think the dude has it in for Leah."

"Nah," Anna said dismissively. "She's just money to him."

"You didn't hear him. He said Gerald's name at the rocks and then went ballistic when Katie said she'd seen a picture of him. It's personal with him," Elizabeth insisted.

"That's a bit of a stretch," Anna said. "He was probably just cold and hungry and tired like the rest of us."

Anna turned away from E and walked

slowly back into the trees. She needed a sling to keep her arm from driving her mad with pain; she needed a drink of water and the last of the aspirin. The list of needs had the potential of consuming the rest of the day. She quit thinking about it.

Heath turned down Anna's offer to share the last three aspirins. Anna didn't argue but washed them down with gratitude. Poor little white pills didn't have a hope of fighting the kind of cruelty the bullet was dishing out. Swallowing them was an act of faith and optimism.

"Now, could some able-armed individual shred my T-shirt into strips?" Anna asked. "Then you can secure this wretched piece of meat to my chest."

Elizabeth started to help Anna pull the T-shirt over her head. "Can't," Anna gasped. "Cut it off."

"Duh," Elizabeth mocked herself. "Right, we're shredding it anyway."

"That which isn't already shredded," Heath added. Eyes moving from Anna to her daughter, Heath said, "We remind me of that painting of the Revolutionary soldiers limping home, one with a bandage around his head."

"Except they could walk," Elizabeth said. "And the guy could hold a fife."

"Can you return children to the breeder if they turn out to have defects?" Heath asked.

"E and I were talking when we went for our morning stroll," Anna said. "The thugs don't know I exist. They think you're dead. Elizabeth is long gone, lost in the woods, for all they know. They probably won't make much of an effort to find us. Probably won't make any effort at all to find us. I think we should lay low until the plane leaves and whatever leftover thugs clear out down the logging road."

Heath, propped up on her elbows, stared at Anna for a second, then said, "You're right. All I can do is die again. You're spent. Another night in the cold will do us both in, and I don't like the looks of E's eye."

Elizabeth stopped her meticulous shredding of the black knit shirt. "You'd just leave Leah and Katie?" she asked her mother.

"There's nothing we can do to help them, E," Heath said. "Hey, look what I found," From the folds of Jimmy's much-abused coat, Heath pulled out a mauled cigarette. "Too bad I lost my lighter," she said sadly. "Leah's husband will pay the ransom and the kidnapper will cut them loose, E. They'll be okay."

"You didn't leave me behind," Elizabeth said.

Heath winced.

Anna wanted to slink cravenly away from the scene and leave it to mother and daughter. "That was different, Elizabeth," Anna said. "That was something we could do something about."

"We could do something to help Leah and Katie," Elizabeth insisted.

"Don't be an ass," Anna snapped. "Two grown men, neither injured, two pistols, a rifle, and a plane on the way? Act your age. There is nothing we can do but get ourselves killed." Rising without assistance, she left the clearing. Had she not been in the forest, she would have stomped out and slammed the door.

Several yards away white pines, tangled with winterberry bushes, provided cover. Anna stepped behind them so Elizabeth could no longer see her.

"I'm sorry Anna snapped at you," she heard Heath say.

"I've never seen her being such a bitch before," Elizabeth replied. Hearing the tears in her voice, Anna felt her own eyes sting.

"She has her days," Heath said dryly.

Turncoat, Anna thought.

"She's right, though," Heath said. "I hate it as much as you do, but we haven't a chance — especially if Anna's lost her nerve.

Throwing our lives away won't help Leah and Katie, it'll just break Aunt Gwen's and Paul's hearts."

Anna counted slowly to one hundred, giving Elizabeth time to process; then she crunched around a bit to announce her arrival and returned to where they sat. "Sorry," she said. "My arm's killing me." She sat down, ignoring the cold emanating from the teenager. "We'll follow the logging road out," Anna said. "It'll take us somewhere there are people and cars."

"Dragging Mom?" Elizabeth asked acidly.

"Can't you carry her?" Anna asked.

"I'd bleed to death, Anna," Heath said. "Leg. Holes on both sides. You remember."

"There is that," Anna admitted. "E and I can go. The faster we get help, the better your chances. Your golden hour is already shot to hell."

"I won't leave Mom," Elizabeth said.

"Then I guess it's me going for help," Anna said. Painfully, she rose to her feet, Four steps later she fell to her knees. "Woozy from blood loss. Once I get moving I'll be fine." This time she didn't make it to her feet before faintness hit. Staggering, she leaned against a tree, shaking her head to clear it.

"Go, E," Heath said softly. "I'll be okay.

Run like the wind. Get us help. Stay in the trees until you're out of sight of the field. If you hear a plane, duck back into the trees."

"Mom . . ."

"Go now before things start to happen. We'll be fine. They'll never even know we're here. I promise."

Elizabeth got to her feet. Anna could feel her staring at her back. "Take the water bottle," Anna said.

"Hurry," Heath urged.

"I love you, Mom," Elizabeth said as she left the clearing. Then, "You, too, Anna. I guess." Fleet footsteps faded quickly in the direction of the logging road.

"You sure raised one stubborn girl," Anna said.

"Yes I did," Heath agreed. "What are we going to do?"

"I have no idea. We wait for an opening. Tie my arm to my chest?"

"Shhh." Heath held up a hand.

Men talking.

Anna slipped back to the fringe of brush around the clearing. Maybe there were fewer leaves than the day before. Maybe she was just feeling more vulnerable. Crawling commando-style, throwing herself to her belly — those marvelous feats were beyond her now. Not all of the fainting and fogging had been assumed for Elizabeth's sake.

Using trees and hoping for luck, she could see the field in its entirety. Reg and the dude had brought the hostages to the center of the cleared area. Their hands had been re-tied behind their backs. The dude was taking no chances. He barked an order that sounded like "Down." Before there was time to respond, he grabbed Leah by the shoulder and shoved her to the ground. Hands bound behind her, she couldn't break her fall and slammed facefirst into the weeds. Katie quickly got down.

Orders were given that Anna could not hear. Both Leah and her daughter stretched their legs out in front of them, feet together, like Barbie dolls on a shelf. Reg knelt and began tying their ankles with strips of cloth. Finally, they had run out of plastic ties.

Anna was mystified. Why leave their nice cozy pen with the food and the fire to stand in the middle of an open field on a cold morning? Unless the plane had left wherever it left from in darkness, it would be a while before it arrived. Satellite phone: The dude would know its ETA to the minute. Was he afraid the pilot wouldn't see them in the shelter? That was absurd. Smoke from the campfire marked the spot beautifully.

The plane was coming in minutes; the

470

thought cut cold through Anna's mind. No. Were the plane imminent, they wouldn't tie Leah's and Katie's feet. They'd have to untie them to get the women into the plane, unless they planned on loading them like gunny sacks full of grain.

Anna tried to put herself in the dude's place. Why would she leave the comfort of the camp they'd made? Because it was a trap. Because she didn't want anybody sneaking up on her from behind the three standing walls or around the corner of the barracks building. The dude must have finally figured out they were not alone in these woods. That, or Leah or Katie had told him she was here; she was responsible for Jimmy's decimation of the troops.

Damn.

Having finished tying Leah's and Katie's ankles, Reg rose to his feet. The dude issued a few more sotto voce orders.

"No fuckin' way," Reg ejaculated.

The dude argued. Reg shuffled.

"You go," Reg said.

The dude had the rifle under his arm. His gun hand twitched toward the pocket of the coat. Reg turned and stared at Anna. She flinched, but he hadn't seen her. His eyes were searching the tree line. The dude knew, or suspected, Anna existed. He was sending

471

Reg to search the area beyond the burned-out plane hulk.

Sulkily, like a recalcitrant teen with an attitude, Reg started in the direction of the plane, the direction of Anna, of Heath.

Anna backed away until she could no longer see him, then turned and walked as rapidly as she dared to where she'd left Heath. There was no way Anna could move her. With luck, she could scrape enough forest detritus over her to camouflage her from a casual glance, no more than that. The red-and-black checkered coat could be buried under duff. Signs of their disturbance couldn't be erased even if she had fifteen minutes. They'd been there too long, rearranged too much.

"They're coming?" Heath asked as Anna walked into their primitive camp.

"Reg," Anna said. "I think the dude knows I exist. He's not leaving Leah and Katie. He's got them tied hand and foot in the middle of the clearing. I don't think he knows you're alive. Can we use that?"

For a minute or more neither woman spoke.

Heath drew in a deep breath and let it out on a sigh. "Give me your pants," she said.

Since Anna had no better idea, she undid the top button of her trousers and let Heath

472

skin them down to where she could step out of them. Working on nothing but trust and hope that Heath actually had a plan, Anna asked, "Do you want my tank top as well?"

"No," Heath said. "I have good breasts. These breasts have been known to freeze men in their tracks for three to five seconds. They should be good for at least half that with Reg, given he thinks they're returned from beyond the grave."

Kneeling, Anna helped Heath pull on her trousers as best she could. With one arm screaming every time she moved, she wasn't terribly effective. "I don't want him to see my legs, the bandage, all that. It will spoil the effect," Heath explained as she zipped and buttoned. "Grab the strips of your shirt."

Anna did as she was told.

"Give them to me." Heath quickly tied three of them together into two ropes each several feet long.

"Help me get up, then tie me to the tree," she said.

The plan finally came together in Anna's mind, the fruition of blind faith. "Got it," she said. With Anna's hand and knee, Heath pulled herself up until she was hanging from Anna's good shoulder, her back against the tree. Overhead was a small branch, no more than two inches in diameter and a few feet long. Anna supported her until she got one hand around it.

"I'm good for a second," Heath said. "Hand me the first strip. Good. You take one end." Heath held her end in her free hand as Anna passed the other around the trunk.

"Brace me," Heath said.

Anna wrapped her good arm around Heath's waist and took her weight on her hip as Heath tied the strips tightly under her breasts and tucked the tails in where they didn't show.

Without awaiting instructions, Anna handed her one end of the second rope, ran it around the tree trunk, then held it in place while Heath tied it tightly around her hips. "That should keep me from suffocating for at least four minutes," Heath said.

"Doesn't matter," Anna said. "He'll probably shoot you on sight."

"See that he doesn't."

Anna turned to go see if Reg was coming their direction.

"Wait," Heath said. "Cross my ankles so I look casual, and hand me that cigarette." She pointed to the disreputable-looking cigarette in the folds of Jimmy's coat.

Anna did as she was told, then threw the coat behind the tree where it was out of sight.

"Go," Heath said.

Holding her rotten arm with the one in slightly better shape, Anna trotted the few yards to the edge of the clearing. Reg, his Walther swinging in short arcs like the cane of a blind man searching for obstacles, was walking warily toward the burned plane. The sun was well and truly up. Autumn sunlight, rich and warm as clarified butter, poured into the clearing.

"Nothing," Reg shouted to the dude.

"Check out the tree line," the dude called back. He put the Colt in the waistband of his pants. Rifle at his shoulder, he watched Reg and the trees through the site.

He did know Anna existed. He was using Reg as bait to draw her out.

Reg circled the rubble, all that remained of the Cessna, and walked in halting baby steps toward Anna. As he closed the distance, Anna slipped back to Heath.

"It's now or never," she whispered. "Wait until I'm set."

The only chunk of anything remotely solid that she could wield with one arm was a pine branch three feet long and slightly bigger around than her wrist. Rot had set in.

Like as not, it would shatter on impact, but it might suffice to give her the time she needed to get his gun.

Might was such a peevish little word.

Backing behind an old oak where she could see Heath but couldn't be seen from any other angle, she nodded.

"Hey, Reg," Heath called softly.

"What the fuck?" Reg said. Anna leaned back until she could just see him through the berry bushes. He'd stopped and was rolling his head around, trying to find where the voice came from. He even searched the heavens in case the gods were calling his name.

"Reg, come over, would you?" Heath asked pleasantly.

Anna marveled at the calm and ease in her voice. The ties had to be cutting off half of her oxygen supply.

"Shit, man," Reg muttered and crept closer to the bushes, his head forward, his gun leading the way.

"God damn it, stop fucking around and get over here," Heath said.

The cigarette between her fingers was shaking as if it had a life of its own and struggled to take flight.

Reg stepped into the trees and was gone from Anna's view. In seconds he would see

Heath. He had to come far enough in so Anna could see him and knock his miserable head off his miserable shoulders. She wished she had two good arms. She wished she had a gun. Most of all, she wished she had her pants on. Defending the right and just was hard enough without having to do it wearing nothing but filthy lace panties.

He walked into Anna's sight line. Heath smiled at him. Raising the cigarette to her lips, she said, "Got a light?"

Reg screamed and bolted.

Anna swung the rotten branch with all her strength.

She struck out. Only empty air remained where once had been a thug.

Fifty-One

The dude had skinned out of his bulky coat and was following Reg's every move with the rifle. Something beyond the tree line had snagged Reg's attention, and he'd followed it until he was swallowed by the half-denuded bushes. Leah eyed the Colt in the waistband of the dude's trousers but could think of no way of getting close to it, except by biting him on his hip pocket.

A scream ripped the fabric of the still morning, a skin-shriveling, bowel-loosening shriek that sounded more animal than man. On the heels of the shriek, Reg burst from cover. Instead of running back toward Leah, Katie, and the dude, he veered left and pelted pell-mell down the old logging road at the end of the clearing.

"Holy smoke," Leah murmured.

"Wolves?" Katie asked.

"Something put the fear of God in him," Leah said.

The dude pressed his cheek to the stock of the rifle and pulled the trigger. A blossom of liquid red bloomed from the top of Reg's skull. He fell in midstride, dead before he struck the ground. With Reg down, a second figure was revealed. Not ten feet beyond where Reg lay was Elizabeth. She was running, not away, but up the old road toward them. Without a change in expression, the dude pumped out the spent round and chambered another, then pressed his cheek to the stock.

Leah toppled onto her side, bunched her legs, and kicked out hard, hitting him in the ankle. The shot went wild.

"Get his gun!" a woman shouted.

Not Heath. Heath was dead. Anna, then. It had to be Anna. Leah had begun to think Anna, like the windigo, was a ghost story told to frighten children on winter nights.

The dude kicked Leah's shins so hard she was spun halfway around. The intensity of the pain tore a squeak from her throat. A scream wanted out, but she didn't want to scare Katie any worse than she already was. Fighting through the waves of pain, Leah rolled to her back and sat up. She needed to see what was happening. Planting his feet, the dude again took aim and fired at Elizabeth. In the instant the crack of the bullet hit Leah's ears, Elizabeth dropped to her knees. Shot, downed like Reg. Leah couldn't bear so much. She tried to shut out the image.

"She's taking his gun!" Katie squeaked.

Not shot, just down, Elizabeth was snatching something from Reg's dead hands. Holding it tightly against her belly, she slipped into the trees.

"Elizabeth got his gun!" Katie crowed.

"Shh," Leah said, afraid the dude would vent his frustration on her daughter.

He seemed unmoved by this turn of events. Leah remembered hearing that it was hard to hit a target with a pistol at any distance, that even people who shot regularly couldn't be sure of hitting a bull's-eye at more than ten yards, or twenty, she couldn't remember exactly. Maybe the dude didn't figure a fifteen-year-old girl, scared half out of her mind, was much of a threat.

Without glancing back to see if Leah was planning another ground assault on his ankles, he calmly twisted the end of a tube that was slightly smaller and shorter than the barrel of the gun, and mounted right beneath it. Pulling the tube out, he looked into a hole. Counting his bullets, Leah realized. The only rifle bullets he had must be in the gun. The thugs hadn't come prepared for an extended ordeal.

He eased the tube back in. Nothing on his face indicated whether he had plenty of ammunition or none. Raising the rifle again, he searched the line of trees and bushes at the edge of the clearing, waiting for Elizabeth to show herself.

Katie was scooting, pulling her rear end along with her heels, moving toward the castoff jacket on the dude's far side. Leah wanted her to stop, to stay still, to stay safe, but there was no safe anymore. Katie reached the coat and fell over on her side. Leah was afraid to ask what she was doing, if she was cold, or going to take a nap. Katie looked at her. Leah raised her eyebrows in silent questioning. The look Katie returned said something important. Leah hadn't a clue what it was.

Her daughter began nosing around in the folds of the hunting jacket like a puppy looking for a place to nurse.

"You said your brother died," Leah said to keep the dude from looking in Katie's direction.

"That's right," the dude replied without stopping his endless scanning.

"Did he die recently?" Leah asked because she couldn't think of anything cleverer.

"He died on the sixteenth of July fourteen

years ago."

The sixteenth of July was Leah and Gerald's wedding anniversary. Fourteen years. Michael had died on their wedding day.

Katie found whatever it was she was looking for. Her nose was burrowing into the checkered wool, into a pocket. Working her jaws, she bit at something.

"Suicide." The realization came to Leah like a punch in the gut. "Michael committed suicide." Gerald hadn't bought Michael out, or cheated him. Michael committed suicide because Gerald dumped him. Gerald had inherited Michael's half of the business when he died.

"That's right," the dude said.

Using her teeth, Katie tugged whatever she'd been nipping at from the dude's coat. The pilot's satellite phone. She pressed her nose on the bottom and the screen lit up. She pressed her nose on an icon and numbers took over the screen. Poking with her nose, she brought up a nine.

Leah stopped talking, stopped breathing.

And a one.

Silence was a mistake. It brought the dude's head around. His boot struck Katie on the side of the face. Her head snapped back, and she fell over without uttering a sound. Dead to the world. Or dead. Another swift kick, and the phone went sailing out into the weeds.

The dude tucked the rifle beneath his arm, pulled the Colt from his waistband, and pointed the barrel at Katie's temple. "I don't need you both," he said flatly.

FIFTY-TWO

"What are you doing here?" Heath demanded of her gasping daughter.

"You guys tricked me!" Elizabeth accused. "You were never going to do nothing."

"Give me the gun," Anna said.

"I got about a quarter of a mile before I figured it out. I can't believe you did this! You lied to me! You wanted me out of the way."

"Of course I want you out of the way," Heath hissed. "Now get out of the way. Go!"

"Give me the gun," Anna said.

Elizabeth held out the Walther. Anna took it. "Hold out your hand," she ordered. Elizabeth held her hand out palm up. Anna released the clip into E's palm. Four bullets remained. "Shove it back in the butt of the pistol until it clicks." Taking the gun gingerly from Anna, Elizabeth clicked the magazine into place, then handed it back.

Armed, Anna walked toward the clearing.

The dude had his back to her. As she watched, he took the Colt from the waistband of his pants and pointed it at Katie, lying motionless at his feet. Leah was talking fast, her face contorted with the effort. Anna couldn't hear the words.

This was the only shot she would get. Resting her wrist on a branch, Anna steadied the gun, took careful aim, then fired. The recoil jerked her hand high and sent shock waves through her damaged arm. Vision grayed out. In this fog, she thought she saw the dude spin, the pistol and rifle flying away from his body.

Gray slid toward black, and Anna slid to her knees.

Elizabeth was beside her. "He's down," she whispered. "He's down, but he's not dead."

Anna tried to raise the hand with the gun and managed a couple of inches. "Shoot him again," she said.

"I can't," Elizabeth said. "I've never even held a gun. You have to get up. You have to wake up."

Anna felt hands tugging on her good arm. She tried to remember where her feet were and failed. "Just point and click," she said.

"Get up! You shot him in the shoulder looks like. The dude is on his feet. F moving. He's going to get his gun. The pistol, I think."

"Shoot at him," Anna murmured.

"I can't! I might hit Leah or Katie."

"Shoot in the air. Anything. Scare him."

Elizabeth took the gun from Anna's hand. What seemed an interminable time passed. Still on her knees Anna lifted her head to see Elizabeth, both hands on the pistol grip, barrel pointed toward the sky. The girl's eyes were squeezed tightly shut and her mouth thinned to a snaky line.

"Pull the trigger," Anna pleaded.

There was a resounding crack as Elizabeth fired into the air. Anna could smell the gunpowder, feel the sound waves crashing around inside her skull.

"It worked!" Elizabeth whispered. "He's down on the ground again. Afraid he'll get shot. He's still crawling, though."

"Get me up now," Anna said. "I can see again."

FIFTY-THREE

A second shot. The dude fell. Leah hoped he was dead. He wasn't. He was moving. The second bullet hadn't hit him. He had dropped to the ground to make a smaller target. For a wasted second or two, she waited for a third shot, waited for Elizabeth or Anna or whoever had the gun to shoot the dude again.

Withering silence filled her ears. Reg had been firing off at anything that moved. Maybe two bullets were all that remained in his gun. His gun was the kind with a clip — magazine — Leah knew. Even if Reg had a second magazine, Elizabeth hadn't had time to find it.

Katie wasn't moving. The dude was. His breath came in short staccato puffs. Despite the lack of gunfire, he wasn't trying to ge to his feet. Leah wasn't sure he could.

"You have been shot," she told him. "Y are dying." She had read once that peo could die of nonlethal bullet wounds if they believed the wound was fatal.

The dude was not people. He kept crawling toward where the pistol had been flung when he was shot.

Rolling and squirming, Leah moved over the ground like a sidewinder over desert sand. She reached the pistol before the dude did. Swinging her legs, she struck it with her bound feet. It skittered a few yards farther from the dude's grasp.

"You have been shot," she repeated. "You are going to die."

The dude crept forward.

"No," she said. "No. No." Working her legs like a jackhammer, Leah pounded his side with each word. Ignoring her onslaught, he crawled inexorably after the gun. Leah flopped to her side, trying to keep his body within striking distance. Her feet lashed out, hitting dirt and grass, knocking it into his eyes.

Eyes half closed, he crawled on, never oking at her. Bright red blood, lots of it, ned the dying yellow grass in his wake. u are losing too much blood. Quarts. ons. Liters," she added, because he was Canada. If she could keep him crawl-e might run out of blood before he kill her, or at least before he could shoot Katie.

To keep her legs at the right angle to kick, she had to stay on one hip, crushing the hands tied behind her back. Once more she managed to hit the Colt, knocking it another few feet. Twice she landed body blows, a shoulder, his ribs. Air gusted from his lungs in a grunt, but he didn't slow down.

Then she was kicking air. He was out of her reach. Hunching and flinging herself, she made a futile effort to catch up. What little strength she'd had was used up. She could barely draw up her knees, let alone kick out with any damaging force.

Gulping air, sweat pouring into her eyes, she stopped. Her flopping had turned her around. The dude was no longer in her field of vision. Katie was. She lay exactly as she'd fallen after the dude's boot struck the side of her head. Her eyes were closed.

Craning her neck, Leah squirmed around until she laid eyes on the dude. He was between her and the morning sun. Eyes full of dust and sweat, he was a humanoid shadow in stark and splintering light. A man of shadow, a black hallowed fallen angel. As she blinked away the illusion, the dude, fighting gravity, dizziness, or pain, struggled to one knee. The Colt was in his hand. All Leah could do was watch. She hadn't even the wherewithal to pray.

Propping his right elbow on his thigh, he made a cradle of his right hand, then placed his left forearm in it, steadying his gun hand. Unwavering, the bore of the pistol pointed between Leah's eyes.

"Charlie," Leah gasped in sudden remembering. "Charlie."

His colorless eyes clouded. Confusion? Maybe fury? Or memory.

"Michael called you Charlie," Leah said.

"Brother Charlie. He called me Brother Charlie." He thumbed back the hammer.

Beyond him, over his shoulder, Leah saw what she believed at first to be a trauma-induced hallucination. A woman with no eyebrows or eyelashes, with a frizzled mass around her face that looked more like staghorn fern than hair, was walking toward them. The woman wore a red tank top, bright turquoise lace panties, and a pair of shapeless dilapidated bedroom slippers. Encrusted with dried blood, her left arm hung lifeless at her side. A single thread of ruby red ran through the black to end in a teardrop on the tip of her forefinger.

In her right hand was Reg's pewter-colored pistol.

"Anna?" she whispered.

The dude turned to look.

Anna shot him center mass. The force of the bullet knocked him over. The thump of his head on the ground was palpable. Keeping the gun trained on him, Anna walked up beside him. With the side of her foot, she booted his Colt out of reach of his lax fingers.

"Is Katie dead?" she asked, staring down at the dude's face.

"I don't know," Leah replied. She didn't want to know she was, and was desperate to know she wasn't. There was no courage left in the middle to ask. "Is the dude dead?" she asked instead.

"I don't know," Anna said, "and I'm not going to get within reach to find out. Is there any food left? I'm starving."

The dude's eyes opened. "Mrs. Hendricks?" he whispered.

"I'm here," Leah said. She sounded nice, caring, like the beloved sister at the bedside of a dying man. She didn't know why she sounded that way. Too many movies, perhaps. Maybe watching a man dying brought out the best in people.

"Building fund," he whispered. "Chapel of the Virgin at the sister house of Marie-Reine-du-Monde. See they get it. Gerald owes him. A suicide. Been in purgatory for fourteen years." Each word was formed separately and pushed up from somewhere deep inside. Blood frothed pink at the corners of his mouth.

"You think you can bribe the Virgin Mary to spring somebody from purgatory?" Anna asked.

Obviously watching a man dying did not bring out the best in everyone.

"I. Never. Met. A woman who —" Weak coughing stopped his words. More blood trickled from the corners of his mouth. "Didn't want me to buy her a house," he finished in a rush of breath.

"I will," Leah heard herself saying. It was true, she would. Not for the dude — Charlie — but for Michael.

"Good," the dude whispered. His eyes rolled until they focused on Anna, where she stood over him with Reg's gun. "You were here, always."

"Yes," Anna said.

"Silly-looking demon," he muttered and closed his eyes.

"Is he dead?" It was Elizabeth; she'd come most of the way from the trees to the battle-ground.

"Getting there," Anna said. "Don't go near him. Dibs on his pants. E, check Katie for a pulse. Her carotid. You know how to do it."

Elizabeth knelt by Katie's head. She put two fingers on her trachea, then slid them down to the carotid. "Alive," she reported.

"Thank God," Leah said simply. "Heath . . . ?" Leah let the question trail off. What did one ask? Did you find your mom's body?

"Alive," Anna said. "Shot in the leg."

Relief so intense it brought tears to her eyes startled Leah. She hadn't known she cared so much. "Will you untie us now?" she asked Anna.

"I can't," Anna admitted. "Can you do it, E?"

From Leah's viewpoint at ground level, Anna leaned as badly as the tower in Pisa. "Why don't you sit down?" she asked.

"Can't," Anna said.

Elizabeth sawed through the fabric that tied Leah's hands together with the sharp edge of the piece of metal she'd salvaged. "Get Katie?" Leah asked. "I can work on my ankles. Why can't you sit down?"

"Won't be able to get up," Anna said. Now the tower was leaning in the opposite direction. "Got to go back for Heath. Need to eat something. Have to —"

"Momma?"

"Katie's come around," Elizabeth said unnecessarily. Leah believed she would have heard that beautiful word ringing like a

493

steeple bell if Katie had whispered it into the wind on the backside of Saturn.

"I'm here, Katie-did." She crawled quickly to her daughter's side. "Here I am." Katie's eyes were open.

"Check the pupils," Anna said in a wispy voice. "See if they're the same size."

Leah held Katie's chin in her hand and, without moving the child's neck, looked into her eyes. "They are!" She was as proud as if she'd invented pupils, as if her child were the first child in the universe to have two of the same size.

"Hands are free," Elizabeth announced. "I have to go back and check on Mom. You can keep my scrap to do her feet." Rising, she dropped the triangle of aluminum beside Leah and trotted off. Trotted, Leah noticed. She wondered if she'd be able to get up more than an old-lady shuffle.

"I'm going behind you," Leah said to Katie. "I'll be right here behind you. I'm going to cut your hands loose, okay?"

"Mom, I'm not five years old, you know," Katie said.

She was going to be all right, Leah thought.

A loud thump brought her eyes up from her work on Katie's bonds.

Anna had pitched forward onto the

ground. The gun was still clutched in her hand.

FIFTY-FOUR

Anna was in ecstasy. Leah and the girls had moved both her and Heath to the warmth of the thugs' camp. There was food. Using a plastic spoon to prove she was civilized, she shoveled cold Wolf chili with beans into her mouth from a can held between her thighs. Aptly named and delicious: Anna promised she would find out who the chef was and see if Leah could get him canonized while she was bribing the Catholic Church for the release of the dude's brother's soul.

Not only was she eating, there was coffee, real coffee. Elizabeth had a pot brewing on a Coleman stove so old, Anna hadn't seen its like in twenty years. Food and coffee, and trousers: Anna was wearing pants. True, they were too long and too big and belonged to a dead man, but then, she was getting used to wearing dead men's clothes. Heath had argued against stripping the corpse, saying it was too gruesome a task for Elizabeth, Katie, or even Leah to be made to do. Once it became clear Anna would have the dude's pants or she'd claim her own back, Heath decided it wouldn't scar them too deeply.

Elizabeth and Katie were still young enough to retain some of the love of the macabre natural to most kids. They didn't seem to mind a bit. At any rate, doing it hadn't damaged Elizabeth's appetite any. She'd polished off a bag of Doritos and was rifling through the box in search of tasty morsels. Leah and Katie, who had eaten breakfast, were out scouring the field around the body trying to find the cell phone the dude had kicked from under Katie's nose. Wily lay near the food box, trusting E to share whatever she found.

Heath was eating a deli sandwich. Her color was better, the leg wasn't bleeding, and she was wrapped from the chest down in the coats of criminals. Warmth, food, and blood flow to the heart.

The sun was shining, the sky was blue, and everybody was alive who should be. Anna thought she couldn't get any happier when Katie called, "Found it!"

"Do it, Katie!" Leah called from twenty yards away, where she'd been picking through the matted grass and weeds.

Katie dialed a one with her nose and they all cheered. Autumn was glorious, but it should have been spring, Anna thought, hunting Easter eggs, rebirth, the return of the sun, baskets of candy and flowers. Katie handed the phone to her mom, and as Leah talked, the two of them walked back to the camp. Neither gave the dude's corpse a glance.

Anna knew that the time for nightmares would come. That she would press her face into Paul's shoulder and speak of the unspeakable things she had done, that she'd be put on paid leave, her badge and gun taken until the incident had been investigated, that Katie would wake up screaming, imagining Sean's hands on her body, his brains splattered on her face. Heath would have health complications for a long time from what her body had suffered. She would shudder at the sight of swift rivers. A scar would mark her cheekbone, and another her arm where the dude had burned her. Elizabeth, whom Anna had most feared for because she had suffered a similar trauma as a child, seemed best able to handle what had transpired. This time she wasn't a little girl; this time she had fought and won. Elizabeth would be made stronger.

Leah, too, had been made stronger, Anna

believed. Before, she seemed oddly out of focus. Anna felt as if she viewed Leah through gauze, as if her colors were unsaturated. Walking over the weeds, her daughter beside her, she was in living color, hair black as a crow's wing, white skin, livid red and purple bruises, the lenses of her glasses catching and reflecting the green of the field. No one would get off scot-free, but none of them would be destroyed by the experience either.

"The cavalry is on the way," Leah announced as they arrived.

"What did you tell them?" Anna asked, talking with her mouth full because she could.

"Just that we had been kidnapped, had gotten free, and needed emergency medical attention for trauma and gunshot wounds, that you were shot in the arm, Heath in the leg, and that Heath was a para."

"Nothing about all the dead guys?" Elizabeth asked.

"I lost them before I got to that part," Leah said.

"Good," Anna said. "Some stories are too long to tell on the phone."

"You lost them?" Heath sounded alarmed.

"They know where we are. That was first. Then, as I was telling them about the injuries, the battery went dead. When the dude — Charlie — kicked it, he broke the case. That may or may not have anything to do with anything," Leah said as she collapsed by the smoldering fire.

"He was messing with the phone all night," Katie said. "Probably surfing for porn. Will we all be arrested for murder?" she asked Anna.

"You sound like you'd relish the experience," E commented.

"It would be something to talk about in homeroom," Katie said.

"There will be a huge investigation," Anna said. "FBI, the whole dog and pony show. Kidnapping is a federal crime. Then we have murder — dude murders Reg, attempted murder about a zillion times, assault, battery —"

"Ruining the word 'fuck' forever," Katie added.

"Theft," Elizabeth said. "Anna's wearing the evidence."

"All that," Anna said. "Our injuries testify in our favor. Sean was killed while trying to commit a felony, the dude was killed in self-defense — there are witnesses to all that. The only iffy one is Jimmy. Cold blood."

"You have the burning-bed defense. Did you see that movie?" Elizabeth asked.

"I will plead extenuating circumstances and hope for the best," Anna said.

"Temporary insanity," Heath suggested.

"That, too," Anna agreed.

"Can't you just say Jimmy attacked you?" Katie asked. "Nobody saw."

"Wily saw," Anna said.

"He's just a dog."

Anna looked at Wily, lounging by the food box in his filthy dented splint, his tongue lolling out of his mouth. "Just a dog," Anna said. Slowly — deliberately, she was sure — one eyelid dropped. Wily had winked at her. She hadn't been crazy.

"Yeah, just a dog," Anna said and returned the wink. "Lying to the law doesn't work as well as people think. Like my mother used to tell us, 'one little lie gets lonely.' You always have to tell others to bolster the first. Before you know it, you've hung yourself."

"Can't you shoot anybody you want? You're a federal law enforcement officer," Elizabeth said. "You're a park ranger."

"That should get me a nice place in the lunch line at the penitentiary," Anna said.

"You won't really go to jail, will you?" Elizabeth asked.

"I don't think so," Anna reassured her. "I expect, when the FBI starts digging, it's going to turn out that our pals were not nice

501

men even before we met them."

"Listen!" Heath said suddenly.

Anna stopped chewing and listened. Faint and far away was the pesky buzz of a small plane's engine.

"Hooray!" Katie shouted. "We're going home!"

"Not yet," Anna said. "Too soon."

"It's the plane the dude called for last night," Leah said. "They've come to get us."

FIFTY-FIVE

The engine's purr paralyzed them. Katie shook it off first. "We could all run and hide in the woods until the Forest Service or whoever comes and rescues us," she said.

"Good thought," Anna commended her, "but I doubt Heath and I are running anywhere anytime soon."

"How many men do you think will come?" Heath asked.

"One," Anna said. "Maybe two. Unless the dude told them different, the kidnappers think they are hauling out four women. Big planes can't land on a field this short. My guess is it's another small plane. No more than six seats."

"Girls, run and hide with Leah," Heath said. "Anna and I will stay here with the guns."

"No," Elizabeth said, with such finality neither her mother nor Anna argued with her.

"No," Leah said. "You go, Katie. It is a good idea."

"Oh, right," Katie said. "Like I'm going to hide under a rock now."

Whoever was in that plane would be armed; Anna would bet on it. Whoever was in the plane would be on guard, but not against the hostages. Against the dude. Leah had told them the dude had asked Mr. Big for his share of the cash and told him he wasn't going north. It wouldn't take a criminal mastermind to suspect the dude had plans he wasn't sharing.

"Get the dude," Anna ordered. "Bring him here, drag him, carry him, cut him into pieces and bring them one at a time, but get him here quick."

"What —" Katie began, but her mother and Elizabeth were running for the corpse. She ran after them, calling, "Wait for me!"

"Make sure he's really dead," Anna hollered after them. "Stomp on his trachea."

"Don't you dare," Heath yelled to her daughter. "Anna, what's the plan? Is there a plan?"

"Sort of," Anna admitted. "Did you ever read *Beau Geste*?"

"You're thinking of the part where the Legionnaires hold the fort by propping up dead men with rifles on the walls so the enemy will think there's a bigger defense force than there really is?"

"Almost hold the fort," Anna corrected. "Eventually they all die but Beau."

"That's a cheery thought," Heath said.

"It's a better plan than tying yourself naked to a tree," Anna said.

"That was a great plan. He just rabbitted before you got your clubbing act together."

"Look at them," Anna said, marveling at the sight of the younger woman and the girls, bruised, dressed in rags, hair tangled, each grabbing a limb and beginning to drag the corpse of the dude over the grass. After so much, it didn't even strike Anna as gruesome. They were young and strong and alive. The dude who had spent so much time trying to kill them was going to save them. "If we had enough like them, we could run the world," she said to Heath.

"They probably wouldn't let us run the world," Heath replied.

"Maybe not," Anna said.

The moment they were within speaking distance, Anna began directing the show. "Prop him up across from me. His face will be away from the plane that way."

It took all three of them to get him into a sitting position.

"Big dude," Katie said. For some reason

all of them laughed and it felt good.

When he was seated, his back braced against the opposite wall, Leah and the girls stepped away and the five of them surveyed the results. The growl of the airplane was distinctly louder. There was little time remaining.

"Something over his lap," Heath said. "He's in his underpants."

"Tighty whities," Katie said. This, too, made them laugh, but with an edge Anna didn't like. Hysteria was burbling up from the depths. Elizabeth took the checked hunting coat from Heath and spread it over his legs.

"Better," Heath said.

"His head won't stay up," Elizabeth said. "He looks like he's asleep."

"Prop his head up. Here." Anna tossed Leah a plastic fork. "Put the tines under his chin and the handle in his chest."

"Good," Anna said. The effect wasn't too bad if you couldn't see that his eyes were closed — or that he wasn't breathing. He looked like a man relaxing by the fire after a hard day's felony kidnapping. "E, give your mom the dude's Colt. It's over with the empty bags. Leah, you take the rifle."

"I have never touched a gun," Leah said.

"Elizabeth?"

"Point and click?"

"You got the idea. I'll keep the Walther. Everybody sit. Hands in laps like they were tied. E, Heath, hide the guns under something."

Heath put both her hands and the Colt beneath the pilot's flying jacket that lay across her lap. Elizabeth laid the rifle along her leg where it couldn't be seen from the front of the three-walled enclosure.

"What do I do?" asked Katie.

"Sit beside the dude. Make his hands move once in a while so he looks alive," Anna said.

"Anna, don't you think that's a little over the top?" Heath asked.

"I'll do it!" Katie said and scrambled to her puppeteer place beside the dead man.

The engine noise swelled. They all looked up as a sleek, white, low-winged airplane flew over. Down its side was a red swoosh the same shape as the Nike swoosh.

"It doesn't have any wheels," Katie said.

"They retract," Leah said.

"Duh," Katie said. "I knew that."

"No numbers," Anna said. "The guy must fly out of a private strip only. The FAA is picky about the numbers thing."

The plane circled neatly around the old camp, flew over again, skimming the treetops, then lined up with the clearing and landed on the grass. The ruin of the first plane effectively ended the ersatz runway. A ways before the wreck of the Cessna, the new airplane turned around and taxied back toward where Anna and the others waited.

It was a Beechcraft, a new one, very clean and shiny. Anna watched the single propeller chopping the air into pieces as it ate its way up the field, and felt nothing. Leah was staring at the plane as if it were a stalking lion, and she a hapless gazelle. Heath was bunching and unbunching her fist beneath the pilot's leather jacket as though, in her mind, she practiced a quick-draw on the Colt.

Elizabeth leaned forward, a bowstring drawn tight. Katie chewed on the edge of her thumb. "Hands in laps," Anna said. Katie put her hand in her lap. Elizabeth lifted hers from the rifle along her thigh and did the same.

The airplane taxied up until it was no more than thirty feet from the fire. The engine was shut off. There was only one man in the airplane. Anna's numbness was stirred by a slight feeling of relief. She waited for fear or anger to follow. Nothing did. She and the dude sat opposite one another, bookends of the dead.

The door opened. "Dude, where are the men?" the pilot shouted. Nerves tightened his voice, giving it a shrill edge.

"Not a sound," Anna whispered, going on with her lunch as if the plane did not exist. She imagined the pilot peering all around, trying to find where the dude had positioned his snipers.

"Dude, it's Mr. Big. I came like you asked. No middleman. Dude?"

Anna nodded fractionally at Katie over the rim of her chili can. Katie, her small hands nearly invisible in the folds of the dude's shirt, her tiny body completely hidden behind his, raised his right arm. The hand came up in a wave like that of the Queen Mother. Katie was poking the dead man's palm with a stick to get the effect.

"Talk about *Weekend at Bernie's,*" Anna murmured to Wily. "Don't tell me. You haven't seen that either."

A brown-wrapped package was pushed out onto the wing.

"Dude, bring the hostages. Here's your money."

The dude waved, this time with definite flippancy. Anna glared at Katie lest she get too carried away with the performance.

"I'm coming out," the pilot called after a minute. "Don't shoot. I'm stepping out of the airplane. I'm unarmed. Nobody shoot."

A hand appeared on top of the gleaming white frame. On the wing appeared a foot clad in a black calfskin loafer with a silver buckle where the penny was in the old days. No socks. Anna experienced an emotion she couldn't put a name to, a sort of internal sneer, the sense that this guy deserved to be treated as less than human. She didn't like feeling as if harming this man would be a good thing, fun even.

The whole man emerged, tall and thin and unfolding. Anna placed him in his early forties. His brown hair was receding at the temples, making a deep, false widow's peak over his aviator's sunglasses. Pinstriped oxford shirt, blue silk blazer, khaki pants with a sharp crease, narrow belt — black to match the loafers — posing on the wing of an expensive airplane: He resembled an ad for LLBean more than a kidnapper. He kept both hands in sight, his left on the top of the plane's door, his right, a metal thermos bottle held in it, resting on the roof of the Beechcraft.

"Dude," he called and smiled. He had a nice smile, natural, teeth crooked but white. Could have been easily mistaken for a nice guy. "Hey! Boys! Come join the party," he hollered at the men he believed to be hiding. Having carefully closed the door, he stepped down off the wing. "What's with the silent treatment, Dude? Hey, I smell coffee."

Jaunty, that was the word for him; this man was positively jaunty. The left lapel of his coat stuck out a tad. Anna guessed he had a shoulder holster.

"Dude," he said as he walked around the fire.

"Ladies," Anna said. The Colt, the Walther, and the .22 appeared. All barrels pointing at the man's heart.

Instinctively he threw his hands in the air. His first rational thought was to go for his gun.

"Don't," Anna said. "We've killed Sean, Jimmy, Reg, the dude, and your pilot. Don't think we won't kill you."

Muscles in his legs and shoulders shifted as his brain shifted gears. He snapped a hard look at the dude, shins bare, eyes closed, a white plastic fork holding his chin up.

"Whoa," he said and turned on his nice smile. It was fraying at the corners. "I have no idea what has happened here. I fly around here a lot. I've never seen anybody in this old camp. Today, when I flew over, I happened to see you down here. Airplane wrecked, no car in sight. I thought you might need help is all. No need for the heavy artillery. Just hoping to do a good deed in return for a refill." He waggled the silver thermos.

He sounded so sane, looked so sane. His face was absolutely guileless. Confusion registered, surprise and concern, but not a single shred of anything resembling guilt or malicious intent. Anna suffered a disorienting sense of wrongness, feeling that perhaps she had fallen asleep for three days and when she woke up she was a stone-cold killer pointing a great damn big gun at the heart of an innocent man.

He took off his sunglasses and beamed at them with clear blue eyes that crinkled at the corners. "Can I put my arms down? I'm feeling kind of silly."

"Barnyard?" Leah asked in an incredulous tone.

The mask slipped. Only a fraction, and only for a second, but Anna saw it; pure hatred flashed from beneath it like a bolt of black lightning.

"Take your gun out with two fingers, just like on TV," Anna said.

"I'd love to help you out, sweetheart, but I don't carry a gun," he said easily, smile back in place.

"Shoot him, Heath," Anna said flatly.

Heath raised the Colt.

"Okay, okay," he said. "I do carry a small personal weapon for self-defense. You should have been more explicit."

"Two fingers. Drop it away from your body." He did as he was told.

"Barnyard — Bernard — Bernard Something," Leah said. She was standing now, as was Elizabeth. Katie, bravado damped, stayed tucked behind the dude's corpse. "I met you. You were a junior partner of Michael and Gerald's."

"I'm afraid you've got me —"

"Sit down," Anna ordered.

"I've been sitting for three hours, but if you say so." He sat on the dry grass between them and the fire.

"Iverson. Bernie Iverson," Leah said. "That's it. You're it. You're him."

"The dude called the man on the phone Bernie once," Katie piped up.

The man laughed and shook his head. "I have no idea what you're talking about."

"Heath," Anna said. Heath thumbed the hammer of the dude's Colt back with its resonant metallic swallowing sound. "You don't understand," Anna said reasonably. "I want to shoot you. We want to shoot you. We've had a real bad couple of days. Are you Bernard Iverson?"

He put the mirrored sunglasses back on. His head turned right, then left, perhaps seeking a way out. Finally his jaw extended a little and he tossed his head, the way a high school girl might to get the bangs out of her eyes. "Yes," he said. Superciliousness cloaked him from the receding hairline to the chin. "I thought it was time I collected what is owed to me."

Part of him thought he was in the right. Given time, he would undoubtedly convince the rest of himself that he'd only been doing what he had to. Anna had known several people like that, sociopaths, but not easy to diagnose, sociopath lite.

"What is owed you?" Leah asked. Anna didn't care, but Leah clearly did, so she said nothing.

"My share. Gerald and Mike shoved me out just before our business was about to take off."

"They bought you out," Leah said. "My designs made the business."

"Momma's a genius," Katie said. "Literally."

"Geniuses are a dime a dozen. Those designs were intuitive," Bernie said. "Gerald didn't give me time."

Leah stared at him, mouth slightly ajar, as

514

if he were an equation that didn't add up.

"So you kidnapped Leah, her daughter, Heath, and her daughter because you think a guy named Gerald owes you, have I got this right?" Anna asked.

"I had nothing to do with these others." He waved a dismissive hand at Heath and Elizabeth. "And Gerald owes me. As his wife, she owes me."

"Because you might have, given time, come up with Leah's designs," Anna said.

"I would have."

"This is unbelievable," Elizabeth said. "We are beaten and dragged all over hell and gone because this creep thinks he *might* have come up with some designs?"

Bernie said nothing. He unscrewed the cap from his thermos, set it on the ground, and tipped the canister. A single drop came out.

Anna did not continue questioning him. Leah would not find relief. Not with this guy. Hitting men like this was like hitting the tar baby; they felt nothing and anyone striking out at them was trapped.

"Now she's planning on putting me out of business," Bernie said, addressing Anna, holding his coffee cup just as if there were coffee in it.

"Leah?" Anna said. Leah shook her head.

"How is she putting you out of business?" Anna asked out of curiosity.

"Selvane," he said, showing a hint of anger for the first time. "My company designs boats. Without selvane I'll go out of business."

"The magic slippery stuff," Anna said. "Leah has the formula in her head. The thugs get the ransom and you get the chemical composition of selvane. Was that the deal?"

"It doesn't matter." Bernie rose to his feet.

"Sit," Anna ordered him. This time he didn't obey.

"I'm going to walk away. If you shoot me, you will be murderers. I'm just a man who happened by to help. Not even that. Nobody knows I'm here. I filed no flight plan. If anyone chanced to see my plane they couldn't positively identify it — no number. I'm unarmed. You can't say you shot me in self-defense. No one will believe you. No one will believe I was ever here."

"Five of us can swear to it," Anna said.

"And I have ten clergymen and judges who will swear I was with them," he said smugly. He looked down his long patrician nose at Heath, Elizabeth, then Anna. "There's no point in shooting me. It will only cause you further harm. I will take my leave now."

"Why don't I just shoot you in the leg," Anna said. "Then, if somebody comes to find us, you can tell them your story yourself. That is, if you don't bleed to death first."

"If you wound me, or harm me in any way, I will sue you, your family, your employer. I will sue Hendricks and Hendricks. I will sue the American government and the state of Minnesota. You will die broke, in a tangle of red tape."

Anna considered this. Bernie Iverson was right. If she shot him, he could keep her at least, and possibly Heath and Leah, in the courts until their lives were about nothing but depositions and lawyers' fees. Based on their stories, the FBI or CIA or whoever dealt with extradition and international kidnapping schemes might pursue an investigation into Bernie's affairs. For a while.

"You're beginning to catch on," Bernie said condescendingly. Anna wanted so very much to shoot him. Earlier, before people and food and sanity, she would have done so. Jimmy, extenuating circumstances. Sean, in the commission of a felony. Reg. The dude had shot Reg, but Heath had the dude's gun. Who was to say who shot whom? A body, here and now, clearly shot down in cold blood; that might skew the investigators' minds toward believing all three were murder. Not the ones who arrived on scene. They would see. Still, detectives, lawyers, judges, and juries on down the line, this would be nothing but words to them.

Anna was not going to shoot him, not even in the foot, and he saw it.

Bernie's mouth nodded to himself, a snort of derision puffed out his nose. He held out the thermos. "Leah," he said. "I can call you Leah, can't I?"

She nodded dumbly.

"Give me a refill and I'll be on my way. In a couple hours I'll need a cup of good coffee." He smiled, but the words were an order, not a request.

Leah's head jerked back as if he'd slapped her. Her hand came out of her pocket and clawed the glasses from her face. She folded the temples and replaced the glasses in her jacket.

Bernie was holding out the thermos.

"Don't give it to him!" Heath demanded.

Leah reached over the fire and took it. Nerveless, she fumbled the bottle and it fell to her feet. Bernie, smile in place, watched while she managed to gather it and the cap up from the dirt.

"Wipe it, would you?" he asked pleasantly.

"Momma, don't!" Katie cried.

Leah wiped the dirt from the mouth of the thermos and the inside of the cup. Without speaking or looking at him, she filled his thermos from the pot of coffee Elizabeth had made, screwed the cap on, then handed it back to him.

Anna could not shoot him. Short of that, she had nothing to say. The others must have felt much the same.

"Thanks, sweetheart," Bernie said. His tongue clicked as he pointed a finger gun at Leah before walking to his plane.

Anna and the ex-hostages watched without speaking as he folded himself back into the cockpit, fired up the engine, turned the plane around, and taxied to the far end of the clearing. The plane turned, the engine revved, and the Beechcraft rushed toward them, the wheels lifting over their camp and vanishing in a roar.

"I can't believe you gave him coffee! I hate you! You let him get away!" Katie wailed.

"I didn't. In a few days he will feel nauseated. Then, for a day or two, he'll feel better. Within a week he will die."

Stunned silence followed this announcement. Then Heath started to laugh.

"What?" Anna asked irritably. "What am I

519

missing?"

"Amanita," Heath said between giggles.

"Destroyer Angel," Leah said.

"You put that mushroom in his coffee?" Elizabeth asked.

"The toxin is water soluble," Leah said. "I broke it and crushed it a little."

"What mushroom?" Anna snapped.

"Leah found a Destroyer Angel," Heath said. "She had it in her pocket."

"There is no cure," Leah said.

"I'm glad," Katie said firmly.

"Bloodthirsty little wench," Heath said, but she was still laughing.

To Wily, Anna said, "*All's Well That Ends Well.* You've got to have seen that."

Again the engine noise of a small plane disturbed the stillness. Laughter dried up. The women froze, all eyes on the sky.

"He's coming back," Katie wailed.

"I'll shoot the son of a bitch," Heath said. "I haven't killed anybody yet."

For a moment they all listened, nerves stretching toward the distant sound.

"No," Anna said and sighed with relief. It was the sturdy growl of the old Lockheeds the Forest Service used. "That'll be our ride."

ABOUT THE AUTHOR

Nevada Barr is the author of the series of *New York Times* bestselling novels featuring Anna Pigeon, a law enforcement park ranger. Her novels include *Winter Study*, *Borderline* and *Burn*. She won the Agatha Award for Best First Novel for *Track of the Cat*. Like her character, Barr worked for the National Park Service as a park ranger before resigning to write full time. She had postings to such parks as Guadalupe Mountains National Park in Texas (where Anna Pigeon was created) and Natchez Trace Parkway in Mississippi. She lives in New Orleans.

The employees of Thorndike Press hope you have enjoyed this Large Print book. All our Thorndike, Wheeler, and Kennebec Large Print titles are designed for easy reading, and all our books are made to last. Other Thorndike Press Large Print books are available at your library, through selected bookstores, or directly from us.

For information about titles, please call:
   (800) 223-1244

or visit our Web site at:
   http://gale.cengage.com/thorndike

To share your comments, please write:
   Publisher
   Thorndike Press
   10 Water St., Suite 310
   Waterville, ME 04901